A DARK HORSE

By

BLAYNE COOPER

Bella
BOOKS

2015

Bella Books, Inc.
P.O. Box 10543
Tallahassee, FL 32302

Printed in the United States of America on acid-free paper.

First Bella Books Edition 2015

Editor: Ruth Stanley
Cover Designer: Judith Fellows

ISBN: 978-1-59493-456-8

Other Books by Blayne Cooper

Dedication

For Bugsy

About the Author

Blayne Cooper is an award-winning author and co-author of a variety of fiction ranging from mystery/romance to outrageous parody. The University of Oklahoma College of Law grad loves travel, reading and spending long, sleepless nights crouched over her computer in search of the perfect words. She's still looking, but having a great time on the journey. She lives in Minnesota.

PART ONE

CHAPTER ONE

"Have a seat, Natalie." Rose ushered her grown daughter to stand in front of a kitchen chair and pressed her into the seat with slightly more force than necessary. "Eat with me. No excuses. Your stepdad has already gone to play dominoes in the park, so it's just us this morning."

The doorbell rang, and Natalie was surprised to see the neighbor girl at their kitchen door. She opened it with a smile. "Good morning, Rebecca."

"Morning." The girl's grin was toothless and far too adorable for her own good. The grade-schooler—Natalie had no idea exactly how old she was—was on roller skates and full of so much energy she couldn't help but roll back and forth a bit even while trying to stand in place. "I'm selling popcorn for the neighborhood park fund. Would you like to buy some?"

"No." Rose's disembodied voice came from behind Natalie.

Rebecca's face fell. Natalie quickly grabbed her purse. "Ignore her," she whispered. "I want some, kiddo. How much?"

Rebecca's expression instantly lit up the kitchen doorway. "Eight dollars, please."

"Done." Natalie handed over the money, and Rebecca dug into a sack that was slung over her shoulder and passed over a brightly colored, but depressingly small, tin of caramel corn. "Hey, has anyone ever told you that you look like the red-haired girl with the pigtails in the Wendy's advertisements? You know—Wendy?"

Rebecca shrugged. "Only the jerks."

Natalie snorted. "Good one. Okay, good luck with the rest of the grumpy old ladies on the block."

She and Rebecca shared a conspiratorial grin and the girl turned on her heels and rolled away. "Thanks, Ms. Abbott!"

Natalie set the tin on the counter and closed the door. "Now I have dessert for after breakfast. And, Mom, you were so mean that I'm not sharing any with you."

"Nobody needs dessert after breakfast," Rose muttered.

"Says the woman who will be trying to sneak some of my delicious, gag-a-maggot sweet popcorn in about twenty minutes." It was the weekend—thank God—and for the first time in longer than Natalie could remember she didn't have anything to do that couldn't wait, at least until that evening. "Breakfast smells great."

Natalie craned her neck, trying to see into the living room to catch sight of her stepbrother. It had been a while since she'd been to the house, she privately admitted, and she half-expected to see the teen sprawled out on the couch, his gangly legs and big feet hanging off one arm of the sofa as he watched cartoons and noisily consumed cereal straight from the box.

But the living room was silent.

She frowned. "Mom, where's Josh? I haven't seen the runt in ages. Is he sleeping until noon on Sundays, even with his job?" He hated being called runt and she supposed, considering he was bigger than she was by several inches and at least forty pounds, it really didn't make sense nowadays anyway. The corner of her mouth quirked upward. "Hey, runt, time to wake up!"

"Shhh. Don't yell." Rose spoke with her back to Natalie as she pulled some silverware from a kitchen drawer. "Josh is what I wanted to talk to you about, honey." Her voice was breezy and even.

Natalie regarded her mother with sudden caution. Clanging alarm bells sounded in her head. That tone of voice and the endearment meant only one thing, Rose wanted something, and whatever it was, Natalie wasn't going to like it. She felt her mood plummet with a great *kerplunk*.

Her mother's kitchen—a place she'd spent endless and mostly happy childhood hours, bathed in morning sunlight, the room filled with the heavenly scent of fresh coffee—could have been a place of sanctuary for her. Well, if it weren't for the presence of her mother. "And...?"

When Rose didn't say another word and instead began to hum quietly to herself, Natalie rolled her eyes. The older woman knew how her daughter hated awkward silences, and knew how to use them to her advantage: to build up the tension of the moment and to make Natalie squirm like a fat worm on a fishhook. *But why?*

Giving in despite herself, Natalie resentfully prodded, "So I'm here… and what does it have to do with Josh?"

"Joshua is gone, honey." Rose began plating the food.

Natalie made an impatient "hurry up" gesture with one hand. "Gone…how? Staying with a friend?"

Rose set a steaming plate of eggs and potatoes in front of her daughter. The scent was divine, but Natalie refused to take a single bite until her mother came clean about why she'd been summoned to her family home.

"Gone to New Orleans."

The blood drained from Natalie's face so quickly spots danced before her eyes. "What?" she roared, jumping up and tossing her paper napkin down onto her plate. Dizzy, she grasped the edge-worn Formica tabletop with both hands. "*What?*"

Rose gave up any pretense of doing this delicately and plopped down into her seat with a great sigh. "You heard me."

"*Mama!* How could you let him? We talked about this! You promised," she hissed.

"I didn't let him." Rose pointed toward Natalie's seat with a stern finger and Natalie hesitated for only a second before sitting down. "He went on his own with stupid Mary or Marcy."

"He has been dating that girl for a year. You know her name is Misty." Natalie licked her lips. "But he's coming back, right?" *Please.* "For school?"

"He decided finishing school wasn't necessary."

"*He* decided? He's only sixteen!" Natalie's face felt hot and her hands trembled. "He's not mature enough to be on his own. He has two more years of high school and can't drop out without parental consent."

Rose suddenly found something terribly interesting about the inside of her coffee cup.

Natalie gasped. "You didn't!"

Rose's pale blue gaze snapped up to meet its twin. "He said if we didn't sign the paper he would just write our names down himself and go anyway. At least this way he came to us and we discussed it first."

"And that makes it better?" Natalie was stunned that things had spun this far out of control. Her goofy, teenage brother was somehow living in a far-off city and no one had gone to bring him home. It was terrifying but not wholly inconceivable. When Josh had hit his teenage years her parents simply decided that they were tired and that meant they were finished parenting. Josh was like a cookie that was still hopelessly gooey in the center, but deemed close enough, and snatched from the oven prematurely.

Her mother's late-in-life marriage to Josh's father was welcomed by them both, but at sixty-five years old Rose was well past the age when she should have been dealing with a kindhearted but willful teenager. Rose had barely been able to keep up with the responsibilities of being a parent during Natalie's teenage years, much less a second child so many years later.

Natalie's attention strayed back to the living room, as though this were a joke and she'd hear Josh burst out of his bedroom and plop himself in front of the family television set any second. "I can't believe he ran away."

Rose scrunched up her face. "At first, yes. But…"

Natalie turned her palms skyward. "But?"

"He ran out of money not long after he arrived, so I convinced his father to let me send him some. And since we helped him, and he has an apartment, and we know where he is, is it still running away?" Rose's words flew out in a rapid burst and for the first time, Natalie caught a trace of real worry in her mother's expression.

"How long has he been gone?"

"Six weeks and six days."

What? " Natalie spluttered for the second time in as many minutes. This time when she jumped up she bumped into the table, sending coffee splashing out of both cups.

"I can't talk to you if you keep jumping up like that. For cripes sake, sit down!" Rose seized a wad of napkins from a wire napkin holder and began to sop up the mess.

"No!" Natalie growled, her temper on a razor's edge. "Tell me every damn thing, and do it before I lose my mind from waiting." *Weeks,* her mind chanted, *he's been on his own for weeks.*

Rose finished wiping the table, then picked up her cup to take a sip of the remaining liquid. Natalie's murderous glare stopped her in her tracks. "Fine." She sniffed dramatically. "He asked if he could quit school and move to New Orleans. We said 'no.'"

Natalie nodded. When Josh had come to her and told her he wanted to drop out and move out she'd forbade it. And with some mild convincing, she'd gotten her parents to agree to do the same thing.

"But he went anyway," Rose continued. "And ran out of money and sounded like he really needed help…so I sent him some, everything we had, really, and…and didn't tell you about it."

Tears filled Rose's eyes and Natalie couldn't help the sickening realization that she wasn't sure whether the tears were for Josh and his future, or the loss of the money.

Rose wiped at her damp cheeks. "I thought for certain he'd be home by now."

Natalie listened, her mind racing as it replayed the same thought over and over. *He's been gone for weeks. Jesus.*

"But he stopped calling ages ago, and we haven't heard from him since."

"Exactly how long is ages ago?"

"Five weeks ago."

Dumbfounded, Natalie had reached her limit. "What the *hell*?"

"I have his address, but you need to go find him and make sure he's okay."

The sound in Natalie's mind was like a screeching record needle. "No."

"Natalie!"

"I said 'no.' I didn't make this mess. You did. Go and get him yourself."

"How can you say that?"

When Natalie just looked at her with a raised eyebrow, Rose groaned. "Please, Natalie. *Please*. It's like he's vanished, and that's not like Joshua at all."

"How would you know?" Natalie's lips curled in disgust. "Have you been paying attention to him at all?"

Rose's eyes flashed. "Have *you*?"

The air fled Natalie's lungs like a popped balloon, her mother's words piercing her heart with unerring accuracy. She sat back down and swallowed hard.

Natalie knew that she wasn't overly involved in her stepbrother's life. Hell, he'd been gone for most of the summer and she hadn't even realized it. But, Joshua was so much younger—16 years—that they hadn't grown up together. She'd been so busy for so long, it was easy to let things like phone calls and visits slide.

For a few brilliant seconds it looked as though Rose was going to apologize for her nasty dig, but instead, she muttered, "He could have at least written us a letter."

Natalie tilted her head and regarded her mother with true disbelief. "Seriously? You thought he was going to write you an actual letter? With a pen?"

"I've even been checking on the computer at the library for a note."

"You mean email?"

Rose narrowed her eyes, and her already thin lips nearly disappeared into a straight line. "I know what it's called."

Natalie glanced at the calendar that was pinned to the refrigerator with magnets in the shapes of fruit. "How is this possible? We texted each other earlier this summer, and I spoke to Josh on the phone a few weeks ago."

"Did you ask him where he was?"

Natalie slapped her hand down flat on the table. "I didn't think to ask him whether he was out of state!"

"Don't raise your voice at me, young lady," Rose snapped. "Spend all that energy finding your brother instead."

When Natalie opened her mouth to protest, Rose stopped her by blurting, "You have to go for us. How can you not ca—?"

"Don't say that I don't care! Don't." Natalie ran a hand through her hair. She gave her head a little shake and allowed the locks to settle haphazardly down her back. "I *love* Josh. Just like you do. It's just not a good time for me."

Natalie turned and dumped what was left of her lukewarm coffee down the drain and began to rinse the cup. "This isn't like the junior college where I taught last year, Mom. Tomorrow is already Monday. UW–Madison expects me to attend departmental staff meetings this week and then maintain regular office hours for the full week before classes start." *Not to mention the cost of a last-minute airline ticket and hotel would kill me this month.*

Rose smoothed her hands down the apron she was wearing over white cotton pants and a bright pink flowered shirt. Then she effectively ignored everything her daughter had just said. "But you don't *actually* start teaching for two more weeks. There's still time. You'll probably set him straight the very first day…or two…and be able to come right home."

"You can go. Or better yet, call the police."

Obviously appalled, Rose's face twisted and her voice boomed. "I would never! I'm not doing anything that will get your brother arrested."

"But—"

"We can't afford to go. I sent Josh everything we had to spare, which wasn't much."

"But, don't you see? By doing that you only made it easier for him to stay away!"

"I will lose my job if I try to go myself, Natalie. I already asked at the grocery store and they said no more time off. Even part-time work is hard to come by at my age. And your stepfather isn't well enough to travel alone."

"Oh, my God!" Natalie threw her hands in the air, but she was starting to lose steam. When her mother was like this, talking to her was like banging her head against a stone wall. "There's absolutely nothing wrong with him, and he's never been sick a day in his life. He's going to outlive us all. We're talking about *his* son here, Mom. *Your* son."

Rose's hard swallow was audible. "If we went we'd need *two* tickets. We can't afford—" the older woman's voice hitched.

"Stop." Natalie released a long breath and held up her hand to forestall any more discussion. She set her cup in the drainboard and moved around to the table to stand in front of her mother. On one hand she recognized deep in her gut that she was being manipulated, but on the other, something still had to be done. "Just...stop." *It's for Josh*, her mind chanted. "I'll go, Mom."

"Lord...Thank you!" Rose jumped to her feet and threw plump arms around her oldest child. "You're such a good girl. So smart and beautiful and responsible. I knew I could count on you."

Natalie ignored the compliments that were given freely when Rose got her way.

Worry bubbled up inside Natalie and despite the shouting match that had just played out, she held her mother a little tighter and rested her chin atop a pile of gray curls that had once been the same shade of deep chestnut brown as her own. "I won't just find him," she reassured softly. "I'll bring him home."

* * *

Tired of fanning herself with her hands, Natalie blew a forceful stream of air upward onto her face in a hopeless attempt to cool herself off. The scorching heat and relentless humidity clung to her like a second skin, even as she sat impatiently inside a weakly air-conditioned waiting room of the New Orleans Police Department. It had been forever and her blouse was just now starting to unstick itself from the perspiring skin on her lower back and chest. She adjusted herself in her seat, more than a little uncomfortable and frustrated.

She'd spent more than two days looking for Josh and her worry was mounting with each passing hour. She was in an unfamiliar city, armed only with an address that had unexpectedly led her nowhere. After looking every obvious place she thought her brother might be, then every place else, she realized she had no idea what to do next. He could be anywhere.

The waiting room was dank, musty and noisy, filled with a cacophony of grumbling people, running and fighting children, and crying babies. Natalie's head was starting to pound.

She glanced at the clock on her cell phone. Another five minutes and she was going to go hassle that enormous uniformed officer at the reception desk. Again. She hadn't eaten yet today and she realized that she'd just missed lunch. At this rate, she'd miss dinner as well.

"You get used to it, you know."

A woman's voice, soft and lilting with a local accent, caused Natalie's attention to snap to her.

"The heat, that is." The woman smiled, showing off perfect white teeth. "At least that's what I hear. But I'm local, so I guess I wouldn't really know."

Natalie sprang to her feet, barely catching her purse as it threatened to tumble off her lap and onto a tired-looking linoleum floor.

The other woman's light, caramel-colored gaze traveled upward to a dusty vent and she stretched onto her tiptoes to give it a good rap with her knuckles. The movement caused her snug, designer T-shirt to slip out from inside low-slung slacks, exposing an immodest amount of pale skin. "Look out," she warned and darted sideways, unselfconsciously stuffing her shirt back into the back of her pants as she went.

With a small gasp, Natalie mirrored the movement and just missed being hit by the light shower of dirt and general gunk that rained down between them. Sunlight poured in from a nearby window, causing the tiny floating dust particles to take on an ethereal glow.

"It would help if they cleaned this place—" the woman narrowed her eyes at the offending vent one last time before refocusing on Natalie— "ever." Then a good-natured smile stretched across her face and lit up delicate features.

"I'm Detective Adele Lejeune." She pronounced her last name "La-Zshoon," giving it a slightly exotic sound to Natalie's ears.

Natalie couldn't help but think that the gun and gold badge worn on the detective's hip didn't fit with the rest of the friendly, girlish picture. It made her feel foolish, but Natalie realized she hadn't been expecting to see a woman or someone her own age.

Adele looked around at the semi-controlled chaos and winced as they shook hands. Today was a particularly loud day. "I hope you're still sane after waiting out here in the snake pit."

Natalie suppressed a tiny chuckle. Grasping the detective's hand, she noted the contrast between the soft skin over slender fingers and the confident, solid grip and shake.

"Natalie Abbott." She slung her purse over her shoulder and wiped moist palms off on the thighs of her jeans. "Thank you for seeing me without an appointment. The woman at the desk told me I'd probably have to come back tomorrow."

Detective Lejeune shrugged. "It's no problem. You caught me at the perfect time. My partner is out with the flu this week, and I was just catching up on some paperwork, which is not my favorite task. I try to spend as little time in the office as possible."

Natalie forced herself not to wrinkle her nose. She couldn't blame her.

"Anyway, I'm with NOPD's Criminal Investigation Division, Juvenile Section."

With a tilt of her head, Detective Lejeune asked Natalie to follow her. They quickly passed through a heavy set of security doors, and began the trek down a narrow, long hallway lined with scratched, mint-green file cabinets that looked like something out of the 1950s.

"My unit specializes in missing children and parental kidnappings. Though I tend to deal more with the former." Adele pointed straight ahead. "There's a private office we can use back here to talk."

The detective turned sideways in the hall to let a cocoa-skinned uniformed officer, who sported a wicked-looking tattoo, pass. "Hey Al." Adele softly smacked his muscular shoulder with the back of her hand as she strode by. "You owe me twenty bucks. I haven't forgotten." She waggled a finger over her shoulder in his direction.

"Hey, Little Mama," the young cop answered happily, the faint scent of musky cologne and sweat trailing after him. "I haven't forgotten either. Don't you worry."

Natalie's focus was wholly transfixed on the fit woman in front of her as she took in the assured, rolling gait that bordered on a swagger. The detective had dirty blond hair styled in a longish pixie haircut that suited her heart-shaped face and slender neck. She was an inch, or maybe an inch-and-a-half, taller than her own five-and-a-half-feet and far more put together-looking than any policewoman Natalie had seen on television.

"It's a bit cooler here than where you just were. But not much," Adele drawled conversationally, not bothering to look back over her shoulder as they walked.

They passed a large room filled with old wooden desks covered with paper files and computers. Inside the room, clusters of men with guns and badges, but in plainclothes, huddled around the desks talking. More than one curious gaze swung their way as they walked.

Glad to be distracted from the reason for her visit, even for a few seconds, Natalie idly noted that it must be difficult for Detective Lejeune to look the way she did in her line of work. *Pretty and so delightfully… unexpected.* But then all thoughts of anything but Josh were whisked away as soon as they entered the nondescript, gray-walled office.

"Please, have a seat." Adele grabbed a notepad and pen from a cardboard box on the floor near the back of the room. She gestured toward a metal chair on one side of a small square table.

Natalie sat and swallowed nervously. She'd never been inside a police station before. It was not only disconcerting, it was so…official. Josh had never been in any real trouble, and rationally, she knew he was probably fine. But his address…maybe her mother had written it down wrong.

"Lorraine at the front desk said that you're here about your stepbrother, who is missing. Will you tell me about him and what happened?" Detective Lejeune crossed her legs and allowed her top foot to bounce up and down a few times, her eyes sweeping over Natalie and clearly drinking in every detail.

Natalie wondered if the detective always had this much restless energy at the start of a case. "Yes," she began, profoundly relieved to finally be doing something productive. "Joshua Phillips. But you can leave the 'step' out of the equation. He's just my brother. He and his girlfriend, Misty Kazik, left home and came here seven weeks ago. Josh is very close to our parents, especially our mom. His birth mother died when he was a baby and my mother has raised him since he was in diapers.

"He and my mom spoke almost every day when he first arrived in New Orleans, and then nothing. He hasn't answered his phone or contacted the family for five weeks now. We think…well, something must have happened. My mom has left him about a hundred voice mails."

When Josh turned thirteen, Natalie added him to her calling plan and purchased him a cell phone so he wouldn't be the only kid in his class without one. She knew what it was like to grow up poor, always peering in hopefully from the outside, wishing for what others simply took for granted.

While she didn't think teenagers needed every little thing their hearts desired, it hurt Natalie to think of Josh doing without. She'd recently gifted him the newest iPhone. "Misty never had a phone. She just uses Josh's." She didn't add that Misty's drunken mother couldn't care less where Misty was now.

Adele nodded thoughtfully as she tapped her chin lightly with the pen. "He *came here*? Not ran away?"

The power of Detective Lejeune's piercing gaze was palpable, and Natalie rubbed one of her temples with her fingertips, willing her headache away.

"He ran away. He told me about his crazy plan to move here at the end of the school year. We all told him no, but he left anyway. My parents sent him money to help him, then stopped hearing from him."

"Ms. Abbott, how old is Josh?"

"He's sixteen and will be for a couple more months. Misty is seventeen."

"And you're just now coming to the police?"

There was no judgment in Detective Lejeune's voice, just curiosity. But Natalie felt the censure all the same. "I just found out," she said flatly. "I've…my parents. I just found out," she repeated in an uneven breath.

Adele nodded and scribbled something on the paper in front of her. "And you're from a northern city, I presume?" She cocked her head to the side. "You, um, look a bit more wilted than our average citizen," she said tactfully.

Natalie rolled her eyes at her undoubtedly bedraggled appearance. "Madison, Wisconsin."

Adele's eyes twinkled. "Home of…cheese?"

Despite her uneasiness, Natalie released a small smile. "Something like that."

"This is a long way from home then."

"Mmm." Natalie dug in her purse for the photo of Josh she'd just had printed at a local drugstore. "Josh plays the clarinet. He's talented and wants to be a musician. Despite testing very well academically, he's never been interested in school."

Natalie clutched at the purse in her lap while she continued to hunt. "When he told me he wanted to drop out and get a GED I was shocked. But he loves jazz and is convinced he doesn't need to understand algebra or chemistry to play his music. He's been dying to come here ever since I can remember." The color rose in her cheeks. "Even Hurricane Katrina didn't deter him. Though that should have kept anyone with any sense away."

"Believe it or not, Ms. Abbott, there are some of us who love living here." Her voice hardened and she kept her eyes on her notes as she spoke. "And even *with* the weather, a few of us manage some semblance of sense."

Natalie's eyes widened and her heart beat faster when she realized what she'd said. And how rude it was. "Oh, my God. I didn't mean...I didn't. I don't doubt that." She winced, knowing she'd offended the detective. "I'm *so* sorry. It's just that it looked so terrible on television, and my family has been concerned about how dangerous it might be to live here after everything. I know there's been so much progress cleaning things up and repairing the city."

When the detective appeared unmoved, the words seemed to pour out of Natalie. "And, I'm scared. And I'm missing work, and I haven't slept well and—"

Adele held up a hand and squared her shoulders. "It's okay. I...I'm a bit touchy to comments from outsiders. It's..." she expelled a slow breath and kicked her legs out in front of her, crossing them at the ankle. "Well, it was a lot to deal with. Still is."

"Of course." Natalie's pale blue gaze conveyed honest regret and Adele breathed a bit easier. "Even with all the rebuilding that's necessary, it's still a beautiful place. I can see that after being here for only two-and-a-half days. I shouldn't have made it sound otherwise."

Adele managed a weak smile and cleared her throat. "Has Josh ever been arrested?"

The transition was jarring, and it took Natalie's brain a few seconds to adjust. "No."

"Trouble in school?"

"No."

"Did he ever run away from home when he was younger?"

"No."

"Fights?"

She shook her head and frowned. Her mother would have mentioned... "He's a good kid."

Adele blinked, then frowned. "Never?"

"Are you saying that if he'd been in a school fight in the second grade that you wouldn't look for him now? He's *missing*."

Adele ignored the question. "What about gang involvement?"

"No. My family doesn't come from money." She glanced at Adele's expensive watch and left the words *like you do* unspoken. "But that doesn't mean we're part of the Hell's Angels."

One of Adele's eyebrows twitched and she locked eyes with Natalie. "What about sexual or physical abuse in the home or elsewhere?"

The way she said it was so matter-of-fact. Like she *expected* the answer to be yes. Like it was somehow perfectly okay if the answer was yes.

A hot rush of anger caused Natalie's chest to flush. "Of course not! Do you think I would traipse halfway across the country to bring someone I love *back* into an abusive situation?" Rationally, she knew these questions were necessary, but that didn't stop their sting.

Adele looked as though she wanted to explain herself, but held back. "Drug or alcohol use?"

When Natalie didn't answer right away Adele pinned her with an even more serious look. "Ms. Abbott?"

"Call me Natalie, please."

"Natalie," Adele amended softly. Her voice took on a sympathetic but firm tone. "You need to be honest with me or I can't help your brother."

"Alcohol, yes. My stepdad let him have beer at home and he abused that privilege more than once. But, it was always just normal teenage stuff, you know?"

"Actually, I don't." Then Adele remained quiet, her expression steady and open, asking Natalie to continue.

Natalie sighed. "Marijuana…probably. I smelled it on him a few times last semester. I confronted him about it. He said he was just around some kids who were smoking it and that it wasn't his. He never got into any trouble, so I let it go."

"Nothing besides pot?"

Natalie didn't see Josh every week or even every month anymore. During her years of study she'd lived out of state and the siblings had drifted apart. Then even when she'd come back to Madison to start her career, they'd stayed that way. Loving, but distant. With a pang, Natalie realized how selfish she'd been. She *hated* that she could no longer answer such an important, simple question absolutely. "I-I don't think so."

"But you're not sure?" Adele prodded. She shifted once again so that both her feet were firmly planted on the floor and she fully faced Natalie, leaning toward her.

This pose was slightly more aggressive and though it was subtle, Natalie's reaction was immediate. One of her hands shaped a tight fist while her jaw worked. "No," she snapped, but the anger she was feeling was directed more toward herself than the detective. "Clearly, I'm not certain of anything at all."

Natalie realized she was still holding Josh's photo in her other hand. She slid it across the table. Grabbing hold of her emotions, Natalie forced the corner of her mouth to quirk upward, but she couldn't stop her eyes from glistening. "Are you sure you aren't a lawyer? A prosecutor maybe?"

Adele's demeanor melted into something that looked a lot like remorse or pity. "It doesn't sound like you deserve to be prosecuted."

Natalie refused to allow the words to make her feel better.

"Did Josh mention a job? Or new friends?"

Natalie searched her mind for everything her mother had told her about their calls. "Not really. He mentioned looking for a job."

Adele leaned back in her chair and tossed the pen on the tabletop. It sounded unnaturally loud in the mostly empty room and they both flinched. "Okay. Let's try something different. Think about the last conversation you had."

"I didn't even know he was in New Orleans at the time. Everything seemed just the same."

Adele chewed the inside of her cheek. "Okay, think of what time of day it was when you spoke. What you had to eat that day. What was on TV. The weather. Everything. The smells. The sounds. Put yourself back in the moment." She waited nearly a full minute before speaking again, until Natalie nodded that she was ready, obviously having done her best to mentally rewind time.

"The phone rings and you greet each other. Josh is…?"

Natalie's forehead creased. "He's…happy."

Adele smiled. "Okay, he's happy he's in New Orleans. Even though you didn't know he was here."

The detective's voice reminded her of a hypnotist's, calm and reassuring, and although the way Adele pronounced *New Aww-lens* tugged at Natalie's attention, she refocused herself quickly. "Yes." She thought for a moment. "He talked about getting a new case for his clarinet."

"Good," Adele murmured. "So he's happy because he's someplace he's always wanted to be. He's enjoying the music scene and dreaming of someday playing his horn in some smoky club. Wishing for a better case."

A nod. "He mentioned wanting a new job. He works at a diner back home but doesn't like it."

"What sort of new job?"

Natalie's eyes widened as a memory suddenly swam to the surface. "He said if he had to be a dishwasher that it should at least be someplace with live music." Hope infused her. "He wanted to work someplace that had live music so he would be near it, even if he wasn't playing himself."

Adele nodded encouragingly. "Good. That's *good*, Natalie. Keep going."

"I—" Natalie chewed her lower lip as she combed through her memories, but drew a blank. "I would have paid more attention if I'd known…"

"I know," Adele soothed and gently steered Natalie back on track. "He wants to work where there is music. He loves it. What else?"

She groaned and covered her eyes with her palms. "I don't remember anything else that would help."

"It's a start." Adele finally picked up the photograph on the table and spent a long moment studying it.

Natalie knew the photo by heart. Josh looked healthy with slightly chubby cheeks, smooth clear skin, and a toothy smile. He appeared a couple of years younger than sixteen and was wearing a maroon marching band jacket and tatty jeans, his arms wound around a beaming older couple.

Adele glanced up. "I know you're not biologically related, but he has your eyes."

Natalie felt a lump rise in her throat. "I know."

Adele pushed to her feet and laid a cool hand on the other woman's wrist. She gave it a comforting squeeze and let a little of the sympathy she felt show. "I have some ibuprofen in my car, if you'd like."

Natalie's eyes closed. The pain behind her eyelids was making her ill and she didn't bother to ask Detective Lejeune how she knew. "That would be wonderful." She let out a shuddering breath, anticipating the relief already.

"Do you have Josh and Misty's last known address?"

Wordlessly, Natalie nodded.

"Good." Adele kindly offered Natalie a hand up, which was graciously accepted. "I've never taken a family member along with me, but today is as good a time as any time to break the rules. We'll start at the address you have. We can talk more on the way. I still have a lot of questions."

Each woman was lost in her own thoughts as they made their way through the building. "Detective Lejeune?" Natalie slid on her sunglasses as the bright afternoon glare assaulted her eyes and a blast furnace of heat ruffled her hair as they moved outside. "He couldn't have just disappeared without a trace, could he?" But even as she said it, she knew the answer.

Adele's expression turned grim and she trained her eyes straight ahead as she walked toward her car. Her silence screamed louder than anything she could have said.

CHAPTER TWO

"Have I said thank you yet?" Natalie unbuckled her seat belt and shifted so she was facing Adele.

"I haven't done anything yet. Well, except ask you about a million questions." Adele had stepped out of her car and adjusted the low-slung belt where her gold shield and weapon were clipped.

"That doesn't matter." Natalie glanced away. "Just…thank you. I'm so grateful for your help."

Pleased, Adele smiled brightly. "You're welcome. This is where you tried earlier, huh?" She took off her sunglasses and stuck them on top of her head. She looked up at the second floor of the building, her mouth shifting into a frown.

The women stood on Governor Nicholls Street, in the French Quarter, in front of a shabby-looking bar, its wooden sign hanging entirely still in the stagnant, heavy air. The clouds had started to move in overhead and Adele was sure it would be pouring rain before the day was done.

Natalie nodded, looking miserable. "The man at the bar told me nobody lives here. He said I must have the address wrong." Her lips turned down. His clumsy attempt at seduction had been repulsive. "Then he hit on me."

Adele rolled her eyes. "Of course he did. Wait here."

"But—"

Adele was already moving inside. "Just wait here. I'll only be a minute."

The bar had a dark cave-like interior and was nearly empty in the middle of the afternoon on a weekday. It smelled like dust, old wood and beer with the faintest undercurrent of vomit. Adele swallowed back a groan. The smell, ever-present, but most commonly found in the heart of Bourbon Street, was as familiar as her own name. And she hated it. It reminded her of her patrol days and the many late nights spent wrangling drunks…and just drunks.

It didn't take *much* convincing for the bar manager, a stocky man with a tragic comb-over. Adele simply flashed her badge, threatened to kick in the apartment door, and finally hinted that if he made things easy for her, she wouldn't cause a stink about his illegal rentals. "It's the silver key," he said gruffly, tugging a couple of keys from his pocket. "First door on the left."

She snatched the keys from his hand and leaned way over the bar until her face was very close to his, cringing at the thought of her clothes coming into contact with the sticky surface. The scent of stale cigarettes emanated from the bar manager's pores.

She pinned him with a flinty glare, not speaking until she saw his Adam's apple bob up and down as he swallowed hard.

Adele's voice was soft but unyielding, like velvet stretched over steel. Anger bubbled up inside her. "You should have helped the nice lady who came asking after her brother. That was an asshole move that I won't forget."

The man lifted his hands in surrender and took a step backward. "Okay, okay. But the apartment is empty now anyway. Stupid shit and the dizzy blond girl stopped paying, so I locked 'em out."

Adele nodded and straightened. She picked up a napkin from a dispenser and grimaced as she wiped the palms of her hands. "How long ago?"

He scratched at a stubbly chin, his fingers making a harsh rasping sound. "Few weeks. Maybe less."

"Don't suppose he said where they were going or left a forwarding address?"

The man gave her a look that said she was crazy. "Hey," he called as she turned to leave. "You're going to give them keys back, right?"

She smirked over her shoulder and kept on walking.

"There are tons of illegal rentals in town, *especially* in the Quarter, but also around the colleges," Adele explained to Natalie as they passed through a nondescript doorway next to the bar. It opened into a shadowy alleyway and finally a tiny courtyard filled with crumbling stonework, garbage cans and a few sad-looking plants.

Natalie's eyes went round. From the outside of the building you would never know any of this was here.

The apartment was on the second floor. Adele put herself between Natalie and the door and then backed Natalie up a few steps. Adele lowered her voice to a near whisper. "The manager says he kicked Josh and Misty out for not paying rent, but stand here and give me a few minutes to check it out before you follow me in."

Natalie's eyes narrowed. "Detective, I'm not here just to stand around in the background while you look for my brother. Besides, Josh would never hurt me."

Adele did her best to sound reassuring, but also to be crystal clear. "I'm not saying he would, but we don't know if the bar manager was telling the truth about the place being empty. There could be someone else in the apartment, and he or she could be armed."

Natalie paled. "I-I never thought of that."

"I shouldn't have let you come along at all, but if you're going to do this with me, I need you to do *exactly* what I say so you'll be safe." Detective Lejeune's expression softened just a fraction. "I know you want to help, and you are, I promise. I'll come out and get you as soon as it's clear." She smiled gently. "Okay? Just to be safe."

Natalie let out a long breath, her resolve visibly melting under Detective Lejeune's tender brand of persuasion. "Okay."

Adele returned to the door and unclipped the safety strap on her gun holster. She gripped the handle of her Glock 42 with one hand while banging firmly on the door with the other.

The detective gave the door three loud raps with a closed fist and called out in a firm voice, "This is the police. Open up." When she was met with only silence, she tried once more before carefully unlocking the door and peering inside, weapon at the ready. Her body was rigid with tension and a wisp of excitement intertwined with the fear that came with stepping into the unknown.

The apartment consisted of a single twelve-by-twelve-foot room with a stained mattress in the corner and two rusty metal chairs that faced a broken window. Empty food containers were scattered across the floor, along with a few pieces of miscellaneous clothing and a fair amount of plain old garbage. Adele scanned the space quickly, then entered the bathroom, clicking the light on as she went. Several bulbs above the vanity were burned out, casting the room in a gloomy glow. The toilet seat was cracked in half, the tank lid was missing altogether, but the tub and sink both looked useable, if grubby.

Still feeling a bit uneasy, even with no one in the apartment, Adele holstered her weapon. She stuck her head outside to wave in an anxious-looking Natalie.

"Oh, my God," Natalie groaned as she crossed the apartment's threshold. It was far hotter inside than out, and she felt as though she'd stuck her head into an oven. "It's disgusting in here." She put her hand over her mouth and spoke through her fingers. "And it smells like rancid cheese."

Adele's voice flattened and her eyes closed briefly as her memory abruptly provided the reason for the knot in her belly. "It-it does." Not long after she'd become a detective, and only months after Katrina, Adele and her partner had entered an apartment eerily like this one, only to find the missing child they'd been searching for, along with the child's noncustodial father, both very dead. Victims of a murder-suicide.

The detective pushed out of her mind the memory of the little girl in a yellow flowered dress, curled up in bed next to her father, black cornrow braids drenched in dried blood, brown eyes open and unseeing. When her eyes swung around to meet Natalie's, Adele's cheeks pinked with embarrassment at the panicky look of concern on the other woman's face.

Adele ran her hand over her mouth and flailed wildly for something to say. "The kids didn't trash the place before they left." She gestured aimlessly at the bare walls, which were a sickly shade of pale green. "No parting graffiti. That's a switch."

Natalie stepped closer, her hand automatically lifting. "Are you—?"

Adele gave a short, dismissive wave, signaling that she was fine and silently asking Natalie to leave it alone. "The manager must have told them to go and let them collect their belongings first before locking them out. This is just junk." She kicked at a torn, neon orange ladies' T-shirt with her boot. The fabric looked to be stained with coffee or tea, but nothing suspicious.

Natalie reluctantly tore her gaze from Adele and eyed the shirt carefully. She squatted down to get a better look. "Is that a uniform shirt? It's hideous, but maybe worn by a waitress and someone spilled on her?"

Adele shook her head. *She's smart.* "Not for anyplace I know about. Unfortunately, I think it was just worn by a slob." She found two receipts for pizza on the windowsill, both paid for with cash. "Did the kids have credit cards?"

"Josh didn't, for sure. And Misty didn't have a job back home or the sort of family who could give her theirs. So I doubt it."

Adele crumpled the receipts and let them fall loosely from her hand. There was nothing here that would help them. "Do you recognize any of this stuff?"

Natalie began to examine the strewn contents of the room, doing her best not to actually touch anything. "No." She shook her head. "Nothing.

He…God this is sickening. My family's home is small and simple, but immaculately clean. We…he never lived like this."

Adele reached out for Natalie's hand and gave it a quick, reassuring squeeze. "Don't look so disappointed. We're just getting started. Let's go back outside before we die in here." She wiped a trickle of sweat from her temple.

"Okay." Natalie lifted her chin a little. "I'll think of something to tell my mother when I update her tonight."

With a sigh, Natalie reached into her purse and shoved aside an enormous paperback novel to dig out a hair rubber band. She quickly swept her hair up into a messy, but somehow fashionable-looking, ponytail. "What next?" She fanned the back of her neck with one hand. "The music clubs?"

Adele locked the apartment door on their way out, then carelessly tossed the apartment keys into an overgrown bush in the courtyard.

Natalie's eyebrows jumped as she watched the keys disappear. Adele didn't offer an explanation for her actions, and at the moment, she didn't care enough to ask.

"Too early for that. Next we head over to Jackson Square. If your brother's halfway decent on the clarinet, then there's a good chance he's on a street corner trying to make money from it. It should be busy there this time of day and I know most of the regulars."

"I just want him to be okay, but—" Natalie's expression went a little sour as they trotted down the courtyard stairs, their feet loud against the metal. "I hate the idea of him begging for money. If things were that bad I can't imagine why he wouldn't call me."

"Ms. Abb—"

"Natalie, remember?"

Adele inclined her head in acknowledgment. If Natalie didn't mind that calling her by her first name was a bit unprofessional, she certainly wasn't going to complain. "Right. Natalie. What do you do for a living?"

Natalie blinked a few times at the seemingly random question. "I'm an assistant professor of Colonial and Revolutionary Period American history. Why?"

Adele wasn't the least bit surprised by Natalie's occupation. She had guessed researcher or librarian or something equally studious, and this was more than close enough. Next she imagined the entire college baseball team vying for a seat in the front row of the young professor's class.

"If you were a sixteen-year-old boy, away from home for the very first time, and doing something your successful, intelligent, older sister is dead-set against, would you call her with your tail between your legs at the first sign of trouble?"

"If I needed help—yes."

Adele pursed her lips and gave her a look that conveyed her doubt.

"You think he wouldn't call me out of pride and that I wouldn't help him to prove a point? That—that's not true!"

"Of course you'd help him." Adele stepped off the stairs and into the courtyard. "But you'd have busted his chops about it first."

Natalie didn't deny it, but still managed to look genuinely offended.

"Please don't take this the wrong way, but you're not thinking like a teenager. You're thinking like a rational adult." *Who looks like she wants to punch me in the face.* "If Josh had spoken to you recently, you might have actually convinced him to come home. I'm *not* saying it's right for him to ignore your mom's calls, I'm just saying I can sort of, maybe, understand why he might be reluctant to touch base."

A crease formed between Natalie's brows. "He didn't want a hard time and he didn't want to be convinced to come home," she murmured so low that Adele barely heard. "Jesus, I didn't mean for him to think he couldn't call me."

Adele felt the pain in Natalie's voice as though it were her own. "Couldn't call and decided not to call aren't the same thing. I'm sure Josh knows you'll always be there for him. Maybe he's not *ready* for you to be there for him just yet."

Her words were greeted with silence and Adele had begun to wish she'd kept her big mouth shut when Natalie spoke up.

"Which do you think it is?" An involuntary shiver passed through Natalie and her voice trembled. "Couldn't call or just hasn't?"

Detective Lejeune sighed. "Odds are Josh is fine. But we both know I'm not certain and that your family can't live with anything less."

"Right," Natalie rasped as though they'd come to some sort of an understanding.

Adele stepped aside as a group of laughing college kids wove between her and Natalie. "That reminds me. Have you checked with your phone carrier to find out if his cell phone is still being used?"

Natalie's jaw sagged. "No. Ugh! I should have thought of that."

Adele gave her a lopsided grin. "Why? Your job is to teach about George Washington. This is my job. We'll do that today too. And as far as begging goes…using your talent to play an instrument, so long as you're not hassling anyone while you do it, is a far cry from begging in my book."

Adele waved Natalie away from her car after tossing her sunglasses on the driver's seat and relocking the door. It was cooler to walk and they could look in on a few places along the way. Adele cocked her ear toward the bright sounds of a jazz band marching near the end of the block. A trumpet solo sang in the air. "Some folks say *music* is the soul of the city."

They were quiet for a few minutes as they walked. This part of the city had an old-world charm Natalie had never seen before, and she found herself wishing she could enjoy it.

"So." Adele tucked her thumbs into the pockets of her pants and smiled to herself. "Have you heard of a website called hotprofessors-dot-com?"

Natalie tripped over her own feet and blushed a shade of red that would make Lucifer himself envious. "Uhh...well...I mean, maybe."

Delighted, Adele snorted and reached out a steadying hand. Maybe Natalie didn't spend all her time with her nose in a book after all. "Oh, my God!" Adele threw her head back and laughed, showing off deep dimples that hadn't made an appearance all day. "Just how many flaming hot chili peppers are there by your name?"

* * *

Evening the next day...

The sun hung low in the summer sky as Natalie sat at a small wrought-iron table in the shadowy courtyard of a small café in the French Quarter. The space was hidden from the street by a tall brick fence and a row of thick green bushes. It felt ten degrees cooler in the shade. It seemed miles away from the hustle and bustle of the street. An oasis. Natalie was glad they'd ended back here after traipsing across the city today.

A waiter moved from table to table as he lit small candles nestled into hurricane glasses. Natalie drew her fingertip through the condensation on her glass of lemonade, absently making designs on the glass as Detective Lejeune, her back to Natalie, chatted on the phone a few feet away.

The sound of trickling water from the nearby fountain was soothing and Natalie tried to allow it to penetrate her frayed nerves. The day had been an unmitigated disaster when it came to finding Josh. When a tiny lead would appear, it would vanish with their very next stop. The teenager, it seemed, had simply evaporated into the evening mist of the city.

Natalie quietly observed Adele, who was clearly unfazed by the heat and long day. Adele looked just as put together in her dove-gray linen pants and crisp white sleeveless top as she had the day before. This was the third phone call the detective had reluctantly stopped to take in the past hour. And Natalie could tell from the occasional snippets of conversation that had carried to her ears that Adele was being pulled from this case.

This call, however, seemed a bit different. Whereas Adele appeared frustrated with the other calls, this time she was frustrated *and* annoyed. Her voice was a bit louder and she gestured vigorously with her hands as she spoke. When Adele finally turned her phone off with a short jab of her finger, she had to take a deep breath to compose herself before turning to face Natalie once again.

Adele ran a hand through her hair, sending the blond locks into slight disarray before absently smoothing them down with one hand. "I'm sorry about that."

Natalie shifted uncomfortably in her seat. *This is where she tells me goodbye and I have to figure this out on my own.* "Is there a problem?"

Adele smiled softly and Natalie couldn't help but return the gesture. "Of course not. I, well…we should talk."

Natalie gave a reluctant nod and sat a bit straighter in her chair. She lifted her glass to her lips but her stomach was churning so she set it back down without taking a sip.

"And we should eat. I'm starving to death." Adele unclipped her badge, gun and handcuffs and stuffed them into a large canvas purse she set next to the table. She placed the phone onto the tabletop, then unceremoniously plopped down into her seat and looked longingly at the outdoor bar. With a quick gesture to the bartender, he began pouring Adele a lemonade of her own.

Natalie eyed the designer purse that now held the gun and badge. "Does this mean you're off duty?"

Adele gave her a knowing, sympathetic look and kicked out her feet in front of her. She crossed her legs at the ankles and sighed with relief. They'd easily walked twelve miles. "It means that I want to get comfortable. But I'm always a detective, no matter what I'm wearing, Natalie. I don't just stop looking for your brother because it's dinnertime or I'm on another case, or because…well, you've gone back home to Wisconsin."

The waiter delivered Adele's drink on his way to a table of laughing tourists near the rear of the courtyard.

"Back to Wisconsin?" Natalie's eyes fluttered closed and her heart sank. "We can't give up." When she opened her eyes again, a few seconds later, Natalie had to blink at the sudden change; the courtyard was now immersed in soft gaslight.

"I'm not. I promise." To Natalie's surprise, Adele looked stricken and reached out to grab her hand. She held it firmly. "But you've done what you can do and it's time for you to go home."

A gust of wind tousled a strand of pale blond hair and Adele absently tucked it behind her ear, the light mint scent of her shampoo moving with the breeze. Candlelight shimmered in warm brown eyes that regarded her with kindness and determination. "Just because you won't be here, doesn't mean you're in this alone."

The errant thought struck Natalie squarely in the chest with such force that for a second she actually forgot to breathe. *She's beautiful on the inside and out.*

"There you are!" a voice boomed.

Adele quickly pulled her hand from Natalie's as a tall man in his early forties, with short dark brown hair that bordered on black and a square jaw, purposefully strode toward their table. He was handsome in a rugged sort of way, with kind green eyes and a squirming child in his arms that looked somewhere between one and two years old. The toddler was dressed in shorts and a Saints T-shirt and adorably chubby.

"Landry, we talked about this," Adele hissed quietly. She stood and Natalie stood with her. "I'm not finished here."

The man glanced at Natalie, their eyes holding steady for a heartbeat before his shifted to Adele. "I heard you the first time on the phone, darlin'." He grinned unrepentantly. "But we were already so close, I thought I'd bring Logan by to say hi to his mama." He took his son's hand in his and waved it at Adele.

Natalie's eyes widened. Detective Lejeune hadn't mentioned a family and Natalie was sure she hadn't seen a wedding ring. But a single look at this gorgeous baby left no doubt as to his parentage. And the man's adoring gaze meant that he and the detective were together. With a twinge of what she knew was unflattering envy, Natalie acknowledged that they were a picturesque-looking family, like the mock photos that came preinserted in picture frames or one of those outdated Stepford-family magazines at the gynecologist's office.

At the word "mama," Logan practically launched himself toward his mother, leaning dangerously far forward away from his father's chest, arms outstretched.

"Hello, little man," Adele cooed as she took the toddler and settled him easily against her. With sticky fingers, he determinedly started reaching for anything he could grab, but her hair was shorn too short for him to do much damage. "Ms. Abbott, let me introduce you to my husband, Detective Landry Odette."

"NOPD homicide department," he added.

"Call me Nat—Wait." Adrenaline surged through the professor and she gripped the side of the table to keep from crumpling to the ground. "Homicide?" *This is why she was unhappy on the phone?* "Oh, my God, Josh—"

"Whoa. Whoa!" Landry's eyes went round. "This is a purely personal visit. Nobody is dead." A pause. "At least that we know about."

"Jesus Christ, Landry," Adele groaned. She could only shake her head.

Landry extended his hand politely to Natalie and let his words sink in for a moment before adding, "Nice to meet you, Natalie. Ella mentioned your case last night. You're the professor from Wisconsin with the stepbrother."

Adele seemed embarrassed as Natalie gave her a curious look and nodded dully.

Landry squeezed Natalie's hand gently as they shook, his eyes kind and inquisitive as they met hers again. "I hope you've had better luck today?"

Natalie looked better, but still had a slightly green tinge to her pallor. "I—not really."

"Don't pass out on us, okay?" Landry said worriedly, shooting an apologetic look to his wife.

"Natalie." Adele took a step closer to the other woman, obviously ready to catch her should her legs give way.

"I'm fine," Natalie murmured, only barely suppressing the urge to swat away Adele's concerned hands, irritated and embarrassed by her visceral reaction. "I'm fine."

Adele frowned and raised an angry eyebrow at her husband.

The color fully back in her cheeks and composure firmly in place, Natalie looked to Adele in question. "Who's Ella?"

Adele made a face. "I never cared for 'Adele' but I use it at work, I guess because I'm too lazy to correct folks." Then she focused on her son. "Ella's what anyone who really knows me and what my friends and family call me." She nuzzled the boy's cheek and he erupted in a fit of giggles that left both Natalie and Landry standing with grins on their faces, utterly charmed. "Isn't that right, sugar?" she said to the toddler as she noisily kissed his rosy cheeks. "And this is our son, Logan."

Natalie reached out to touch Logan but pulled up short. She was never very good with babies, and he seemed so happy at the moment that the last thing Natalie wanted to do was make him cry. She settled on saying, "Hi, Logan."

Logan looked at her with his mother's intelligent, caramel-colored eyes. "Bye-bye," he said enthusiastically, waving one fist. "Bye!"

Landry laughed. "So close."

"No," Adele corrected gently, adding a kiss to Logan's forehead for good measure. She adjusted him a little higher so she could look him in the eye. "*Hi.* Not bye-bye."

His new position, on his mother's hip, put his gaze directly in line with the gas lamp near their table. Utterly distracted, Logan flopped his head down on his mother's shoulder and began to chew on his fist, his drool promptly pooling against the bright white cotton of Adele's shirt.

Adele pinned Landry with a serious look, absently running her fingers through her son's dark hair. "Has he eaten yet?"

Natalie stood by, feeling awkward in the midst of the familial exchange.

A guilty look flittered across Detective Odette's face. "We had a late lunch."

"Landry!" Adele's exasperation was clear enough that even Natalie winced at the man's impending demise.

Landry held up both hands in good-natured surrender. "We're on our way now. We just wanted to say hi. You eat too and we'll see you tonight." He lowered his voice and nudged Adele with his hip. "I'd like to spend at least a little of our day off together."

Natalie shifted uncomfortably, guilt assailing her. Detective Lejeune had spent her entire day off with her. When she caught up with Joshua, she was going to hug him for a week, then kill him. Slowly.

Adele passed her son back to Landry then rose to her tiptoes to brush her lips against Landry's cheek, scrunching her nose up as she placed a second kiss against the heavy five o'clock shadow on his chin. "I still need to go to the Dixie Brewery."

His expression darkened. "Ella—"

"I'll be fine." Adele's tone left no room for argument, but she squeezed his forearm in a gentle show of affection. "Now feed him and yourself, and I'll see you later."

Landry looked like he wanted to argue, but then thought better of it. "It was nice meeting you, Natalie." Landry settled his son against his broad chest. "If anyone can find your brother, it will be Ella, here. She's one of the NOPD's brightest stars."

Adele rolled her honey-brown eyes, but looked pleased at her husband's obvious pride.

"You too, Detective Odette." Natalie glanced at the baby who was babbling happily to himself. "Bye-bye, Logan."

Hearing his name, he sat up, suddenly alert, and waved one hand wildly. "Hi!"

Adele rolled her eyes again and puffed out a loud sigh, but both Landry and Natalie couldn't help but chortle.

Alone once again, the women sat back down and a waiter discreetly placed two menus before them. The sun had completely disappeared, providing a blessed respite from the heat, and the courtyard was bathed in the golden glow of flickering flames.

Cringing, Adele situated her purse at her feet. "I'm sorry for that. I told him I was working, but he was only a half a block away at his mother's souvenir shop when he called. I don't think he could help himself."

Natalie waved away Adele's concerns. "Don't be sorry. I don't blame him for wanting to see you. He's adorable, by the way."

Adele's eyebrows crawled up her forehead. "Landry?"

Natalie's lips curled. "I was thinking Logan. Landry isn't my type, but…" she tilted her head to the side, her hair shifting over her shoulder, "at least he wasn't drooling."

A burst of laughter had Adele nearly choking on her lemonade. She lifted her napkin and dunked it into her water glass and made a face as she blotted the damp spot on her blouse. "Don't let Landry hear you say that. He thinks he's *everyone's* type."

Not everyone's. Natalie held in a sigh. For a few minutes, neither woman spoke. The courtyard was starting to fill with couples and small groups for dinner, their conversations animated and lively. It was a comfortable silence during which Natalie listened to the wind as it gently rustled the bushes near their table, bringing with it the faraway scent of rain and a feeling that this fruitless day was finally coming to a close. Almost. "You mentioned someplace called the Dixie Brewery…"

Any lingering mirth remaining in Adele's expression instantly dried up. "It's my stop right after dinner."

"But—"

"*My* stop. As in police only." Detective Lejeune paused as though waiting for another objection, not bothering to hide her surprise when Natalie conceded with the tilt of her head. "It's an old, abandoned beer brewery in Mid-City where the down-and-out, mostly addicts and nonfunctioning alcoholics, go for a place out of the rain or where they can sleep."

Natalie's jaw sagged.

"I know a lot of the regulars and they know me. The uniforms clean it out fairly regularly, but the regulars just keep cutting through the fences and coming back. It's not a nice place, but it's where I sometimes find runaways or older teens who are too spaced-out on drugs to do much more than lay around." Adele set aside her menu with a deep frown. Apparently, they'd both lost their appetites.

Natalie swallowed thickly. "Addicts? Nonfunctioning alcoholics? But-but that's not Josh."

"I doubt this will pan out, but I'm going to check there to be sure. Kids somehow find their way there. It's the last obvious place to look."

"He won't be there." Natalie scrubbed her face with her hands, her skin feeling unnaturally warm. "I don't want him to be someplace horrid like that, but then I do, because I can take him home."

Adele's eyes softened. "Natalie."

Natalie held up a hand. "I'm sorry. My emotions are all over the place." She licked her lips nervously and blinked back the hot sting of tears. "We aren't going to find him, are we?"

"I don't know," Adele whispered, voice unexpectedly thick. She reached out for both of Natalie's hands, cupping them carefully between hers, as though they were being held there for safekeeping.

Even though Natalie had already surmised that Detective Lejeune was a tactile person by nature, often reaching out to make contact as she spoke, *this* gesture was somehow oddly intimate for virtual strangers, and Natalie felt a corresponding tightness in her chest at the comforting sensation.

Adele squared her shoulders and warned off their approaching waiter with a single unwavering look. "Are—are you ready for me to tell you what I really think?"

"Not even close." Natalie let out an uneven breath. "But tell me anyway."

Adele nodded slowly, reluctantly, compassion shining in her eyes. "We've already checked all the usual places. I've put out feelers all over the city to every one of the contacts I've made in my five years as a detective. We've been to all the hospitals, and I-I checked the morgue."

Natalie flinched as though she'd been slapped. Thoughtfully, the detective had done that outside her presence.

"He hasn't pawned his horn, there is no money or employment trail, we have no reason to suspect foul play, and he hasn't used his phone in a few weeks. He's old enough to get around on his own, and he's not alone. As far as we know, he is with his girlfriend. If he was just living his life normally and oblivious to the fact that his family is desperate to reach him, we probably would have already run across at least one of them by now. This means that if he's still in the city, chances are he does not *want* to be found. And, I'm sorry, Natalie, if that's the case, we probably won't find him until he's ready."

Anger and fear boiled sickly in Natalie's stomach and she laid a flat hand against the clenching flesh. "So I just stop trying? Jesus, he's my *brother*. How do I just go back home and go to work as if everything is just fine?"

"I didn't say that you give up on him." Adele's soft drawl was deeper than normal, and more fervent. "It's not giving up to go home and live your life. Josh needs to come to you now. Doing what we've been doing will *not* find him if he doesn't want to be found."

Adele reached out and tenderly wiped a glistening tear that had escaped down Natalie's cheek. "You won't forget about Josh, and neither will I. And, Natalie—" Their eyes met and held. "I never give up. And I never stop looking. It's who I am." She smiled reassuringly, the gesture brimming with resolve. "It's what I do."

PART TWO

CHAPTER THREE

Two years and one month later...

Rain emptied from the sky in great sheets, drenching New Orleans in a gushing blanket of warm water. Thunder boomed so loudly that it drowned out the sound of the rain and shook the broken glass panes in the windows of the Dixie Brewery.

Built in 1907, the old brick factory stood in ruins, a haunted relic of better times...of times before an apocalyptic hurricane, and looters, and promises of repair and refurbishment that never came. Old, ruined machinery, garbage, and shredded, water-damaged furniture was strewn about in chaotic piles.

Doors, long torn from the hinges and tossed into splintered piles, provided an all-access pass to the sprawling building. Crumbling walls gave way to uneven stacks of bricks and lowly burning fire pits used by its residents. There was no need for heat in the late summer night, but the fires provided enough light to walk through the rubble and acted as gathering points for homeless companions.

But on this night the sky lit with such frequent bursts of blinding lightning that, at times, it seemed like afternoon, and the pits sat dark and moldering, unused.

Misty laughed hysterically as she and Joshua Phillips flopped down into a pile of dirty blankets. They missed the soft landing they'd anticipated as the cardboard boxes they were aiming for shifted out from beneath them. Her voice echoed in the cavernous room.

"Oh-oh-oh, shiiiit," Josh slurred, rubbing his bottom with two hands. He'd landed in a shallow puddle and his dirty jeans were now soaked. "Not funny." Dazedly, he struggled for a moment before he pulled his cell phone from his back pocket and put it onto his concaved belly to save it. He smacked dry lips together. "Got any more Pepsi? Hey, you okay?"

Lightning flashed, illuminating the brewery, and Misty scrunched her nose up at the disgusted, slack-jawed look on Josh's face. Affectionately, she ruffled his long, stringy dark hair with one hand. "Yeah. 'Cept for my ass is wet too." She sat back, enjoying the feeling of ice running through her veins as the drugs in her system fuzzed the world around her and cranked up the blessed white noise in her head. An overwhelming sense of peace enveloped her.

Josh's head lolled sideways and he stared at his girlfriend, his glassy eyes blinking with exaggerated slowness and glinting in the low light. He plucked at the dank tank top that clung to her body like a second skin. "Your everything is wet and I want a kiss." He puckered up and made a kissing sound, but lost interest in the kiss only a second later.

She snorted and tried to snatch away his cell phone, but missed when he shifted away. His clarinet, and everything else they'd owned had been sold ages ago. Everything but his stupid phone…that he didn't even use. "Gimme it!" she whined. "I want to take your picture, and then we need some tunes."

"Why?" Josh regarded her skeptically before staring at the ceiling, his mouth sagging as he continued to stare off into nothing, looking like a zombie.

"Damn, Joshie." Misty chuckled. "You shouldn't have taken that second hit." She tried to sit up and made it on her third attempt. "You're *too* wasted."

Eventually, a slow smile formed on his face—the only outward sign that what she'd said had registered—and he laughed quietly at himself. "Yeah."

Lightning flashed, and for a second Misty caught a glimpse of the husky teenage boy who'd come to this city with her more than two years before, instead of the emaciated, scraggily bearded man next to her. Then she blinked, and the normal Josh was back. "Whoa," she whispered to herself, her eyes going owlish, wondering what exactly was in the heroin they'd just taken. "Fuck-fucking f-fentanyl. Holy shit."

"Mmm?"

"Gimme the phone and say cheese." This time she managed to snatch the phone off his belly and take a sloppy picture, pushing random buttons until the flash went off.

"Don't!" Josh hissed. Guardedly, he glanced around, suddenly hyperaware of his surroundings. "Someone'll steal it."

"Who's gonna take it? It's raining too hard for anyone to be out, and it's practically deserted in here tonight." From their place in the shadows, Misty did her best to follow his line of sight. The room was empty except for her and Josh, and a sleeping drunkard named Crisco, who was sprawled out on the floor nearby, snoring. She'd nearly overlooked him. Like one of the many dilapidated pieces of furniture that littered the floor, Crisco spent so much time in the brewery that nobody even noticed him anymore.

Misty squinted when she heard a noise coming from the far end of the room. A lone man entered, but stayed along the far wall, splashing through several puddles as he walked.

Josh reached out for the phone, but let his arm fall to his side when Misty stepped away. "Gotta pee," she giggled quietly, and headed toward a tall concrete pillar a dozen feet away.

She staggered as she walked, intent on using the phone as a flashlight but unable to work the buttons in time. It wasn't easy to see enough to navigate the floor, but in between the blinding flashes of lightning that brightened the room it wasn't pitch black, but an eerie, inky blue tone that made her shiver. She managed to situate herself behind a concrete pillar before peeling down her Daisy Duke denim shorts, and began to squat. Suddenly the scent of stale urine and feces wafted up to her and made her gag. Someone else had used this spot as a toilet recently, and she aborted her mission with a grunt of revulsion.

Afraid of what she might step in, she moved a large step away and began to tug up her shorts to find a better location. With one hand she pushed her wet hair out of her face and glanced up to see a second man had joined the first at the far side of the room. They spoke quietly for a few seconds. A burst of lightning chased away the darkness just in time for her to see the shorter man hand something in a thick white envelope to the other.

Unfazed by the apparent drug deal, she unsteadily lifted her foot to check it for shit, human or otherwise. She silently hoped for dog shit, which smelled far better. A crack of thunder exploded directly overhead, startling her, and Misty let out a surprised squawk as she tipped over. The phone flew out of her hand when she hit the ground, landing on all fours.

"Ugh." She blindly felt around for the phone, hoping she wouldn't find the crap pile first. Grabbing the phone, she stuffed it into her front pocket. The fall, and the stench, and mostly the drugs coursing through her system caused her stomach to lurch and she leaned back against the pillar. Panting slightly, she closed her eyes as the coolness of the pockmarked concrete seeped through her clothes and its roughness bit into her damp skin.

"Hey!" Josh piped up from the darkness, his voice sounding wobbly.

She opened her eyes and was about to answer her boyfriend, when she saw one of the men from the drug exchange snap his head in their direction at the sound of Josh's voice, then freeze. The other man strode out of the room without a second glance and disappeared into the night.

"How about some for me?" Josh said loudly, his words slamming into each other.

Misty felt the hair on the back of her neck stand on end when the remaining man strode deliberately in Josh's direction. Halfway there, he stopped, his head turning from side to side. He'd clearly lost Josh in the shadows.

Misty remained silent and bit her lower lip as she quietly situated herself so that her body was behind the pillar, but she could still see her boyfriend and the stranger. A few more seconds passed, and all she could hear was the pounding of her heart and the pouring rain as it lashed against the building.

"Hello?" the man said quietly, his voice deep and scratchy, his eyes searching the darkness, his neck craned.

Josh didn't answer, and Misty held her breath.

Then, just as the man began to turn to leave, lightning flashed again, illuminating the entire room, including a smiling, reclining Josh, who was scratching his neck with both hands.

"Were you talking to me, kid?" This time the man's voice was loud and clear as he strode over and stopped right in front of Josh. The stranger tilted his head to the side like a curious puppy as he peered down at him.

"How about sharing some of that dope?" Josh asked, laughing as though the mere fact that he was asking was the funniest thing in the world. "It's nice to share."

Misty's eyes widened. Josh never stuck his nose in other people's business. They'd seen all sorts of things, horrible things, in the places they'd crashed around the city. But they didn't really *see* them because they were minding their own business. That kept them safe. They had learned to be alone…together. But tonight Josh was so, *so* trashed, that he was being stupid.

Rooted in place, the man let out a deep sigh and rubbed the back of his neck with the palm of his hand.

"By the way, nice suit. But we don't have a dress code." Finding himself terribly funny, Josh laughed riotously. "Never mind, buddy," he garbled. Josh briskly waved his hand in front of him like a king dismissing his unworthy subject. "Beat it."

Earsplitting thunder roared so loudly it was as though the sky itself was breaking in two.

"No, no." The man shook his head. "I have something for you." The stranger bent over and picked up a large brick from a pile next to

Josh's feet. Without another word, he hefted the brick over his head and brought it crashing down with all his weight behind it, careening it into Josh's skull with a sickening, squishing thud.

The sound of Josh's head being split wide open was like a watermelon exploding against a wall, splatter making it all the way against Misty's pillar. Misty clamped her hand over her mouth, her head already thrown back in a silent, horrified scream.

Hot urine streamed down her legs, and her entire body shook.

Lightning flashed and the man noticed a bum unmoving, passed out cold on the floor nearby. With the dripping, bloody brick still held tightly in his hand, he gently placed it into one of the bum's limp hands. He righted himself, and with his clean hand, plucked his cell phone from his pocket to make a call.

Misty felt her world turn upside down amidst crackling thunder.

The man's calm voice grew fainter and fainter as he exited the Dixie Brewery.

* * *

Detective Lejeune sighed as she hit her left turn signal and eased onto Tulane Avenue. "I know, I know, Landry. I'm sorry." She wanted to turn up the volume on her cell phone but gave up, her eyes narrowed in concentration as she navigated the nearly empty streets through the pounding late summer storm. It had been raining for hours, and anyone who didn't want to get soaked was already tucked safely inside somewhere.

Thunder rolled overhead, and she had to repeat her apology. It was 10:30 p.m. and Adele should have been home hours ago, but a last-minute clue was calling her to make one more stop before she got up close and personal with a glass of white wine, her favorite chair, her son's sleepy murmurs and her husband's warm lips.

Landry had been dealing with a grumpy three-and-a-half-year-old alone all night. He was an excellent father, who never complained about doing chores like laundry or vacuuming. But Adele, whose hours were much more predictable than the homicide detective's, was the designated "bath giver and reader of bedtime stories" and when she had to work late, Landry struggled on his own.

Adele worriedly chewed her lower lip. "Did you feed him something healthy for dinner and give him a kiss good night for me?"

An indignant snort filled her ear. "Course I did."

The healthy dinner part was a lie and she knew it. Left to his own devices, Landry, much to Logan's delight, would have definitely selected pizza. Adele was quite convinced that she had the only daycare-age child in New Orleans who could order pizza on the telephone and never forgot to ask for extra cheese and light sauce. She smiled inwardly.

"Hey, we both have the day off tomorrow. How 'bout we do some fishin' on Lake Ponchartrain?"

Adele stopped at a red light and looked skyward. "Are you planning on building an ark tonight?"

"Oops. Right. Okay, the movies then."

"Deal."

"But no cartoons. We watched the *Little Mermaid* tonight. Twice."

Adele snickered. "He *loves* that movie. And don't pretend you don't know all the songs by heart too."

"Ugh!"

She could practically hear his frown.

"It's not a very manly movie for his favorite."

"Well, he's not a man yet, so I'm not too concerned. He can learn to enjoy your beloved *Reservoir Dogs* when he's…never, actually. That movie is disgusting."

Landry laughed.

"Okay, hon, I'm almost there." She hit the accelerator. "Unless I get very lucky, I'll be home in about forty-five minutes."

"I should have my girlfriend out of here by then."

"If she's cute, don't have her leave on my account."

"Ha. Ha."

"See you soon." Arriving at the Dixie Brewery, Adele hung up and pulled in behind an empty police cruiser with its red lights flashing.

"Jesus," she muttered to herself. "What kind of douche bag cops toss people out into this sort of storm?" She grabbed an elastic band from her bag and pulled the wavy hair that nearly hit her shoulders into a messy ponytail.

Adele had finally started getting used to working without a partner. Hers had retired three months ago and the department had yet to assign her someone permanent, allowing her to work alone as an experiment, of sorts, in the face of ever-shrinking budgets. She liked it, and was as productive as ever, but there were times, like this, when she wouldn't have minded a little backup. Just in case.

Having worked through the entire night before, she was bone-tired. Being tired, she knew, led to mistakes that could be deadly. Adele mentally pumped herself up for a few seconds before leaving the car.

The detective entered the brewery cautiously, her powerful flashlight carving a path through the darkness. She kicked away an empty syringe and a few beer cans with a look of disgust as she scanned her surroundings carefully. Halfway into the room, Adele heard a low keening sound that increased in volume as she went. By the time she hit the doorway to the adjacent room, the keening had turned into outright screams.

Gun drawn, she sprinted forward.

"Keep whoever it is back!" a male police officer boomed, sending his partner to intercept Adele.

Adele's eyes widened as she watched one of the two uniformed cops, Officer Jay Morrell, who, unfortunately, she knew from her academy days, deliver a stunning kick to Crisco's chest.

Crisco's screams shifted to broken howls and coughs, and he struggled to crawl away from Morrell, who yanked him back by his hair.

"What the *hell*, Morrell?" Adele roared. "That's just Crisco!" Every cop in the city who wasn't fresh off the turnip truck knew that Crisco was essentially harmless.

Morrell kicked Crisco in the stomach and Crisco began to vomit. "Let's try this again," Morrell snarled. "Why'd ya kill 'im?"

Thunder shook the walls.

"Stop right there!" a young officer with a short Afro and wide, scared eyes barked at Adele. "Stop!" Dutifully, she froze, and in that same second, the officer seemed to realize she had a gun in her hand and drew his, his hand unsteady.

Lightning flashed.

Adele quickly threw her hands in the air, her mind split between what Morrell was doing and saying and trying to keep this obvious rookie from shooting her. "Whoa! Hang on! I'm NOPD. A detective." With an exaggerated motion, she glanced down at the badge on her belt. "Detective Adele Lejeune, CID, Juveniles." She rattled off her badge number a little frantically.

Doubt overtook the rookie's face, and he looked over his shoulder at his older partner in question. "Jay?"

"Tell him who I am, Morrell," Adele growled as she ever so slowly holstered her weapon.

Crisco killed someone? That made no sense at all. Even from where she was standing she could smell the booze over his general body stench, which was saying a lot. She doubted Crisco could even stay upright for more than a few seconds at a time, much less harm anyone.

Lightning flashed again, and this time Adele caught a glimpse of a body on the floor behind Morrell. *Crap.*

Crisco began to squirm in Morrell's grasp and the cop tightened his hold, twisting his fingers into Crisco's greasy blond hair. Then he grunted unhappily at his partner. "She's a cop. A *de-tec-tive*." Childishly, Morrell drew out every syllable of the word, making it clear that he resented the fact that he had yet to receive his own gold shield.

Crisco held his arms up weakly as if to ward off future blows, but the effort only drew Officer Morrell's attention back in his direction. The cop stuck his face close to Crisco's and hissed in a low whisper, "Remember what I said about takin' back what you…"

But the last of Morrell's words were lost to the sound of the thunder.

Then, in a move so quick that it was over before she could intervene, Morrell slammed his fist into Crisco's face. The crashing blow was so brutal that several teeth flew from Crisco's mouth and scattered across the floor. He went sprawling, face-first, into a sludgy puddle near a broken window.

Adele flinched at the extreme violence and fury sang through her. "What the blue fuck, Morrell? He's not even fighting you! You haven't even cuffed him!"

She moved to stop Morrell's attack when the rookie put himself in Adele's path once again. Hackles rising even further, her eyes flashed dangerously. "Lay a single finger on me, rookie, and I will break. Your. Nose. And put your stupid gun away before you shoot yourself," she ground out.

He obeyed instinctively.

"I don't care if that swine Morrell is your partner, we need to stop him."

"Get over yourself, Lejeune," Morrell spat. "This drunkard was in the middle of confessin' to killin' that nasty junkie over there when you interrupted us. Wasn't he, Billy-Boy?" He rolled his eyes when his partner opened his mouth with an affronted look. "I mean, *Officer* Hobson."

"Y-yes." The rookie seemed a little confused, but immediately backed up his partner. "Yes. Absolutely. I heard him." He nodded decisively at Adele. "Crisco hit that guy with a brick and bashed his head in. And that's a fact."

"Shit." Morrell kicked at Crisco, whose jaw was barely out of the water and resting at an unnatural angle. "He's unconscious."

"I wonder why!" Adele elbowed Officer Hobson out of her way then stalked over to Morrell and shoved him back a step. It was like trying to move an oak tree. "Have you lost your mind? Are you trying to kill him?" With a growl, she spun and bent to check Crisco for a pulse. Her eyes fluttered shut in relief when she found one.

She gave the unconscious man's shoulder a small, apologetic squeeze, but didn't try to move him. He was okay for the moment, and she had no idea what injuries were brewing below the surface. From what she'd seen already Crisco would be lucky to walk away with missing teeth and a broken jaw. God knows what had happened before she arrived.

Morrell lifted his chin defiantly. "He was resistin' arrest. Look at my hand."

She shined her flashlight on the appendage in question and did, in fact, see what looked like a small bite mark.

Morrell shivered with distaste. "Now I'm gonna need a rabies shot."

"Bullshit!" she shot back, straightening. "If Crisco was resisting anything, it was getting his ass beaten by you." Livid, she clenched her jaw and did her best to control her temper. Her knuckles whitened around her heavy flashlight. It was all she could do not to knock that smug look off Morrell's face.

"Come near the suspect again, *Officer* Morrell, and I *will* arrest you." Turning, she pointed an angry finger at Officer Hobson. "Call an ambulance. Why isn't Homicide here?"

"He doesn't need an ambulance," Morrell insisted. "He's in this shithole brewery passed out drunk half the time, and nobody sends him to the hospital then."

Officer Hobson drew a nervous hand over his chin, unable to pull his eyes away from Detective Lejeune's harsh glare. "We only got here a few minutes before you did, Detective. I was just getting ready to call this in." He swallowed with a loud gulp. "Umm…I'll go and call…I'll just go."

Hobson practically bolted from the room.

Adele trained her flashlight on Crisco again to make certain his chest was still rising and falling. She caught sight of something that made her do a double take: a large, bloody, red brick covered with bits of skin, hair and general gore. She changed the angle of the flashlight. Blood was also caked onto one of Crisco's limp, outstretched hands and formed a broken droplet trail that led back toward the victim. Footprints smeared the trail, hopelessly breaking up the natural pattern.

The fire in Adele's belly burned even hotter. "Christ, Morrell, you've totally ruined the crime scene by stomping through the splatter with your muddy boots!"

With a quieter *boom*, the thunder seemed to finally be heading somewhere else. After a few seconds' delay, lightning filled the sky. The rain, however, still lashed relentlessly against the brewery.

"Maybe. But it won't matter," Morrell said confidently, adjusting his utility belt with both meaty hands. He bent and picked up his hat, which had fallen off during Crisco's beating, and settled it back on his shaved head, cocking it a bit to the side. "We found the murder weapon clutched in Crisco's grimy ole paw. And when I questioned him—"

"You mean when you *beat* him."

Morrell had the nerve to look offended. "When I *questioned* him, he confessed to tryin' to rob that junkie kid before killing him. Case closed. Next."

"Kid?" Adele's ears pricked and she swore under her breath as she carefully navigated her way over to the body. "Why didn't you mention that before?"

Morrell snickered. "He's not young enough for the kiddie police to care about."

"Asshole. We're not done here." Taking extreme care where she stepped so as not to further disrupt the crime scene or trip on something sharp, Adele finally squatted in front of the body. She swung her flashlight up to get a good look at the unlucky victim's face.

Adele immediately clamped her mouth closed to stop the bile that shot up from her stomach from spewing forward, though she couldn't prevent the overwhelming, coppery scent of blood from clinging to her nostrils. A large chunk of the victim's head, starting at the hairline at his temple, had been crushed. Gray matter and blood had spilled down the young man's forehead and formed grisly, red rivulets that carved crooked paths down his face. "Jesus Christ."

Morrell sniggered darkly. "Feelin' a little less sorry for Crisco yet?"

Adele brushed off his words as her gaze traced the victim's thin cheeks. Both his eyes were open and fixed, and his dark hair was longish, dirty, and as unkempt as his scraggly beard, which was also matted with sticky blood. Adrenaline made it hard to keep her hand steady as she moved the beam of light down bare arms covered in track marks. The victim was young and a mess and there was no way to tell for certain whether he was a juvenile by looking at him.

Adele wanted to reach into his pockets, but the scars on his arms made her think better of it. She wasn't willing to have a chance encounter with a dirty needle. "ID on the vic?"

"Nope. I had Billy-Boy check. And no library card either."

"Why are you even here? You work the Tremé neighborhood, unluckily for them."

She spoke absently as she continued to examine the body without touching it. An uneasy feeling that went beyond general queasiness over the gruesome gore on display began to overtake her. Her pulse, which was already clipping along at a fast walk, climbed to a vigorous trot.

"An anonymous tipster called in a disturbance. We're on nights this week and were on the way to Betsy's Hole-in-the-Wall for dinner. We were nearby, so I said we'd check it out. I never expected a goddamned corpse. Or to miss my dinner. This—"

But Adele had already tuned him out, her stare riveted to the victim's ruined face, recognition warring with the doubt and fuzziness that comes from the passage of time. She couldn't quite place the face…but… Then she focused on his blue eyes and a memory plucked a chord inside her so loudly that she felt a little unsteady on her feet. Her pulse rate exploded into a full gallop.

Adele had seen those eyes before, just on a prettier face. Realization crashed like a tidal wave, and her mouth dropped open. "Oh, no. No. No. No. *Shit.*"

"What?" Morrell stepped closer, his voice eager. "You know who the druggie is?"

"Shut. Up." But her roiling gut had already answered with a resounding, terrible yes. This was Joshua Phillips. The teenager from Wisconsin. The one she couldn't find. Guilt settled over her, cloying and heavy like a wet blanket.

Now Adele had only one thought. *How in the hell am I going to tell his sister?*

* * *

"Why are you doing this?" Detective Landry Odette's voice was nearly a shout as he paced around an interrogation room that held him and his wife.

They'd sequestered themselves in the small room for privacy, but their raised voices made the matter moot. Luckily, the squad room was mostly empty.

Landry sat down at the table across from Adele with a tired sigh. It was nearly four a.m. He'd been assigned to the murder at the Dixie Brewery and after dropping Logan off at his in-laws, visiting the crime scene, and having a short conversation with Crisco in the hospital, he met a seething Adele at the police station. "Ella?"

She sniffed and even after all these hours she swore she could smell the faint, metallic scent of blood. "What?" she snapped, profoundly hurt that he was trying to talk her out of doing what was right.

"You know nothin' will happen to Morrell in a case like this. Let it go."

Adele knew exactly what he was trying *not* to say. Crisco was a loser bum with no money and no family connections. His injuries, while painful, weren't life threatening. And he was accused of murder. If ever there was a case where the brass would look the other way, especially after the years of fallout over police brutality in the wake of Katrina, this was it.

"Yes, Crisco has a broken jaw and nose and a few missing teeth, that were already rotten, I might add. But otherwise he's fine," Landry went on. "At least now he's getting food that doesn't come in the form of a Budweiser, and he won't be sleeping in piles of garbage. Whether that dickhead Morrell roughed him up or not, Crisco still killed that boy. Crisco *told me* he did it...well, more like mumbled it. His jaw is wired shut."

Adele's lips turned up in a disbelieving sneer. "Are you seriously trying to get me to believe that what happened to Crisco was for the best? And dammit, Landry, since when do you call an eighteen-year-old a *boy*? When it's someone who is a suspect in one of *your* cases, that's a grown man."

Landry avoided her eyes and instead looked down at his hands, which were resting on the table.

"I won't be manipulated, especially by you." Her gaze turned beseeching. "I need to trust you."

"Oh, my God! You *can* trust me." His entire body began to vibrate with frustration. "That's why I'm trying to stop you!"

Furious. That was the only way to describe how she felt at this second. Full of fury. "Crisco is afraid of Morrell. Morrell practically threatened him not to recant right in front of me. You can't believe what he says now. That confession was literally beaten out of him."

Landry reached for one of Adele's hands, but she snatched it out of his way. Rejected, he curled his hands into fists. "Why are you taking this so personally?"

"Why aren't *you*? We can't torture suspects to get them to talk. You didn't hear him tonight." Her stomach twisted at the memory. "Crisco was screaming like a cat frying on an electric fence."

"Crisco confessed again in the hospital to me." He jerked his thumb toward his chest. "*Me.* Morrell was nowhere in sight."

"Don't you get it? Morrell doesn't have to be in sight because he already threatened Crisco and showed him what he can do to him if he doesn't abide by the threats."

"You told me yourself that what Morrell actually said could be interpreted to mean anything!" Landry threw himself back in his chair, the metal groaning, his face flushed. "You're talking about going against one of our own for someone you don't even really know."

Adele shot to her feet and stared at her husband as though he was a total stranger. "It's not just about Crisco. I can't believe you're going to ignore what happened. And you want me to ignore it! Since when don't you care about justice? You're not that kind of cop!" *You're not that kind of man.*

Landry shook his head and bolted upright just as quickly. He slapped his palms down on the table between them. "Don't make me the villain!"

The sound reverberated so loudly in the small space that it reminded Adele of the night's merciless thunder.

He glared down at his wife, challenge etched into every line on his face. "You can't ignore that Crisco committed murder. And not only did he confess to the crime, the murder weapon was found in his goddamned hand. He *did it*, Ella."

She closed her eyes. "Probably. But—"

"What Morrell did was wrong, dead wrong, but what do you want to do? Go after him officially and get Crisco's confession tossed out? That could cost us the conviction of a guilty man if this goes to trial." He threw his hands in the air. "You already went to the hospital and told Crisco to lawyer up. You believe in justice so much? Where's the justice for the victim or his family in any of that?"

Adele felt the sting of her own words being thrown back at her. "We can't rely on Morrell when he says he'd Mirandized Crisco. I went to the hospital to help. Despite what you think, I *don't* want our case thrown out. But it should be based on real evidence."

"Hobson backs up Morrell's version of what happened."

Adele rolled her eyes. "I checked. Hobson's been out of the academy for all of eight weeks. He almost peed himself in that factory tonight and doesn't know whether he's coming or going." She decided not to mention the fact that she was lucky the rookie hadn't accidentally put a bullet in her. "If Morrell told him to jump off a bridge, the only question Hobson would ask is whether he could lick his partner's boots before taking the plunge."

Landry crossed his arms over his thick chest. "You know you can't prove what you're alleging."

"That doesn't make it less true."

"Ella," he bellowed, scrubbing his short, rain-dampened hair with both hands. "Do not throw a grenade into our case and turn yourself into a rat in the process! You'll ruin your career."

"I've already talked to my lieutenant." Dejectedly, she leaned against the wall with one shoulder. *That* had not been a pleasant phone call. Her eyes were tired and gritty, and she blinked painfully as she wrapped her arms around herself in mute comfort.

Landry frowned, visibly torn between scooping up Adele and holding her close or strangling her.

Their eyes met, and Adele ached to lose herself in the comfort and safety of his sturdy embrace, and feel his lips murmur against her forehead that everything would be okay. But not while they were so far apart on this. Not when she could barely recognize the man she went to bed with every night.

Landry lowered his voice and reined in his emotions. He perched at the edge of the table. "I take it the conversation didn't go the way you wanted?"

Adele chuckled humorlessly. "He gave my current caseload away and told me to go home, to take a few days of vacation to cool off. Said that he'd talk to Morrell's lieutenant and that they'd deal with it internally and in a way that wouldn't compromise the case." Her boss had given her the verbal equivalent of a pat on the head, and it galled her to the core.

"I'm sorry. But he's right. Just…Let me drive you home. You've been up for nearly two days." Landry finally opened his arms to her, but once again she skirted his grasp.

Jaw set, he didn't try again. Instead, he lashed out, his own hurt on display. "Your pretty face shouldn't look so wounded. I never took you for naïve, Ella. Did you really expect anything different from the brass?"

Bitterness filled her mouth. "I *expected* more from my boss, but I *deserve* more from you."

Landry's spine stiffened at her words.

"I need you with me on this." She hated that she sounded so needy, as though she was pleading, but why couldn't he see how important this was? She didn't want to just look the other way. She wasn't sure she even could.

Landry let out a slow, defeated breath. "I can't support this. I won't. We're supposed to stick together."

It was clear the "we" he was referring to was not the two of them, but their brothers in blue. Landry had been a marine before he joined the NOPD. *Semper Fidelis* was in his blood. *Always faithful.* And she loved that about him. But for the first time in their marriage, Adele was forced to wonder where exactly she sat in the pecking order when it came to that unshakable allegiance. "*We*," she gestured between them, "are supposed to stick together too."

Her eyes glittered with unshed tears and Landry had to turn away, his own eyes glassy. "At least take some time to think about what you're doing, Ella. Promise me."

Reluctantly, she gave him a quick nod, the anger inside her warring with the hurt.

"Do you want me to contact the victim's family for a positive ID?"

"Right now, Landry, the only thing I want or need from you is the one thing you're unwilling to give." Sickened and her heart aching, she strode out of the interrogation room and into the larger squad room. With a violent kick she sent the first wastepaper basket she encountered sailing across the room, crumpled paper and empty coffee cups flying in all directions. "And don't you dare make that phone call!" she shouted without a backward glance.

* * *

A light groan came from the naked body lying nestled in a tangle of baby-blue sheets next to Natalie. "Who would call at this hour, babe?" A whimper. "It can't be morning." It was still dark out and they'd stayed up so late. "Even if it is, I'm not teaching today."

"Shh…" Natalie drew her fingers through the redhead's long hair before reaching over her bedmate to the nightstand to retrieve her phone. "Go back to sleep," she breathed, her voice little more than a sleepy whisper. Distracted by miles of skin, she kissed a slender, bare shoulder, her lips lingering there for another shrill ring of the phone before she grabbed it.

Natalie's own skin felt hot and hypersensitive, the tender flesh between her upper thighs still damp from her night with Hannah. She didn't bother to cover herself as she groggily stumbled out of bed and pressed the phone to her ear over a shock of messy chestnut hair. "M-Mom?"

"Ah…no. Is this Ms. Abbott?"

Still half asleep, an unconscious smile stretched Natalie's face as that soft, barely there accent rolled over her in a sensual wave. She moved to the open living room window and peered lazily out into the quiet night, her eyelids already starting to droop again, the faint sound of crickets in the yard barely registering. "Wh-who is this?"

A pause.

"This is Detective Lejeune with the New Orleans Police Department. I'm the detective that—"

Natalie snapped awake so quickly she had to reach out and grab the windowsill for balance. She cleared her throat. "I-I remember you, Detective. Of course. I'm sorry." She held the phone out in front of her, glaring at it as though it would give her a preview as to whether this was the call she'd prayed for or had been dreading for the past two years. She made her way to the sofa on wobbly legs, her heart pounding against her ribs. She placed the phone back against her ear. "Have you found him? Josh, I mean?"

"I believe so."

A split second of shining hope was replaced by a stunned look as Natalie listened to Detective Lejeune speak, her face growing more and more ashen with each passing second.

"A young man was killed in the Dixie Brewery tonight. I'm so, *so* sorry, but I believe the victim was your brother." Detective Lejeune's voice was gently authoritative and calm, but still audibly upset.

Natalie didn't remember sitting down.

She had no right to feel shocked. How could she? Even if Josh was the type of kid to run away, he wasn't the type to simply disappear and stay gone. Even if he didn't want to come home, he loved his family and would have reached out eventually, even if only to touch base or ask for money. Horror tinged with disbelief swept over her, swamping her senses. "I-I see. How?"

"It looks like he died from massive blunt force trauma to the head, though we won't know that for sure until the autopsy results are in."

"What does that mean? He was k-k-killed? Like an accident?"

"I—No. Murdered."

Silence.

"Natalie?"

The sound of her own heartbeat roared in her ears. "I'm still here. Was—OhmyGodohmyGod…was he alone?"

"Misty wasn't with him, if that's what you're asking. Natalie, we need a family member to identify the body. I can call his mother or father instead, if you'd like?"

Natalie looked skyward with pleading eyes. "No."

"Okay, then. I-I also wanted to say again, from me, that I'm *so* sorry."

For a few seconds the only sound on the line was the sound of uneven breathing.

"Natalie?"

Detective Lejeune's voice was so achingly gentle that it actually hurt. Natalie placed a hand against her chest, on top of her heart, as though she could somehow touch the source of the searing pain.

"Are you still there, Natalie? Is there someone there who can help you now?"

Natalie turned toward her bedroom, her forehead wrinkled. Her chin quivered as she spoke. "I...I'm not sure."

There was another awkward pause. "Your mother? Maybe you could call her."

Natalie shook her head sharply. "Not until I see him and we know for sure." Her voice trailed off as the lump in her throat grew too big to speak around. *Oh, Josh.* "I—I..."

"Do you have any questions?"

"Yes. No. I mean—" she stopped again. *I should have questions.* But she just...didn't. What was left to say? Everything was too late. Josh was dead. Detective Lejeune had said that they couldn't positively identify Josh from just the photo she had, but Natalie already knew deep in her heart that going to New Orleans would be nothing more than a formality. She could hear what the detective wasn't saying.

Then the tears began, scalding and fierce. They splashed onto her bare breasts and then the floor with a delicate plinking sound. Natalie swallowed hard a few times before she found her voice. "I'll be there..." She cast through her memories, trying to recall if there was a nonstop, early morning flight. She told herself not to think about telling her mother and stepfather. Not now, not yet. Because surely that would drive her to her knees. "I'll be there as soon as I can."

CHAPTER FOUR

"I'm so-sorry, Det-detec-tive." On her hands and knees, Natalie lurched forward and brutally retched into the toilet in the ladies' room at the New Orleans morgue. They hadn't made it there in time the first time Natalie had vomited, or the second. This was round number three. Her stomach was long empty and cramped viciously as her body ignored that fact and tried to turn itself inside out.

"Don't apologize." Adele held Natalie's hair out of the way with one hand and rubbed small circles between her shoulder blades with the other. "It's okay," she said softly, her lips near the back of Natalie's head. "Just let it out."

Detective Lejeune had told Natalie that Josh looked different now. She'd said in hushed, almost reverent tones that Josh had been through a lot and for her to be ready to be shocked and disturbed and a million other things. She'd warned her that the teenager was unkempt and very thin and that his body showed the wear and tear of someone who'd lost themselves to drugs and ultimately violence.

And Natalie had listened closely, nodded numbly, and girded her emotional loins as she told the morgue attendant to raise the curtain that separated her and her brother. And now, only a few minutes later, she understood that *nothing* could have prepared her for this.

Nothing could have prepared her to see the boy that she had taught to ride a bike, who loved peanut butter cookies, and hockey, and fuzzy slippers that resembled Sasquatch feet, looking as though he'd been living under a bridge or in a concentration camp. Nothing could have set her mind on the path that would allow her to accept seeing him stretched out on a cold steel slab, a white towel covering the ruined half of his head and a pristine sheet draped over his skinny body.

This was so *beyond* what she knew and could process that she'd asked the morgue attendant to look for several known scars to convince herself that she even knew this sad, dead boy at all.

Natalie sat back on her heels and drew in a shaky breath. Then another. Until the spasms in her stomach began to ease. "I didn't mean to do that. The mess I made…the morgue floor…I'm sorry."

Adele gently squeezed her arm. "Don't be embarrassed about that." She moved away and plucked a few paper towels from the dispenser and ran them under cool water.

When Natalie tried to get up to join the detective at the sink, Adele said, "S'okay. I locked the door. Nobody will bother us." She pressed the cool towels against Natalie's clammy, hot forehead and let her sit there on the bathroom floor as long as she needed.

Natalie's eyes fluttered closed as she greedily sucked in the comfort the way a man in the desert attacks a tall glass of water, knowing that once she got home no one would take care of her like this again, not without expecting something from her in return. Her mother and stepfather were out of the question.

And Hannah was a lot of things…attractive and brilliant, chief among them, but their relationship was…complicated. Natalie knew she'd be lying to herself if she said Hannah was her safe passage in a storm.

Natalie experienced a rush of not only gratitude, but also affection, for the detective, and after a moment more, felt a bit more like herself. A bit more in control. The worst was done and she would deal with the rest. "Thank you." She took the paper towels from Adele's hand, folded them in half, then used them to wipe her mouth and chin.

Adele merely nodded and graced her with a kind smile.

With a groan, Natalie teetered to the sink to wash her hands and rinse her mouth.

Adele never left her side, then seemed to remember something, and pulled a roll of breath mints from the pocket of her cotton slacks. She held them out to Natalie, who gave her a grateful look.

Natalie popped two mints into her mouth and began to chew, the flavor and strong scent already helping to quell any lingering nausea. "Do all the family members who come here get this sort of attention?"

Adele looked a little flustered and refused to take the roll of mints back from Natalie. "I don't know. Luckily, I don't have to come here often, but when I do, I help out however I can." She shrugged lightly. "It's my job."

"Somehow, I don't think holding my hair while I vomited multiple times is in your job description, Detective."

"I didn't mind."

Natalie found herself envious of Detective Landry Odette as she wondered what it would be like to have someone in her life on a full-time basis who was capable of such tender devotion. She threw away the paper towels and mint wrappers and brushed her hands off on her pants.

"Any chance you'd like to get some tea to settle your stomach? It always makes me feel better after I've been sick."

The questions that wouldn't come at half past four in the morning now flooded Natalie, and she nodded. Suddenly, she wanted more time together.

"Good," Adele said, obviously relieved.

For the first time, Natalie noticed the wrinkled clothes and dark circles under the other woman's bloodshot, honey-brown eyes.

"I know just the place."

* * *

"Have a seat. I'll be right back to make us that tea in just a minute." Adele ushered Natalie into a tall paisley highboy chair in her living room, then moved to her thermostat and turned up the air conditioner.

Outside, the sky was a stunning blue, and hot sunshine beat down on large, steaming rain puddles. The air was heavy and smelled like ozone and muddy water. To Natalie, New Orleans was like being on the inside of a giant, tropical volcano.

Grateful for the sudden blast of cooler air from a nearby vent, Natalie gave Adele a watery smile when Adele said, "Make yourself comfortable," before padding out of sight down a dim hallway. Her already light footfalls grew quieter with every step.

Natalie glanced around Adele's living room, a little overwhelmed. Okay, a lot overwhelmed. Without permission, tears filled her eyes and then spilled over. She brushed them away with shaky fingers, and when they wouldn't stop, she just let them come. Natalie didn't want to fall to pieces but wasn't sure she could stop herself.

She couldn't get the image of Josh's dead body out of her head. No matter what else was in front of her, there it was in her mind's eye, festering. Then there were the drugs. Detective Lejeune had said Josh had most likely been using heroin. *Heroin.* Just the word was terrifying.

Jesus, what kind of insane death spiral had her brother been living? And why couldn't she help him? Why wouldn't he let her?

Adele returned a few minutes later and crouched down in front of Natalie. "Where are you staying?" she asked softly. She handed the other woman a box of Kleenex.

Mindlessly, Natalie's hand reached out for the Kleenex box of its own accord. Dazed, she frowned. "Huh?"

"What hotel?"

"I-I don't know. What?" Then the words seemed to register. "No place yet. If it hadn't been him…I mean, at the morgue…" Tears continued to stream down her face, and it was Adele who snatched a tissue from the box and began to tenderly wipe Natalie's cheeks. "I wasn't sure whether I would fly home tonight so I-I-I bought a one-way ticket and didn't get a hotel room."

"We have a guest room. You can lie down there."

"N-no." Natalie's frown deepened. "You weren't expecting a guest." But the idea of staying suddenly called to her with the strength of a dozen sirens. She felt safe when she was with the detective, as though everything would somehow end up all right, even though the time for that had long since passed.

"You're more than welcome in my house, Natalie." Adele extracted a few more tissues and attentively continued to tend to the never-ending stream of hot tears. "In fact, maybe you'd like to lie down now?"

Yes. And pull the covers over my head and block out the entire world.

"You're tired too," Natalie said, as though somehow it wouldn't be right for her to rest if Detective Lejeune didn't. She leaned in to the other woman's touch.

"I am tired," Adele agreed in a weary murmur. "But I can't sleep quite yet anyway. I have to pick up Logan from daycare. Then there's his dinner and bath and we need to spend a little time together." She stifled a yawn. "But we'll be going to bed as early as I can manage."

Natalie's shoulders caved in on themselves, the tension falling from her body in visible waves. "Thank you. I d-don't want to be alone." She sniffed.

"You're not alone."

"But…" Natalie didn't know why she was trying to find a reason she couldn't stay when she so desperately didn't want to go. Like maybe she didn't *deserve* to feel safe and peaceful when Josh wouldn't ever feel anything again. "Your husband might not want…he might not want you to-to bring your work home with you."

Adele released a heavy sigh. "You're not *work*, Natalie. You're a person. And Landry will be fine."

There was an edge to Adele's voice that Natalie didn't understand.

"C'mon." Adele gently tugged her from her chair and led her down a hall to a modest-sized guest room. She gestured to a side door. "Bathroom is in there."

Restless but drained, Natalie lay down on top of the bed, her eyes closing immediately, though the tears didn't seem to want to stop. "Wake me. Wake me when you're ready to pick up your s-s-son, and I'll find a hotel. And—"

"Shh…" Adele took the tissue box from Natalie's already limp hand and set it on the nightstand. "We can talk later."

Natalie's mind began to drift. Part of it here, basking in the other woman's strong presence, part of it holding Josh's small hand the first time the little boy braved the cold water of Lake Mendota, and part it of it back home, in *her* seat, in her mother's kitchen.

She heard the light click off and the door creak closed, and in the next few breaths Natalie floated into an exhausted slumber.

* * *

Deep purple clouds had moved in and hung over New Orleans in the dark hours before dawn when Natalie awoke.

It took a few seconds to remember where she was and why she was here, and her stomach twisted into a painful knot when she did. "Oh, God," she hissed lowly, wishing this had all been nothing but a bad dream.

Natalie knew she should have called her parents yesterday afternoon or evening. But between a drive from the city morgue to the detective's house—where she vacillated wildly between silent numbness and gut-wrenching sobs—and when she practically collapsed in Detective Lejeune's guest room, the right moment never came.

A phone call at this hour would surely frighten her mother. Then again, Natalie pondered with icy logic, what the older woman would be afraid of was that someone was dead. And someone was.

But how could Natalie tell her mother that Josh was dead over the phone? It seemed cruel. Especially when she still wasn't sure exactly what *had* happened to him. Detective Lejeune had only given her the barest description of a possible robbery gone bad, promising more when she got to New Orleans and then delaying that discussion again until after their trip to the morgue. After that, Natalie had been in no condition to do much of anything but cry.

Even after what had to have been twelve solid hours of sleep, she felt fatigued, but too uneasy to go back to bed. Eager to think of anything but her brother's murder, she softly crept from the guest bedroom and began to explore the silent house, grateful for this respite before dealing with her parents.

Natalie had never been able to process strong emotions quickly. And even though Josh had been gone for two years, and she'd wondered a hundred times if the worst had happened, now that it actually had, it felt a little like the sky was falling all at once.

When Adele had offered her a drink to settle her stomach, Natalie assumed they'd head to one of the hundreds of cafés in the city, not the detective's own home. Being here now, especially in the middle of the night, felt very personal. Oddly so. The more Natalie considered it, the more she realized the characterization fit their relationship perfectly. Oddly personal. Adele was professional, of course, but she exuded so much warmth and empathy that Natalie couldn't help but see that as something that came directly from the woman, and not simply as part of her job.

In all honesty, Natalie had never met anyone quite like Adele.

The short amount of time they'd spent together now, and two years ago, was so intense for Natalie, as though her chest had been cracked wide open with nothing to block Adele's view directly inside. On one hand the vulnerability was mortifying. Unacceptable. On the other, the detective had never stopped trying to jam a life preserver over her head even as Natalie floundered.

Natalie thought about the day before and the horrors that had piled on top of each other, one after another, and recalled how Detective Lejeune had held her hand the entire time. *Ugh. Think of something else! Something simple.* So she exited the hallway and examined the living room and its contents in the bluish light of predawn.

The space wasn't at all what she expected from two police detectives with a small child…or maybe it was child*ren* now? Two years was a long time. If pressed to guess, Natalie would have said Detective Lejeune inhabited a newish apartment that was more fashionable and modern than classically pretty. And she would have been completely wrong.

The bright yellow house with white and turquoise trim was what Adele had described as an 1850s Creole Cottage and was located in the Faubourg Marigny neighborhood of the city. It wasn't large, but Natalie hazily recalled that it looked to be the nicest property on an old block. And judging by the number of houses under renovation and the detailed paint jobs in progress, it was a street in transition.

Natalie ran her fingertip over a dust-free bureau top as she walked. Either the detectives had the mother of all housekeepers or one of them was seriously anal retentive about messiness. No toys or magazines or dishes marred the sense of pristine order that she had to admit felt comforting when everything else around her was so out of control.

The living room was furnished with mahogany antiques that complemented the rich ochre walls and sage green cloth accents that looked mostly gray in the dim light. Silver-framed photos of smiling people dotted most of the available surfaces, and an enormous Oriental rug covered dark wood floors and dominated the center of the room. Several shuttered side windows were filled with stained glass that allowed ambient light from other houses and streetlights to stream in. During the day, she imagined, the late afternoon sunshine would scatter colored light beams everywhere.

The vibe of the room was one of quiet refinement, a comfortable mix of masculine and feminine, function and old-world class.

An elegant cop. Who knew?

* * *

Adele appeared behind Natalie, her hair a little messy from sleep and hanging freely around her shoulders. A thin, melon-colored T-shirt and heather-gray gym shorts had replaced her designer slacks and silk blouse, and showed off long, lean legs and bare feet. Adele's face had long since been scrubbed free of makeup, and her gun and badge were locked safely away.

What had happened at the Dixie Brewery and then her confrontations with her lieutenant and Landry left her feeling like the outside layer of her skin had been peeled away. But even so, she couldn't stop thinking about Natalie and how crushed she'd be in her shoes. When Adele heard the light creaking of the floors she'd been meaning to fix, she left her room to make sure it wasn't Logan walking the halls.

She knew it wasn't Landry. He hadn't come home at all.

Hidden by the shadows, she'd observed Natalie peacefully exploring and decided to fetch that long-promised cup of tea to give the professor a little more time on her own. Natalie seemed almost content and Adele was loath to interrupt the moment of desperately needed peace.

Both cups now in hand, she decided to make herself known.

"Do you like them?" Her voice low, Adele smiled at the windows a little nostalgically. "A friend of the family, who was an artist, made the stained glass when I was a little girl. I couldn't wait until I had a place where I could use them."

She handed Natalie a bone china teacup full of steaming liquid.

Natalie looked startled to see her, then stared at her for several seconds longer than was strictly polite, her eyes just a little wider than normal.

Adele bit back a chuckle. She'd experienced the same thing once when she was a child and had seen her grade school teacher at a local service station, pumping gas. Seeing her out of her element, in sweatpants and a hoodie, just seemed *wrong* somehow, as though she wasn't a regular person who should exist beyond the confines of her job.

Adele clicked a small table lamp to its lowest setting.

Natalie seemed to collect herself, though her cheeks had already turned a lovely pink. Her gaze captured Adele's and held it. "Anyone would love them. They're beautiful," she said, her voice ringing with heartfelt candor.

Adele was the first to look away. "I appreciate that…thanks."

Natalie glanced down to see Adele's bright coral-colored toenails. "Cute. I'm not sure how early you get up to go to the station, but it doesn't look like you're dressed for work."

"Nah." Adele sat heavily on the sofa and gestured for Natalie to take a seat as well.

And Natalie did, but at the far end of the sofa rather than the highboy from the afternoon before.

Ignoring years of lectures on manners, Adele kicked her feet up on the coffee table. "I was on vacation yesterday and will be for the next few days. So only the most comfy clothes for me. Although I might manage to dress up a bit more than my pajamas."

Adele chewed on her bottom lip when Natalie didn't answer. She'd invited Natalie here on a whim, something she'd never done before, because as much as she dreaded it, she knew they needed to talk and she didn't want to do it at the station or in public. But now she was starting to wonder whether this was a mistake. "I hope this isn't weird."

"You should have woken me up so I could go to a hotel," Natalie accused without any heat in her voice.

"Why? We all needed some rest, and we got it. There was no reason to disrupt that by moving you to a hotel, unless you really wanted a mint on your pillow?"

The corner of Natalie's mouth curled upward just a hair. But she was clearly too sad to do much more. "I didn't."

"Good."

"But as far as being weird," Natalie raised a disbelieving eyebrow, "you spent the day picking me up at the airport, comforting me, holding my hand in the morgue, and watching me barf and bawl. And the entire time you could have been at home with a good book or parked in front of the television? That is the very *definition* of weird, Detective."

Adele burst out laughing but covered her mouth quickly when she remembered why Natalie was here in the first place, and that she might wake her son.

Natalie's smile trembled. "It's okay. Don't stop yourself from laughing." She sighed. "It sounds really nice. And *that's* not weird. It makes me feel…good, I guess. It's good to know that someone is on my side in all this."

Thoughts of Landry, Crisco, Josh and Officer Morrell along with a heaping ladle of guilt crashed together in Adele's mind and mixed toxically with Natalie's words. She suddenly felt ill. Looking away, Adele set her cup down and began to get up. "I should have asked. How do you take your tea? Milk or honey or—?"

Natalie waved her back down. "This is fine." After a small sip, she looked for a plate or coaster or even a book to set the cup on.

"Just put it right on the table. I'd rather get it refinished every few years than worry about coasters. Besides, Logan uses the table to play cars on, so it's already under severe abuse." She drew her finger along several prominent scratches that somehow didn't distract in the least from the wood's natural beauty.

"Where is he?" Natalie glanced around warily as if expecting the preschooler to come barreling out from behind a piece of furniture at any minute.

"Sleeping."

"Ah…of course."

Seconds ticked by, and Adele couldn't think of anything else to say. She didn't want to talk about Josh's case yet, but it loomed so large in her mind that it was hard to focus on anything else. For the moment, however, Natalie didn't seem to be in a rush to get to the hard stuff and needed a distraction.

Natalie tilted her head to the side and regarded Adele curiously. "You've grown out your hair."

Surprised that she'd noticed, Adele's dimples made an appearance. "I cut it short when Logan was born, but I," she paused, "and by I, I mean mostly my husband, missed the length. So I've been trying to leave it alone for the past couple of years." She ran a hand through the blond hair naturally flecked with gold and light brown strands. "It's been hell. I've nearly cut it all off again about a dozen times, but now that it can go comfortably into a ponytail that doesn't look like a three-year-old's pigtail, I think I'm finally past the danger zone. I think."

Natalie nodded knowingly, then made a face. "Been there, done that. I cut mine into a short and highly disastrous shag during undergrad, and it took four years to get it back to the way I wanted it. If I ever cut it off that short again, it's staying off. I don't have the fortitude to grow it out anymore. Was yours always this wavy?"

"Nah. The waves come mostly with the length."

Natalie absently drew her finger along the lip of her cup. "It's nice, Detective."

"Thanks." Adele shifted uncomfortably.

"You were right."

"About what?"

Natalie scrunched up her nose apologetically. "This *is* weird."

Adele released her words on a single rushed exhale. "Thank God you think so too! I thought it was just me."

"Ah…no."

Their laughter mingled together softly and they relaxed a tiny bit more. Adele let her gaze sweep over Natalie and she felt an unexpected rush of protectiveness and warmth. She honestly liked her. But there was so much about Natalie that she'd forgotten. She hadn't remembered that Natalie's face could transform into something that could stop traffic when she laughed, or that her jawline was so sculpted and strong, or that her eyes, especially when shiny with tears, were such an intriguing shade of light blue.

"Detective—"

Caught zoning out and staring, Adele snapped to attention. "Oh, Lord, wait. I can finally say this." She didn't think she needed to mention it was because she was no longer working her brother's case. "*Please* call me Ella. My mother calls me Adele, but everyone else calls me Ella. And you've been killing me with the constant 'Detective, Detective, Detective,' ever since you insisted that I call you Natalie. Fair is fair."

"Okay," Natalie said, her voice still raspy from a day and night spent in tears. "I guess I know how you feel. Try having students only a few years younger than you, or someone who is older, calling you 'professor' all day long. Ugh. When I first started teaching I felt like such a poser."

"But you really *are* a professor, not a poser."

Natalie shrugged one shoulder. "It just all seemed so stuffy and formal, like a kid dressing in her mother's clothes and trying to be a grown-up. Giving me the title didn't make me feel like one of them." She tilted her head from side to side. "Though I guess I did get used to it, eventually."

"That much school must have taken forever. Your folks must be so proud of you."

Natalie's expression flattened, but tears still leapt into her eyes. "I suppose."

Aww, shit. Mentioning Natalie's parents when she still had to call them about Josh's death was stupid. Adele wanted desperately to fix her blunder, but Natalie's voice cut into her thoughts before she had the chance.

"What about you? College?" Natalie asked carefully, as though she didn't want to insult Adele in case she hadn't gone to college at all, but was dying to shift attention away from herself.

Adele couldn't blame Natalie for being wary. But rotten cops like Officer Jay Morrell notwithstanding, things in New Orleans were changing faster than television shows intent on focusing on voodoo, racism, and poverty led people to believe. Even the cops could be educated. "I went to Tulane and have a BA in philosophy and a master's in social work."

Natalie let out a low whistle, misty eyes round and appreciative. "Wow. Those are challenging degrees." A sniff. "*Your* parents must be proud."

"They are proud, I think. It took a while for them to get used to the fact that I'm a cop, when everyone else in the family somehow works in retail. But they did, even though I'm the odd duck."

They both stopped talking for a moment and took sips of their tea. And this time the silence wasn't as awkward.

It felt, Adele realized, surprisingly good to truly start to get to know one another. It reminded her that she needed to work fewer hours, not just for Logan or Landry, but also for herself. It had been far too long since she'd made a real friend.

Natalie wrapped her slender fingers around the cup that was almost too hot to hold that way. "Being able to call you Ella makes one thing much nicer for me."

"It's got less syllables?"

"It makes it easier to really say thanks," Natalie corrected mildly.

Adele's smile slipped away. "No. It's not—"

The look on Natalie's face was incredulous. It not only silently asked Adele whether she was for real, it stopped her cold. "You're not going to try to actually stop me from thanking you," Natalie said unequivocally.

The corner of Adele's mouth twitched at Natalie's boldness. She crossed her legs, one bare foot dangling. "Was that a question?"

"Not really." Natalie's eyes flashed with resolve. "I know you haven't met them, but this is coming from my parents too. Thank you, Ella, for everything you've done. And I don't care what you say, you helped far more than was required by your job."

Natalie gestured at the room around them. "Here I am taking yet *another* one of your days off, drinking tea that you made for me, and sitting in your living room at the crack...no *pre-crack* of dawn." Natalie shook her head and spoke with utter conviction. "*Ella* has been the one helping me, not just Detective Lejeune, and for that I am deeply and profoundly grateful."

Adele's throat tightened and tears pricked the back of her eyes. Yes, she'd tried to be kind. But she hadn't helped Natalie or her family. Not really. She hadn't found Josh until it was far too late. Now to make matters worse, she was nothing less than a coward for not officially reporting or even arresting Morrell. But how could she do that now with Natalie looking at her like she was some sort of damned savior?

"I know you feel badly that you didn't find Josh before now."

Adele's eyes widened.

Natalie gave her a knowing look. "You're not that hard to read. Even though I'm far better with words than feelings." She sighed. "Not finding Josh wasn't your fault."

That was empirically true. The problem was it didn't make Adele feel better or even less frustrated. For months, when she was between other active cases and even when she wasn't, she'd followed up on Josh. But nothing had worked. "I *really* tried."

"I *really* believe you."

Adele's mouth was too dry to swallow, and she forced herself to finish the last of her tea, ignoring the fact that it was still a bit too warm to drink so quickly.

"Hey." Natalie moved closer, not stopping until their thighs were touching. She set her cup on the table, her entire focus on the detective. Natalie lifted a hand, and for a second Adele thought she was going to cup her cheek. But her hand fell away before she made contact. "Are you okay?"

Adele rubbed her eyes. "I think I'm just overly tired."

"Then you should go back to bed." A frown flitted across Natalie's face and she moved to stand. "I can call a cab and—"

Adele grabbed both of Natalie's hands to stop her. "I didn't say I was tired of *you*. But I'm beat." That was an understatement. The day before her tank had been utterly and completely empty and Adele was only slightly better now. She knew it was playing hell on her emotions. "And I know you're beat too."

Natalie tilted her head in acknowledgment. "I've cried more in the past twenty-four hours than I have in my entire life. Even after twelve hours of sleep, I'm not still just tired, I'm *exhausted*."

"So let me help you by telling you what I know. Then you can get some real rest without any more wondering. You've wanted to ask me more about Josh since the morgue." She squeezed Natalie's hands in encouragement. "Ask."

"Okay, Ella." Natalie's eyes closed for a second before she reopened them and soldiered on. "Who killed my brother?"

Adele was anxious and relieved at the same time. "We think it was a man named Crisco...I mean, Otis Etienne. He's a fifty-five-year-old, homeless alcoholic, no family, and no job. He sometimes hangs out on street corners, begging drivers for spare change. He's lived in abandoned buildings or under the overpasses for years and years."

"Why d-do you think he did it?"

"He was found passed out near your brother and in possession of the murder weapon. And..." Adele's voice petered out before she was done.

Natalie waited, but when it became clear Adele wasn't going to continue she prompted her. "And?"

Detective Lejeune, not Adele, squared her shoulders and chose her words with extreme care. She spoke as though she was on the witness stand. "And the arresting officer and homicide detective assigned to the crime, who happens to be Landry, both obtained confessions."

Natalie let out a groan of relief. "You caught him and he confessed! That's wonderful!" She pulled Adele into a bone-crushing hug that seemed to surprise them both. "This is going to make things easier for my parents." Natalie's lips were pressed so close to Adele's ear that when she spoke Adele shivered. "It won't bring back Josh, but just knowing that the man who did this to him is going to be punished will help."

Adele closed her eyes and took in an unsteady breath full of Natalie's light floral perfume, trying not to feel the guilt that was coiled around her chest like a boa constrictor. Landry was right. Natalie and her family *did* deserve justice. And she was selfish for considering any action that would deny them that.

Natalie gave Adele a firm squeeze, her hands blazing hot against the thin cloth covering Adele's back. Adele barely resisted the overwhelming desire to melt into the embrace. This was the divine comfort she'd so desperately needed the night before, only from the entirely wrong person.

Both women pulled away at the exact same second.

With a self-conscious look, Natalie moved a little farther back down the sofa.

Adele licked her lips, grateful for the space to breathe. She wished she had some tea left in her cup to distract her. "I didn't catch the suspect, but I was there when he was arrested."

Tears stung Natalie's eyes for the umpteenth time since that morning and she wiped at them futilely with the back of her hands. "Why did he kill Josh?"

Seeing pain painted in stark colors across Natalie's face made Adele want to hug her all over again. The urge was nearly irresistible. "We're unclear on that." She wished she'd remembered to bring more Kleenex along with the tea. The top of Natalie's blouse was soaked with tears, and she looked more than miserable.

"It could have been a robbery and then a fight over that," Adele continued. "Or maybe just a fight. The suspect is being released from the hospital today or tomorrow and then he'll go into a cell. The police will also question him again, maybe more than once. So unless he refuses to cooperate, we'll get more information soon. His time in the hospital will delay the upcoming deadline for his arraignment, but that will happen within the next few days too."

"Hospital?"

Adele's skin began to crawl. *Tell her.* She opened her mouth but nothing came out.

Confused, Natalie searched the detective's face. "Did Joshua do something wrong? Did he attack the man first and that's why they fought?"

Adele sat on her hands, her heart sinking. She was making everything worse. "Don't think that, please. The investigation has just started, but we have no reason to believe Josh did anything wrong at all. He was just unlucky."

An unhappy, vertical crease in Natalie's forehead eased. "Then why is the suspect in the hospital?"

"The suspect, Crisco, was injured while resisting arrest." It was out before she could stop herself. *The first outright lie.*

"Serves him right," Natalie said bitterly, her face suddenly granite. "No matter how badly he was hurt at least he's still alive. He must also be a *stupid* murderer if he actually fought the cops."

Adele's tone was dull. "Right."

"So what happens now? You said an arraignment?"

"Yes. Crisco will go before a judge and plead guilty or not guilty."

Natalie's eyes clouded over with a look that said her sharp mind was going a mile a minute. "But he confessed so he'll plead guilty, right? If he was going to make the state prove their case, there would be no reason at all to confess."

"Right." Lie number two. *This is what drowning feels like.*

"Can I be in court for the arraignment? To watch?"

Adele nodded reluctantly. "You can. But you don't need to be. He'll plead guilty, and then the judge will set a date for sentencing in a few weeks or so. You won't miss much if you go home." *Please, Natalie. Go home.* "Your job—"

Natalie dismissed the idea abruptly. "A teaching assistant can fill in for me while I'm gone. I'm in no shape to work and this is more important." She had to take a few breaths before continuing. "That man *murdered* my baby brother." Her words were like broken glass, causing her to bleed right before Adele's eyes. "I want to see him. I *need* to see him and to feel sure that he's going to go to jail for a very long time. Forever."

"Okay," Adele rasped, her expression pained.

The anger melted away from Natalie's eyes and her demeanor softened. "You look as wrung out as I feel. I should go."

Adele pinned Natalie with an intense look. "Nuh-uh. You should stay. The hotels will still be there tomorrow. Or the day after. In fact, stay here until you go home. I'd like it if you stayed here."

"Okay," Natalie whispered, looking a little overwhelmed again. "And, Ella," she said, emotion seeping into her voice, "just knowing that you're helping to put Josh's killer away means everything to me."

Don't let her keep saying things like that! "Don't-don't mention it." Adele knew she should tell her about the coercion this very second. There would never be a better time than now, and there was always a chance that Natalie would understand. But even as she tried to convince herself, Adele knew that was bullshit. Crisco killed Natalie's brother. No legal technicalities or moral quandary would ever touch that.

Torn between her conscience, Natalie's pain, and the idea of what was right, which was growing fuzzier and fuzzier with every heartbeat, Adele decided to sleep on her decision about Morrell. Maybe everything would look better after some rest.

Natalie stood, still eyeing Adele carefully.

Adele could see that Natalie knew something was wrong and Adele fought not to squirm under the attention. But there *was* something wrong, so she let it be.

Natalie ran a nervous hand through her hair and looked as exposed as Adele had seen her. "Ella?"

"Hmm?"

"Do you have many friends outside work or your family?"

It made her sound pathetic, but she was too tired and raw to care. "No."

"You have a new one today, okay?"

One tentative smile reached out and met its twin.

"You too, Natalie. You too."

CHAPTER FIVE

It was just after eleven a.m. the next day when Adele marched into the NOPD Homicide bullpen and all but yanked Landry out of his seat by the arm.

"We need to talk," she whispered harshly. "Right *now*."

"What the hell?" Landry bit out, his arms spinning to keep from falling backward. The tips of his ears pinked under a chorus of loud snickers and chicken squawks from his coworkers that signified he was henpecked.

Balance restored, he stood and glared down at his wife, fire in his eyes. "*Ella.*"

"Don't 'Ella' me." Adele glared right back. "We can do this here or someplace else," she declared, hands on hips. "But it's happening now."

Their eyes dueled for a few long seconds then Landry grabbed her forearm and pulled her in the direction of an interrogation room.

"Let's go outside instead." Adele yanked her arm from his grasp and began to lead the way by striding toward the door, her already confident gait quick and elongated. As livid as she was, she'd already embarrassed him in front of his colleagues and she didn't particularly want to put on a show for the entire homicide department. Interrogation rooms were fitted with two-way mirrors and cops were notorious, gossipy busybodies.

Landry shot a murderous scowl at his remaining tormentors, but followed his wife. "Fuck. It's raining outside."

"Don't be a baby." It was barely sprinkling, but neither of them had an umbrella.

"Was that really necessary, back in the bullpen?"

"Yes."

Now his entire face was red. "I have to work with those men!" Once safely outside and well away from the front doors, Landry tugged Adele to a halt. "This had better be good."

Adele tried not to sneer, but was pretty sure by the look on Landry's face that she hadn't managed it. "I'll bet you won't guess where I just was."

"Helping Crisco pay for an attorney to beat this rap? Or maybe braiding Natalie Abbott's hair in our living room?"

So that's how it was going to be. They were both incensed. Good. Adele wondered briefly how he knew that Natalie was staying with them, but didn't care enough to ask whether one of the neighbors was his spy. "I just came back from talking to Morrell's lieutenant and Lt. Xavier."

Some of the antagonism evaporated from Landry's face. Resentment filled the gap. "I told you to leave this alone!"

Incredulous, Adele blinked. "You *told* me? Did I miss the part of our relationship where you became my daddy or my boss?"

Landry's eyebrows jumped up his forehead and stayed. "Don't pretend you listen to either one of them either."

A gust of warm, wet air tousled Adele's hair. Irately, she shook her head to dislodge a lock that stuck to the damp and sweaty skin on her neck. "How could you tell him that? How could you tell Lt. Xavier, my *boss*, that you'd *handle me*," she nearly spat out the words. "You know how hard I worked for my gold shield. How hard it is to get everyone's respect. Xavier was actually surprised to see me because you were supposedly taking care of my *little problem*." She curled her fingers into air quotes.

Landry looked chagrined but unapologetic. "I never used those exact words. I only told him I'd talk to you and try to get you to see reason about Morrell." He frowned and shook his head slowly. "And I can see that you still haven't."

"You would have known that if you'd bothered to come home last night."

Landry pushed his shoulders back. "I was working."

Adele's disappointment was written all over her face. "You were hiding at your mama's house."

He shrugged one shoulder. "It was nice to spend the evening with someone who didn't hate me for being realistic and doing my job."

Adele's jaw worked. "I don't...I don't hate you." She stepped off the sidewalk to allow a woman pushing a stroller to pass. "I'm just furious with you!"

Landry followed Adele, rubbing the back of his neck with one hand. "Somehow, Ella, I'm having trouble telling the difference."

With effort, Adele lowered her voice. "Why were you even talking to Xavier?"

"Morrell does need to be dealt with. I know that. But I also want to keep you from making a huge personal and professional mistake. And I'm not ashamed to say I want to keep my case alive."

Adele stiffened as something he said registered and felt suspiciously close to an ultimatum. She also noticed that the day before this had been "our" case. Today it was "his." "Are you trying to tell me if I pursue this it will hurt our marriage?"

"It will hurt everything!" Landry looked at her as though the very question was inane. "You're a cop. You're married to a cop. All our friends are cops." He hesitated. "Morrell was one of the cops who stayed during Katrina and not one of the bastards who ran away. And you know that means something."

"So that gives him a free pass to act as though the laws don't apply to him?"

"No. But he gets one of his *own* people to set him straight without compromising the entire job we're here to do in the first place!"

"This is important to me, Landry. To do the right thing. I don't want to be the kind of cop who looks the other way."

His demeanor softened. "So you said. But you *didn't* look the other way. You've gone to Morrell's boss, and yours. You've done enough, Ella. Now let everyone else do their jobs."

"And what about Crisco?" She blinked slowly as she thought of the rap sheet she'd pulled right after his arrest. Crisco had several arrests for domestic battery, with one that actually stuck, and multiple counts of vagrancy spanning nearly twenty years. He was neither angel nor devil, but did that even matter? This wasn't just about him.

Landry's expression cooled. "You mean the *murderer?* At least he's got a life ahead of him, hopefully one that's entirely in prison. Or better yet, he'll end up on death row. Joshua Phillips has been on ice to keep from rotting during his dissection. I heard his sister had a hard time seeing him that way in the morgue yesterday."

Adele's eyes flashed. That was a surprisingly low blow. "Landry—"

They both abruptly stopped talking when a couple of uniformed officers walked past them with mumbled greetings and strange looks. The meager raindrops were beginning to soak through their clothes.

Adele turned away from her husband but threw her words back at him like barbs. "Xavier isn't going to initiate an investigation of Morrell and neither is Morrell's boss—Luna. They both made that clear. Is that your doing?" She held her breath, not sure what she would do if Landry's answer was yes.

"Fuck. Of *course* not."

She could hear the hurt but also the truth in his voice. Landry didn't want his case compromised. But if the brass decided to go after Morrell, he would support that as wholeheartedly as he was trying to talk her out of officially reporting Morrell now. *Always the team player.* "How'd we wind up on different sides?" she murmured to herself, surprised to find that her indignation was edging toward sadness.

"Huh?"

"Nothing." She shook her head and turned back to face Landry. "Lt. Xavier—"

"Did exactly what we both knew he would," Landry finished. "But he told me confidentially that once Crisco is sentenced he's going to talk Lt. Luna into pulling Morrell from the field for a few weeks and make him go through sensitivity training again. And not just the usual two-day class, either. Some major, three-week, bullshit training course from hell. It's a punishment. Apparently there have been a few problems with Morrell's behavior and attitude in the past. Luna's also going to assign him a more veteran partner. Someone who can help keep him in line."

Adele rolled her eyes.

Landry threw his hands in the air. "Do you need a pound of flesh too? You know that training is torture."

"No, Landry, you know what is torture? *Actual* torture. Like getting your teeth knocked out. Or bones broken. Or kicked in the chest while you're begging for it to stop. *Those* things are torture. Not watching lame videos from 1988 on how you shouldn't call grown women 'girls' and stare at their tits while you talk to them!"

"Forensics came back. At least with the preliminary results."

It took a few seconds to get over the case of mental whiplash that came with the apparent change in subjects. Adele lifted a skeptical eyebrow. "That was fast." When Landry looked down at his feet and nodded, she immediately suspected the rush in processing wasn't accidental.

"Everything was just as it appeared. Cause of death was blunt force trauma to the head. Brick was the murder weapon. Vic's blood on Crisco's hand and Crisco's bloody prints on the brick. But—" Landry hesitated.

"But?"

He released an explosive sigh. "That's *it*. The crime scene was a mess. Crisco ended up tits down in some mud puddle and ruined any other forensics on his clothes. Every other test for fibers or fluids or anything else remotely useful came up inconclusive."

Adele's eyes widened, though she wasn't entirely surprised. Morrell had been beyond careless and ruined the evidence a jury would expect to see. All those stupid procedural crime shows set unrealistically high expectations when it came to forensics. And disappointed juries often didn't convict.

"Ella, we didn't find any of what we think were Josh's possessions on Crisco. No wallet. Or money. Or even drugs." Landry growled in frustration and for the first time that day Adele took a good look at him. The rain had soaked through his pale blue cotton shirt, and it was plastered to his broad chest. His eyes were bloodshot and he looked like he'd slept in his clothes.

"We're still waiting for toxicology to come back," he went on, brushing a few droplets of rain from his face. "But the medical examiner says he only expects it to show the vic was high. Yesterday, I scoured the area and talked to anyone who frequents the brewery. Nobody saw anything. The rain kept them all closer to downtown that night. So far, other than the brick, there's not a single link between Crisco and the victim."

Adele's jaw dropped. "Holy shit. You can't even prove robbery. You have no witnesses or motive for a fight or anything else."

Landry looked as though he wanted to argue, but couldn't. He stuffed his hands into the pockets of his slacks, his expression darkening.

Adele wiped her hand down her face and stared off into the distance, eyes unseeing. "Christ, even a hopeless defense attorney could make a jury at least consider that Crisco might have stumbled onto Josh after he was murdered and stupidly picked up the brick. Maybe even because he wanted to help Josh. Then he passed out drunk."

She swallowed a few times, the implications sinking in. "You have no case."

"That's not true."

She looked up sharply.

"We have a confession. We *need* that confession." When Adele didn't say anything to that he asked, "What are you going to do?"

Adele's lips thinned, and she held her tongue for fear she'd say something truly damaging to their relationship.

"Dammit, I don't like this sword hanging over my case!"

"Morrell put it there, not me."

"At least tell me if you're going to unleash hell into this so I can prepare for the fallout." He pointed an accusing finger straight at Adele's chest. "You owe me that."

They owed each other so much *more* than that. But it should be a two-way street.

In her heart, she believed Crisco had killed Josh. If it walked like a duck, and quacked like a duck, in her experience, it was a goddamned duck. Yes, a lot of potential evidence had turned out to be inconclusive, but she'd seen why with her own eyes. The remaining evidence tied Crisco to the murder weapon. But *none* of that made his confession viable. And that was now the linchpin of the entire case.

"What are you going to do?" Landry repeated, his impatience winning out.

"I-I don't know," Adele said honestly. And even if she did, at this point she didn't think she could tell Landry about it. How could she trust him after he went to Lt. Xavier behind her back? How could she let Morrell get away with what he'd done? How could she crush Natalie and her family and potentially let a killer get away with murder?

She wanted to scream.

Neither her boss nor Morrell's would pursue her claims. She knew that now. That left her with the choice of doing nothing or filing a complaint with the NOPD Public Integrity Bureau. Or what was unkindly, but commonly, called The Rat Squad.

Landry moved in close and cupped her cheek with a sturdy hand that felt hot on her damp skin. She couldn't help but lean into the touch as his familiar scent washed over her. Her heart jumped wildly when his olive-green eyes captured hers. "Baby, let me help you. Please."

She let out a shuddering sigh, relief infusing her every cell. This was what she'd been craving. "Yes. Please. I need your—"

"Let me help you keep from doing something *stupid*."

His words sank in and then came to land in the pit of her stomach with a sickly thud. Wounded to the core, she stepped away. He wasn't even trying to understand. "Say hello to your mother for me tonight, Landry." She walked away.

* * *

"Ella! Wait up. Hey." A young uniformed officer grabbed Adele's arm as she began to open her car door.

She spun around to face him, eyes blazing. "Not right now, Al!" Her temper was a razor's edge after speaking with Landry, and she was fighting to get away from the station before the tears that had been threatening since her argument with Landry could fall.

A very light rain dotted the concrete all around them.

Al backed up a step and raised two placating hands. "Damn, Little Mama, don't shoot. I was just checkin' on you. You looked all upset, like you were marching out of the PD on the way to shoot someone. I figured I'd better go along to, you know…" He shrugged as though the reason was obvious.

"Hold my bullets for me?"

"Why you gotta make a servant joke to a black man, Ella? You know, there's room in this world for *both* of us to be bad-ass motherfuckers."

Despite herself, she smiled.

"I was going to say, I would go with you to keep you out of trouble."

"Shouldn't you actually be someplace…like on duty and working? Or home taking care of those kids that are way too cute to actually be yours?"

Al scowled playfully. "Their mama says the same thing. I'm on nights this week and am actually just getting off duty. And now's not the time to get all picky about who holds your bullets. If you're going to kill someone you'll also need a strong partner who can lift the body to wherever you're going to dump it. So I'm your man."

Something about Al's bright smile always made her feel better.

He was all raw muscle, tats, and street attitude...with everyone but Adele. They'd known each other since Al was a boy and she was a fresh-faced beat cop. Each one's devotion to the other went bone deep. Though there were no blood ties, theirs was a relationship that straddled the line between friendship and family effortlessly.

Adele let out a shuddering breath. "I'm not going to kill someone. I'm-I'm sorry I snapped. Landry and I just...we aren't seeing eye to eye on something."

"Get in." He gave her a gentle shove into the driver's seat of her car. "I'll come around."

Adele made sure the passenger door was unlocked so Al could slip inside, his wide shoulders seemingly too big for the seat. He took off his hat, and she waggled her finger at him. "Don't you shake the rain off yourself like you're a wet dog, Alonzo. I don't want to have to wipe down the inside of all my windows again."

He rolled his eyes, and Adele reached out and scrubbed the bristly top of his high fade haircut. Al gave her a long-suffering look but still endured her rough affection without complaint.

He chuckled quietly, then for a moment there was only the sound of two sets of breathing and the light pitter-patter of the rain. "Now tell me what's really going on? I've been hearing rumors."

Adele dug out her keys and popped them into the ignition, where she left them dangling for a moment then fired up the car for the air-conditioning. "What have you heard?"

His gaze went so serious that for a second Adele was struck with the duality of Al's personality. One minute he could be joking and playful and the very next, as intense as anyone she'd ever known.

"That you're stirring up questions of police brutality and coercion against Morrell over the beat down he gave Crisco."

Adele snorted derisively. "That's not a rumor. That's the actual truth."

"Ella, what trouble are you getting yourself into?"

Frustrated that he seemed to be taking the same attitude as Landry, she muttered, "None. But that doesn't mean trouble won't happen."

He stuffed his hat back on his head and opened the car door. Glancing over his shoulder, his warm smile was back. "Doesn't matter. I've got your back either way."

Adele waved at Al, but her smile melted away before he was out of sight. Why hadn't Landry said that?

* * *

When Natalie awoke for the second time, the skies were bright enough that it was obvious morning had arrived. She reached over to the nightstand and checked her phone. 11:45 a.m. Natalie couldn't remember the last time she'd slept so late. She lay there for a moment, listening. The house was so silent that she was reasonably sure she was alone.

She shifted onto her side and groaned, feeling closer to sixty-four years old than thirty-four. Her back was sore from lying in bed for too long, and a tension headache was brewing just below the surface. She was dehydrated from crying so much, and the skin around her eyes felt sore and puffy. And with all that, she was quite certain that today would be far better than the day before.

"Time to get up, Nat," she mumbled to herself.

On a chair near the guest room door she spied her overnight bag with a tented note perched carefully on top. Leaning over so far she nearly fell out of the bed, Natalie snatched up the note. The handwriting was a pretty cursive.

Natalie,
Pick you up at 12:30 for lunch?
— Ella

Detective Lejeune, she determined, could be a woman of few words. And she appreciated that. Natalie's colleagues could pontificate for hours and hours, often just to hear themselves speak. This direct, simple communication was a refreshing change of pace.

Twenty minutes later she emerged from the bathroom, dressed and ready, to hear footsteps in the hall. Natalie stuck her head out in time to see a very wet Adele, oddly barefooted, walking slowly toward the far bedroom. It looked like every step was a chore. Her clothes were sopping and her hair was hanging in messy waves around her face.

Natalie cleared her throat, and Adele turned. Her eyes were red-rimmed, as though she'd been crying. "Hi," Natalie said, feeling a little bit awkward after their intimate late-night talk.

"Hey." Adele smiled valiantly, but it didn't quite reach her eyes. "You're up."

"Just barely," Natalie admitted self-consciously.

"You needed the sleep. Don't feel bad about that."

Adele was right. She had needed it and especially the support she'd gotten from the detective. "Okay. I won't. Umm…" She gestured at the detective's sodden body. "Did you decide to take a swim in the

Mississippi?" Natalie didn't really feel like teasing, but Adele looked equally down, and she didn't think she could take them both feeling low.

Adele snorted. "Not exactly. I decided to have a conversation outside in the rain. Not quite as stupid, but still pretty dumb. Hungry? I can be ready in just a few minutes. Too many late-night calls for work have given me the ability to change and shower in less than fifteen minutes."

Natalie's stomach growled at the mention of food.

Adele laughed as she heard the ferocious rumble, and this time the gesture looked natural and came easily. "Okay, then." She tilted her head toward Natalie's belly. "Let's feed that. Meet you out here in fifteen."

"Just us for lunch?" Natalie was a bit surprised that Landry hadn't come by, and she assumed that Logan was in preschool.

"Just us."

Natalie nodded. She retrieved her purse from the bedroom then took a seat on the living room sofa. The cell phone inside her bag mocked her. Stomach suddenly roiling, she plucked the phone from her bag and stared at it. She had a few minutes until Adele finished showering. That meant she could do this, and do it quick.

Her fists clenched and unclenched as she decided what to do. "Okay, okay," she finally mumbled. She lost track of how long she stared at the phone before dialing her mother's number with shaky fingers.

It rang so many times that Natalie felt as though she had dodged a bullet and almost hung up. But then…

"Hello?"

Suddenly Natalie's throat wouldn't work.

"Hello?" Rose's voice was irritated. "If this is one of those prank calls, I'm calling the police."

"No…" A swallow. "No, M-Mom. It's me."

Rose sighed in obvious relief. "I thought it was those stupid kids playing on their cell phones. They practically get them when they're babies nowadays. How their parents can afford that I'll never—"

"Mom, I'm calling from New Orleans."

There was a long silence on the phone before Rose said in a dull voice, "He's dead, isn't he?"

Natalie felt like an elephant had parked squarely in the center of her chest. "Yes. I…" Tears pooled in her eyes then spilled over. "Yes. I'm so sorry," she croaked. She might have been sick again if there had been even an ounce of food left in her stomach.

Rose's sigh sounded different this time. "I know, honey. I'm sorry you had to make this call."

Natalie let out a sob. Given a million years, she still wouldn't have expected this reaction. She felt the strongest yearning to be in her mother's arms, and she could hear the other woman sniffing back tears.

"I assume it was the drugs."

"I-I-" Natalie dropped the phone and stared at it as though it was a snake. She felt dizzy, but picked it back up and pressed it to her ear. "What-what did you say? The drugs?"

Rose sniffed loudly a few more times, and Natalie heard her blow her nose. "You're going to be mad."

"Oh, no, no, no." Natalie closed her eyes. "What have you done now?"

"Don't get smart! Especially—"

"Mom!" Natalie barked, patience gone. "What made you think it was drugs?"

"He called me a year ago from Houston and then six months ago from New Orleans, asking for money."

Natalie stood and looked skyward for assistance. "And you didn't think to tell me?" She wiped futilely at her eyes. "Why wouldn't you tell me?" Her voice sounded shrill and desperate to her own ears. Thank God she wasn't in the same room as her mother now. She wanted to strangle her.

"I didn't want his father to know that Josh was hooked on dope. It would crush him." Now Rose openly wept as well. "How am I going to break this to him? He loves that boy to a fault."

"He's not the only one."

"How can you say that? Believe you me, I was only trying to help."

"Not again," Natalie gasped. Though she knew it was ridiculous to continue to be surprised by the same action from the same person. "Tell me you didn't give him money to buy drugs."

"He said the money was for rehab! The first time it didn't take, but I heard that Dr. Drew on TV say that sometimes it takes several tries. Josh told me it had *almost* worked the first time. He promised to come home as soon as he got out of treatment. He was trying to get better! Was I not supposed to help him?"

Rose sounded so bereft and confused that Natalie didn't have the heart to yell and lash out the way her guts were demanding. Instead, she sat back down heavily on the sofa, gripping the phone so hard that her knuckles turned white.

"It wasn't drugs, Mom." Natalie looked around for some Kleenex only to have a sympathetic-looking Adele appear out of nowhere and offer a fresh box. She thanked her with her eyes. "Josh was killed in a fight of some kind. The police are still investigating, but the man who did it confessed."

When Adele moved to leave the room, Natalie motioned for her to stay.

"Murdered?" Rose shrieked, as though this news was somehow much worse than Josh overdosing on drugs. She wept for a long moment before calming enough to say, "The police ha-have him? The killer?"

"Yes."

"Good," Rose said, her voice loaded with bitterness. "Then the man will get the electric chair," she announced with one hundred percent certainty.

"The electric chair?" Natalie swallowed, feeling sick. She glanced at Adele who shook her head no. "I don't…they don't do that anymore, Mom. At least not that way."

Adele looked as ill as Natalie felt.

Rose ranted on about killers and justice, and Natalie held the phone away from her head with a deep sigh. She let her mother vent for a moment before interrupting. "He won't get away with Josh's murder. I'm staying here a couple more days to make sure."

"Good. Whatever it takes to keep that monster off the street. Is that nice detective who helped you before helping you again? The one who is a girl?"

Natalie gave Adele a watery smile, well aware the other woman could hear her mother's voice, even though the phone wasn't on speaker. "She is."

Rose sniffed and her voiced thinned. She sounded so old that Natalie almost didn't recognize her. "Natalie?"

"Yes, Mom?"

"You'll bring him home *this time*, right? You won't let me down again?"

Adele winced.

Natalie's dry swallow was audible and she could feel the blood draining from her face. "Yes."

"I have to go talk to Josh's father now…" And without saying goodbye, Rose hung up.

Adele looked at a loss for words as Natalie stared at the phone in her hands. "I'm so sorry, Natalie. That was—" she floundered for something to say that wasn't…the truth.

"That was *horrid*. Sometimes *she* can be horrid. Though she doesn't mean to be." Natalie's eyebrows drew together. "At least I don't think she means it."

Adele moved a little closer to Natalie. "I didn't mean to intrude on a private family moment. I heard you crying and was…I was concerned."

"I—I actually feel a little better." Natalie grabbed her small pile of tissues and clutched them tightly in one hand. "I was dreading that call. And now that it's over…well, at least it's over." But even as she said it, her face crumbled.

"I wish I could do something," Adele whispered tenderly. "Something to make you feel better."

"I…" Natalie knew without a doubt what she wanted. "Maybe… please—" And she wanted to beg for it too, but somehow couldn't bring herself to do it.

More tears spilled over Natalie's cheeks and Adele didn't bother waiting. "C'mere." She wrapped Natalie in a fierce embrace, pressing their bodies tightly together, stroking Natalie's soft dark hair with one hand. "Cry all you want. I'm not going anywhere. And I bought six more boxes of Kleenex."

Natalie snorted despite herself and returned the hug with all her strength, melting into it with every fiber of her being. "Thanks, Ella."

"You're welcome," was the whisper in her ear.

A few minutes later, Natalie's tears had dried, but she hadn't relinquished her hold on the detective. She felt a buzzing against her hip, but it wasn't her phone, it was Adele's.

"Are you okay?" Adele whispered before pulling away.

Natalie nodded, moving away reluctantly. "Yes. Of course. Answer your phone. It could be important."

Adele reached for the phone and looked a little surprised at the name that flashed on the screen. "Al?" A pause. "What? An hour? Okay. Okay." She hung up.

"What's wrong?"

"They've moved up Crisco's arraignment to this afternoon." She glanced at her watch. "C'mon. We have to go."

* * *

Adele sat in the back of the courtroom with Natalie as Crisco and his attorney, a public defender she'd seen many times, took the very front seats of the small courtroom. Crisco's entire face was black and blue, and he limped as he walked. She didn't expect his arm to be in a sling, but it was. His poorly cut hair had been slicked back, and his face was clean-shaven for the first time in what was probably years. He was wearing pants that were too long and a much-used tan blazer that Adele recognized as one his defense attorney routinely loaned out to his clients.

Adele prayed Crisco wouldn't find her in the back of the courtroom. She didn't think she could sit there quietly if he so much as glanced in her direction.

The lack of windows, a security precaution, left the room poorly lit. It smelled like sweat and was so dusty that Adele had to wrinkle her nose to keep from sneezing. "Are you good?" she asked Natalie out of the side of her mouth, her volume low.

Natalie's eyes were glued on Crisco. "I just want this to be over."

"Me too."

"That's who killed Josh." Natalie gestured at Crisco with her chin. It wasn't a question.

Adele nodded.

Natalie stared at Crisco, intense anger written on her every feature.

In fact, Adele figured if looks could kill, Crisco would be a smoldering pile of ashes right now.

"I thought he'd look more like a murderer. Instead, he just looks like a sad, beat-up old man."

Adele's attention was drawn to the prosecutor as she took her seat.

Before the judge could bang the gavel to open the proceeding, Landry snuck in the back of the room and took a seat on the opposite side of where Adele and Natalie sat. His blue suit jacket was stretched tight across his back as he leaned forward, elbows on knees, his necktie hanging loosely in front of him.

Across the courtroom, their eyes met and held and Adele saw anger and pain and love all wrapped up together in a terrible package.

He was the first one to look away.

The preliminaries only took a few minutes. Before Adele knew it, her pulse began to pound, and the judge asked, "And in the matter of the *State versus Otis Etienne*, how does the defendant plead?"

A quiet hush came over the courtroom. Crisco's mumbled voice broke the silence, loud and strong. "Not guilty."

Adele's jaw sagged. She heard Landry's "Oh, shit," from across the room.

"What happened?" Natalie asked, confused. "Why would he do that?"

Adele didn't bother to stay to listen to the judge deny Crisco bail, instead she bolted out of the courtroom after Landry who had stormed off the second the words "not guilty" left Crisco's mouth.

The hallway outside the courtroom was busy with men and women with briefcases hurrying about and uniformed cops coming and going. But her husband was nowhere in sight. Adele fought the urge to burst into tears. Everything was falling apart. Now it wouldn't be enough to keep quiet about Crisco's beating. She couldn't just stay quiet. Unless Crisco got a plea, she'd have to lie on the stand.

She wrapped an arm around her stomach, glad she'd missed lunch.

"Ella?" Natalie appeared behind her, flustered and perplexed. "Where'd you go? What happened in there?"

Adele held in her sigh. "I'm sorry. I didn't mean to ditch you. I wanted to catch Landry."

Natalie frowned and did a quick scan for the homicide detective. "He looked upset."

That was an understatement. Landry looked homicidal. "We all thought Crisco would plead guilty, Landry included. Crisco might just be trying to work out a better plea bargain with the prosecutor, probably to take the death penalty off the table. But he might actually want to take his case to trial."

"Trial?" Natalie's face fell. "That could take months, couldn't it?"

"Yes."

"I can't stay here that long."

"I know." Adele continued to look around, hoping to catch sight of her husband's head above the others. "Look, I need…I have to find Landry and then get Logan. I want to talk to the prosecutor too." She gave Natalie a sympathetic look.

Natalie swallowed hard and nodded. "Okay, well, I have to arrange to take Josh home, so I'll go do that."

Adele could feel her panic building. She raked a hand through her hair. "Then take care of that now. I'll meet you back at my house, okay. Then we can go get something to eat and talk about all of this."

"I'm not—"

"Me neither. But we have to eat *eventually*. Take my car." She began digging through her purse for her keys but Natalie stopped her by laying her hands over Adele's.

"I'll just take a cab. You can text me the address?"

"Of course." Adele frowned. "I would go with you if I could, you know. To help you so you wouldn't have to go back there alone. But—"

Natalie squeezed Adele's hands and then lifted her chin and took a step back. "You've done nothing but help me for days. Please do what you need to do and I'll see you later."

Adele nodded, grateful. "Thank you."

"Ella?"

"Yeah?"

"It's going to be okay. Crisco did it. He confessed. Like you said, he's probably just dragging things out now to get a better deal. I'm not exactly surprised that a killer isn't interested in making things easier for anyone but himself."

Nothing about this was easy. "You're probably right."

* * *

The next morning, Natalie finished blow-drying her hair and drew a brush through it enough times to bring it back to its usual order. Adele hadn't met her for dinner the night before. In fact, when the clock had struck nine p.m. in Adele's living room, Natalie finished purchasing her airline ticket online and went to bed. The house felt bigger, the silence more ominous when she was there alone, and she realized that it was the detective's presence that made it feel homey.

While she felt a bit out of sorts in Adele's home without her, Natalie had also been exhausted again and welcomed the chance for an early bedtime. Even though her mind was crying out for rest, thoughts of Josh, her mother's tears, and musty courtrooms plagued her sleep.

With a frown, Natalie wondered whether she'd see Adele again today before she had to fly home. Her heart ached a little at the thought that she might not. She owed her so much and Adele had been so kind.

Natalie tucked a thin, snug white tank top into slim-fitting, threadbare Levi's and wiggled her toes comfortably in her well-worn sneakers. Then she layered a baby-blue chambray short-sleeved shirt over the tank. She applied a touch of mascara and clear lip gloss and left her makeup at that, foregoing everything else, including the usual powder she used to cover the light smattering of freckles across her nose and cheeks.

The overall result, Natalie decided with brutal honesty, was nothing to write home about. She still had dark circles under her eyes that would simply take time to erase. Her outfit was what she'd intended to wear on the plane ride home, where no one from work or even the NOPD would see her. This was "weekend Natalie" and under these horrible circumstances she needed every possible comfort. Even from something as silly as a pair of well-loved sneakers.

Natalie padded back into the guest bedroom, hands full of toiletries that she stuffed into her travel bag and zipped closed. It was 9:08 a.m., later than she'd normally sleep even on the weekends. She could hear Adele and Logan's laughter coming from the living room. They'd obviously been up for a while. She listened for Detective Landry Odette's deep baritone, but couldn't pick it out among the muffled words and squeals.

A cool breeze blew in from the open window that Natalie didn't remember opening. Adele must have come in while she was in the shower. Overnight, the rainy weather front that had stalled over the city passed, causing the temperatures and humidity to plummet. This morning was sunny and breezy and even the birds outside seemed to have renewed energy in the face of the much cooler day.

Natalie sucked in a deep breath of fresh air that felt heavenly. She was still sad, devastatingly so. But already things were feeling more manageable. Emotions like guilt, shame and regret were being compartmentalized. And lists of things she still needed to do were being organized in her mind.

There'd be a wake, funeral, graveside service and reception at the house full of church members whose names only her parents would know, neighbors bearing various hot dishes, and shirttail relatives who would show up out of a sense of guilt, curiosity, and for the free booze.

Natalie didn't want to attend a single one of those things. She wanted to say goodbye to her brother in her own way and to grieve without an audience. But her parents would need her, and like always, she would put aside her own wants and needs and try not to disappoint.

Mid-thought, Natalie's nose twitched and she spied a steaming cup of coffee waiting for her on the nightstand. A genuine smile bloomed.

Coffee in hand, she put aside thoughts of things that would happen another day and wandered out to the living room. She found Logan spread out on the floor wearing shorts, shoes, but no shirt, and playing with a large plastic dinosaur. The chubby three-and-a-half-year-old was having a ball as he and his mother traded what Natalie assumed were dinosaur roars. Then again, who knew what dinosaurs really sounded like?

Adele was on the floor near Logan, her back resting against the sofa, the morning newspaper spread out in front of her, coffee mug at the ready. Her hair was tousled and worn in a loose ponytail and her face still held remnants of creases from her pillow. She was wearing a T-shirt and shorts again, with the addition of a thick pair of white socks.

Maybe Adele and Logan hadn't been up for that long after all.

Adele glanced up and smiled warmly at her guest. Or at least she tried.

Natalie immediately sensed something was wrong.

"Good morning," Adele said her voice still sleepy, her eyes not quite meeting Natalie's. "Did you sleep well?"

A polite lie was on the tip of her tongue, but she quashed it. She felt close to Adele and didn't like the thought of even the white lie between them. "Not particularly. You?"

Adele flashed a low-watt, but genuine smile at Natalie's bluntness. "I got a few hours in."

Natalie raised her coffee mug in acknowledgment. "Thanks for this."

Adele dropped her gaze to stare at the face of her watch, suddenly finding it terribly interesting. "No problem. I'm sorry I missed dinner last night. I had to run some errands that went crazy late, and my mom ended up picking up Logan for me. Then I had to get him from her. I was—" She glanced up, seemingly realizing that she was uncharacteristically rambling. "I was delayed." She took a deep breath and shifted a little to center herself. "I didn't want to wake you last night, but I really need to talk to you about yesterday."

Worry brewed in Natalie's belly at the solemn look on Adele's face. "Okay," she said reluctantly.

"Your flight?"

"This afternoon."

Adele nodded, lower lip between her teeth.

"Mama?"

Adele turned to her son, who hadn't even looked up from his toy when Natalie entered the room and gave him a little nudge. "Logan, this is Ms. Abbott."

The boy stopped what he was doing, but kept his dinosaur gripped tightly in his hands as he marched over to Natalie and boldly said hello. He held out his toy for Natalie's closer inspection. "See? It's a dinosaur. My favorite."

Natalie crouched down to his level and forced herself not to think of Josh at this age. If she did, she'd burst into tears. "Hi, Logan. He?" she paused, asking Adele with a tilt of her head whether it was a boy or girl dinosaur.

Adele merely shrugged and gave her a half smile that said she had no idea.

"*She* is an *excellent* T-Rex, Logan. Super scary and loud." Natalie didn't touch the toy for fear the little boy would start to shriek like he was being kidnapped. She hadn't been around small children for a while. But fool her once...

He beamed an enormous grin and nodded, then released his own very enthusiastic dinosaur roar, bouncing a little on chubby feet.

"What's her name?" Natalie wondered aloud, pointing at the toy.

"T-Rex," he said proudly, eyes bright.

Okay, perhaps he wouldn't grow up to be a fiction writer.

Natalie was nervous in the preschooler's presence, but also a little charmed. He strongly resembled his mother, but this smaller male version of the detective had none of his mother's keen intensity. Instead, he simply looked relaxed, full of energy and happy. The way a child should.

Natalie fought the desire to reach out and tickle his exposed belly.

Abruptly, Logan lost interest in the visitor and flopped back down on the floor with his toy, making the reptile march across the rug and then over his mother's lap.

"Sorry," Adele murmured. She gave Logan a mischievous pinch on his bottom as he and the dinosaur scooted away. "Sometimes he's a bundle of energy with the attention span of a flea." She shrugged again, this time sheepishly. "He probably gets that from me."

Natalie spied Adele's fidgety hands, and privately agreed, but chose not to comment. "There's nothing to apologize for. He's obviously thrilled to spend this time with you." She was surprised to find herself feeling a little envious. Though Natalie wasn't sure whether it was of Logan or Adele.

Natalie couldn't remember being as young as Logan, but suddenly a faint memory came into sharper focus. She was five or six years old and at a summertime tea party on a blanket in the backyard with her mother. The sun was shining and there were cookies to go with their lukewarm tea. It was a nice memory, one that warmed her insides in a way she hadn't felt in too long. Natalie wondered briefly when the harder times with her mother had begun to overshadow the sweeter ones in her mind.

But the memory quickly faded, and Natalie found herself squarely in the present.

"Is everything okay?"

"I think I need to ask you the same thing."

Adele's expression clouded over further. "Let me put on a movie for Logan and then we can talk—"

Suddenly, the front door exploded open.

* * *

The front door banged hard enough to shake the glass in the windows and startle everyone in the living room. Natalie instinctively placed herself between Logan and the door and Adele jumped in front of both Natalie and Logan, reaching for a gun she wasn't wearing.

Red-faced, Landry stalked deeper into the room, and headed straight for Adele. "Why can't you ever listen?" he roared.

Alarmed by the crashing door and his father's yelling, Logan's lower lip began to quiver and tears filled his brown eyes.

"Landry!" Adele scolded, suddenly as enraged as her husband. "What are you doing?" But she knew exactly why he was here. She cursed herself for not waking Natalie to talk to her earlier.

Landry stomped over to his wife and motioned angrily at Natalie. "She's still here?" He snorted. "How'd you manage that after what you did?"

Adele ignored the venom in his voice and scooped up her son, even though he was getting too tall to comfortably rest on her hip. "Honey, it's okay," she murmured against Logan's cheek as she kissed him.

The boy sniffed a few times, and Adele bit her tongue to keep from lashing out at Landry in front of him. "Daddy was just playing and got too noisy."

Landry looked suitably shamed and lowered his voice. He gave Logan a reassuring smile. "Hey, buddy. Everything is fine."

"Logan, can you play in your room for a few minutes and then I'll come and get you?" Adele set Logan down then reached for his dinosaur and handed it to him.

"Daddy, play *with* me." Logan extended his T-Rex to his father. He hadn't seen him in a couple of days and his excitement was evident.

But Landry ruffled the boy's hair instead and said, "Go to your room and find another dinosaur for us both, and I'll be in there in a minute. Then we'll go to the park." His hand drifted to Logan's exposed belly. "And pick out a T-shirt too."

Natalie watched the exchange, eyes wide and confused as Logan darted toward his room.

"What the hell was that?" Adele hissed, making sure Logan was out of earshot before she spoke. "Are you drunk?" She leaned forward and sniffed the air, obviously trying to check for alcohol.

"Are you trying to commit career suicide?"

When Adele just looked at him, hands on her hips as she waited for an answer to her question, Landry rolled his eyes. "I'm not answering your stupid question. And I don't need to be drunk to be pissed at you! You didn't listen to a goddamn word I said!"

"Umm…" Natalie backed away toward the guest room, wanting to be anywhere but in the middle of a domestic dispute. "I'm just…yeah. I'm going—"

"Oh, no. You should stay here, Ms. Abbott." Landry sneered at Adele as he spoke. "Right, Ella? After all, this concerns her more than any of us."

Landry blinked at Natalie's obvious surprise. He turned back to his wife. "Well, well. That's why she's still here. You haven't told her."

"Landry." Adele's voice was a warning.

The tall man let loose a bark of unexpected laughter. "You know what's funny? No, it's not just funny, it's hilarious." He jerked a thumb at Natalie. "I've been jealous of her."

Stunned, Natalie's mouth dropped open while Adele's eyebrows crawled up her forehead and stayed. "What?" they both exclaimed.

"Why not?" he scoffed. "The last time she was here, Ella, you mentioned her for days after she left."

With wide eyes, Natalie turned to Adele. What was he talking about?

"Landry, we both discuss *all* our cases. That's what we do."

Landry didn't just look livid, he looked devastated, and the sight made Adele's stomach twist.

"Something was different about this case and you know it. And now she's back and you invite her to stay in our house? In our house, Ella! Since when do you do that?"

Adele shot Natalie an apologetic glance then focused on her husband. "Landry," she tried again, her tone softer. "I—"

"And I drove by here the other night. You know, to check on things. And you two were up talking in the middle of the night. All cozy in the living room. Arms wrapped around each other."

"Are you insane? She's just lost her brother! I gave her a *hug*, Landry. I do it all the time!" As Landry's other words soaked in, Adele's expression hardened. "Wait. You were spying on us?"

"It's *my* house too," he reminded Adele bitterly. "That's not spying."

Brown eyes narrowed. "You can't see inside the living room from the street."

He threw his hands in the air. "So what if I got out of the car? I saw a light on in the middle of the night. I wanted to know why."

"Jesus, Landry, listen to yourself! You're being ridiculous."

His bristly cheeks were beet red and he laughed again. The sound was high-pitched and out of character. "You're right! I was being totally stupid. Because if you cared about her *at all* you would never have ruined the case against her brother's killer."

Dead silence.

Adele and Landry glared at each other with fire pouring from their eyes.

"What..." Natalie swallowed thickly before she continued, "what does he mean...ruined the case, Ella?"

More dead silence.

Heart in her throat, Adele opened her mouth but it was Landry who spoke. "Detective Lejeune, here, thought she'd play Superwoman and right all the wrongs in the world herself!" he thundered. "Of course, she didn't actually right *anything*. Instead, she just made everything worse."

Adele sighed and rubbed her forehead with both hands. "You can be a real jerk when you want to be, Landry."

"Me? I *begged* you to tell me before you did anything stupid. I begged you and you were too stubborn to listen."

"I tried to tell you!" Adele's volume matched her husband's. She pointed an accusing finger at him. "I couldn't find you because you didn't want me to find you."

"My brother...?" Natalie's voice was soft and puzzled and didn't penetrate Adele and Landry's shouts.

"Landry, I ran after you at the courthouse and looked for you the rest of the afternoon. Your phone was off, and nobody knew where you were!"

"I got called in for damage control while you were still spilling your guts to The Rat Squad," he shot back. "And this morning it's already all over the station!"

Adele groaned loudly. She knew her accusations wouldn't stay quiet for long, but they couldn't have had time to even start investigating. "How?"

"Morrell's partner, that stupid fuck Hobson, shot off his mouth about being called in for questioning when he came off the nightshift and it spread like wildfire." His eyes flashed dangerously. "You didn't *trust* me to wait. I can tell."

"You're right. I didn't."

Adele saw her words stab Landry right in the chest, felt it as keenly as if the knife were twisting in her own. What she said was unequivocally true, and she regretted it instantly.

"Landry, I couldn't wait to say something. I'd already waited too long. *Please* understand. When I couldn't find you, I called the prosecutor. He told me that Crisco's attorney called him right after the arraignment. He thought he was going to have to drop the charges and, instead, Crisco's lawyer proposed a deal. Life in prison, if the death penalty was off the table. The prosecutor agreed on the spot."

Landry shook his head and crossed his arms over his chest. Adele could see shutters going up behind his eyes. "No shit, Ella. Putting bad guys in jail is his job."

"I needed to say something fast, or it would have been too late. I couldn't know when they'd schedule the actual sentencing hearing."

"Nothing happens *that* quickly," Landry ground out.

"Everything is happening too quickly!" Adele's cell phone rang. She snatched it up from the coffee table and saw that it was her lieutenant. With the push of a button she sent the call directly to voice mail. She threw the phone on the sofa and watched angrily as it bounced on the floor. Adele was going to be yelled at over and over again today. "Landry—"

"My brother's killer?" Natalie tried again. "I don't understand why the case is ruined if there is a deal." But Adele and Landry were only focused on each other. "Hey!" Natalie finally shouted, coming to stand directly between the detectives.

Landry looked at Natalie as though he just realized she was still in the room.

The tension in the air was thick and dangerous, and Natalie instinctively shifted to the balls of her feet. "Now, someone please tell me—"

"Daddy!" Logan burst into the room, two dinosaurs held awkwardly in one hand, wadded shirt in the other. "I'm ready!" The smile slid off his face at the sight of the livid expressions and rigid bodies around him.

"C'mon, son," Landry said. He took the shirt and toys from Logan with one hand and grasped the boy's small hand with his other. When he spoke again his voice was barely above a whisper, betrayal carved into every word. "You don't know what you've done, Ella. I don't care what you think you know, you don't. It was *naïve* and *reckless* and *selfish* and it's going to hurt us all."

Every word felt like a slap to the face and Adele flinched at "selfish."

"Ms. Abbott?" Landry's gaze slid sideways.

But Natalie's worried stare was glued on an ashen Adele. "Yeah?"

"I'm truly sorry about your brother." With that, Landry lifted Logan into his arms and strode out the front door, which was still hanging wide open.

Adele dropped back onto the sofa, her face in her hands as she tried not to cry. "Shit."

* * *

Natalie slowly crossed the room and shut the door, as much to give Adele a few seconds to collect herself as anything. When she turned back the detective was staring at her, eyes glittering, and obviously upset. "I know he's your husband and all, and I don't really understand what's happening," she sat down next to Adele, "but I'd sort of like to punch him in the nose."

Adele let out an unexpected burst of laughter. "You and me both." Then she sighed. "But I think I'm the one you'll want to hit after I explain what's going on."

Natalie smiled reassuringly, nervous about what was to come, but sure that Adele was on her side. Boldly, she took one of Adele's warm hands and held it firmly in hers. "So explain."

Adele drew in a shuddering breath. "When I arrived at your brother's crime scene I found the arresting cop, Officer Jay Morrell, assaulting Crisco. Not roughing him up, Natalie. Sadly, that sort of thing happens all the time. This was *bad*. The way Morrell was hammering him, he could have easily killed him. And Crisco wasn't resisting arrest, and he wasn't fighting back, he was just screaming and begging for it to stop."

Natalie's nostrils flared. "You saw this happen?"

Adele nodded.

"You stopped it?"

"Yes, but not before Officer Morrell got in another couple of good hits and a vicious kick. He knocked Crisco out cold. Morrell told me that Crisco had confessed to killing your brother just before I came in, but Crisco couldn't even speak coherently by the time I arrived."

"Then the cop should be punished for abusing his power." Natalie's free hand shaped a fist. "I know I should be more upset that he hit Crisco, but Crisco *killed* my brother." A tiny growl escaped. "If I could back over Crisco with my car and get away with it, I would."

Adele said slowly, "I know." Guiltily, she released Natalie's hand.

Natalie inclined her head curiously. "I don't understand why this would ruin my brother's case."

Adele swallowed hard. "Crisco's confession, if he made one initially at all, was coerced. It should be thrown out because it can't be trusted. And if it's gone, there is no case."

Natalie's eyebrows drew together, and adrenaline began to surge through her as she finally and fully grasped where this conversation was headed. *No. No. NO!* "But you said Crisco confessed before you arrived. How do you know it was coerced?"

"Morrell was *still* beating him when I arrived. If I did to you what Morrell did to Crisco, I could make you say anything, Natalie." Adele lowered her voice. "*Anything* I wanted. We can't believe what Morrell says because he's a dirty cop and we can't believe what Crisco says either. He was being tortured."

Natalie leaned away from Adele, both captured by and furious with the earnest look in her eyes. "Why would he confess if he wasn't guilty? No one would do that!"

"I know it sounds crazy, but you're wrong. People do it all the time."

Natalie struggled to wrap her mind around what Adele was saying. "But-but why in this case?"

Adele shrugged helplessly. "I don't know why, except that Crisco's deathly afraid of Morrell."

"This doesn't even make sense! You're the police. Why are you trying to get a confession thrown out?" She didn't give Adele a chance to respond before she asked incredulously, "So, I'm supposed to believe there is some sort of big conspiracy against that old down-and-out drunk?"

Natalie stood, needing to put some distance between herself and Detective Lejeune. Betrayal bubbled up into her throat and burned like acid. *She's helping the bad guy? I thought…I thought she was helping me…*

"I don't think there's a conspiracy, but I do think there is a rotten cop and that Morrell threatened to do something to Crisco if he took back the confession." Adele sprang to her feet and took a step toward Natalie, trying to stop her retreat. "Please, Natalie. Try to understand. I couldn't just stand by and do nothing after what I saw and heard."

Natalie covered her mouth with her palm for a few seconds as her mind spun furiously. "But you told me yesterday that they found the murder weapon on Crisco. And you said the forensics back this up."

Adele nodded miserably.

"Then I don't understand! Are you saying Crisco *did* or *didn't* kill my brother?"

Adele paused and looked down at her hands. "I don't know for sure. I—"

Natalie bared her teeth. "What do you *think* happened?"

"I think Crisco most likely killed Josh, and that Morrell forced him to confess."

"If he's *guilty* then who cares? A guilty man will go to prison, right where he belongs."

"Somebody has to care. *I* care." Adele's jaw worked for a few seconds, her entire body vibrating with frustration. "Going to the Public Integrity Bureau with this information was the right thing to do."

Natalie's mouth dropped open. "The right thing for whom?"

"I-I-I…" Adele stared at her with watery eyes, unable to answer the question.

"Oh, my God." Natalie bent at the waist, feeling sick. "Landry was right. You did this for yourself. You did this so you wouldn't feel guilty. You're going to help my brother's murderer go free to ease your conscience."

Tears filled Adele's eyes. "The police just can't attack people. We're supposed to *protect* people. You're supposed to be able to trust us."

"What are you talking about?" Natalie cried. "I *did* trust you! And look what happened."

Adele's frustration leaked into her voice. She wiped at her eyes with the back of her shaky hand. "I-I don't know what you want me to say. I agonized over this, but it had to be done. More than...more than anything, I wanted to help you and do my job. I wanted to do both."

Adele's phone rang again, interrupting them a second time. This time she savagely yanked it up from the carpet without looking at who was calling, and slung it across the room with shocking speed.

Natalie jumped when it hit the far wall and exploded into a dozen pieces, plastic and glass flying everywhere. Her voice went eerily flat. "You said you were a philosophy major in college. This is just some sort of esoteric, theoretical case study of what is and isn't justice to you, isn't it?"

Adele looked stricken. "No, Natalie."

"I have news, Detective," Natalie mocked, her chest constricting. "This isn't a philosophy word problem. This is about Josh being murdered! He was a real live, breathing, good person, who is now dead! He will never have a career or his own family or do all the things he dreamed about doing. He's *dead!* And you knew you were going to ruin the State's case this entire time?"

Adele closed her eyes. It took her several shaky breaths to find her voice. What emerged was a broken whisper. "I didn't know what to do."

Anger swelled in Natalie like the incoming tide, then crested. She'd been lulled into a sense of safety when she was most vulnerable, only to have the rug ruthlessly yanked out from beneath her. "I don't believe you. How can I believe anything you say?"

"I never lied to you!" Adele reminded her severely, her hands gesturing wildly as she spoke. "And I didn't want to hurt you or your family."

Natalie's eyes widened with realization and she took another step back. "These last couple of days...I wondered who would be so kind to a stranger. But you've been so helpful because you felt bad about what was going to happen! About what you were going to do." She shook her head quickly, full of disbelief at her own stupidity. "God, I feel like an idiot." Embarrassment mixed with raw anger. "I trusted every goddamn word out of your mouth and all the while you were just softening the blow."

The breath flew from Adele's chest as though she'd been punched in the gut. She gasped. "No, Natalie! I truly wanted to help you. I still do."

"You were right, you know."

Adele tried to change gears. "I-I...what?"

Natalie glared. "I do want to hit you."

Adele looked away, long wet lashes fluttering over dark circles.

"You dried my tears, and held my hair, and told me everything was going to be okay. Why? I don't...You could have stopped us from starting to become friends!" *You should have stopped me.*

"I didn't *want* to stop it." Miserable, Adele reached out for her. "I'm still your friend."

Reeling, Natalie lifted her hands to ward off Adele from coming any closer. The movement stopped Adele in her tracks. "Don't. Please." Their eyes battled for several fierce seconds. Neither woman blinked. "You were never my friend. Did you even look for Josh after I left New Orleans?"

Adele inhaled sharply. "What are you talking about?"

Natalie lifted her chin a little. "Did you bother to look again?"

"How can you say that?" Adele growled. "I looked for weeks! He wasn't my only case, but that didn't mean I ever completely stopped."

"Why would I believe that? You don't care about him now. You don't care about his killer paying for his crimes. You don't care about what your actions will do to his family. You. Only. Care. About. You!"

Deeply wounded, Adele allowed her arms to fall loosely at her sides. She looked a little shell-shocked by Natalie's venomous words. "I'm so—"

Turning on her heel, Natalie bolted from the living room, silent tears trailing down her cheeks as she grabbed her bag and threw the strap over her shoulder. She marched out of the house without looking back.

Adele was hot on her heels, but stopped in the doorway of her home even when Natalie didn't.

Natalie was simply finished.

"Natalie."

Finished feeling like a fool.

"Natalie, wait."

Finished with New Orleans.

"Dammit! Please!"

Finished with police stations and morgues.

"Natalie!"

And most especially finished with Detective Adele Lejeune.

CHAPTER SIX

Six months later…

Gun drawn, Adele crept around the side of a rickety old structure that was more shack than house. Katrina had devastated the neighborhood, located in New Orleans' notorious D-block in the 6th Ward, and years later almost forty percent of the houses still sat abandoned and in ruin. The sound of gunshots wasn't uncommon, and on this street the police were about as welcome as a raging case of the clap.

It was just past twilight and the dark bluish tint of the evening sky had shifted into a deep black-purple. Sporadic lights inside the tiny houses began to pop on up and down the street, but there were no streetlights for illumination. This was the last house on the block. It rested a bit farther from the street than the others, and the impending night seemed to want to swallow it whole.

With her back pressed lightly against the house, Adele moved deeper into the shadows, and headed for a back window and the faint light that emanated from it.

She could hear voices coming from inside the house. The voices she'd been looking for.

Annie and Milo Olmstead had been missing for nearly a week. The four- and five-year-olds' parents were in the middle of a cutthroat divorce. Their father, Reggie, a nasty piece of work who was only a few months out of prison for attempted robbery and assault with a deadly weapon, had picked up the children from school one day and simply never took them home. Then all three of them had disappeared.

Adele had leveraged every street contact she had, spent hour after relentless hour interviewing everyone who even knew Reggie or his wife, and followed every wild goose chase until she had meticulously traced the children and their father to a dilapidated house that belonged to Reggie's old girlfriend's cousin.

Her hard work was about to pay off...

She let out a soft curse as her feet sank into the spring mud and one boot made a loud squelching sound when she lifted it and gave her leg a little shake.

"Where are you?" she whispered softly to herself. Her focus drifted back to the darkening street. Adele had called for backup more than fifteen minutes ago, but so far she was still alone.

Resentment ate away at her like a disease. This wasn't the first time her fellow officers had taken their sweet time coming to her aid. She scarcely wanted to give dispatch her name anymore when she called for backup. It was as though there was an NOPD labor strike...but the "blue flu" was focused solely against her. "Fuckers."

Then the voices inside the small house shifted into yells and the sounds of crying children. She strained to see down the street again. "C'mon!" Crouched low, Adele kept moving until she was right below the cracked window and the voices became clearer. The side of the house was damp and the moisture soaked into the back of her shirt and bra. She listened carefully, a nervous sweat trickling between her breasts.

"Daddy, no!" a young boy's frantic voice pierced the night and Adele closed her eyes, her heart racing. Every muscle in her body itched to propel her inside the house to grab those kids.

"Shut up!" There was a loud crash and a muffled shriek.

"I'm sorry," the boy sobbed.

Reggie, Adele thought with disgust. She was going to enjoy throwing that prick into jail.

"Where is it?" Reggie bellowed.

His voice thundered so loudly that even Adele flinched. *Those poor kids must have just wet their pants.*

"I don't know, Daddy!"

The words trembled and were soft enough that Adele could barely make them out. Her eyes narrowed. *Annie.*

"I asked you a question, little bitch!"

Anger bubbled up in her so quickly that Adele couldn't stop herself from raising her head and peering inside, even at the risk of being seen. A single light bulb cast the small kitchen in a dull yellowish glow, and dark, jagged shadows shot inward from the corners of the room. The room was filled with hazy smoke from a lit cigarette smoldering in a small tin ashtray by the sink.

Adele couldn't locate Milo, but in the center of the room, she saw Reggie shaking Annie as though the little girl was nothing but a rag doll, her head flinging wildly from side to side. Adele didn't wait to see more. She sprang up and sprinted for the back door. She had to get inside right *now*.

Annie screamed when her father slapped her. Hard. He lifted her by her slender biceps and shook her again, her blond head flopping against her shoulders. "I told you not to touch the fuckin' lighter! How am I supposed to smoke? Huh?"

Adele burst through the back door with so much force she had to stop herself from skidding directly into the kitchen table. "Freeze!" she shouted, her Glock pointed straight at Reggie's head. "Let her go." She pinned him with a flinty stare and lifted the gun a little higher. "Slowly," she instructed precisely. "Let her go *slowly*." Her heart pounded furiously in her chest.

The whites of Reggie's eyes grew so big that his pupils nearly disappeared. "Who the fuck are you?" But instead of lowering the girl slowly, he simply opened his hands, sending her crashing to the floor and onto bony knees.

The girl released a shrill cry.

"I'm the police," Adele growled, her darker instincts demanding retribution for what she'd already seen. Her voice dropped an octave. "You really should shut up."

Grabbing hold of her emotions, she spoke gently to the sobbing girl. "Honey, you're Annie, right?" Adele didn't bother to ask her if she was okay. She clearly wasn't. The girl just looked at her, too rattled to answer, but Adele recognized her from her photo. "Annie?"

"Y-yes?" she sniffed. Blood dripped from her nostrils and over her lips.

Adele's chest ignited. "Step away from your father and over to me, sweetheart. That's it. I won't hurt you. I'm the police. I have a badge, see?" She gestured toward the gold shield on her belt.

Reggie sneered at the child as though she was a traitor when she began to move. "You little—"

"I said, *shut up*! On your knees. Hands on your head! Now!" The gun suddenly felt hot and slick in Adele's sweaty hand. She realized with nauseating clarity how badly she wanted to pull the trigger and simply rid the world of this piece of filth.

Reggie reluctantly dropped to his knees with a loud thud and laced his fingers behind his head. He glowered at her, his gaze glinting menacingly. "These are my damn kids. I didn't do anything wrong."

Adele cocked her head to the side. "What part of shut up is unclear, dumb fu—?" Then she remembered the little girl, quaking at her side. "Reggie." Adele released one of her hands from her pistol and used her fingers to softly tilt the girl's chin upward to look into her eyes.

Annie looked confused and dazed. It was hard to see in the dim light, but her eyes were the lightest blue Adele had ever seen, and her pupils looked as though they were different sizes. *Concussion.*

Adele bit her tongue and glanced around expecting to see Milo cowering in a corner, but he wasn't there. A sense of unease washed over her. She hadn't been able to clear the house. She had no idea who, besides Milo, might be hiding there.

"Milo," she called out gently. "Milo, you can come out. This is the police."

There was no answer.

"Run, son! Go grab Daddy's twelve-gauge!" But Reggie whimpered when Adele took a menacing step toward him, her patience at an end.

"I'm going to take you back to your mama, Milo," Adele tried again. "She misses you and your sister."

"That junkie whore?" Reggie laughed bitterly. "She's bat-shit crazy."

Adele ignored him and cautiously moved a little deeper into the room, keeping her gun trained on Reggie, while trying to see into the darkened hallway. Annie was practically plastered to her leg and they moved as one. "Milo? You can come out. It's safe."

"S'okay, Milo," Annie warbled.

The boy instantly and silently poked his head out from around the corner, startling Adele who quickly swung her gun in his direction.

"Thank God," Adele mumbled and retrained her weapon on Reggie.

Milo's mouth was bleeding. The blood had formed a lurid red pattern on his dingy white T-shirt that looked like a demented Rorschach test.

Adele felt another surge of anger. She should have come inside sooner. "Come stand with me and Annie. It's okay." She extended a hand and motioned him forward with curled fingers.

Milo tiptoed around his father and came to rest next to his sister. Ignoring the adults completely, he offered the sleeve of his T-shirt for his sister to wipe her bloody nose.

Adele extended her hearing outside. Still no backup. *What the actual fuck?* But again, she couldn't wait. It wasn't safe to leave things as they were. She still hadn't patted down Reggie for weapons. "Annie and Milo?"

Two sets of terrified blue eyes swung up to meet her gaze. "Is there anyone else in the house besides the four of us in this room? It's very important that you tell me the truth."

"Don't tell that pig anything!" Reggie spat, sitting back on his haunches. "You can't make them talk!"

"I'm not making them," Detective Lejeune said calmly. She beamed a kind smile at the children. "I'm asking them nicely. Are we alone?"

They both nodded silently, and Adele huffed out a relieved breath. "Okay, listen closely, kids." Her volume was low, but the children couldn't mistake the intensity in her voice. "I want you to go wait outside on your front porch. Do *not* go anyplace else. Especially don't go near the street. Hold hands as you walk through the house. And stay together. If you need me, yell. I'll hear you. But no matter what you hear from inside the house, do not come back in. Stay where you are."

She gave first Milo, then Annie, a tender, one-armed hug. "More police officers are coming, okay?"

The children's fear seemed to multiply at Adele's words.

"No, no, no," said murmured. "The police are coming to *help* you. I promise." She ran a reassuring hand softly down Annie's long hair. It felt like silk against her fingertips. "Do you believe me?" Adele couldn't let the kids out of her sight if there was even a hint that they might run.

"She's lying!" Reggie roared, glaring at Milo and Annie like a dog that was about to bite. "I warned you about the asshole cops. They'll shoot you if they get the chance."

Adele rolled her eyes and let the children see it, then she forced out a light laugh. "That won't happen. The police *help* people. And they'll be wearing uniforms so you'll know exactly who they are. Your mama sent us to come get you." She smiled again. "She's going to be *so* happy to see you." Privately, Adele wasn't so sure. Their mother, a hot mess in her own right, seemed angrier that Reggie had taken the children than the fact that they were gone. She only hoped Milo and Annie didn't know that. "Okay?"

It took a few seconds, but both children warily agreed.

"Good," Adele murmured. "Go now. Quickly."

Milo quickly grabbed his sister's hand and walked from the room. They trembled when they, once again, had to walk past their father, even after Adele moved to put herself between them and the beefy man.

When she heard the last of the pounding of their small feet, and the front door open and slam closed, Adele reached around behind her with one hand and retrieved her handcuffs, her gun still trained precisely on Reggie. Standing well out of his range of motion, she dangled the handcuffs in front of his face.

"Time for your favorite accessory. On your belly, you ugly bastard," she commanded. She nudged one of his elbows with the toe of her boot when he tried to reposition himself. "No. Keep your hands on your head."

He spoke directly into the dirty floor. "Bitch."

"You have the right to remain silent."

"Fuck you, bitch!"

Adele sighed and wished that just once someone would listen to the "remain silent" part and take it to heart. She moved behind him and pressed her knee squarely into the center of his back for leverage. As she spoke, she silently holstered her weapon.

"You said that already, Reggie." She grabbed one of his hands and quickly pushed it up his back until he yelped. Then she brought the other down to meet it. With a quick click, one shackle was on, but before the next heartbeat, Reggie began to squirm and howl like he was on fire. He spun them in a half circle as though he was a bull Adele was riding at the rodeo.

"Dammit! What are you doing?" she ground out. "That's a good way to get your arm broken." Quickly gaining the upper hand, Adele dug her knee just below his shoulder blades and pressed hard enough to hear the air expel from his lungs. But before she could secure the second cuff she caught the sound of the floor creaking behind her.

Her head snapped sideways, and she reached for her gun just in time for something to explode across the side of her face, sending glass and sweet iced tea flying everywhere. Adele's body toppled over Reggie, and she saw stars as she went sprawling across the kitchen floor face-first and into the kitchen table, blasting the kitchen chairs in all directions the way a bowling ball scatters pins. Her gun flew from her hand and skittered out of sight as a wiry, clawing body landed on top of her with stunning force.

She felt searing pain at her temple and forehead, and a warm gush of blood ran over one eye and down her nose in a steady stream. A quick shake of her head sent blood scattering everywhere. She turned sideways, her arms coming up to block the blows raining down on her.

"Let him go!" a woman with crazy eyes and wild red curls shrieked. She dropped the remains of the handle from the glass pitcher she'd smashed against Adele's head and jumped onto the detective. Her flailing legs sent another chair crashing sideways. "Don't hurt him!"

For a split second Adele was disoriented, then her heart began to jackhammer. Adrenaline sang through her veins at lightning speed as her fight-or-flight response kicked in with full force. The women began to wrestle fiercely, broken glass cutting into Adele's shoulders and arms as they fought.

"Stop it!" Adele snarled, recognition dawning. She knew this woman. "What the hell?" But she could tell by the woman's savage, reckless movements, and the way she didn't seem to care if Adele hit her, that she was too high on drugs to listen.

"Denise?" Reggie cried, sounding as surprised at Adele felt. "How'd you find me?"

Reggie's wife, Milo and Annie's mother, slashed her sharp fingernails across Adele's cheek, tearing the skin in a jagged line and drawing blood. Adele hissed loudly and landed a solid elbow squarely against the woman's jaw. The strike was hard enough that it couldn't be ignored and with a blood-curdling scream, Denise sagged forward and grabbed her face just long enough for Adele to shove her completely away and half under the kitchen table.

"Denise?" Adele shouted, confused. "What are you doing? I'm helping you! I found your kids." But there was no way they were going home to this crazy bitch tonight. Or ever if she could help it. Suddenly, the faint sound of sirens coming from somewhere outside registered. *Thank God.*

Reggie, who was so shocked that he froze for several seconds as the scene unfolded in front of him, finally lumbered to his feet. He glanced at the open back door, but instead of running outside, decided to try to run past the fighting women toward the front porch. Where his children were waiting.

"No!" Adele's hand darted up as he passed, and she grabbed the dangling handcuff. From her knees and using all her body weight, she jerked the cuff sideways with such force that she heard the man's wrist snap.

Howling, Reggie dropped to the ground and clutched his hand to his chest. "Fuck!" Spittle flew from his mouth as he wailed.

Adele had to blink blood out of her eyes before she could see him clearly. She wobbled to her feet, her muddy boots slipping until she managed to use her smaller size to her advantage and maneuver behind him in the tight kitchen. She pulled hard on the dangling handcuff as he began to fight her again. "Stop it!" Another hard jerk and she dislocated his shoulder, his screams ringing in her ears as she shoved him facedown into the floor and secured the second cuff tightly in place.

Adele could see the flashing lights of a police car reflected in the side window and hear adult voices on the porch. "C'mon!" she yelled, spitting away the blood that had dripped into her mouth. "Inside!" she called out, her eyes scanning desperately for Denise. "Help!"

Then, out of nowhere, Denise was on her again and fighting like a banshee, her momentum pushing Adele almost on top of Reggie. As they grappled, Adele caught a glimpse of something shiny and metallic in Denise's hand. Her eyes widened when she thought of her gun. Fear exploded inside her. She wrapped a hand tightly around Denise's wrist, pinning it down. With the other, she wound her fingers into Denise's hair and yanked hard, successfully wrenching the other woman off her chest.

Reggie, who was still facedown, helped his wife by kicking wildly at Adele with both legs. After a few attempts, one of his big sneakers caught Adele in the ribs just as she freed herself from Denise.

"Christ!" Adele cried out again as she felt something snap inside. A wave of nausea rushed over her and she instinctively tucked her elbow against her body to protect her ribs from more damage.

"You're sleeping with him, too!" Denise wailed, dilated eyes blazing.

Adele finally saw what was in Denise's hand…a second too late.

Denise plunged a long, slender boning knife into the flesh high on Adele's leg, below her hipbone, burying the blade to the hilt before savagely twisting it and yanking it out with such force that she stumbled backward, screaming, blood dripping from the blade and down Denise's arms. The woman looked equal parts horrified and thrilled at what she'd just done.

"*Fuck!*" The pain that tore through Adele was so intense that dots danced before her eyes and the room blurred. An inhuman cry ripped itself from her chest and her hands flew to her leg. Hot blood pulsed between her fingers in time with her pounding heart. "Argh!" Her mind screamed along with her mouth. *Shit. Shit! This is bad.* Blood spurted out of her and she couldn't stop it.

Then, even though she couldn't tell exactly how much time had passed, everything seemed to happen all at once.

Two uniformed police officers burst into the room.

Adele heard gunshots and shouts. Denise went silent, and Reggie's screams sounded different, more desperate and higher pitched. His legs, which had been tangled up with Adele, slid away. *Was that my gun that went off?*

Her vision grew fuzzier. She shook her head again to clear away the blood from her eyes, but her vision wouldn't focus. Her eyelids began to droop, and try as she might, she couldn't help but let them slip closed. *Just for a minute. S'okay. I'm awake. I'm…awake.* Her limbs felt thick and weighted down like they were dissolving into the floor. For the first time Adele noticed that the room smelled like cigarettes, mud, and gunpowder mixed with something cloying and metallic.

The linoleum around Adele grew slick as the pool of brick-red blood continued to grow, circling her. She couldn't keep pressure on her leg any more and her hands limply fell away. One hand landed on a tiny sliver of glass and she felt it prick her skin almost gently and accompanied by a tiny sting, which registered as odd in the face of the nearly overwhelming pain in her leg, ribs, and face.

She thought she heard someone call her name. But then the voice seemed to be a whisper.

Hands touched her, but she couldn't stop them. She hoped they weren't Denise's or Reggie's.

An unwilling voyager, her mind began to drift. Handcuffs. That was her mistake. Not getting those damn handcuffs on right the first time when she cuffed…him.

The buzzing from the refrigerator grew louder and overtook the voices in the room. And the floor felt cool against her back, much cooler than it had seemed before. The pain was still there, but it was distant and disjointed as though she was dreaming. She felt wet everywhere. Mud. Tea. Like a scene from a horror movie, blood was everywhere.

She thought of the kids on the porch. She should have come inside sooner. Before he'd hurt them. The blood spatter on the little boy's white T-shirt looked like a butterfly. She liked butterflies. The orange ones especially made her think of picnics in summertime. And she thought of Logan who'd fallen and knocked out a tooth and how she'd promised him the tooth fairy would visit in the morning. She hoped she had quarters in her purse. The gas station would have quarters.

Was she being lifted or was she floating?

She prayed the kids were okay. She should have come inside the house sooner.

Even though she didn't feel like she was on the floor anymore, her body grew heavier and her movements more lethargic, as though her mind was disconnected from her limbs. Then Adele's gasping breaths and furious heartbeat simply dissolved into nothing.

PART THREE

CHAPTER SEVEN

Two years and nine months later...

It had been less than ten days since Thanksgiving and a thick blanket of snow already covered the yard in front of Natalie's townhouse. She'd survived another of her least favorite holidays. The food was divine, she had to give her mother her due, but an entire day at her parents' house among a sea of extended relatives who only found time for one another once a year, and over someone else's turkey, was something she could live without.

Christmas, she convinced herself, would be a bit better.

It was Saturday morning, and she sat on one corner of her sofa, alone, wearing warm flannel pajamas and a weary smile. Her hair was swept up in a haphazard ponytail. A hot cup of coffee was cradled in both hands, its aroma surrounding her. She gazed out the window, eyes unfocused as large snowflakes gently drifted to the ground. Natalie had gotten lucky and been assigned one of the earliest days possible to give her final exams, and now three tall piles of completed tests sat on her coffee table awaiting her judgment.

She began to mentally map out her day and her smile slowly slid away.

Natalie had no plans for this first Saturday of the school winter holiday and it irked her. Only last week she'd achieved one of the major milestones of her career, one she'd worked tirelessly toward. She'd not only been promoted to associate professor, but granted tenure. In the face of never-ending university budget cuts and a depressingly low number of tenure-track positions within her department, the achievement was substantial and while she was thrilled, she also felt a little aimless.

Now what? Even with her nose to the grindstone, something she excelled at, full professorship was at least five years away. While the salary was better, having already achieved tenure, the role carried more prestige than anything else. Her next promotion would require a sharper focus on research and publishing, something Natalie heartily enjoyed, but it also meant she still had years more in front of the classroom, something she tolerated but had come to accept she didn't really love.

With a grimace, she recalled her own education and the many professors she'd had who clearly didn't want anything to do with the students. Natalie was far from that, and would never allow her students to suffer for her work preferences, but she wasn't exactly happy either.

She'd made a conscious decision to place her career above her personal life years ago, and so here she sat, having reached a major life goal, and at a crossroads in her career, but with no one to share it.

The tradeoff left her cold and contemplative.

Most of her friends had families of their own and would be enjoying the day with them—holiday shopping, or sledding, or perhaps hanging Christmas decorations. Of course, she could do those things herself. Well, if she actually had Christmas decorations or did any shopping that wasn't handled completely online, or owned a sled. It was really too bad that she hated cats, she decided. For the first time in her life she saw the appeal of their mindless, yet judgmental company.

She slipped on her reading glasses, a new and unwelcomed addition to her life that seemed to mark the passing of time even more than the calendar, and picked up the first exam off the pile. It was for a freshman-level course that was required for almost all the liberal arts degrees. Meaning: almost nobody who was in the class had selected it voluntarily and out of interest.

She sighed and gnawed on the cap of her red pen. Half the answers were blank and the others were filled in with handwriting so bad it was utterly illegible. She did see a few smiley faces and LOLs among the words, which was odd and slightly amusing considering the questions covered the impact of disease on the Continental Army at Valley Forge in the winter of 1777–1778.

Natalie took off her glasses and tossed them on the table, deciding to wait to grade the exams until she could give them the attention they deserved. Reluctantly, she forced herself to fight the nearly overwhelming urge to just give everyone an A. Not a single student would complain, and she could call it a day. Her cell phone rang. Still in teacher mode, she absently answered as though she was in her office and not at home.

"Professor Abbott." Natalie's voice was gravelly from disuse.

"Professor? Wow. I forgot about that, Nat."

Natalie spilled her coffee down the front of her and almost dropped her phone. Only her brother called her Nat. "Ouch! Dammit! M-Misty? Is that you?"

A sigh. "Yeah. Hi, Nat. I mean Natalie."

"Holy...I mean, holy *shit*!" Natalie shot to her feet and began to pace, pulling the hot, coffee-soaked flannel away from her stomach. "Where have you been? Christ, I figured something awful had happened to you. Are you okay?"

"Something awful did happen. A lot of somethings. I mean, I was really messed up for a very long time."

Tears leapt into Natalie's eyes. She was never close to Misty, but Josh was and that, if nothing else, was enough to engender genuine concern. The sting of the loss of her brother welled in her chest. "Are-are you still messed up? Are you okay?"

"I'm...a lot better now. It's taken a long time, but things are good. Or at least they're getting to be good."

Natalie nodded to herself, not missing the regret that laced Misty's words. Josh's autopsy toxicology results had been appalling. If Misty had gotten only half as deep into drugs as Josh had, her life would have been more nightmare than mess.

"Where've you been?" Absently, she stripped off her pajama shirt and wadded it in her hand as she used it to sop the coffee from her skin.

"New Orleans mostly. For like what, five years? I waitress in a bar on Magazine Street now, and it pays the bills."

Misty seemed to be forcing herself to talk, and Natalie began to get nervous. *She's going to bolt.*

After a beat, "I'm sorry. I think I should go now. Maybe this is a mistake. I shouldn't have bothered you and I shouldn't—"

"No, please don't hang up!" Natalie perched on the sofa arm, trying not to panic. She pressed the phone so tightly to her ear it hurt. "I have so many questions. Please, Misty."

"I...okay."

"Thank you. Thank you." Natalie let out a shaky sigh. "Okay, I tried to find you and Josh that summer you left. I went to the police for help, but somehow you were just gone."

"We...we ran out of money and did some really bad things, Natalie. We, um, fell in with some homeless kids who drifted around town and slept in abandoned houses. We started using drugs. Then we couldn't stop using." Misty laughed softly, but it didn't carry an ounce of joy. "Not that we wanted to stop. We didn't have the money to fund the habit, so we started doing favors and running small errands for our dealer and then his friends."

Natalie heard a dry swallow. Misty was a pretty, if vapid, girl and she didn't want to think about what exactly those favors might have entailed. It was so repulsive to consider, Natalie wouldn't even let her mind go there when it came to Josh.

"By the end of that first summer we were going back and forth to Houston, picking up drugs and bringing them back to New Orleans."

Natalie sucked in a breath. "I'm so sorry."

"None of that was your fault. We were dumb. Dumber than you'll ever know."

"Do you…" Natalie paused to wipe at her eyes, "do you know what happened to Josh?" Hearing her brother's name, even from her own lips, caused a pang deep in Natalie's chest. Her parents, unable to cope with the loss, barely acknowledged what had happened, and she hadn't said or heard his name in more than two years. But that didn't mean Natalie didn't think about him often, along with every mistake she'd made along the way to his death.

"That's why I called. I need to…to tell you that I was there that night."

Natalie's eyebrows drew down. "The night he was killed?"

"Yeah. At the Dixie Brewery. We hung out there sometimes."

"And that means…you saw it happen?"

"Yeah. I wish to God I hadn't. But I did. I mean, I was so high, and Joshie was too, but it's like it's burned into my brain. It's killing me."

Natalie frowned. "So you saw Crisco hit him?"

"I-I need to tell you about that. Crisco didn't do anything. He slept through it all. He was passed out cold, I think."

"Misty." Natalie's frowned deepened. "Maybe your memory isn't as good as you think. The police caught and arrested Crisco that same night. He had the murder weapon. He confessed. He did it."

"No. He didn't."

Natalie looked at the phone in confusion. "I don't…I don't understand."

"Crisco didn't kill Josh. He didn't do it."

Natalie's stomach dropped to the floor, and she groaned loudly. "Jesus Christ! What?"

Misty burst into tears. "I was too afraid to say! I saw it all. It wasn't Crisco. I swear it wasn't."

"But—"

"What happened to Crisco was all over the news, especially after that one detective ratted out the cops."

That detective. Natalie looked skyward and closed her eyes.

"But I was too chicken to do anything about it or go to the police. You have to understand. *Please*, Natalie. What could I say? I was strung out all the time. If I wasn't using myself, I was a pack mule. At least until I was so messed up I couldn't even carry dope back and forth. I didn't talk to the police back then, I ran from them."

Natalie's hands trembled. She hit the speaker button on her phone and set it on the coffee table so she wouldn't accidentally hang up. *Detective Lejeune. Ella. Oh, shit. Oh, shit.* Regret bubbled up so quickly she thought she might be ill.

"Are—are you still there?" Misty asked worriedly.

Natalie gritted her teeth. "Tell me what happened."

"We saw a drug buy go down between two guys. No—no biggie. We'd seen a million of them. By that time we were mixed up with some really bad people. I stepped away from Josh so I could, you know, take a leak. It was raining that night. God, was it raining."

"Was one of the men in the drug deal Crisco?"

"No! Like I said, Crisco was asleep. I'd seen Crisco at the brewery lots of times before. He was always dead drunk…passed out."

Natalie couldn't believe it. She didn't *want* to believe it. It was as though someone came back after the fact and rewrote a piece of history that you knew in your heart was true. Only now it wasn't. "Go on."

"Josh teased one of the men from the drug buy. I don't know why. He never did stupid shit like that. But he was so damned trashed that night. Worse than ever before. The man walked over…" Misty sniffed loudly and her next words came out in a rush. "He picked up a brick and hit Josh in the head." She sounded a little astonished, even now. "He hit him so hard."

Natalie's eyes fluttered shut again. She tried not to picture what Misty was describing, but it was impossible.

"The man couldn't see me, but I could see him. After he hit Josh, he took the brick and put it in Crisco's hand and just walked out like nothing happened. Oh, and he made a phone call on the way out, but I couldn't hear what he was saying. That's it."

"Oh, my God, Misty. Why didn't you say anything at the time? The police arrested the wrong man!"

"I did! I ran out of the brewery and bummed a phone off a guy at the strip club a couple of doors down and made one of those calls where you don't give your name."

"Anonymous?"

"Yeah. That kind. I said there was a really bad fight and the cops needed to break it up. It wasn't until days later that I saw Crisco had been arrested and there was a massive shit parade going on about brutality in the NOPD. I couldn't go to the cops then. I was afraid they would put me in jail."

"His confession wasn't true," Natalie murmured, heartsick and consumed by guilt. "She told me it couldn't be trusted, but I didn't believe her. Or maybe I just didn't care."

"Huh?"

Natalie scrubbed her face. "Never mind. Why are you telling me all this now?"

"Because I'm getting my life back on track, and for the first time in forever I can see things clearly. I know I need to go to the police. But I'm- I'm still afraid. Maybe it's a bad idea, you know? It's been years. It's over and done with. Josh will still be dead whether I do this or not. And that Crisco guy was released from jail or something. I saw it on a TV in a bar. I know the cops won't want to believe me, but I can tell them everything."

"Misty—"

"Lately I dream about him," Misty carried on, sounding a little frantic. "About Josh, I mean. About how his killer walked out of the brewery like nothing had happened. And—"

"Go to the police."

"I-I *want* to do that." But doubt colored Misty's words.

"Then let me help you. We owe it to Josh." *And I owe it to Detective Lejeune.*

"I'm not—not sure, Natalie."

"Give me your address. I can be in New Orleans by tonight." Her gaze swung outside. The snow was falling even harder. She'd need to leave for the airport right now.

"Okay, okay, yeah. I'll call the cops today to set up a time, and then you can go to the station with me when you get here. You have to promise you'll go with me. I'm really scared. I can't go alone."

"You won't have to go alone. I promise to go with you, but you need to promise me you won't run before I can get there."

For a few seconds the only sound on the line was two sets of heavy breathing.

"I really loved Josh, you know."

The non sequitur caused Natalie to lean a little closer to the phone, but remain silent.

"Maybe you don't think I know what love is because we were just kids or because of the drugs, but I did and I do. He stayed for me." Misty's voice cracked piteously. "When everything got horrible, and it was just stupid to stay, he did anyway. He knew he could come home to you, Natalie. But I couldn't do the same thing. My mom…well, there was never anything for me back in Wisconsin. So he stayed in New Orleans for me."

Natalie felt a little light-headed at Misty's words. To know that Josh at least knew he could come home was an unexpected gift. But now that she finally had a target for her frustration, beyond herself and her parents, she wanted to blame Misty for what happened. She wanted to lash out and lay everything at her feet like a horrible, tragic offering to youth and stupidity and addiction.

But she couldn't.

Misty hadn't forced a needle into Josh's arm. Natalie was still having trouble coming to terms with it herself, but deep down she knew that despite everyone else's failings, hers included, it was Josh's own decisions that led him to the Dixie Brewery that night. So Natalie said the only think she could think of. "He loved you too."

"I...Thank you for that. Natalie?"

"Yes?"

"Please hurry."

* * *

Twenty-four hours later, Natalie stepped out of a cab in front of a tiny shotgun-style house on North Roman Street in the Faubourg Tremé. The home looked ancient, but the tiny patch of grass outside was well taken care of and held several pots brimming with purple and red flowers. Paint was peeling from the walls, and the house sat a little uneven on its foundation. But someone had made an effort. The vibrant colors of the flowers looked foreign but beautiful to Natalie, having just come from the frozen tundra where this time of year everything seemed beige.

As she ascended three crumbling concrete steps, Natalie stretched a little. She was exhausted, and her back was sore and stiff. Her connecting flight had been delayed by a snowstorm at O'Hare where she'd been forced to spend the night in a hard plastic chair, both dreading and anticipating seeing Detective Lejeune again, and running through contingency plans in her mind in case she had to abandon the airport completely and simply drive through the storm. Luckily, the morning had dawned clearer and she'd been filed onto a later flight.

Misty had seemed so jumpy on the phone that Natalie half-expected no one to answer the door when she knocked. She wasn't wrong.

After knocking, then pounding, then barely resisting the urge to kick the door in, she let out a frustrated sigh and checked her cell phone. She had the right address. *Okay, plan B. Be bold.* Shoulders squared and looking as though she was comfortable breaking into people's houses every day, Natalie simply opened the door and strolled inside, a little shocked to find the door unlocked.

"Misty?" she called out loudly. She set a small duffel bag and her purse near the front door. "It's Natalie." She glanced around quickly, scanning the messy living room. Frowning, her attention was drawn to the blaring television, the laugh track from *Friends* filling the small space. A tiny bolt of worry shot through her. Who goes out, but leaves on their TV? Loud. Purely out of habit, she reached for the remote control that sat on a ratty love seat and turned off the TV, plunging the room into silence.

"Misty?"

Still no answer.

Maybe Misty slept like Josh had. A freight train pulled by wild horses couldn't stir him. Natalie passed a sink filled with dirty dishes without pausing. The bathroom, too, was empty. The last door to what she presumed would be the bedroom, was open a crack.

Feeling like a thief in the night, Natalie stuck her head inside. The curtains were drawn so it was dark in the room, but she could still make out a figure lying on top of a partially made bed, blond hair fanned out gently on her pillow. "Thank goodness," she mumbled, grateful that she wouldn't have to spend the day scouring every bar on Magazine Street to try to find where Misty worked.

"Time to wake up." Natalie wondered whether Misty'd been so nervous about going to the police that she'd gotten drunk the night before. "C'mon. I know it's early, but up and at 'em." Gently, she reached out to softly shake her awake. But the second her hand touched the other woman's skin, she knew something was dreadfully wrong. Misty felt unnaturally cool and rigid.

"Wake up!" Natalie said loudly, shaking Misty's shoulder a little harder with a trembling hand, still expecting her to bolt awake. The movement caused Misty's head to roll sideways so that the younger woman fully faced Natalie, gazing up at her with dull, unseeing eyes. Natalie gasped and yanked her hand back as though it had been burned. "Jesus!" She retreated so quickly her back slammed against the bedroom wall. A framed picture near Natalie's head rattled off its nail and crashed to the floor, glass shattering.

For several seconds Natalie stood there, dumbstruck, the blood draining from her face, both hands clamped over her open mouth in stunned disbelief. She forgot to breathe, or even blink, as her eyes began to adjust to the light and the scene came into sharper relief.

Misty's face looked much the same way she remembered only a little thinner and tinted gray. She was fully dressed in jeans, T-shirt and sneakers. A thick rubber band was tied around her right bicep, and the appendage was a deep purple. A syringe and needle, still half-stuck in the flesh at the crook of Misty's arm, hung limply against a pile of wadded sheets.

"Oh my God. Oh my God." Natalie's eyes flicked around the room as though there was someone she could ask for help. But she was alone.

Misty was clearly dead, but she had to be sure, right? Biting her lip, Natalie reluctantly made her way back to the bed, each quiet step sounding unnaturally loud to her ears. This time she leaned down, and the scent of stale urine and feces wafted up. With a grimace, she pressed her fingers against the cool skin at Misty's throat to feel for a pulse.

Nothing.

Natalie's mind jumped into hyperdrive. Had Misty been so stressed about going to the police that she'd needed to get high to make it through the night? Then an even more disturbing thought reared its ugly head. What if Misty simply couldn't cope with what she was about to do and she'd overdosed on purpose? Would the poor kid really do something so horrific? Natalie honestly had no idea.

Shock gave way to disgust, which quickly slid into anger, all in the span of a few seconds. Natalie wanted to scream. "Why is this happening?"

The words sounded petulant, even to her ears, and especially when faced with someone who was having a *significantly* worse day than she was. Natalie was suddenly furious at everyone and everything: the snowstorm, for causing her delay, Misty, for doing something so incredibly stupid, herself, for not having found a way to arrive in New Orleans sooner. And even, to her surprise, Detective Lejeune. Because even though Natalie still half hated her, she needed the detective's strong, calming presence with her now, and she wasn't there.

Forcing her shaking hands to still, she clicked on the bedside light. Natalie tore her attention from Misty's haunted face, already knowing that it would hang alongside the portrait of her brother on a steel morgue table in a particularly gruesome gallery in her mind. "No, no, no," she murmured, wishing fervently that she hadn't set foot inside this house. She was already anticipating the nightmares.

More than willing to drop to her knees to feast on an enormous piece of humble pie, Natalie grabbed her phone and began to scroll through her contacts, looking for Detective Lejeune's number, when something on Misty's bedside table caught her eye: it was a cell phone. One she recognized instantly as the phone she'd purchased for Josh just before he'd run away from home.

Natalie moved to the other side of the bed and reverently picked up the device. The green and gold Green Bay Packer cell phone case was cracked, and chipped, and scratched but still wrapped around the phone. She turned it over to find that the engraving she'd added to her purchase had survived as well. Joshua Edward Phillips.

Natalie ran a single fingertip over the cool, dark screen, her throat constricting. Misty had kept it all these years. The pity she felt for Misty intensified. Another life wasted. None of this had to be this way.

Natalie wanted this small memento of her brother, and while she wouldn't have begrudged Misty holding on to it, she didn't want it to end up in some garage sale held by Misty's drunken mother. Absently, Natalie slipped it into her purse, and began to scroll for the detective's number on her phone. Her finger hovered over the screen, unable to hit send.

She recalled the look of raw hurt she'd intentionally put into glistening brown eyes the last time they were together.

A phone call wouldn't do.

Instead of calling Detective Lejeune, Natalie dialed 911 and stepped outside into the bright sunshine. Adele might be able to avoid her phone call, but she couldn't keep from speaking to Natalie in person, not if Natalie simply wouldn't go away until she did. Or at least she hoped that's how it was going to happen. In any case, Natalie was sure that whether or not she was successful in getting Adele to forgive her, or better yet, enlisting the other woman's help in finding Josh's killer, the rest of the day was going to feel like sticking her hand into a blender.

Natalie sat down on the front steps of Misty's house and watched a bee buzz around the pretty flowers as she waited for the police to arrive.

* * *

Natalie had spent almost an hour with the police at Misty's house and then another hour being questioned at a police station she hadn't been to before. The officers were respectful and easygoing. Somehow she thought their questions would be a bit more intense, but the police had taken one look at the scars up and down Misty's arm and the needle sticking out of it and quickly decided she was nothing more than a loser junkie who had overdosed. It was a simple case and something not to be overanalyzed.

Drug paraphernalia found in the bathroom medicine cabinet, and a small amount of dope in Misty's bedroom dresser, backed up the police's assumptions about Misty. It would be up to the medical examiner to decide whether the death was an accidental or an intentional overdose. The only thing that seemed to pique the police's interest for even a moment was the broken picture from the wall, that is, until Natalie admitted that she'd done that herself.

When Natalie explained why she'd come back to New Orleans and what Misty had seen at the Dixie Brewery the night of Josh's murder, the police had listened politely, and then promptly told her to go home and forget about what Misty had said. Apparently, junkies weren't reliable eyewitnesses. Natalie pressed, but quickly hit a stone wall. The entire case around Crisco and Josh's murder seemed to be an old, but still very raw nerve that no one in the NOPD wanted to aggravate.

When Natalie mentioned Detective Lejeune's name during the interview, she was met with cold, closed faces and arms crossed tightly over chests. Things had wrapped up quickly after that.

Exasperated and appalled, Natalie stormed out of the station and hailed a cab. Natalie wondered briefly if she had somehow, in another life, wronged the City of New Orleans.

* * *

"How can she not live here anymore?" Natalie asked as she stood outside Adele's Creole Cottage. The stained glass windows that the detective had loved were gone, replaced by clear glass. So it must be true. Still, it didn't want to register.

A young Asian woman—Sun Kim, according to her introduction—stepped out onto the porch and repeated what she'd just said. For the third time. "Mr. Odette sold us this house about two years ago. I'm sorry, I never knew his wife. But I did see him with a cute little boy once when we came by to look at the house. *We* live here now." She gave Natalie a stony-eyed stare. "And we keep a gun in the house."

Natalie blinked a few times. "Okay. But do you—"

"I don't know where Detective Odette and Detective Lejeune moved. Or have a forwarding number."

"But—"

"Try Google." And with that, the woman ran out of patience, walked back into her house, and slammed the door behind her.

Natalie's head snapped back. "Fine!" Trudging to the curb, she plopped down and dropped her bag next to her. Taking a deep breath, she bit the bullet and dialed Detective Lejeune's number, only to be greeted by a canned message stating the number was no longer in service. "Where are you?" Unwilling to give up, Natalie found the nonemergency police number and tried that.

"I'm sorry, ma'am, we don't have a Detective Odette or a Detective Lejeune with the NOPD."

"Yes, you do. Lejeune is spelled L-E-J—"

"I know how it's spelled. I'm sorry I can't help you, ma'am."

"Do you have a number—?"

"I'm sorry."

"Stop saying that! Please. Someone must know something!"

"Look," a deep sigh, "I've never heard of Detective Odette, but Detective Lejeune hasn't worked for the NOPD for more than three years, which is two years longer than I've been on the force. I heard the name, is all. That's all I know. Well, that, and she's not a cop here anymore."

Natalie murmured her thanks and hung up. She looked skyward and squinted into the bright blue, more than a little surprised that it wasn't storming. She felt the deluge and thunder keenly, just on the inside. Elbow resting on her knee, she cradled her chin with her upturned palm and fought back tears. Things were falling apart. How could Detective Lejeune not work at the NOPD when it was so obvious that she was dedicated to her job?

It took a moment to collect herself, but she did, and refused to allow the tears to fall. She dug through her bag and pulled out a small laptop. "Okay, Sun Kim, I'm taking your advice. Please don't have a password protected Wi-Fi connection."

Her search query was simple: "Detective Adele Lejeune" & "New Orleans." What she found left her rooted to her spot on the curb for the next hour as she read. This time her tears fell unbidden. Finally, still upset and bone-weary, she stood and crammed her computer back into her bag as she took stock of her situation. Natalie had already missed her flight back to Madison.

Pulling out her cell phone, she called the number she'd programmed moments before. "Hi. I'd like to book a room, please."

* * *

It was only a ten-minute walk from Adele's former residence to the Touro Street Inn, a brightly colored and unusually large Creole home from the 1860s that sat behind several tall crepe myrtles and an exotic-looking palm tree. The midafternoon sun had sent the temperature into the mid-sixties and Natalie stuffed her jacket into her bag as she walked. Clad in a simple V-neck, lightweight sweater and faded skinny jeans she shivered even though she was far from cold. Natalie climbed the three wooden steps to the tiny porch, and then maneuvered around several tall bags of planting soil and a few odd garden tools, to ring the doorbell.

When no one answered, Natalie followed the instructions she'd been given on the phone and went inside. She kept walking straight through the house and out the back door until she entered a lush, green courtyard. Black slate flagstones created paths that cut through generous beds of plants, and several small clusters of wrought-iron tables, chairs and benches made for cozy seating areas. A gurgling fountain stood proudly in the center.

Natalie's eyes instantly fastened onto the back of a woman who was pouring fresh dirt into a bed of deep purple blooms. She let go of the door and jumped when it let out a high-pitched squeak, then slammed shut. Natalie's stomach flipped and she set her overnight bag down and wiped damp palms against her jeans.

"I know, I know." Adele waved a careless hand in the air and dropped to her knees so she could gently spread the soil around the flowers. "Ugh. Next I'll take care of that noisy door. But first, Georgia, could you bring me some different gloves, please? Somehow, I ended up with Landry's. Mine are under the sink, I think." She pulled off the too-big gloves and tossed them onto a trash pile a few feet away.

Natalie swallowed hard at the sound of Adele's gentle drawl. That voice. It was as silky and feminine as a tender caress and every bit as lovely as she remembered. But she suspected it would only stay that way for a few seconds more. "Sorry," Natalie began, "I didn't see Georgia when I came in, but I'd be happy to go back inside and get your gloves."

Adele's head snapped sideways at the words and her eyebrows crawled so far up her forehead they disappeared behind tousled golden bangs. Natalie noticed the detective's hair had been shorn into the longish pixie cut she'd favored five years earlier.

Wordlessly, Adele sat back on her heels and stared at Natalie with an icy expression as though she was the last person on earth she expected to see walking toward her. And that probably wasn't far from the truth.

"Hello," Natalie said quietly, completely unable to read Adele's closed face and trying not to stare at the thin, slightly jagged scar that ran from Adele's temple to almost the corner of her eye. Natalie's stomach clenched at the thought of how that must have hurt. "I called earlier and spoke to the inn's manager, Georgia, I think. She said you weren't available to come to the phone."

Adele inclined her head, her curious expression the only sign of a thaw. "We're closed for the month for renovations. Leave."

Natalie blinked a few times. *That was quick.* "I—"

Adele's eyes turned to slits. "Why are you here?"

"Well, I—"

"Nope. Nope. Let me guess," Adele said with sudden faux brightness. "Another missing sibling is lost in my fair city, and you're here looking for someone to blame if he or she doesn't make it home in time for Santa?"

Natalie winced. "No," she replied needlessly.

"No? Then you must be here to rub salt in my wounds. Again. But you're way too late to inflict the maximum damage. My life hit rock bottom almost two years ago."

Callous sarcasm didn't look good on Adele. *But that's my fault, isn't it?* A lump rose in Natalie's throat, but she refused to take the bait. "I'm here because we need to talk."

"*We* don't have anything to say." Adele returned to her flowers, presenting Natalie with her back and effectively dismissing her.

"Okay, then I think you'll want to hear what *I* have to say," Natalie tried again, her frown deepening.

"You thought wrong."

Flustered, Natalie opened her mouth and let it slam shut before finally saying, "I want to apologize."

"I must not be making myself clear, Ms. Abbott."

Ouch.

"I'm not interested in what you want. And I'm not interested in apologies."

"Please—"

"No!" And just like that, ice turned to fire. Adele growled, the sound vibrating from deep within her chest.

Natalie felt a sliver of apprehension. She'd experienced Adele's gentleness, but never her wrath. She was only hoping not to be thrown out on her ear before she'd had a chance to explain. "Okay, I can't make you listen. But I'm going to say this anyway. I'm sorry for what I said to you the last time we were together. I was cruel and I was wrong. I didn't mean it, even then, but I said it anyway to hurt you."

Forgetting about her gloves, Adele plunged her hands into the sack of dirt and began to fill in a bare area of the flowerbed as though Natalie wasn't even there.

"I was angry and I let my mouth get away from me. You were nothing but kind to me."

Adele clenched a fist, compacting a handful of dark soil into a ball. She let it fall from her fingers and leaned forward on her hands, making deep impressions into the soft, loose dirt. "You should see yourself out."

"When you told me about turning in Officer Morrell for what he'd done, I was afraid. I was afraid that I couldn't handle things if they somehow got worse and Josh's killer didn't go to jail. Crisco getting caught right away and confessing to the crime, was one of two bright spots during the worst time in my life. It was like a tiny life preserver in an ocean of heartbreak that I could take back to my parents."

Natalie could see Adele struggle with herself. She watched the rise and fall of Adele's shoulders and saw her ribs expand through her thin T-shirt as she drew and then released a deep breath. Heart hammering, Natalie waited for the inevitable detonation, but it never came. Instead, Adele simply stared straight ahead like a statue.

"The other bright spot was your unexpected friendship," Natalie said, remembering, and allowing the comforting feeling to fill her. "And it came at a time when I needed it *so* much. Then, I felt like I lost both of those good things in the very same instant and I reacted horribly."

Adele still wouldn't look at her.

Natalie tilted her head toward the heavens for assistance. "I'm so, *so* sorry. When I accused you of not continuing to look for Josh…" She sighed. "Well, that was just bullshit."

Adele finally turned to face her. The look of cold anger she had worn only seconds before had been replaced by an open, injured expression. "You were an asshole."

"Yes," Natalie agreed unequivocally, hating the look of hurt even more than anger. "But this asshole is truly sorry. She knows she was wrong and is doing her best to beg for your forgiveness."

Adele ran her hand across her forehead, smearing it with dark soil. She hesitantly admitted, "You're, um, you're not doing too badly, I guess."

"Good. I'm just getting started."

"But what you accused me of… " Adele's face twisted as though she was hearing the cutting words all over again. "I would never use you just to try to make myself feel better, and I would never give up on a kid who needed me. Never."

"I know," Natalie said solemnly. *Now for the hard part.* Even though Adele had been proven right, and Natalie was sorry, a tiny part of her still felt conflicted and resentful. But she knew she had to get past it. "Turning in Morrell, it was the right thing to do. I was just too wrapped up in my own suffering to realize or even to care. It felt like you were picking Crisco over Josh and over me. It didn't seem fair or just. It just hurt." She wanted to elaborate but the sudden flashing of Adele's eyes stopped her.

"You think you were the only one hurt?" Adele's normally light voice was low and severe. "You have no idea. And you kicked me in the teeth while I was down."

Natalie nodded. "I did."

"Natalie!" Adele let out an explosive exhale. "How am I supposed to have a fight with you if you agree with everything I say?"

Natalie almost let out a burst of inappropriate laughter at Adele's truly distressed expression. "I want to make up. I don't want to fight with you."

Adele just grunted. "Maybe *I* do. You walked out during the last one."

"Okay," Natalie allowed carefully. "Then this is your chance to say anything you want. I won't run away even when the truth hurts." When Adele still didn't seem satisfied, Natalie added, "Or we can duke it out, if we must. But you should know that I bite."

Adele grudgingly rolled her eyes.

Finally, Natalie felt confident enough to allow the barest hint of a smile to chase its way across her lips. "Can we at least really sit down and talk? I'm more than willing to continue to grovel, but you don't look very comfortable perched in the dirt while I do it."

Adele was obviously torn, but after an uncomfortably long period of deliberation that had Natalie literally squirming, she finally nodded. "Yeah. A chair, for a few minutes anyway, would be good."

Natalie didn't want to be on some sort of timer for their conversation, but she bit her tongue, acknowledging that this was progress and she'd be an idiot to do anything to mess it up. She extended a hand to help Adele up, but the other woman waved her off.

Instead, Adele's hand disappeared into the flowerbed and she drew out a wooden cane with a large silver ball that served as a handle. With visible effort, she pushed unsteadily to her feet.

Natalie's eyes widened. The scar was bad enough, but this? She'd read online that Adele had been injured in an arrest gone wrong, but she had no idea…

Adele walked slowly to one of the small iron tables, leaning on the cane as she went. She stood tall and proud, but her limp was pronounced and each step looked painful.

Dismayed, Natalie gaped, not knowing what to say, but feeling the sting behind her eyes that signaled impending tears.

"It's worse than normal today because I've been up and down a bunch of times," Adele admitted as she sat down heavily, obviously aware of Natalie's internal struggle. "Some days I don't even need the cane at all until the evening or when I get tired."

Natalie was astounded to find that the budding affection she'd felt for her new friend all those years ago was still there, and so strong that she had to stop herself from pulling Adele into her arms and fiercely hugging her. She hated the fact that Adele had been hurt so badly. All was clearly not forgiven yet, but they would get there and then move forward. Natalie promised herself that right then. "That still sucks."

Adele chuffed out a laugh and looked pleasantly surprised that Natalie's reply hadn't contained a trace of pity, just the unvarnished truth. "Yeah, it does."

Natalie moved to stand directly in front of Adele and gave into what she'd wanted to do for the last couple of moments. Daringly, and with painstaking slowness, she placed two fingers gently under Adele's chin and lifted it a bit higher.

Their eyes met and locked.

With every ounce of tenderness inside her, Natalie brushed Adele's cheek and forehead with the pad of her thumb. The corner of Natalie's mouth quirked. "You, uh, you have some dirt on your face." The skin beneath her thumb was achingly soft and grew warmer with the tender touch.

It was Adele's slightly confused, brown-eyed stare that dropped away first. Awkwardly, she cleared her throat a little before speaking. "Thanks."

With an inward sigh, Natalie withdrew her hand and took a seat across from Adele. She still had so much to say, about Misty, and Josh, and a million other things, and so much she wanted to ask about Adele's injuries, and her job and family, and this inn. And she still had to get Adele to forgive her and truly mean it.

It would have all been overwhelming except for one thing: for the first time while in the city of New Orleans, Natalie Abbott was exactly where she wanted to be.

CHAPTER EIGHT

Adele listened patiently and emotionlessly as Natalie explained Misty's overdose, the phone call that prompted Natalie's trip, and Crisco's innocence when it came to Josh's murder.

It was clear that Adele's nonreaction left Natalie floundering. Natalie squeezed the sides of her own head in disbelief. "What do you mean you don't care?"

Okay, saying she didn't care was a lie and Adele knew it. But what really set her blood aflame was that clearly Natalie knew it too.

It wasn't that Adele didn't care about Misty's death. That was tragic. It wasn't that she didn't care about who really killed Josh. His death hadn't just been a low point in her career, she'd felt it deeply, and it had kicked off a chain of events that still had Adele reeling. And it wasn't that she didn't believe Josh's rightful killer should be behind bars. That was so obvious it was insulting to think otherwise. It was the fact that Adele couldn't do anything about any of those things that left her hollow.

Adele wanted to tell Natalie that there wasn't a realistic chance of solving the crime after all this time, and even if there was, she wasn't the woman to do it. Instead, Adele ignored Natalie's question and did everything she could to erase the tiny bit of progress they'd made only minutes earlier. Adele'd been in self-destruct mode for so long now, it'd become a habit she didn't know how to break.

"I knew there was a real reason you were here." Adele pinned Natalie with a penetrating glare as she searched for the lie.

Natalie's pale gaze softened. "Yes, I came back because of Misty and what she said. And yes, I would like…no," she shook her head a little, acknowledging her predicament, "I *need* your help. But I did come to apologize. It's not the only reason I'm here, but that doesn't make it any less real."

Adele wanted to believe Natalie. She couldn't help it. She liked Natalie and the fact they'd connected so easily and comfortably. Adele craved even the chance to go back and start over. At the same time, she didn't feel like sticking her neck out again, only to risk having her head lopped off. She crossed her arms over her chest and raised a single eyebrow. "Uh-huh."

Natalie threw back her own disbelieving look. "How can you not want to know what actually happened that night? How can a detec—"

"Don't call me that," Adele snapped harshly. "I'm not a detective anymore."

Taken aback by the poison in Adele's voice, Natalie licked her lips nervously. "Okay, fine." She held up a placating hand. "Ella—"

"You don't get to call me that either." Adele pushed to her feet, cursing under her breath when her cane rattled to the ground.

"Then what am I supposed to call you?" Natalie asked reasonably. "You mentioned before that you didn't like to go by Adele." She quickly reached for the cane, but Adele beat her to the punch and nearly snatched it from Natalie's grasp.

"I can get it myself," Adele bit out, hating the petulant way she was acting but unable to stop herself.

Even when they'd parted three years ago, Adele had been more hurt than angry at Natalie's words. Natalie's reaction to everything that had happened hadn't exactly been unexpected. But something in Adele didn't want to let Natalie know that. Adele had lost so much already—nearly everything she held dear—that she wanted to keep any tiny kernel of pride that still remained and not give in as easily as her heart demanded. The problem was, with every earnest, apologetic look from Natalie, she felt her resolve weakening.

She loathed feeling weak and Adele fairly shook with the need to explode. With every fiber of her being she wanted to raise her voice and yell at the top of her lungs. She wanted to feel the satisfaction of causing pain instead of stinging from it. She wanted to push all the frustration, hurt and anger she felt outward instead of allowing it to fester inside. Adele knew her reaction to seeing Natalie again was out of proportion with what had happened, but she was spoiling for a fight and Natalie wouldn't engage!

"Only my family and friends call me Ella," Adele rasped. "And remember? You made it clear that I was never your friend. So I guess that leaves you with nothing." *Just like me.*

Natalie sucked in a sharp breath. "I told you…I didn't mean what I said."

Voila. Adele saw the flash of hurt she was looking for, but it only left her feeling empty. With effort, she consciously lowered the volume of her voice. "Go home or go back to the police, Ms. Abbott."

Natalie shook her head. "You calling me that isn't annoying me as much as you're hoping. And I already explained that the police wouldn't help me. It's obvious they aren't interested in taking things any further with Josh's case." She sighed. "You're the only one who can really help."

Outwardly, Adele shrugged. Inwardly, she seethed at her former coworkers' apathy…and her own lack of capacity. "Then I guess you'll have to go home now…disappointed again. I hear third time's the charm."

"Jesus Christ!" Natalie shouted, hitting the wrought-iron table with two flat hands, her temper finally flaring out of her control. "I may go home disappointed, whether you help me or not, but I won't go home until *after* I at least try to find justice for Josh."

"There is no justice here." Adele turned away.

Natalie barked out a harsh laugh. "Drama queen! That's the biggest bullshit drama queen answer I've ever heard!"

Adele spun back, eyes blazing, grasping her cane with both hands until blood fled from her knuckles. "What did you call me?"

"You heard me." Natalie shot to her feet. When Adele tried to turn away from her again, Natalie followed her and inserted herself directly in front of Adele no matter which way she moved.

Adele suddenly felt cornered, and an unexpected surge of panic caused her breathing to shallow and a cold sweat to erupt across her back.

At the flash of stark terror on Adele's face, Natalie's eyes widened and she took a big step backward. "Oh, my God. I'm so sorry. Are—are you okay?"

Adele wet her lips and glanced away. That hadn't happened in a long time, and it was unnerving that it could still sneak up on her. "I'm fine," she said quietly.

"But—"

"I said, I'm fine! If you're finished now—"

"I'm not finished."

Adele groaned. "Natalie."

"No matter what you say, I don't believe that you don't want to do everything you can to make things right now. Not when you risked everything to do it before. And I sure as hell don't believe you don't want to be vindicated over Crisco."

The mere thought of it sent a bolt of longing through Adele, but she pressed her lips together in a thin line and refused to acknowledge it.

"And I don't know what happened to you. At least not more than what I could read online. But this," Natalie waved her hand around the yard, "isn't you! I *know* you were dedicated to your job and helping people. I could tell that was your *life*. And now I'm supposed to believe that you don't care about one of your cases and that you'd rather spend all your time plucking weeds and making dinner reservations for tourists?"

Adele felt that one squarely in the chest. "You think I *wanted* to leave my job? I had no choice but to leave the NOPD!" she hissed, her face mottled.

"Your leg—"

"You don't know anything." Adele bared her teeth. "Even if I were one hundred percent healed and healthy, I couldn't be a cop. Not here."

Carefully, and telegraphing her every move, Natalie reached out and wrapped warm hands around Adele's biceps and squeezed hard. For a second, Adele was certain she was going to shake her. Because it didn't catch her off guard, she didn't have the slightest urge to pull away. Instead, and despite herself, Adele wanted to lean in to the touch.

"I don't need just any cop," Natalie said, voice quivering. "I need you."

Just then, a reed-thin black woman in her early sixties, wearing a crisply pressed navy blue shirtdress, and carrying a can of WD-40, breezed through the back door and into the courtyard. "Ella, I brought you some—" she paused at the scene before her.

Natalie immediately stepped away from Adele, looking at her hands as though they'd acted completely without her permission.

More unsettled than she cared to admit, Adele set her cane on the table and leaned against the cool wrought iron, letting her eyes slide closed. She'd been itching for a fight, and now that she had it, she felt as though she was the one walking away bruised.

"I'm Georgia Trotter." The woman held out her hand. "You must be Ms. Abbott."

Natalie nodded, her mouth clamped shut as though she didn't trust her voice to speak.

"Am I interrupting something?" Georgia asked, though it was obvious she was.

Adele pushed away from the table with a grimace and reclaimed her cane. "Ye—"

"It's nothing," Natalie broke in with sudden brightness. "We were just catching up. And I got excited about our upcoming plans."

Adele's eyebrows shot upward.

"You know each other then? Ms. Abbott didn't mention that on the phone." This time Georgia made a point of looking at Adele for an answer.

Adele only shrugged one shoulder. "Vaguely."

Natalie shot Adele a covert glare. "We're old acquaintances who are about to get to know each other better."

"That's great. Things are working out perfectly then." Georgia's white teeth gleamed with her welcoming smile. "Sorry I wasn't here to greet you. I had to make a quick run to the hardware store. But your room is all ready."

Adele's eyes popped wide open. "What? She can't stay here!"

Georgia waited for Adele to elaborate.

"We're...we're closed!"

Georgia nodded. "I explained all that to her, and she was such a doll about it. She found us on the Internet. Ella, I told you that picture of you on the 'About' page would help drive business."

Adele's eyes rolled at the memory of another battle lost.

"And Ms. Abbott insisted she wouldn't mind the noise or that there wouldn't be housekeeping or breakfast service. And she even insisted on payin' full rate for the entire week in advance."

Adele's mouth dropped open. "A week?"

Obviously thrilled with this arrangement, Georgia beamed at Natalie. "Isn't that right?"

Natalie smirked openly at Adele. "That's right. And please call me Natalie."

Adele started to protest, but Georgia stuffed the can of WD-40 into her hands before she could argue. Georgia lowered her voice to a whisper. "You wanted to look for ways to offset some of the renovation costs. And this fell into our lap. What luck, huh?"

Adele could only shake her head in disbelief. "Yeah. I have amazing luck."

Georgia smiled again and patted Adele's shoulder affectionately.

The older woman had known Adele since she was in diapers, and their relationship went far beyond that of an employer and employee.

"After you finish the flowers you can fix the door," Georgia said. "I'll show Ms. Abbott to her room."

Natalie grabbed her bag and slung the strap over her shoulder. She followed Georgia across the courtyard toward the back door, stepping around a rake and garden hose as she moved. Natalie waved over her shoulder without looking back. "Will I see you for dinner, Adele?"

Georgia clucked woefully and spoke from the corner of her mouth, "Didn't she tell you she doesn't like to be called that?"

Natalie chuckled unrepentantly as a large dirt clod sailed through the air and came dangerously close to hitting her in the head as it exploded against the side of the house. "Yes."

* * *

It was nearly midnight that same evening when a cold December wind invaded the city like a conquering army, and the temperatures plummeted into the high 30s.

Wearing the only other clothes she'd hastily shoved into a bag as she packed for the airport, a pair of sweatpants, and a cardinal red and white UW–Madison T-shirt, Natalie wrapped her arms around herself, a little shiver running through her as she padded in socked feet through the dark, silent house in hopes of finding something to eat. The fourteen-foot ceilings, while probably a godsend in the smoldering summer months, helped a cool draft travel through the house with ease. Natalie rubbed her hands up and down over the goose bumps on her arms in a vain attempt to warm them.

Her hair was loose, and more than just a little disheveled, as it flowed over her shoulders and several inches down her back. She'd considered hiding in her room the remainder of the night and burrowing under the covers until the next morning, but her hunger drove her up and out of bed after this endlessly long day. She poked her head around each dark corner, hoping to find Georgia still awake or at least a fruit bowl she could raid.

Natalie hadn't seen Adele at dinner that night. In fact, she hadn't seen Adele since their argument in the courtyard and had skipped dinner entirely—and breakfast and lunch for that matter—because her stomach had been in knots. Feeling a little queasy after everything that had happened, Natalie had collapsed on the luxurious bed in her room, intent on planning out a strategy for what she was going to do next about finding Josh's killer, or at least how she might jump-start the police. Problem was, Natalie had no idea where to begin.

In the end it hadn't mattered, because instead of strategizing, the lack of sleep from the night spent in the airport, and the stress of finding Misty's body, talking with the police, and arguing with Adele caught with her all at once. The moment her head hit the pillow, she promptly fell into a deep, dreamless sleep that lasted the entire evening. Feeling oddly hungover, even though she hadn't consumed a single drop of alcohol, and having had the longest nap of her life, Natalie gave herself permission to worry about tomorrow…tomorrow.

The sudden delectable scent of chocolate caught Natalie's attention and led her into the darkened kitchen. Moonlight shone into the room through a large window above the sink and cast the room in deep shades of indigo. Full of hope, she headed straight for the oven, confident that even blindfolded she could identify the smell of freshly baked brownies.

Natalie's mouth watered. She wasn't sure exactly what she would do when she found the brownies that were teasing her. Steal them? Yes, she decided, she could live with thievery in extreme circumstances. But sadly, the oven was empty.

"They're on the cooling rack by the fridge."

Natalie nearly jumped out of her skin. Hand flying to her chest, she gasped and jumped at the same time. "Jesus! You scared the crap out of me."

Adele, who was sitting in her pajamas on a barstool in the darkness, a cup in her hands, chuckled softly from across the large kitchen island.

For a few seconds they stared at each other, unsure whether their argument from the afternoon would roar to life and shatter the peaceful atmosphere in the kitchen.

It didn't.

"Sorry about that," Adele murmured, blowing gently across the top of her mug of cocoa. She tilted her head toward the brownies. "Hungry?"

Natalie nodded vigorously. "God, yes."

"You missed dinner."

"I fell asleep."

Adele hummed a little. "Today's been insane, huh?"

Slowly, Natalie nodded in disbelief. She never thought she'd hear from Misty, or be back in New Orleans, or speak to Adele Lejeune ever again. Yet here she was, doing just that, in the middle of the night, in socks, and with bed head. "That pretty much sums it up. Yeah."

Adele took a sip of her cocoa. "Do you, um, want some real food to go with the brownies?"

"I thought meals didn't come with my stay."

Natalie was smiling when she said it so Adele's response was equally playful, if still a bit awkward. "They don't. But I'll make an exception just this once." Adele set her mug on the granite-topped island and slid off her tall barstool.

It was only a couple of steps to the refrigerator, but Natalie noticed Adele's cane was nowhere in sight.

"How about a turkey sandwich?" Adele's head disappeared inside the fridge, the harsh refrigerator light causing them both to squint.

Natalie opened her mouth to answer, but her growling stomach beat her to the punch.

Adele laughed softly. "Well, okay then. I'll take that as a yes." She began setting sandwich fixings on the countertop. She spoke with her head still inside the refrigerator, "Cabinet to the right of the sink has the plates and glasses."

Natalie nodded and retrieved them, not missing Adele's laser-like focus on the plate of sliced turkey covered in plastic wrap that she had placed next to the brownies. "Uh...do you want a plate too?"

Adele hemmed and hawed mentally for a few breaths before declaring, "Definitely." She held up a jug of milk with one hand and a jug of orange juice with the other and waited.

Natalie pointed to the milk.

For a few minutes the women worked wordlessly, preparing their own sandwiches, using only the light that streamed in from the kitchen window to guide them. Things were much less tense than earlier that day, but Natalie still longed for the easy camaraderie she'd gotten just a taste of on her last two visits.

Natalie had come to a decision as she watched Adele scavenge in the refrigerator for mustard. If the former detective couldn't be persuaded to help find Josh's killer, Natalie wouldn't allow that to keep them from being friends. *I could use someone like her in my life. An honest-to-God good person.*

Time, Natalie decided, was what they needed. Time to get to know each other not as a detective and the brother of a crime victim. Time as who they were now, beyond those two things.

The grandfather clock in the hallway chimed, signaling the witching hour as Natalie watched Adele sip her cocoa and pick at her sandwich. A tiny part of her mind had wondered when she saw Adele again, if she'd associate the other woman with worry, or grief or pain, since the only times they had been together had been rife with one or all of those emotions. Instead, Adele brought to mind strength, security and determination. *Not to mention she's freakin' beautiful.*

"You're up late," Natalie observed with intentional casualness, all the while trying not to inhale her sandwich, which was proving impossible. It was delicious and she couldn't help the little moans of pleasure that escaped her as she ate.

Adele released an amused smile at Natalie's groans of satisfaction. "I couldn't sleep. Too much work outside today." She pointed downward. "My leg is killing me."

It was on the tip of Natalie's tongue to ask more about Adele's injuries, but she held back. "I'm sorry."

"How are your folks?" Adele asked, quickly changing the subject before wiping some mayo from the corner of her mouth with a paper napkin.

Natalie cleared her throat and smoothed her shirt as if preparing to make an official proclamation. She affected her best Wisconsin accent. "Ya know, thanks for askin'. Things up nort' in Wuh-Skaaaahn-sin, dere real good."

Adele smiled softly. "You don't speak like that."

"No." Natalie chuckled. "I suppose not. At least not too much. But you should have heard my grandparents and, to a lesser extent, my mom.

I spent my late teens and up until I was almost thirty years old out-of-state and on the East Coast where I went to school and did my postdoc. So I've lost a bit of my Sconnie street cred. Then again, I've been known to enjoy a good tailgating party with brats and a couple PBRs for supper as much as the next gal." Cautiously, she peered over her shoulder as though someone might overhear the conversation. "Don't tell anyone about the Pabst Blue Ribbon, okay?"

A tiny smirk appeared. "Scout's honor."

Natalie's gaze dropped to Adele's mug. "Hot chocolate *and* brownies? You're a girl after my own heart. Your sweet tooth is epic."

Adele shrugged sheepishly. "Comfort food."

Natalie frowned a little and wondered if it was the chill in the air that brought on Adele's need for warm comfort or something more sinister. While their argument had been unpleasant, it wasn't cause for the lingering look of sadness in Adele's eyes. Natalie was concerned and interested, but she also knew she needed to be patient. Now was not the time. Adele didn't trust her enough to share anything too personal.

Natalie searched her mind for a neutral subject. "Does, um, Georgia live here too?"

"Nah. She has a place with her husband in Bywater." At Natalie's blank look Adele clarified, "That's a neighborhood right nearby. She rides her old-school bicycle to work every day. You know the kind with the big wicker basket on the front and a shiny horn with a rubber ball on the end." She shook her head with mock worry. "The way she uses that horn, I see a road rage incident in her future."

Natalie smiled at the fondness in Adele's voice when she talked about Georgia. "She seems really nice and is clearly crazy about you. She's not shy about showing it. Let's see…" Contemplatively, Natalie tapped her chin with her index finger. "You're such a smart girl. And *such* a good mother. And you have such a green thumb. And the inn's customers all love you." The light was too dim, but by the way Adele ducked her head, Natalie guessed she was blushing.

"She said *all* that while showing you your room?" Adele groaned, clearly horrified.

"And she said that you dance really well…" Natalie waited a beat before adding, "for a white girl."

Adele gaped, then spluttered, "She did not say that!"

Natalie laughed softly, inordinately pleased with Adele's flustered reaction. "Okay, she didn't. But I'm guessing it's true." She'd seen that swagger the last time she was in New Orleans. *Anyone with a walk like that is bound to be fabulous on the dance floor…and killer in bed.* The tail end of that unexpected thought caused Natalie's cheeks to flame.

"I, uh…I wasn't too bad before."

For a second Natalie stared wide-eyed, suddenly feeling hot all over. Then she realized that she hadn't actually said the "in bed" part out loud to Adele. But why did Adele suddenly look so serious? Natalie replayed the conversation in her mind and the answer hit her like a ton of bricks. *Her leg. Oh, shit.* "So, um, now you'll just have to focus on slow dancing instead and leave the crazy break dancing moves to someone else," she said, and gave Adele a soft, apologetic smile.

Despite Natalie's faux pas, Adele seemed to relax a bit more. "I will."

Natalie leaned back toward the oven. It was still warm, and the scent of the food reminded her of weekends as a child when her mother's cookie baking was a given. She didn't bake for herself as an adult, knowing she'd only end up eating the entire batch of whatever she made. But that didn't mean she didn't miss the cookies.

Natalie finished her sandwich and milk in two large swallows. Her stomach was happier and had settled. "It's nice in here." She glanced around the kitchen, though it was hard to see much in the wan light. "Comfortable and relaxing."

"Thanks. We renovated it last year. I've got tons of fancy furniture in the rest of the house, but lots of times I find myself on one of these barstools instead. Our customers aren't normally back here, so it's set up the way I like it and not so much for anyone else."

It seemed so strange to Natalie to think that Adele owned this inn and this was her life now. In her mind Adele was a detective. She didn't *just* carry a gun and badge, those things were the trappings of the job, albeit essential ones. Adele helped people for a living. And anything other than that seemed out a place, as though Adele had settled for something less than who she was meant to be. It was like Sherlock Holmes taking a job as a kindergarten teacher, or a lion being employed as a house cat. It just didn't work. Period. End of story. *And just think how she must have felt to give it all up.* The thought made Natalie's heart ache.

"Are you sure you own this place?" Natalie asked, feeling as though she must be missing some part of this puzzle.

Adele's eyes went round. "Yeah, I'm pretty sure. If I don't, I've been paying someone else's light bill for two years." The edge of her mouth curled. "Do you know something I don't?"

"No. I guess…" Natalie lifted one hand and let it drop. "I know you said you're not a detective anymore."

Adele's spine straightened.

"No, don't get mad…I remember you said you didn't want to talk about it. And I'm sure this is a great job." Natalie motioned around the room. "And this inn is gorgeous." She'd always suspected Adele had means beyond what a couple of detective salaries could provide. Owning this place, unless it was leveraged to the hilt, and really, even if it was, was proof.

"The Jacuzzi in my room?" Natalie closed her eyes and let out a low whistle of appreciation. "*If* I ever get married," she paused and lifted a dramatic eyebrow, "and *if* you included meals—" Adele snorted— "I could totally have my honeymoon here." Although, she acknowledged grimly, at some point remembering the horrible things that she'd seen in this city would likely kill the mood.

"Lucky me," Adele said dryly, one leg bouncing casually and restlessly to the beat of some internal drum in a way that Natalie keenly remembered. "Shall I book your rooms now? Or wait for swans to deliver the message that you've found your Prince Charming."

Natalie smirked. "Don't hold your breath for the swans." Then her brows drew together. "Are you sure you're not secretly a private detective, or bounty hunter *in addition* to being an innkeeper?"

Adele rolled her eyes. "I'm sure."

Natalie warmed to the subject. "Or assassin? Or spy? Or ninja? Or—"

"Again, pretty sure. Why do you insist that my life must be an episode of *Charlie's Angels*?"

"I shouldn't," Natalie agreed. "But what about undercover social worker? Isn't that what you went to school to do?" As far as she was concerned, those people pretty much fell into the superhero category. Natalie had no idea how they coped with such difficult jobs and circumstances. And that sort of work just seemed so...Adele.

Adele shifted uncomfortably, and Natalie cursed her new, and astonishing, inability to successfully engage in small talk. "Of course, maybe your interests have changed," she rushed to add. "I get that." The current state of her own career flashed through Natalie's mind, along with the hard choices she knew she needed to make. "Boy, do I get that."

"I'm finished with that part of my life." Adele's voice was serious, and Natalie wished that she'd turned on a light before she sat down. She wanted to study Adele's eyes. "I'm none of those things you just mentioned, though I guess I'm flattered you see me that way." Adele's smile was genuine but a little melancholy. "It's delusional, but I'm still flattered."

Natalie nodded with relief. Yes, that's what she meant. Thank goodness Adele understood. Well, not the delusional part. But the part where she'd meant her joking questions as a compliment and maybe, admittedly, a gentle nudge toward an explanation.

"Do you want one of those brownies?" Adele gestured to the pan that was still on the cooling rack. "They're cool enough to eat now. But I think I'm going to wait until tomorrow for mine. Especially after the hot chocolate." She poked at her own perfectly flat stomach. "Gotta spread out the cavities and calories..."

Natalie gave her a disgusted look. "Ugh. You don't need to spread out anything. You're one of those lucky, almost-mythical women who can eat whatever she wants, aren't you?"

"Not always."

Natalie shook her head sorrowfully and sighed. "*I* am not so lucky."

"Whatever," Adele scoffed. "We're probably the exact same size."

"Probably," Natalie admitted, though she couldn't help but notice that Adele was a little bustier, though neither one of them was underdeveloped in that particular area. "But I *suffer* for it. So I'll wait too." Natalie smiled warmly. "Thanks for the sandwich. I was about to faint from hunger."

"That won't be the case for long. New Orleans is nothing if not the center of the world for delicious food. We have fabulous restaurants on every block. Trust me."

Natalie twisted her fingers together. "Will you show me one of those restaurants, tomorrow maybe?" When Adele didn't answer right away she panicked enough to fill the silence. "That is, if Landry will be okay with me hogging up more of your time. I want us to have a fresh start. I meant my apology, and I get that you don't want to help me now, and that's okay."

Adele scowled and opened her mouth, but Natalie plowed ahead. "I'm not trying to change your mind about that. At least not right this second," she admitted with blunt honesty. "And I do want us to be friends and spending some time together would be a good way to start, don't you think?"

Adele nodded once. When she spoke, her voice was nearly a whisper. "Landry won't mind."

Natalie let out a relieved breath, remembering how uncomfortable she'd felt when Landry had announced his jealousy. Poor Adele had looked like she wanted to crawl under a rock. "Great. I, um, I can be a good friend when I want to be. I'm not the hothead my last departure from New Orleans made it seem."

Adele leaned forward, her elbows resting on top of the cool granite of the kitchen island, and her eyes picking up a glint of light from the window. "No?"

Natalie shook her head, collected Adele's dishes without asking, and loaded them into the dishwasher. "I'm really not. I was embarrassed by the way I had acted by the time I got off the plane in Madison, and I should have been."

Natalie nibbled on her lower lip for just a second before adding, "Even the woman I was dating at the time told me I was being a baby for running out in the middle of our conversation. She said I was lucky you were ethical and not some robot cop who didn't care about the people she was serving." Her stomach clenched as she steeled herself for Adele's reaction.

After only the briefest of hesitations, Adele looked down at her hands and swallowed. She glanced back up and quietly asked, "What did you do then?"

The tension melted from Natalie's body so quickly that she felt a little light-headed. "Broke up with her." She didn't bother to add that Hannah had been about as supportive as a bag of hair during that very difficult time.

A rogue laugh burst from Adele. "Yeah, I can see that you aren't a hothead."

Natalie winced. "Okay, maybe that wasn't the best example of what I'm trying to say. But if it helps, I realized I was being a jerk again and came crawling back to apologize a few days later. I've been much better since then. Honestly."

Adele sighed and nodded. The grandfather clock chimed again, and she stretched her arms over her head, twisting a little. "I should go to bed."

Natalie wasn't especially looking forward to closing her eyes again because of what might be waiting for her on the other side, but she could only put it off so long. "Me too."

Both women headed out into the hallway with Adele in the lead. "Adele?"

Adele winced at the use of her given name. "I was angry before, and not just at you, when I said not to call me Ella." She gave Natalie an apologetic look. "But, please do, okay?"

Natalie's grin was so broad it stretched her cheeks. "Ella, would you mind pointing me in the direction of someplace I can shop for clothes tomorrow? Once again, I packed poorly. You'd think I would know not to come down to New Orleans with less than a full suitcase...ever."

Adele thought about it long enough that Natalie began to grow uncomfortable, then she nodded and began walking slowly down the hall to her suite of rooms at the back of the house. Her limp was still very present, but not as bad as it had been directly after working in the yard. "Sure. I know just the place. Good night, Natalie. Have happy dreams tonight, okay?"

Natalie watched her go and prayed that Adele's request came true.

CHAPTER NINE

The next day…

"If you're making enough to share, don't you think you should let her know so she can get it while it's hot?" Georgia said, giving Adele a little glare from her spot on the barstool that Adele had occupied the night before. "Never mind. Instant grits are a sin anyway, having them cold couldn't make them taste any worse."

The bright morning sun lit Adele's face as she added grits to boiling water, then moved to cut up some fruit. She'd gotten a little color yesterday and her cheeks had a rosy glow. "They'll keep. Besides, there's no hurry. Natalie had a horrible day yesterday, and I'm not gonna be the one to wake her up." She shook her knife in Georgia's direction. "And you're not either."

Georgia sniffed haughtily. "I would never wake a guest."

Adele made a face at Georgia's statement. After last night, Natalie didn't feel like just a guest at the inn, she felt like her guest. "Speaking of that, we're not charging her for her stay. Our rooms aren't cheap, and it's not like she's down here on vacation. You can just put the money back on her credit card or whatever."

"We're priced just exactly right," Georgia challenged with mock indignation. Room pricing was a familiar argument between them, and Georgia had won the last round. "What does she do for a living that makes us too expensive?"

"College professor. And I'm not saying she can't afford it. I'm saying we don't need to charge her."

"That pretty girl is a professor?" Georgia's eyebrows jumped. "She must be a smart one."

Adele hummed her agreement. "For sure. And she's not a girl. We're almost the same age. If thirty-seven is a girl, I'm looking forward to living to be a hundred and twenty."

"I thought you were just acquaintances? Since when do acquaintances stay for free?"

"Since now."

Georgia's dark eyes narrowed. "And since when do acquaintances look like they're gonna strangle each other? I couldn't believe my eyes yesterday. I haven't seen you throw dirt since you were six years old. What's next? Makin' her eat worms?"

Adele smiled as she sliced a banana, then gathered the pieces into a glass bowl alongside some strawberries. Wiping her hands on a towel, she gave the grits a quick stir. "I only did that to Jackson once."

"Ha!" Georgia stuck her fingers in the bowl to steal a strawberry slice. She popped it into her mouth, humming a little. "You only got *caught* feeding your brother night crawlers once, you mean."

Adele's smile turned mischievous. "Same thing."

"Somebody's in a good mood."

"Does it happen so rarely that you notice immediately?"

Wisely, Georgia remained mute on the topic, though that in itself was an answer.

The teakettle began to whistle and Georgia hopped up and gently bumped Adele out of the way with her bony hip as she reached for it. "So what's the story with you two? I know it's somethin'."

Adele sighed and looked out the kitchen window with unfocused eyes. "Her brother is…was Joshua Phillips."

Georgia froze. "What?"

"Do I really need to repeat it?" The grits began to simmer. Adele turned down the flame beneath them and absently continued to stir.

Georgia shook her head and went back to the island with the kettle and two teacups in hand. "I guess not. But I thought you walked away from all that, Ella."

When Adele didn't immediately confirm Georgia's statement, she looked a little put out. "Please tell me you're not going to do anything that will—"

"None of what happened at the NOPD was her fault, Georgia." Adele's tone was resigned but firm.

"I know. I just worry about you."

"I get it." Adele turned and pinned Georgia with a serious look. "I'm fine, okay? So nobody needs to worry. And since I know you report back on how I'm doing to Mama and Daddy, could you share that tidbit too?"

"It doesn't make me an informant just because I tell your daddy and mama how you're doing. It's called conversation." Georgia pursed full lips as she handed Adele a steaming cup. "But whatever you want. You're the boss."

Adele snorted, and her shoulders relaxed. "Since when?"

Georgia let loose a loud guffaw. "Well, at least you know who's actually in charge. When I worked for your mama she used to tell me the same thing." She winked at Adele. "It takes a big person to recognize the woman behind the woman. And since everyone's in agreement that I am in charge, I'm decreeing that you take the day off."

Adele's pale eyebrows rose. "What? We have too much to do."

Georgia eyed Adele speculatively. "Make that two days."

"I can't!"

"You can," Georgia disagreed with utter confidence. "And even if we were too busy, you overdid it yesterday." Her expression took on more than a hint of worry and she examined Adele carefully. "I haven't seen you limp like that since you quit the rehab center."

"Georgia…" Adele warned. "I already have parents. And, I told you, I'm fine."

"Yes. Yes." Georgia waved a hand in the air. "You're fine and you and your 'acquaintance' can go be fine together, away from the house. I have Ross coming over to put a bid on the paint job anyway."

Adele's eyes narrowed and she began to erratically stir the grits. "You know I don't like that man. He's a messy old perv who spends more time flirting than working."

Georgia gave her a crafty grin. "*I* enjoy the flirtin', especially if it gets us a discount. Besides, you won't be here to see it."

Silently admitting that a day off wouldn't be the worst thing in the world, Adele tossed the banana peel in the trash. "You're lucky that I was going to be gone for a while this morning anyway."

"Aha! I thought you were dressed too nicely for replacing the trim in Suite Four's bathroom."

Adele looked down at her sand and black, raglan Helmut Lang sweater and black leggings. She self-consciously smoothed back a lock of her hair. "You'd better stop or I'm going to tell your husband about your flirty ways and Ross." Adele shut off the stove's burner and moved the pan half off the grates to allow the grits to continue to thicken.

"He knows my ways are harmless, little missy. Besides…" Georgia winked. "How do you think I snared him?"

"I've always wondered—" Adele was interrupted by a light knock at the kitchen doorway.

"May I come in?" Natalie asked a little shyly. "I heard voices."

"Sure." Adele made a conscious effort to give Natalie a welcoming smile. "C'mon in."

Georgia and Natalie exchanged cordial greetings.

"Tea?" Adele asked, holding up the kettle.

Her hair still slightly damp from a shower and wearing the same clothes as the day before, Natalie sat down on a stool next to Georgia. "That would be great. Thanks." She glanced around. "Are Logan and Landry gone for the day already?"

Adele paused mid-pour, then resumed. "They're out for the day together."

Georgia stood and smoothed her dress. It was almost identical to the one she'd worn the day before, just in green instead of navy blue. "Enjoy your breakfast and your day, girls. I'd better dig out those paint swatches you like before Ross gets here. And I need to go fix myself up a bit and freshen my lipstick." She primped her short black hair that was threaded with gray. "I'm shooting for forty percent off."

A tiny laugh exploded from Adele, and Natalie gave her a curious look.

On the way out of the kitchen Georgia picked up Adele's cane from its place behind the door. She carefully, but pointedly, placed it down on the edge of the island. "Natalie, will you make sure Ella uses this when she needs it today? No matter what she says, she's hurting."

Natalie's eyes darted to Adele, who was giving Georgia a withering glare, and then back again. "Uh, I'm…" She blinked several times in rapid succession. "Well, I'm sure she'll use it as she needs it?" The question was meant for Adele, who kept shooting bullets with her eyes at Georgia.

Georgia shook her head in disbelief. "Ella?"

Much to Adele's frustration, Georgia waited patiently until Adele finally unclenched her jaw and gave her an eye-rolling nod.

Natalie remained silent. She watched the scene intently as she sipped her tea and Georgia slipped from the room.

"So," Adele started self-consciously. "Breakfast then shopping?" She held up the pan of grits.

"But I thought—"

"I was eating anyway." Adele began to pour the grits onto a plate, and pushed the bowl of fruit to Natalie. "Besides, I'm going to add it to your big fat bill."

Natalie grinned and picked a napkin from a pile in the center of the island. "Deal."

* * *

The women stepped out of a cab onto Royal Street in the heart of the French Quarter, in front of an upscale clothing boutique called Amelia's. Adele paid the driver as Natalie stared longingly at the shop window and the beautiful clothes on display.

"So this is why you always look so great," Natalie said absently as she bent to examine a pair of strappy black Prada pumps.

Adele beamed at the unexpected compliment. "I, um…" Suddenly nervous, she drummed her fingertips against the handle of her cane.

Given the excuse, Natalie slowly raked her eyes over Adele. She laughed softly at Adele's sudden embarrassment. "You really do."

She felt Natalie's gaze drag over her as though it were a living, breathing thing, and Adele's skin tingled in its wake. "Thanks." Adele swore she heard Natalie release a breathy sigh. She couldn't decide whether it was disconcerting or titillating. Maybe both.

"You're welcome. You have wonderful style," Natalie said with a wistful smile and a hint of envy.

"Amelia's has great stuff, but we won't get to see it if we just stand on the sidewalk instead of going inside."

"Great stuff that I can't afford, I'm afraid." Natalie tilted her head toward a chocolate brown sweater that was proudly worn by an anorexic mannequin. It was $249. And that was the sale price.

"Don't worry about that. They have some more economical things near the back. I promise. And lots of casual items too."

"Really?"

Natalie's look was so hopeful that Adele had to suppress a laugh. "Really."

The inside of the shop was much larger than it appeared from the street, and from floor to ceiling, it was a vision of shades of gray and bold blocks of white. The monochromatic palette made the clothes and their splashes of color practically pop off the racks. It was modern and sophisticated. The ringing of the bell that signaled their entry still hung in the air when a blond woman, who was a little older, and a little heavier version of Adele ran across the store, her high heels clicking furiously.

She wrapped Adele in a hug so tight Adele began to wheeze. She pressed her cheek against Adele's as she spoke. "I've been waiting for you since we opened, Ella."

Adele squeezed back and drank in the familiar scent of Shalimar perfume with a warm sense of nostalgia. "You only opened ten minutes ago. Am I the only one with any patience in this family?"

"I haven't been able to get you in here for over a year. Ten extra minutes at this point is ten too long." She gave Adele a playful sock in the arm. "And your friend here must be Natalie."

Adele rubbed her arm with a bit of a pout. "Natalie, this is my *much* older sister, Amelia Belmont."

"What?" Amelia shrieked indignantly. "Only three years older!"

"Amelia, this is Natalie Abbott."

"This is your shop?" Natalie gazed around the store with wide-eyed admiration. "It's beautiful!"

Amelia laughed and wound her arm around Adele's. "I'm glad you think so."

"You must be so proud of Ella. I mean, not everyone has a sister who is a hero and who has helped so many people."

Amelia's face exploded into a mega-watt smile. "Absolutely."

And just like that, Adele thought wryly, Natalie won over her very hard to please older sibling.

Still grinning, Amelia said, "My sister called me this morning and told me that you're here in New Orleans with pretty much just the clothes on your back and you're in dire need of a week's worth of things to wear."

Adele frowned playfully. "I didn't…I never used the word 'dire.'"

Natalie grimaced. "But, it's true."

Amelia smiled broadly. "We've got you covered." Tongue between her teeth, she gave Natalie an appraising look.

Adele rolled her eyes. "Amelia, she doesn't want to be your life-size Barbie doll and stand here while you play swami. She just wants to shop!"

Amelia continued as though Adele hadn't spoken at all. "Size six for dresses and jeans. A snug in the cup thirty-four-B for bras. Medium for blouses. Size eight on the shoes. Yes?"

"Wow." Natalie's eyes turned into saucers. "Perfect except for the shoes. I wear a nine."

Amelia grinned conspiratorially. "I knew that. But I always guess a size lower on the shoes. For some reason, women are weirdly self-conscious about their feet."

Natalie laughed.

"Please look around and let Carla," Amelia paused and gestured toward an immaculately dressed, petite black woman who was fussing with a display of Michael Kors handbags, "…help you with anything you need while I catch up with Ella. Oh, and Carla will show you the stash I've been saving for Ella. But since my sister hasn't bothered to come to see me in ages…"

"Hey," Adele protested grumpily. "That's not completely true."

"You get first dibs, Natalie," Amelia continued blithely. "Just about anything I put aside for Ella should fit you, except the shoes and maybe the bras. She's got Sasquatch-like feet and is a C cup all the way." Amelia put her hands out in front of her chest as though she was holding a melon in each one. "For someone so slim, she's got—"

"Hey again!" Adele blushed to the roots of her hair, but wasn't really angry. If anything this made her realize how badly she'd missed her sister. They'd tormented each other constantly growing up, and it felt as natural as breathing. Adele spoke through gritted teeth. "Stop talking about my boobs, Amelia!"

Natalie clamped a hand over her mouth to keep from laughing.

"Any clothes that you like," Amelia went on, "you can purchase at my cost. And since you're the only person Adele's ever brought in here," she shot Adele a disapproving look for waiting so long, "I'm happy to extend the family discount to you. Just tell all your friends where you got them."

Adele gazed at her sister with undiluted affection. *Thank you, Amelia.*

Natalie's mouth sagged. "I—I can't do that."

"Of course you can," Amelia assured her with a little pat on the arm. "And once you see what my cost actually is, you're going to be furious with every store you've ever shopped in."

Natalie glanced questioningly at Adele, silently asking if it was really okay to take Amelia up on her offer.

Adele shrugged good-naturedly and grinned. "I do it without guilt. You might as well too. I consider it payback for the perm she gave me when I was in the sixth grade."

Brimming with excitement and clapping her hands together, Natalie jumped up and down a little. "Oh, my gosh! Thank you!"

Amelia murmured something into Carla's ear about paying attention to Natalie's light eyes and brainy vibe before pulling Adele over near the register and pushing her into a tall chair. She took her cane and placed it behind the cash register for safekeeping. Then Amelia unrepentantly stared at her sister.

"Don't look at me that way," Adele groaned piteously. For the second time today she felt like a bug under a microscope. "Just because I haven't been in the shop for a few months…"

"Not a few months. A year," Amelia corrected sternly. "You used to meet me here, and we'd go to lunch every other Tuesday, Ella. We did it for *years* and then you stopped when—"

"I know when I stopped." Adele didn't like feeling guilty, but her sister was doing an excellent job of heaping it on. "Maybe I haven't been in the shop for a year, but that doesn't mean we haven't seen each other in that long. I saw you a couple of months ago at Daddy's birthday." She winced hearing how lame the words sounded even to her own ears. She and Amelia had always had a good relationship, and she'd neglected it horribly.

"That was almost four months ago, and we live four miles apart! We should see each other way more than that, and you know it." Amelia lowered her voice and her eyes began to shimmer. "I love and I miss you, Ella. We all do." She gave her younger sister's golden hair a little tug to drive her point home.

Adele looked away. "I know. I'm sorry. I've been busy."

With one hand, Amelia gently guided Adele's chin back so they were looking at each other. "Busy licking your wounds?"

"You say it like it's not a full-time job."

Amelia sighed. "Ella."

"Okay, okay." Adele lifted a placating hand. "I'll come by again soon, okay? I promise. Lunch every other Tuesday. Starting next week."

Amelia's face transformed with a bright smile. "I'm going to forgive you. And do you know why?"

"You're not the spiteful harpy I've always seen you as?"

"No, of course I am." Amelia's demeanor softened. "It's because I've seen you smile more in the last five minutes than I've seen in the past three years."

Adele scowled, and Amelia clearly knew that the younger woman had been pushed to her limit on the subject. "Okay. Now tell me about your friend. Are you—" She made a vague gesture with one hand and wiggled her eyebrows lasciviously.

"What? No! Of course not!"

"Why not? She's gorgeous, and she's been sneaking looks at you as we've been talking. Not that you haven't been doing the same." Amelia's eyes took on an evil gleam. "If you and her were to," she waggled her eyebrows again. "Well, let's just say I'd pay good money to see the look on that rat bastard Landry's face."

Nobody could hold a grudge like Amelia. Adele groaned. "When are you going to forgive him?"

"When I'm dancing in the second line parade for his funeral, I'll consider it," Amelia said simply and without even a trace of guilt. "Now details, please."

They both watched as Natalie and Carla headed toward the dressing rooms each holding a pile of clothes. Adele hoped Natalie remembered to get something warm for the evenings. Maybe they could eat on the patio if...

Amelia kicked Adele's stool, causing her to jump a little. "Earth to Ella."

"Oh, right." Adele steeled herself for a negative reaction. "She's Joshua Phillips's sister. There's been a new development in his murder case, but the NOPD has their heads too far up their collective ass to care. Crisco is most likely innocent, which means somebody else killed her brother. Natalie wants someone to look into it, so she came to me."

"Wow." Amelia let out a gusty breath and leaned against the wall. She ran her hand down her face and studied Adele closely. "I didn't see that coming."

Adele looked a little shell-shocked. "Me neither."

"So you're going to help her." Amelia's voice held a note of certainty. "Good." Her indignation rose as Adele's words sunk in. "Those goddamn rotten cops!"

A customer milling around a rack of scarves sent a disapproving look in her direction, and Amelia lowered her voice. "You were too good for them back then, and you still are!" she hissed like an angry alley cat. "They crucified you, and you were right all along."

Adele's eyes snapped upward, and she gave her sister a skeptical look. "You aren't going to warn me off helping Natalie? Tell me it's too dangerous, blah, blah, blah?"

Amelia winced. "Georgia?"

Adele nodded grimly.

"She was just channeling Daddy and Mama. And you *should* be careful. But I know how much you loved doing what you did, and how good it would be for you to get back into the saddle. Plus, there's no way you're going to give up the chance to be vindicated. Natalie was smart to come to you. I knew I liked her."

Adele rolled her eyes at herself. "Smart because she knows that I want to scream 'I told you so!' at my old lieutenant, and just about every other cop on the NOPD, at the top of my lungs like a six-year-old?"

"Smart because you were the best detective in the city."

Adele smiled, embarrassed, but then quickly looked offended. "Not in all of Louisiana?"

Clearly thrilled, Amelia gave Adele a robust, one-armed hug. "There's the immodesty I've missed!"

Adele chuckled softly.

Amelia's wry grin turned sympathetic. "I know things haven't been easy."

Adele swallowed thickly and shook her head in silent agreement.

"So I say, if helping Natalie Abbott makes you happy, and you get a chance to make things right for yourself, even in a small way, you go for it."

Adele lifted her chin stubbornly, but she couldn't mask the underlying fear in her expression, not from someone who knew her so well. "I don't think I can do it, Amelia. I need to accept that this is my life now and move on and let go."

Amelia regarded her sister seriously. "Moving on doesn't have to mean stopping everything you love."

"I-I don't know how to feel about it," Adele confessed and felt a tiny bit of the pressure inside her chest ease. "I thought I closed that chapter of my life for good. Now it's like she's come back to town and cracked the book open again and I'm afraid to want it." She clasped her hands together tightly. "What if I can't really do much because of my leg or because the NOPD puts a brick wall up in front of me? Or what if I fail just because I'm not good enough?"

Amelia's eyebrows hiked up her forehead at her sister's admissions, which had uncharacteristically poured out of her in a fast-moving stream.

"What if I don't fail, and then it ends, and it hurts twice as much to go back to living without being able to do what I love or be what I want to be?" Adele gave her sister a raw, vulnerable look. "I just can't do it, Amelia. I—I'm scared to death."

Amelia let out a groan of unhappiness at Ella's words. "I know you are, sweetie. And if I could do something about it that wouldn't land me in the clink, I would. You know that, right?"

The corner of Adele's mouth curled upward. "I do."

"Good." Amelia's gaze was full of warm understanding. "But, Ella, your confidence has been shaken, yes. But it's not completely gone. *All* those what-ifs you mentioned were bad. I like my list better. *What if* you do this, and it makes you happy?"

Adele waited, but Amelia didn't offer anything else. "That's your entire list?"

"Does it really need to be longer?"

Adele scowled. "But—"

"Look," Amelia held up both her hands, palms out, and stopped Adele, "if you just need more time to figure things out," she shrugged, "far be it for me to burst your bubble of denial."

"I hate it when you're smug."

"You hate it when I'm *right*."

Adele narrowed her eyes. The truth was her resolve to *not* help Natalie was already weakening and it had only been a day. But Adele also meant what she said. If she didn't move on now, she was afraid she'd never be ready.

"Now," Amelia picked up Adele's cane and shoved it into her hands, "there's an olive-green Burberry coat in the back that I saved from last fall's collection. If I were Natalie—"

But Adele was already standing, glad Amelia knew when to give her some space. "I'm on it." Slowly, she began to head toward the back of the store, using her cane lightly. Halfway across the room, she turned back.

"Amelia." Coloring, she licked her lips nervously, "You won't mention to Natalie about the…well, you know how you do that…thing."

Amelia laughed and walked over to buss her sister's cheek. "I promise not to tell Natalie that I put colored dots on the inside labels of your clothes so you'll know which things go together."

Relieved, Adele grinned sheepishly. "Right, that…thing."

"What thing?"

"Exactly."

* * *

It was after eight o'clock that evening when Natalie and Adele finally settled down on a bench on the walkway that lined the Mississippi River. It was still cool outside, but warmer than the night before. The breeze was light enough that it only occasionally ruffled Adele's short hair. They sat close together, but there was still space between them. The bench was chilly against the backs of their legs, and the scent of damp earth and water filled their nostrils.

"Oh, my God," Natalie groaned, wishing it wouldn't be humiliating to unbutton her jeans. "I'm so full I can't move." They'd just eaten at Galatoire's, a place Adele had described as a local institution. The food had been marvelous, and afterward they'd still managed to squeeze in a slice of bourbon pecan pie from a bakery near Jackson Square.

Adele chortled lightly. "I told you. We have many problems in New Orleans," she drawled in a slow, relaxed way, her accent thicker than usual. A smile broke out on Natalie's face as she listened. "But access to good food is not one of them." Adele shifted in her seat and kicked her legs straight out in front of her, her lips suddenly thinning.

Natalie frowned. She could see that Adele was hurting. They would take a cab back to the inn instead of walking, even if she had to insist. "We walked a lot today. My feet are tired."

"Yeah." Adele's reply was barely audible.

"I have pain tablets in my purse." A memory of Detective Lejeune offering her the same thing the first time they'd met floated to the surface.

Adele sighed. "I took one when we left the bakery. It should kick in soon. But thanks."

Natalie nodded, then slumped down a little in her seat and stuffed her hands into the pockets of her new olive-green Burberry coat. "Ella?"

"Mmm?" Adele's attention was focused on the way starlight created a crust of diamonds on the surface of the dark, lazy river.

"Thank you for today. I really needed to do something fun." She gestured to the bags seated next to her feet. "And the clothes. I got all these beautiful outfits for the price of one or two, thanks to you and your sister." Her smile turned sulky. "But I can't eat like I did tonight again or I won't be able to fit into any of them."

Adele's teeth flashed white in the darkness. "I don't think a little good food will do you too much harm."

"There was nothing little about my meal tonight." Natalie glanced at her cell phone. It was probably already past Logan's bedtime. "Shouldn't we be heading back?"

"If you'd like." Adele pulled up the collar of her jacket, looking a little contemplative. "But I'm not in any particular hurry."

"What about—"

Adele's eyes tilted upward and Natalie saw the moon shimmering in their depths, making them appear every bit as mysterious and fathomless as the black water. "Logan is with Landry in Baton Rouge. That's where Landry lives and works now. He's on their police force. We, um, got divorced almost two years ago. Logan won't be back until Christmas Day."

Taken aback, Natalie's tongue felt heavy in her mouth as she struggled for an appropriate response. She remembered how Logan and Adele had interacted and could only imagine how awful any separation would be for them both. Christmas was nearly two weeks away. "I'm sorry, Ella. That's awful."

Adele's jaw worked for a few seconds as she tried to shrug away the hurt. "I get him most of the time. So fair is fair, I guess."

"There's nothing fair about you being away from him at all," Natalie ground out with enough bitterness to surprise Adele and herself.

"We share custody, but Logan spends most of the school year here with me and most of the summertime and holiday breaks with Landry."

"It's not my business what happened." Natalie shook her head. "I mean, I know Landry was angry the last time I saw him, but..." She didn't really know how to finish that sentence.

"Things got ugly in the months after you left. *Really* ugly. I pretty much ruined his life."

"You wouldn't do that."

"You'd be surprised."

"Ella, c'mon."

"I wouldn't have done it intentionally. But I still did it."

Adele abruptly stopped her narrative, and Natalie decided not to push her to continue. Instead, Natalie let the sounds of the evening penetrate her consciousness: huffing joggers as they ran past, the faint, but mournful wail of a jazz saxophone from a bar down the road, the light tinkling of bare tree branches as they gently collided with the occasional gusts of wind, and the muffled laughter as a group of tourists bustled down the street in the distance.

Natalie burrowed a little deeper into her coat. She wasn't really cold, but she was disconcerted, and it felt safe and comfortable inside the warm cloth. The thought of Adele's suffering upset her on a visceral level she struggled to understand.

After a long, easy silence, Adele simply began to speak. "The Public Integrity Bureau ran with my accusation against Officer Morrell and somehow that exploded into a department-wide investigation."

"Why?" Natalie prompted gently and carefully, as if she was drawing out a wounded animal closer for inspection. For help.

"For it to make sense, you have to understand, Natalie, we were under so much scrutiny during and after the Danziger Bridge shootings investigation. It went on forever, and the entire NOPD was dragged through the mud because of the actions of a few bad apples. The public lost most of their faith in us. The brass and city officials, at least *some* of them," she amended mockingly, "were desperate to get that respect back and were willing to do whatever it took to make that happen. Appearance became more important than reality. It became everything."

Adele's eyes fluttered closed, and she suddenly looked impossibly weary. "God, it was just a mess. Parts of it are still stuck in court or indefinitely on hold, and it's been almost ten years."

Natalie scrunched up her face as she thought. "I think I remember seeing something about that on the news. It was some sort of police cover-up for some shootings during Hurricane Katrina, right?"

Adele nodded stoically. "That's the gist of it. It sort of set the scene for everything that came later. Once the PIB started digging into what Morrell did to Crisco, all sorts of other incidents came to light, most especially, the NOPD's ongoing nasty habit of squelching internal allegations of abuse of power. Important people were embarrassed over the Danziger Bridge shootings, and somebody needed to pay for it. And this was their chance. Then things got passed along to our pit bull of a prosecutor and all hell broke loose.

"By the end, the investigation shifted into a witch hunt. Sixteen officers lost their jobs or voluntarily left the NOPD as part of a plea bargain. Careers over. Pensions gone. Everything. Some of them were nothing more than thugs that needed to go. I still don't know how they avoided jail time." Adele looked close to tears. "But not all of them deserved what happened to them. The net cast by PIB was just so wide...they didn't care about collateral damage at all if it meant making their case."

"But that's not your fault! You had nothing to do with that."

Adele smiled a little at Natalie's indignation. She tucked her legs under the bench and leaned forward, her elbows resting on her knees as she gazed out at the water again. Adele sniffed and wiped her eyes with the back of her hand. "That never mattered. The department was like a big bundle of dynamite, and my allegations were the match that lit the fuse."

Natalie blinked a few times. She had never imagined anything beyond her brother's case. She just now realized that, for Adele, it was only the very tip of an enormous and very ugly iceberg. "So Landry was mad or upset?"

"Mad or upset?" Adele's tone was jaded. "He took shit for what I'd done every single day for months, and it wasn't just teasing or name-calling. What other cops did to us both was cruel and dangerous. He got into a half-dozen fistfights with other officers because of what they said about me. There were threats to blow up our house. Our cars weren't just keyed, they were ruined. And none of that even touches what Landry personally thought of me afterward."

He loved you. Natalie had seen it in his face so plainly, even while Landry was furious and yelling at Adele, there was an undercurrent of caring and fear. Still, Natalie was irrationally angry with him for not supporting his wife when she needed him most. Natalie knew with guilty certainty that she'd reacted horribly to what Adele had done to Josh's case. *But I wasn't her husband!*

"Landry comes from a family of cops. His daddy and granddaddy were cops. His brother is a sergeant in Property Crimes. He's got two cousins in Traffic and another in the State Highway Patrol. This damaged, if not ruined, his relationship with all of them. Well, except his granddaddy, who was already dead. His own family was furious with him for being married to a traitor."

Anger pounded through Natalie's veins. "That's not fair! You're the most loyal person I've ever met."

"That depends on who you ask, doesn't it?" Adele nearly sneered. "None of it was fair! And to make matters worse, everything Landry warned me about turned out to be true. Every. Single. Thing. But I wouldn't listen. All along he warned me that I couldn't count on backup from other cops. That it was too dangerous for me to stay on the force."

Natalie's eyes were drawn to Adele's cane as it leaned harmlessly against the bench.

Adele's hands shaped fists. "But did I listen? Of course not! And so while a crazy woman, whose kids I was trying to find, was stabbing me, the officers who'd been dispatched to the scene as my backup were taking their own sweet time getting there. I heard later through the grapevine that they'd stopped for coffee on the way to the scene."

Natalie closed her eyes and felt the slightly sick sensation that came from the blood draining from her face. *Stabbed?* "Jesus, Ella." She started to wonder whether the news articles she'd read online had intentionally downplayed what had happened.

"I'm actually a little surprised they bothered to staunch my bleeding enough to save my life. I guess they drew the line at actually watching me die."

The extent of Adele's loss hit home. *She lost everything.* "So you couldn't go back to the NOPD, even without your injury?"

Adele let out a shuddering breath. "Not ever. Not if I want to stay alive. Anyway, Landry filed for divorce the day I came home from the hospital. The day after that he moved to Baton Rouge and took Logan with him. He said I'd get Logan back when a judge ordered him to do it."

"What?" Natalie sat up straight. "He just *took* your son?"

Adele nodded mutely.

"Christ, he's lucky you didn't shoot him!" Then she faltered. "You didn't, right?"

Adele snorted. "The thought crossed my mind. Honestly, I was worried about what my family would do. We're not good at taking things lying down. Anyway, Landry knew he screwed up and brought Logan back a couple of days later. Ever since, we've actually gotten along pretty well. He's been supportive from afar and is a good dad."

Natalie reached out and covered one of Adele's hands with her own. "I'm so sorry. You didn't deserve any of that."

"But, Natalie, if I would have—"

"No." Natalie's eyes blazed with anger. "You're not to blame for the bigger investigation, and you were right to instigate the smaller one."

Dismayed, Adele said, "I don't know how I can believe that after I hurt so many people, including myself. I've permanently and negatively altered Logan's life. I lost my career, my ability to walk and not look like Quasimodo when my leg and hip get tired, my nearly ten-year marriage to a man I loved, and most of my identity." Adele drew in a breath and affected a cheerful expression. "So…what have *you* been up to?"

Wet with unshed tears, the women's eyes met and they both burst out laughing. It was so horrible that if they didn't laugh, they'd weep.

The tension in the air dissolved.

"I haven't been up to anything nearly so interesting, Ella. And I think I'm grateful for that." Natalie looked down at their joined hands. Adele's skin was soft and surprisingly warm, even in the chilly air, and Natalie gave in to the urge to stroke the back of Adele's hand with her thumb. Natalie wanted to take every ounce of Adele's pain away and…her gaze dropped to Adele's lips and her heart began to race.

Natalie wanted to kiss her. She wanted to take Adele's mouth with hers again and again until rational thought was impossible and nothing else mattered. The nearly unstoppable urge hit her so suddenly that she could barely breathe.

"So, Natalie?"

"Yeah?" Natalie whispered hoarsely, a swarm of butterflies taking flight in her belly.

"Tomorrow we start working on your brother's case, okay?"

Natalie's eyes snapped up to meet Adele's. "I, um, I thought you weren't interested."

Adele's voice dropped an octave. "I'm interested."

CHAPTER TEN

The sounds of gut-wrenching screams woke Natalie from a dead sleep. Confused and disoriented, she threw off her bedding and jumped to her feet. She wobbled a little as she whipped around in a frantic circle, trying to locate the source of the noise and decipher what was happening.

Then it stopped.

Heart pounding, Natalie sagged against the wall, her body trembling from an instant cold sweat that left her feeling clammy and unsettled. "Shit." Then she pressed the heels of her hands against closed eyes. "Just a dream. It was only a dream."

Then another ear-piercing scream caused her to nearly jump out of her skin. The screams weren't part of a dream. They were real. *Ella?* One scream blended into the next and the next. Natalie flung her suite door open and flew out of her room in a dead run toward the back of the house.

It sounded like someone was being murdered.

"Ouch!" She crashed into a small table in the hallway and fumbled with a vase, trying to right it before it crashed to the ground. But the vase didn't matter, and she let it fall in the next heartbeat because it was slowing her down. Her socked feet slipped on polished wood floors and she skidded as she ran.

Following the sounds of the shrieks, Natalie bolted down a short hallway off the kitchen and burst into another set of rooms she'd never seen. A living room, she thought, but it was hard to tell in the dark.

She scanned the space, her gaze flicking around the room at a frenzied pace. "Ella?" The screams were louder here, but it was still hard to tell exactly where they were coming from. "Ella?" she called out forcefully.

But, just as abruptly as before, the cries stopped completely and silence enveloped the room.

Natalie had to hold her breath for a few seconds to listen. She couldn't hear anything over her own panting and the blood rushing in her ears. On the heels of the panicky screams, the dead silence was almost more terrifying. Finally, and with forced slowness, Natalie exhaled. For a second, she stood rooted in place, trying to calm herself. Then she snatched up a slender, metal umbrella stand and began opening doors.

A child's room.

A large bathroom.

A closet filled with miscellaneous household items. A vacuum. A broom.

The last door opened into a bedroom. Ella's bedroom. Natalie lifted the umbrella stand overhead and carefully peered into the room as she crept slowly and silently inside. Immediately, she located Ella in bed, the moonlight illuminating one side of her still face, the other side cast in black shadows.

Natalie's eyes widened. Ella wasn't moving. At all. *She can't be...* "Ella?" she said, her voice breaking. Her mind flashed to Misty's dead eyes as she felt her knees threaten to give way. "Ella!" she shouted, still brandishing the umbrella stand like a batter awaiting a pitch. She began to panic. "*Ella!*"

With a loud gasp, Adele jerked awake and bolted upright, causing Natalie to shriek and jump back.

In one swift move, Adele reached under the pillow next to hers and extracted a gun and a clip. In the blink of an eye, Adele inserted the clip and pointed directly at Natalie, her aim as steady as a rock. Adele cocked the gun. "Stay back!"

"Don't shoot!" Natalie pleaded, dropping the umbrella stand as though it was red-hot. It clattered to the ground. "Don't shoot. It's me!"

"Don't come any fuckin' closer," Adele growled harshly, the animalistic sound seeming to emanate from the very pit of her stomach.

Natalie softened her voice, her heart in her throat. "I won't. I pr-promise."

Adele's eyes looked wild and unfocused and glinted dangerously. It was clear Adele had no idea who was standing before her.

Oh, my God. She's going to shoot me. "Ella, it's me. Natalie. Josh's sister. Natalie Abbott."

Bewildered and breathing as though she'd just sprinted a mile, Adele squinted at the figure at the foot of her bed. As recognition slowly dawned Adele's expression shifted from fear to anger, then back again. "Nat-Natalie?" She instantly lowered the gun and dropped it on the bed beside her.

Natalie flinched, half expecting it to go off.

"Fuck, Natalie, I thought you were…" Adele shook her head briskly as if to dislodge whatever evil thoughts were still lingering inside. "Christ!" She grasped at her throat and winced in pain.

"Thank you." Light-headed, Natalie let out a shaky breath. "Thank you for not shooting me."

Adele looked around the room as if trying to piece together what had just happened, her mind clearly muddled. "Why? Why are you in my bedroom with an umbrella stand?" Her voice was raspy like sandpaper. She blinked rapidly and laid her hand back on the gun, rhythmically clenching and unclenching the handle. "You looked like you were going to hit me with it."

Natalie swallowed hard as she tracked Adele's every move. "I would never!"

Adele's cheeks were tear-stained and glistened in the wan light. Fresh tears spilled over, but she didn't seem to notice them at all. She just sat there, guardedly, waiting for an explanation from Natalie.

She's terrified. "I-I…You were screaming. You were screaming your head off. I thought you needed help."

"What?" A V formed between Adele's eyes, and her gaze grew distant. "I couldn't get away. I tried—"

"You were screaming, Ella, because you were dreaming. A nightmare."

"Oh." Adele sounded utterly lost, then upset with herself. "God, please put your hands down."

Natalie suddenly realized she still had her hands in the air and she lowered them cautiously. "Are you okay?"

To Natalie's surprise, Adele was completely honest and shook her head no. "I don't think so." She pulled her knees up to her chest, wrapped lean arms around them and buried her face against them.

"It's gonna be okay," Natalie said softly. She took a step closer to the side of the bed, but paused midstep, foot still in the air. "Is the gun gone?" She hated guns and didn't want to come anywhere near it.

"Yes. I mean no. Wait." Adele glanced down at the weapon next to her, then carefully picked it up, ejected the clip, and placed the gun and clip on the nightstand next to her bed. On the same stand sat a small heavy-glassed, Tiffany-style lamp and Adele flipped it on to its lowest setting, bathing the room in a faint warm glow. "I'm sorry I woke you."

Even though the light was weak, it was enough to make both women flinch.

"It's not a problem," Natalie said, doing her best to be calm and reassuring. She decided in that moment that she'd take to the grave the knowledge that Adele's screams had been one of the most terrible things she'd ever heard and that her own heart was still pounding wildly in her chest.

Adele looked up, her eyes a tiny bit clearer than before. "I'm still so sorry. I didn't mean...In my dreams, they were after me. I-I don't know who. Just...someone. But I was running. And the next thing I knew, there was someone at the foot of my bed, holding a weapon of some kind."

Natalie could see that Adele's T-shirt was completely soaked through with sweat. Her temples and neck were also wet with perspiration and her eyes looked haunted.

"Ella."

"I'm sorry," Adele's voice broke.

"Shh...it's okay. You don't need to apologize. It was just a dream." For the moment, Natalie put out of her mind that she'd just had a gun pointed at her face. She gestured to the bed, whose covers were strewn half on and half off the bed. "Can I?"

"Y-yes," Adele stammered. "Of course. Sit. Please. I'm sorry. I—"

"Stop. You didn't know it was me." Natalie sat on the edge of the bed and fought the urge to hug Adele. She didn't look ready to be touched in any way. Frustrated with herself, Natalie acknowledged her own mistakes. She knew, at least partially, what Adele had been through. Sneaking up on her, and then startling her in the middle of the night, wasn't the smartest thing she'd ever done, even if she'd meant well.

But when she saw Adele lying in bed, and so unearthly still, she was petrified. For a moment she wondered whether Adele had really been lying that still or whether she was the one who was seeing things that weren't there.

Natalie tried to smile and hoped it didn't look as much like a grimace as it felt. Inwardly, she was every bit as shaky as Adele appeared on the outside. "I don't know what I'd do if I woke up with a stranger standing at the end of my bed. Yes, an umbrella stand is probably better suited to a game of Clue than it is a real-life weapon, but still, I'd probably have a heart attack."

At the words, Adele managed a quick half grin and then pressed her hand to her own rapidly rising and falling chest. "I might have."

"I called your name and you didn't answer. I thought you were hurt or maybe..." Natalie swallowed thickly. Against her will Misty's lifeless body and dull eyes, and then Joshua's still form resting on the table in the morgue, reappeared in a macabre montage in her head. "Thank God, you're not...I'm just glad you're okay."

For the first time, Adele looked down at herself and noticed her disheveled, overheated state. "Ugh. Gross." She pulled at her damp shirt, her face scrunched up in disgust, her voice still a little rough from sleep and her screams. "I haven't had nightmares like that...since before I bought the inn."

Natalie frowned and suppressed the desire to tuck a wild strand of blond hair behind Adele's ear. "It's because you agreed to help me work on Josh's case, isn't it?" Guilt caused a bitter taste to rise from her belly and into her mouth.

Adele shrugged, upset. "Who knows? It doesn't really matter. Sometimes, I'm a mess," she admitted, glancing quickly at Natalie's face to gauge her reaction. Then without a word, she got up and headed for her bathroom.

Natalie wondered if Adele had been diagnosed with PTSD, but now wasn't the time to ask. She could hear the water running in the sink. Then, damp washcloth in hand, Adele limped past her and disappeared inside a walk-in closet.

Suddenly a T-shirt came flying out of the closet and landed on the floor at the foot of the bed. Next came a pair of flannel pajama bottoms. "I guess I need to add sound proofing my room to the list of renovations, huh?" Adele emerged from the closet wearing a new blindingly white T-shirt and a soft pair of black cotton boxer shorts. Her skin damp and wiped clean, she grabbed the dirty clothes and washcloth and threw them all into the hamper near the closet door. Then she stared grumpily at her bed.

Guessing what she wanted, Natalie stood and offered to help. "It's easier with two people."

Adele gave Natalie a wan smile as she made her way back inside the closet. "Thanks," she said softly, her eyes conveying that it was for more than just offering to help change the bedsheets.

"It really is okay," Natalie promised as she tugged the blanket from the bed and let it pool gently by her feet. "Do, um, do you want to talk about it? The dream?"

Adele emerged with a stack of freshly laundered pale yellow sheets and pillowcases. "Not much to say." But she spoke anyway. "I used to get nightmares like that maybe four or five nights a week. The first few months back home from the hospital after I got stabbed were the worst. God, I was so tired all the time."

Right when Landry left you. Bastard! Natalie seethed inwardly.

"They were...bad." Adele paused, and Natalie could tell she was severely editing her story. "I finally had to start playing music in Logan's room at night so I wouldn't wake him. But they did taper off and eventually stopped." She nibbled her lower lip as she passed Natalie a clean pillowcase. "Or so I thought."

Natalie gave her a sympathetic look. She felt horrible that she'd dredged up so much inner turmoil in Adele that it was literally pouring from her in her sleep. "Maybe you shouldn't—"

Jaw mostly clenched, Adele muttered, "Don't say it. I should, and I want to do it."

"But—"

"I need to help you, Natalie. And Josh."

"But—"

"The last few years I've lost control of everything. Don't decide for me what I can or can't handle." A hint of vulnerability slipped through her pique. "*Please.*"

That, along with the raw look on Adele's face, stopped Natalie's protests cold. Things were upside down. Cats were barking and fish were walking and Adele Lejeune wasn't just asking if she could help her, she was practically begging.

"Besides, maybe your brother's case has nothing to do with the nightmares coming back. Maybe I just ate too much and too late." Adele's smile didn't quite reach her eyes.

"Thanksgiving night must be treacherous at your house."

"It's not." But the protest was weak at best.

"Believe me, I'm plenty grateful that you didn't shoot me." Natalie hesitated for a moment, but decided to ask anyway, very aware that she was about to tread into dangerous territory. "I saw the way you were gripping that gun. What if it had been Logan who had come in?"

Adele didn't seem irritated by the personal question, but her shoulders slumped a bit. "I know it might sound bad, but Logan's not allowed to come into my room on his own at night. When he's not with Landry, I lock my door when I go to bed. If he wants inside, he knocks until I open it for him. That way I know that I'm awake. He's also the reason I keep the clip separate from the gun."

Natalie trusted Adele, but couldn't help but feel relieved at the precautionary steps.

Once the bed was remade, Adele climbed back inside. "Man, I feel like I've run a marathon." She closed her eyes, but patted a space for Natalie to sit next to her again. "Thank you for trying to help me. Even if it was crazy." Her tone was deadly serious, but her gentle smile softened her words. "If you ever think I'm in danger, you should run the opposite direction, Natalie, and go for help."

Natalie actually snorted, dropping down onto the soft blankets and feeling the last few minutes catch up with her. She was exhausted. "Hardly."

"It's the safest thing to do."

Natalie's face fell. Was she supposed to ignore that Adele might have needed her? "But I thought we were becoming friends."

"We are. But—"

"So you wouldn't come help me if the situation was reversed?"

Adele looked mortified. "Of course I would. But I'm a—"

Natalie was sure the word cop died an inauspicious death on Adele's tongue.

"You're a good person," she finished, fighting the urge to fuss over Adele and tuck the covers under her chin. "And occasionally I try to be one too, okay? So give me my ten seconds of glory as a would-be hero."

Without warning, Adele sat up and gave Natalie a quick, but tender kiss on the cheek. Her lips lingered for a few seconds, then Adele shifted and pressed her cheek against Natalie's, her breath hot against Natalie's ear. She grasped Natalie's biceps and gave them a soft squeeze. "If I ever need saving, I'll know I can count on you. And that means everything to me."

Natalie shivered at the feeling of the soft mouth, strong hands…and the words.

"Grab an extra blanket from the closet in your room if you're cold," Adele said quietly, pulling away very slowly, her eyes twinkling just a bit. Invitingly, she inclined her head and smiled. This time her eyes were completely clear. "See you tomorrow?"

Natalie had to remind herself to breathe. *I'm not cold.* She needed a few seconds to find her voice. "Yeah," she rasped, resolutely ignoring the way Adele's grin grew with every second and those goddamn cute dimples appeared in her cheeks. "In the morning."

* * *

The next day…

Adele shook her head no. "He's with Landry."

"For real, Little Mama? Why don't you go back to court and get your son away from that douche bag?"

The heated words seeped into Natalie's ears before she finished descending the several steps into the courtyard of the Touro Street Inn. Adele was arguing with a muscular, mocha-skinned man in a bold pin-striped gray suit and gold tie.

He was Adele's height, sported an ultra short Afro, and looked to be somewhere in his midtwenties. It was a toss-up as to what was the most striking feature about the man: his pale green eyes, or his tattoo of a sinister-looking fanged snake that slithered from just below his ear, wrapped around his neck, and then disappeared beneath the collar of a fitted hot pink dress shirt.

Adele threw her hands in the air. "C'mon! Not this again."

"Not what? I was there when he took Logan and left you alone to deal with everything after the stabbing. He's a dick. Weren't you the one who always told me that a good father sets an example for children by treating his baby-mama right?"

"If I was alone, it was because I wanted to be."

"You make it sound like being depressed was some choice you made!"

Adele's mouth clicked shut, and she squirmed at his words.

"When he left, everything changed! You stopped trying and pulled away."

"You're wrong," Adele said simply, her eyes willing him to understand. "Everything changed because of *me* not Landry."

He and Adele were practically nose-to-nose as they quarreled.

At the sound of the back door slamming, two sets of angry eyes swung in Natalie's direction. She had the distinct urge to turn on her heels and run back inside the house, but she held her ground. Wisconsin, Natalie decided, was a distinctly less confrontational place. "Is everything okay back here?" she asked with a steady voice, her own gaze sweeping over Adele to make sure she was all right. She gripped her morning coffee mug a little tighter.

"Yes," Adele piped up, glaring at the man.

"No," he said at the exact same time, looking just as stubborn.

Natalie shifted her weight from one foot to the other. "You're, um, you're not going to actually fight or something, right?" She narrowed her eyes at the stranger. "If this guy is bothering you, Ella, I can call the police."

"As if the cops would come to this address." Adele snorted and turned back to the man. "And fight? You mean physically?" Their eyes met again. Then they burst out laughing, their argument suddenly taking a backseat to a statement they both found especially ridiculous.

Adele pinched him playfully on the shoulder. "Maybe I should smack you around a little, Al. I would if I thought it would make you listen to me." She was clearly joking, but there was still an undercurrent of intensity in her voice.

He rubbed his arm with a faux pout. "I always knew you were secretly violent."

Adele rolled her eyes.

Natalie let out an explosive breath. Why was Adele always scaring the daylights out of her?

"Natalie," Adele began, gesturing for her to come closer, "this is Officer—"

Stuffing his hands in his pants pockets, the man cleared his throat loudly and gave Adele a dirty look. "Ahem."

"I mean, *Detective* Alonzo Rice. But you can call him Al." Adele smoothed over the suit coat that covered the area of solid muscle she'd just pinched. "I still can't believe you got your gold shield. I'm so proud I could burst." Her expression turned a little wistful. "I wish I could have been there when you got it."

This time it was Al's turn to roll his eyes, but it was obvious he was pleased by Adele's statement. "Aww, don't be that way. I texted you a picture."

"I know. I printed it and framed it." Adele sheepishly turned to Natalie. "I'm sorry if we were too loud. Georgia must be fit to be tied." She gave the man a chastising look. "Al was just sharing his feelings about my ex-husband with me. Again."

Al's face darkened. "What he did was—"

Adele patted his chest as she interrupted him. "I know, Al. But it's time for us to both move on. It's not like I didn't let Landry know how I felt about what he did at the time."

A burst of laughter escaped Al, then he winced as he pressed his thighs together, twisting a little in automatic male sympathy. "I hope his balls *still* hurt."

"Let it go, okay?" Adele dropped her voice a little below its normally, soft lilting register and volume. "Please?"

He looked pained for a second, then resigned, as though he was wholly unable to resist Adele's request. He groaned loudly. "Fine."

Natalie watched the interplay with interest. There was obvious affection between Adele and Al, but there wasn't a scintilla of romantic or sexual tension in the way they interacted. In fact, if pressed, Natalie would have said it was closer to the way Adele appeared with Amelia or even Logan. Siblings? There was no way she was old enough to have a grown man for a son, right? She began doing the math in her head.

"Al, this is Natalie Abbott."

The smile slid off Al's face at the mention of Natalie's name, one he clearly knew. He whipped his head back toward Adele. "What the hell, Ella? Is there something you forgot to tell me?"

"Al." Adele's voice was all warning. "You don't need to be more involved than you already are."

"What's going on?" Natalie wondered out loud. Detective Rice wasn't one of the policemen who questioned her about Misty's death or even Josh's murder.

Adele picked up a manila folder that was resting on the wrought-iron table near her. "I asked Al to bring me the police file on Misty's death along with the preliminary autopsy results."

Al crossed his thick arms over his chest, his suit strained at the shoulders. "You lied to me. I can't believe the first time you called me, instead of just texting, in almost a year was to lie to me! You said this Misty woman was the friend of a friend and that you wanted to know what happened."

A single blond eyebrow lifted. "That wasn't a lie."

"Ella!" He angrily scrubbed the top of his head with both hands. "You left off the part about this having to do with the Joshua Phillips murder."

Adele looked regretful but resolute. "It was selfish of me to call you at all, but I don't have anyone else at the NOPD that I trust. Even so, you're not a homicide detective, Al. You didn't have anything to do with Josh's case. This doesn't concern you."

He appeared crushed by her words. "You concern me. I always have your back, Ella! But, what you can't do is trick me when I do."

Ouch. Natalie frowned.

Adele flinched as Al's remark hit home. "You need to trust me, Al. You're going places with your career. I don't want you involved with things that will only hold you back."

"You mean things like you?"

His words were met with pained silence.

Anger bubbled up inside Natalie at the sudden look of poorly veiled hurt that seeped into Adele's face. She was about to say something when Al stepped forward and crushed Ella tightly against him in a hug so fierce it was almost desperate.

Natalie's eyes widened at the unexpected sight.

"Shit, Ella. I'm sorry." Instantly contrite, he seemed to forget that Natalie was even present as he poured his heart out to Adele. "I didn't mean that. You know I didn't. I'm just…" He sighed. "I'm mad at the NOPD. But we're not all against you, no matter what you think. And I'm mad at Landry because…well, he's an asshole. And I'm mad at you because we don't see each other enough. And I wish you would have trusted me enough to tell me the truth. We're supposed to be *tight*."

Adele swallowed a couple of times before speaking. "We are tight." Her voice broke ever so slightly on the last word. "And I'm mad at all those things too. But it's getting better, I promise." She pulled away gently. "You don't have to apologize, Al. What you said is the God's truth. And I do trust you, I just don't trust the NOPD. You know it would be bad for you if folks knew we were still friends."

He looked ready to explode again at her words, but before he could, she added, "But that doesn't mean I'm giving you up. I'm never giving up on you. We'll find a way, okay?"

Relief made Al's entire body relax, though there was still a hint of resentment in his eyes. "Goddamn! I've been waiting ages for you to say that."

Adele chuckled ruefully. "I've made a mess of things, and I'm sorry I made you wait for me to even start to get my shit together." She sat down heavily at the wrought-iron table, her back to both Natalie and Al.

Natalie noticed that Adele's cane was nowhere in sight.

"Ella—" Al began as he glanced worriedly at the file.

"Thanks for the file, Al. Are these copies or should I have this sent back to your house tonight?" It was clear that Adele was done talking about herself.

Al closed his eyes for a few seconds then said, "Copies."

Adele nodded approvingly. "Good. I'll burn this tonight."

He laid a large hand on her shoulder and Adele reached up and grasped it.

"Ella, are we cool?"

Adele gave his hand a squeeze. "We're always cool, Alonzo. Georgia knows where Logan's school pictures are and will give you one inside. You say hi to Latisha for me, and give the kids a kiss. We'll see each other again before New Year's, even if we have to meet out of town to do it safely. Stay safe, all right?"

Still a little dismayed, he nodded. "Okay. You too, Little Mama. Promise me?"

Adele turned and winked over her shoulder at him. "I'll do my best."

He shook his head and groaned. "You're going to open up another shit can of hell-worms aren't you?"

"If I'm lucky."

Al looked skyward for assistance. "Jesus, I'd better buy some extra bullets."

Natalie's eyes widened. *Please let him be kidding.*

"I'll text on Fridays, like always," he promised.

Adele turned back to the file on the table. "Hey, Al, you still owe me twenty bucks."

He chuckled, and his words flowed out like a well-worn answer before Adele had even finished speaking. "I haven't forgotten."

Adele squeezed his hand a final time, then opened the manila folder and began to read.

Al murmured an apology to Natalie for raising his voice earlier and disappeared inside the inn.

"Sorry about that," Adele said once Al was inside. She let out a deep breath and closed the folder, letting a little more of her feelings show on her face now that he was out sight.

"Shaken" was the first word that popped into Natalie's mind. She frowned, confused over an exchange that clearly carried more meaning than she could understand. After hearing snippets of multiple conversations, it was clear that over the last few years, Adele had closed herself off from most of the people who loved her. Even more disturbing was that someone so strong, and who had a solid support system, Landry aside, had still somehow plunged into an emotional free fall. "That was intense."

"Yeah," Adele grunted.

Natalie took a seat across from Adele and set her coffee down. It was too cold to drink now, anyway. Natalie tilted her head up to allow the morning sun to warm her face. She didn't miss the snow in the least. The December breeze was cool but the sun felt wonderful in contrast and she hoped Joshua enjoyed it while he was living here. "You guys seem like you have a…complicated history."

"I'm not sure it's complicated, but it's important to us both." Adele's expression turned thoughtful. "I've known Al since he was thirteen years old, back when I was still a beat cop. I arrested him for running his mama's prostitution earnings back to her pimp."

"You arrested a thirteen-year-old?" It was hard for Natalie to picture Adele, a champion of children, hauling them to jail.

"Hell, yes, I did. He was old enough to already have that hideous gang tattoo, and I wanted him away from that woman…his so-called mother." She sneered and put air quotes around the word. "There was no dad in the picture at all. Al was smart and sensitive and an exceptionally pretty boy, with those big green eyes of his. I was worried his mother would turn him out."

"Wait, you mean sell him for prostitution?"

Wordlessly, Adele nodded.

A wave of disgust swept over Natalie. "Jesus."

"On one hand, she still had her hooks deep into him. He was just a boy. On the other, he was already essentially living on his own and just getting in with a gang from the Calliope Projects."

"So you helped him?"

Adele nodded, her gaze drawing inward as she spoke. "I kept coming around and checking on him. Over and over. I hauled him in for shoplifting, petty theft, vandalism, anything I could, really. Even when I wasn't dragging his butt to the cop shop, I talked to him as often as I could. But I pretty much made zero headway in helping him. He was going to end up dead or in prison. I was sure of it.

"But then his mama was killed, and I spent months doing everything I could to make sure he ended up in a decent home and with a good foster family. I wanted to take him in myself," she admitted quietly. "But I was dating Landry at the time and Landry convinced me that Al needed more supervision than I could provide. In hindsight, he wasn't wrong, I guess. But…" Her eyebrows drew together. "I would have made it work somehow."

Natalie felt a surge of kinship with Al. No matter what Adele said to the contrary, Landry was definitely a dick.

"Al's foster parents lived in another part of town, which got him away from the project and the gang, and they made sure he attended school. I helped with that," she paused, a little lost in a memory, the corner of her mouth quirked upward. "It proved nearly impossible for a while, but I never quit, and eventually he came around. Over the years we got close." Then her face seemed to light from within. "I couldn't believe it when he ended up enrolling in the police academy."

Natalie couldn't help but smile at the pride in Adele's voice.

Then Adele glanced back at Natalie with a look of such openness that it made Natalie's heart twist. "Along with Amelia, I have a brother of my own, but we were never very close. Different interests, I guess. But with Al...it was like we had an instant connection. Knowing him changed my life, and he's one of the reasons I wanted to work in the Juvenile Division in the first place."

Still, Natalie couldn't help but feel a little protective of Adele's feelings. "He hurt your feelings today with what he said."

"Maybe a little," Adele acknowledged reluctantly. "He hasn't forgiven me for pulling away from him after I left the force." Her nostrils flared. "But I didn't have a choice. I was covered in stink and I didn't want it on him. He's a good cop that shouldn't suffer because of me."

Natalie's heart broke a little. Adele had made choices that were best for everyone but herself.

"He misses you."

"I know," Adele replied gravely. "Like I said, I messed up. Do you remember when I said I was worried about what my family would do to Landry when he moved to Baton Rouge and took Logan with him?"

Natalie nodded and leaned forward a little in her seat.

"I was including Al in that statement. Between him and Amelia, I'm actually surprised Landry is still breathing." Adele suddenly seemed to realize that she'd been talking for an uncharacteristically long stretch. A flush stained her cheeks. "Anyway, enough with my boring history, right?"

"Ella, there's *nothing* about you that I find boring."

Adele smiled and looked a little flustered as she focused on the file in front of her.

Armed with new insight, Natalie felt like she knew Adele that much better. "Josh and I, we reminded you of you and Al?"

The look on Adele's face told Natalie she was right. "I take all my cases personally." Adele's face softened. "But, yeah, you and Josh were... are special."

So are you.

Adele began to read. "Misty's death is being ruled accidental." She flipped the page. "A diacetylmorphine overdose leading to respiratory failure."

"What's dia-whatever?"

"Smack. You know, heroin."

Natalie shivered, the image of Misty with that needle sticking out of her arm embedded in her brain. "God. How horrible."

"Mmm hmm…and there was more than enough in her system to kill her." Lines formed on Adele's forehead as she continued to skim the report. "Wow. Seven hundred milligrams."

Adele glanced up from the page, suddenly angry. "That's way too high a dose for anything to be accidental unless she had a really high tolerance, which wouldn't be unusual for an active junkie. Still, with a dosage like that, I can't believe NOPD is ruling this accidental so quickly," she said disgustedly. "Unless the final tox screens show something different, no one will ever look at this case again."

Natalie's frustration with the NOPD came rushing back with a vengeance. "They took one look at her track marks and crappy house and didn't care what had happened." She cocked her head curiously. "But did you expect to see something else in the report?"

Adele leaned back in her chair and slowly shook her head. "I didn't know what to expect. I guess I was just hoping for a clear-cut answer. And this doesn't give us one. When Misty spoke with you, and she said she was getting her life together, did you take that to mean she was clean?"

Was it only a few days ago that she'd spoken to Misty? So much had happened that it already felt like ages. "I guess so. She seemed really scared but sort of positive too. She was trying to do the right thing. She didn't seem suicidal to me."

With a puzzled huff, Adele refocused on the pages in her hands. "Did she mention a boyfriend?"

"You mean, Josh? Well, yeah."

"No, no, a boyfriend now. Someone she was living with. The notes say, and I quote, 'a tweaker named Kurt Mosley.' Apparently the police questioned him."

Natalie shook her head. Even now, it was hard to imagine Misty with anyone but her brother. They'd been joined at the hip as goofy teenagers. "No. Nothing. But, Ella, Misty can't help us now. So how does any of this get us closer to finding out who killed Josh?"

Adele closed the file and pulled her blue cardigan sweater closer around her body to ward off the breeze. "Except for the murderer, Misty was the last and only person who we're certain saw what happened to Josh. Even dead, she's still the best resource we have. Besides, maybe she told the current boyfriend something about that night that she didn't tell you."

Both women stood, and Adele began to walk. "Natalie, go grab your coat and let's see what we can find out, okay?"

"Ella?" Natalie reached out a hand and stopped Adele. "What about Crisco? Misty said he was passed out that night, but maybe he really did hear something."

Adele stopped and gave Natalie a curious look. "You don't know?"

"Know what?"

"I always assumed you kept up with him because of your brother."

Natalie made a face. "I did until the charges against him were dropped. After that I tried to forget everything about New Orleans so I wouldn't lose my mind."

Adele sighed unhappily. "Crisco's dead. He got crazy drunk one time too many and ended up facedown in a ditch with a few inches of water in it. He drowned about three months after being released from custody."

Natalie's mouth dropped open. "Holy crap. What about Morrell? Do you think he made good on his promise to hurt Crisco if he recanted his confession?"

"I talked to the medical examiner myself. The death was accidental. No one saw Crisco fall, but there were plenty of witnesses who saw him that same day and in the area, drinking himself into his typical stupor. There was nothing else unusual about his body except that he had advanced cirrhosis. Considering his alcohol intake that wasn't a shock."

Natalie blanched and sucked in a breath between clenched teeth. "So Misty is another accidental death surrounding Josh's murder? I know it's years after the fact, but this seems…" She searched for the right word.

"Off?"

Natalie nodded warily, her apprehension multiplying.

"I know."

"Are alarm bells starting to go off in your head too?"

Adele's lips formed a grim line. "Alarm bells have been going off in my head since the day you showed up at my inn." She wound her arm around Natalie's, grinning a little when Natalie encouraged her with a smile and subtle shift of her body to lean on her for support as she walked without the cane. "C'mon. Let's go meet Kurt Mosley."

"Ella?"

"Hmm?"

"What exactly is a tweaker?"

CHAPTER ELEVEN

It was just past eight p.m. when Adele shut off the ignition of her silver Jeep Cherokee on the block behind Misty's house. She'd changed her mind about going to see Misty's boyfriend that morning. Instead, she decided to wait until dark.

"I will not wait in the car!"

"Natalie, please."

"No. Why did you bring me here if I was only going to sit outside?"

That was a good question, and Adele hated the simple answer. *Because I wanted to spend more time with you.* "I wasn't thinking when I asked you along." When it came to Josh's case Adele realized she'd been treating Natalie like a work partner, someone who would know how to handle herself if things got messy. That wasn't fair or safe.

Adele shifted in her seat to face Natalie. "I'm not sure if Kurt Mosley is dangerous. I'm trained to handle dangerous people. You're not."

"Be that as it may, I'm still coming with you."

Adele raised an eyebrow. Apparently, Natalie was obstinate when she wanted to be. "If Kurt isn't home, I fully intend to break into Misty's house and see if I can find any evidence that will help us. That's why I decided to wait until dark."

"Still coming with you," Natalie said defiantly. She glanced up and down the street warily. "And, honestly, isn't sitting in the car in this dodgy neighborhood at night *more* dangerous than coming with you?"

Adele faced forward and looked out at the tired-looking street and the somewhat rough-looking residents. She gripped the steering wheel tightly. Natalie had a point. Time for the big guns. "Breaking and entering can get you ten years in prison in the state of Louisiana. You'd be someone's prison bitch inside a week."

Natalie thought for a moment, her smile nearly held in check. "But if I get caught, you got caught too." Her eyes didn't waiver when they met Adele's. "You'd help me in prison so that I wouldn't end up someone's bitch."

Adele's voice dropped to a frustrated growl. She intended to flat-out lie. She intended to say that if Natalie insisted on doing this, it was every woman for herself. Instead, what came out was, "How do you know you wouldn't be *my* bitch?"

The words shocked them both. The silence in the car was deafening.

Natalie's tongue darted out as she slowly licked her lips and swallowed. Her voice was suddenly husky, but crystal clear in the quiet car. "How do you know that I'd mind?"

Heart pounding and unexpectedly aroused, it was Adele who looked away first. She shifted awkwardly in her seat, torn between wishing she could shove her words back into her mouth and being desperately intrigued by Natalie's answer.

Natalie eyed Adele for a long moment before she sighed. "Ella, once I made the decision to stay in New Orleans to try to find Josh's killer, I was a hundred percent committed. Short of intentionally hurting someone, I'll do whatever it takes to see this through to the end. Besides, isn't it illegal for me to sit in this car and act as your getaway driver too? Aren't we at least accomplices at this point?"

Goddamned logical professors with pretty blue eyes and smoky voices. "Well, yes, but you wouldn't—"

"Please, can you be finished fighting me on this?"

"Do I have a choice?"

"Not really. I'll just follow you anyway."

Adele groaned, believing the stubborn woman would do exactly that. "Okay, fine. But you do *everything* I say."

Solemnly, Natalie nodded. "Everything."

"I'm not kidding." And she wasn't. She actually felt a little panicky at the mere possibility of Natalie somehow getting hurt. Nobody knew better than Adele how a situation could go from bad to deadly in a matter of seconds. "I will literally use my cuffs on you." Adele's cheeks turned beet red at her own words as a stunningly sexy image of Natalie penetrated her brain without her permission.

"As long as you're not sending me away, it's a deal." Natalie tilted her head to the side. "Are you okay?"

"Yes." Adele scrubbed her face with one hand. She cast about for a neutral subject. "You didn't tell me Misty lived in the Tremé, although that doesn't excuse me for not noticing the street and block in the police report."

"Is that important?"

"Jay Morrell's always been assigned to Tremé. Still is. Only now he's a sergeant here." *And if he catches us doing something illegal and tries to lay a hand on either of us, this night is going to end in the emergency room.* "I heard from Al that Morrell got promoted about a year ago."

"Promoted?" Natalie blinked owlishly. "How can that be? Wasn't he one of the cops who lost his job after the investigation?"

"He was exonerated." Even now when Adele thought of the good men who'd been forced out of the NOPD, and the fact that Officer Morrell had survived the nuclear winter like the proverbial roach that he was, fury surged through her.

Natalie's mouth opened and closed helplessly. "Wh-what? How? Argh! *Bullshit!*"

"My thoughts exactly." Adele glanced down the street, every part of her itching with nervous energy as she contemplated what answers might lay inside Misty's tiny rental house. "Let's go. Stay right behind me."

Natalie nodded, and they both exited the car.

The street was dark but surprisingly loud. Music of all genres poured out of the houses and from passing cars, the vehicles threatening to shake apart from the vibrating bass. Raised voices, some laughing and some yelling, slamming doors, and barking dogs made the block feel as though it pulsed with life as they threaded their way between the houses.

Adele gripped her cane tightly, hoping not to have to use it on one of the barking dogs that sounded terrifyingly close. She peered inside one of Misty's side windows, thankful her fellow residents seemed to eschew curtains and ignore their plantation shutters, and unsure whether or not she was hoping to find Kurt Mosley at home.

But there was a man inside the house, wearing nothing but a pair of ratty boxer shorts. He gave off a mangy vibe that some women actually liked, and Adele could never truly understand, and had the body of a hardcore marathon runner.

Beer bottle in hand, he tore the room apart, obviously searching for something. Thankfully, he looked relatively harmless, or at least without a place to hide a weapon on his body.

Adele narrowed her eyes. *Hoped he was gone*, she decided with a distinct sense of disappointment. "Okay, no burglary tonight."

Natalie nodded, looking relieved and just a little bit guilty for even contemplating it. "What now?"

Adele shrugged. "Now we knock on the door." Before Natalie could ask anything else, Adele headed toward the front steps, only lightly leaning on her cane.

She gave the door several *very* firm knocks with her closed fist.

"What are you doing?" Natalie hissed. "This isn't a raid."

Adele blinked, not understanding what the problem was until she remembered that regular, non-law enforcement people didn't bang on the door of someone's home. "Sorry."

The porch light flicked on and when the door swung open, Kurt Mosley's glassy-eyed expression swiftly changed from furious to pleased, especially when his eyes lit on Natalie. His movements were lethargic and just this side of sloppy. He hiccupped. "Well, hel-*lo*."

Adele rolled her eyes. She hated dealing with drunks. "Aw, crap."

"Kurt Mosley?" Natalie inquired politely.

The man appeared to be in his early twenties and maybe five foot nine. His tangled rust-colored hair was a few inches too long to be stylish, and he was perilously thin with freckles covering every inch of exposed skin. He openly leered at Natalie and pulled an ugly purple afghan he had wrapped around his shoulders a little closer. "Who's askin', honey?"

"I'll take that as a yes." Adele abruptly inserted herself between Natalie and Kurt. "We're friends of Misty and would like to ask you a few questions." She tacked on an unconvincing, "okay?" to make it sound a bit more like she was asking and not ordering.

Kurt gave Adele a disgusted look. "Hell, no. I'm done talkin' to cops. You assholes already tore the place apart, and now I can't find a goddamned thing!"

He was in the process of closing his door when Adele inserted her cane between the door and the frame. She scowled and did her best not to grind her teeth. She might as well have a neon sign around her neck that said cop. "I'm not with the NOPD."

Natalie stuck her head around Adele's shoulder to speak. She smiled brightly, and Kurt instantly mirrored her. "We're not the police, I promise. As my friend said, we're friends of Misty."

Kurt reluctantly opened the door fully and then moved forward out of his doorway. He effectively backed them to the limit of the tiny porch, his anxious stare darting between the women and lingering on the scar on Adele's face before moving suspiciously out to the street beyond them. "Since when?"

Adele's pulse began to climb. *He's too close.*

"For years. Since she knew my brother Josh."

His eyes suddenly overflowed with anger and his mild-looking face contorted into something truly scary. "The dead boyfriend? Christ, I'm so sick of him," he wailed, swinging his arms so wildly that beer sloshed over his hand, the pungent scent filling the air. "Misty was always talking about him. Josh was so talented on the clarinet. Josh was so nice! Josh was so funny!" he mimicked in a falsetto voice. It was obvious that he'd forgotten that the women hadn't even introduced themselves yet.

Natalie stiffened.

With more bravado than she felt, Adele gave Kurt a look of warning that must have registered even in his intoxicated state. He quickly backed up half a step, giving her enough space to breathe. "She talked about the night Josh died?" Adele prompted, her emotions swingy wildly as she simultaneously reveled in an unexpected surge of excitement over the hunt and worried that she wouldn't be able to defend herself and Natalie if needed.

"No," he corrected harshly. "She *cried* 'bout that night, but never talked about it."

Like a balloon with a pinprick, Adele deflated, but did her best not to show it. She turned up the collar when a cool breeze cut through the fabric of her jacket. "Not anything?"

Seemingly unconcerned with the brisk wind, a barefooted Kurt chugged his last few sips of beer, then unceremoniously let the bottle fall from his limp hand. It cracked when it hit the porch, then rolled away and onto a soft patch of grass. "Just that he got hurt and died." He eagerly stepped sideways to get a better look at Natalie.

Adele rolled her eyes, but couldn't exactly blame the guy. Natalie was worth a second and third look.

"You're Natalie, right? The lady who was coming down to visit Misty from someplace up north? Iowa or somewhere, right?"

Adele didn't quite manage to suppress a snicker at Natalie being called "the lady," as though she was ancient. But more importantly, Kurt's use of the word visit implied he didn't know the real reason Natalie was here. Misty hadn't told him about her plan to go to the police.

Natalie gave him a small smile and covertly nudged Adele with her shoulder. "Close enough."

Kurt blinked with exaggerated slowness. "The police were askin' after you."

Adele's gaze sharpened. "What did they want?"

Kurt waved a dismissive hand. "You know, some stupid bullshit like always. How did Natalie know Misty? Was anythin' out of place or missing? Was she here to bring Misty drugs? Blah, blah, blah." He snorted loudly. "Like they even have drugs on goat farms or whatever the fuck they have in Iowa."

He tugged up his drooping boxer shorts with one hand, his prominent hipbones only barely holding them up. "Hey, you two wanna come in for a beer? We've got a few more. And if we run out, when Misty gets home I can—" Then his bloodshot eyes filled with tears. "Aww, shit." He hiccupped again. "Never mind."

Kurt was a hot mess, but that didn't keep Adele from experiencing a pang deep in her chest at the sight of his unshed tears.

"Umm..." Natalie inched even closer to Adele, warming her back. Several teenagers who were walking down the sidewalk a dozen feet away had stopped and were now openly eavesdropping on their conversation. She whispered into Adele's ear. "Should we ask to go inside instead of having this conversation on the porch?"

Adele turned her head slightly and gave Natalie a dubious look. She muttered from the side of her mouth. "I don't want to be stuck in the house with him, do you?"

Kurt had gone from talking to them to muttering despondently to himself. He fluctuated wildly between fury and gut-wrenching sadness.

Natalie shivered against her back.

"Good point."

Adele turned and pointed at the teens on the sidewalk and without an ounce of hesitation barked, "Beat it. Now!"

After a few nasty comments, that included some profanity so uniquely filthy that Adele was sure she'd be explaining it to Natalie later, the teens lost interest and slowly strolled away, hurling insults as they left. Natalie's words tickled Adele's ear.

"Do you want to come back when Kurt's sober?"

"Let's not give up yet," Adele muttered quietly. Though he was clearly inebriated, other than being rail thin and a bit unkempt, Kurt didn't seem to have any of the obvious signs of being a meth addict. Adele still hoped to get some useful information out of him. She consciously softened her demeanor. "Listen, Kurt—"

"If you haven't heard...Misty's dead." His voice was flat and he sounded utterly lost. "It doesn't seem real."

Natalie sucked in a ragged breath.

"We heard," Adele said softly, realizing that if the police had explained that it was Natalie who found Misty's body, Kurt was too drunk to remember it. "It's terrible, and we're truly sorry."

Suddenly, Kurt was angry again and his cheeks turned a splotchy red. "She didn't kill herself!"

The astoundingly livid look on his face alone caused Natalie to take a giant step backward. He was about to explode.

Adele reached one open hand back and Natalie grasped it. She squeezed it firmly, trying to assure Natalie that things were okay even though Adele could feel her own uneasiness coiling up within her like a snake that wanted to be free from its cage. And, Natalie, she was sure, was only seconds from bolting.

Adele willed her voice to remain calm and steady. "How can you be sure, Kurt?"

"What kind of stupid question is that? I see...I saw her every single day." He grabbed a tuft of his hair in each hand and pulled down as though his head might pop off if not for his hold. "I would know if she wanted to die!"

"What about the drugs she was taking?" Natalie asked, joining Adele in her fishing expedition.

"What drugs? She's been clean for more than six months. Me too." Defensive, he let go of his hair, which stayed sticking out and gave him a Bozo the Clown-like hairstyle. He held up two hands as if to ward off Adele. "Yeah, okay, I've fallen off the wagon a couple of times, but the little bit of smack the cops found here wasn't mine. I swear! We used everything we had months ago." He grunted loudly. "Trust me, we didn't leave anythin' behind."

Adele kept her voice light, but interested. "If there were drugs here with Misty when the police came, why weren't you arrested? Are you sure the drugs weren't yours?"

Kurt shook his head forcefully. "No way, man! I stay here sometimes, but this isn't my place." He shrugged, seemingly as surprised as Adele. "So the cops didn't arrest me. They said the drugs were Misty's."

"But they weren't?" Adele prodded a bit more urgently. She'd learned over the years that it was okay to make someone she was interviewing repeat himself again and again. It was amazing how often a slight change in her wording could yield a completely different answer.

"No!" His eyes widened and he looked confused. "I mean, I don't think so. I mean, no. She didn't do that stuff anymore."

With a final squeeze, Adele let go of Natalie's hand, noting that Natalie remained practically glued to her back. "Did Misty keep a diary or journal?"

He laughed. "You mean one of those things with a lock and a tiny key that stupid middle school-age girls have? No way."

"That's not accurate at all!" Natalie sounded truly and unaccountably upset. "Some highly literate and intelligent adults—"

"Natalie," Adele muttered under her breath harshly enough that Natalie got the message and clamped her mouth shut. "Kurt, did Misty have any enemies?"

"You mean who'd want to murder her?" Kurt clarified brutally as he glared.

Adele nodded.

His face relaxed and he stumbled a little as he moved back into the doorway and leaned heavily against it. "Yeah. Totally."

Adele did a double take. That wasn't the answer she expected.

Kurt grinned with sudden admiration. "Oh, Misty screwed more than one dealer out of product or money over the years. And screwed 'em hard. She knew just how to freakin' do it, too. Had it down to an art form. And she moved every few months because of it. But she could never leave town." His smile fell away and his stare grew distant. "She loved the city too much to let it go, even though…even though for years it was killin' her."

He gazed longingly back inside the house…to where the beer was.

He doesn't seem violent, Adele told herself. *He's just a drunken idiot. She'll be okay.* Making a split-second decision, she began to shift from one foot to the next. She made a face then moaned loudly.

Puzzled, Natalie asked, "Are you okay?"

"No," Adele whimpered and pressed her thighs together as she twisted like a miserable four-year-old in line at a ladies' room. "I have to go to the bathroom."

"What?" Natalie asked incredulously, looking at Adele as though she didn't believe what she was hearing. "Now?"

"*Now.*" Adele's voice was filled with urgency. "I'm not kidding." She smiled pleadingly at Kurt. "Would you mind—?"

"Huh?" He looked at Adele, his ginger brows heavily furrowed.

"Thank you!" Adele gushed, not giving him a chance to say more. "Don't worry, I'll find the bathroom myself." She swept past him as though going into the house had been entirely his idea in the first place.

"What the—?" Kurt muttered after her, but didn't follow. Adele heard Natalie pick up the ball by enthusiastically asking Kurt about his favorite beer. She figured she had two minutes before he would come in search of her, or try to kiss Natalie, or figure out that he had no chance in hell with Natalie and get bored. She began counting in her head so she wouldn't lose track of the time. *One Mississippi. Two Mississippi.*

Apparently Kurt wasn't much of a housekeeper. The room smelled sour and like rotten food. Adele tried not to gag. Guiltily, she headed straight to the bedroom in the back the house. She knew Natalie was afraid and now she'd gone and left her alone with a drunken stranger. But this might be her only chance to look for anything Misty could have left behind. Something where Misty might have mentioned more about what happened the night of Josh's death.

Adele opened and closed the drawers quickly and quietly, finding nothing but wrinkled clothing and junky trinkets. "Seventy-five Mississippi," she whispered, moving from place to place and cursing her bad leg. "Shit!" She opened the closet door and had to kick the clothes off her feet as they fell off the top shelf.

She did a quick sweep of the living room only to come up empty. *One-twenty Mississippi,* she finished in the bathroom, frowning when nothing turned up there either. Adele flushed the toilet and headed back outside as quickly as her cane would allow.

Adele returned to the porch to find that Natalie had stepped closer to Kurt and was smiling coyly at him. Natalie hung on his every word.

He appeared as enchanted as a moonstruck cow.

"Whew!" Adele said, fanning herself. "That was close. I'm so embarrassed. Kurt, thank you *so much*. I wouldn't have made it to a gas station."

Natalie instantly sighed in relief and backed away from Kurt, her expression shifting from interested to wary (tinged with grossed-out) in the blink of an eye.

Kurt didn't appear happy at the interruption.

Knowing that, at most, they had a moment or two more of his attention, Adele hurriedly cut to the chase. "What did Misty say about the night Josh died again?"

The second his face turned to stone, Adele knew their discussion was over. "I don't want to talk about him anymore!" And this time Kurt's invitation was solely aimed at Natalie. "Are you coming in for a drink or what?"

"No, thank—"

The slamming door interrupted Natalie's words.

* * *

Natalie and Adele settled comfortably on the sofa in Adele's living room. Feeling grungy after talking to Kurt, both women had taken hot showers. Natalie had opted to change into sweats and a long-sleeved T-shirt, while Adele had changed into yoga pants and a thin zip-up-the-front hoodie.

A small fire lit the room and provided welcome warmth on the cool night. Georgia was long gone for the evening, and the old Creole home seemed cavernous and quiet with just the two of them inside.

Adele gingerly tucked her legs up underneath her, and next to her Natalie copied the relaxed pose. They sat close to one another, but not so close that they were touching. "I'm not sure that talking to Kurt helped very much," Natalie began.

"Not much," Adele agreed. She stared at the fire, lost in its golden glow. "It's hard to believe that Misty told Kurt all those things about Josh, but then completely omitted anything about the night he was killed, don't you think?"

Natalie shrugged helplessly. "I have no idea. My family never talks about Josh. I tried to when I first came home from New Orleans after his death and was completely shut down. I guess it's as simple as it hurts and so we ignore that he's really gone for good. It's like he's just off to college or something, and we pretend to forget about the fact that he's never coming home again."

Heartsick, Adele shifted to face Natalie, her face half cast in dark shadow. "I wanted to find him. I'm so sor—"

"No more apologies, Ella. I told you that already. Nothing that happened was your fault. And I didn't mention my screwed-up family's reaction to Josh's death so you'd feel guilty. I mentioned it because I don't think I'm the right person to ask what a normal reaction to any of this should be," she said, making air quotes around normal before she shuddered and wrapped her arms around herself in comfort.

Adele shifted and leaned sideways so she could bump her shoulder against Natalie's. Natalie smelled like Ivory Soap, and Adele inhaled the clean scent with pleasure. "You could talk about him to me, if you like. About Josh, I mean. Anytime."

Natalie's face brightened at the offer. "That would be…great. I'd love that, Ella."

"Me too."

Natalie's warmly indulgent smile caused Adele's insides to melt. She wondered self-consciously if some of the budding affection she felt for the professor was showing plainly on her face. When Natalie's grin grew, she was certain she'd been found out, but after another deep look into intense, soulful blue eyes she found herself unable to care.

Natalie had swept her hair up into a loose ponytail and the light from the fireplace brought out her reddish highlights. Adele stared. Mesmerized like a treasure hunter gazing directly into a pot of gold, Adele lifted her hand to reach out and touch it before she caught herself and let her hand fall awkwardly to the back of the sofa.

The silence between them grew. Adele tore her gaze away from Natalie long enough for her mind to replay the events of the evening. "Six months isn't very long when it comes to beating heroin, and Kurt waffled pretty quickly when it came to whether the drugs the police found were Misty's. Misty was scared and worried about going to the cops about Josh. If she was afraid of being arrested, that might have been enough to send her into a tailspin and start her using again."

Natalie scrunched up her face. "Do you really believe that?"

Points for perceptiveness. "My gut tells me no. I think by the time Misty got up the nerve to call you, she'd already made her decision to go forward. Meaning, most of her soul-searching would have already happened."

Adele absently picked at the back of the sofa as she spoke. "And I don't believe a drug dealer showed up out of pure coincidence on the day you were to arrive and managed to inject Misty with a fatal dose of heroin all while not leaving a mark on her. Dealers can be ruthless, and sometimes they kill on a whim. But getting away with this sort of murder would require planning and smarts. It doesn't make sense to waste this much effort on a petty mule or user, even if she was filching a little product. Bullets are cheap and plentiful, and a knife in the kidney is free."

Adele hated to say the next part, even though it was the truth. "Short of a witness coming out of the woodwork, I don't think we're going to ever know what happened to Misty on her last day."

Natalie wrung her hands. "Should I have told her to just forget what she saw the night Josh was killed and move on with her life?" she asked a little desperately. "I encouraged her even when she was terrified."

Adele's chest twisted with sympathy. She was intimately aware of the damage that regret could do. "Don't even go there."

Natalie swallowed hard. "But—"

Adele reached out and gently squeezed Natalie's arm. "Just don't."

Natalie pinched the bridge of her nose and nodded. "Okay. I'll try."

Adele didn't like the guilty set of Natalie's shoulders so she drew her attention to something else. "Our next step tomorrow is tracking down Billy Hobson, Morrell's rookie partner at the time of Josh's murder. If we can't work backward from Misty, we'll work forward from that night."

Still appearing as if at least a portion of the weight of the world was on her shoulders, Natalie allowed herself to be distracted. "Is he still Morrell's partner?"

Adele didn't bother to remove her hand from Natalie's arm. She liked it right where it was. "He quit the force not long after the PIB investigation went into full swing. I have no idea why and no idea where he is today. But we're going to use one of the best tools I had at my disposal as a cop to find him."

Curious, Natalie leaned forward a little. "Informants?"

"Google."

Natalie grudgingly chuckled. "*That* I can actually help you with. And that reminds me, I, uh, I'm sorry I nearly jumped off the porch tonight. I don't much like drunks. They're unpredictable, and they scare me. Thank goodness he wasn't actually on drugs. I think I underestimated how frightening that would be. Next time you tell me to wait in the car, I'll take it under advisement."

"Advisement?" The corner of Adele's mouth quirked.

Natalie lifted an eyebrow. "You don't want me to lie about it, do you? For some reason, on this trip I'm finding myself tired of doing what I *should* do and opting for what I *want* to do instead."

"Mmm…sounds like an intoxicating sort of freedom."

"That's the problem. It is."

Adele untucked her bad leg from beneath her and stretched it out with a groan. If it hadn't been so late she'd have taken a long hot soak in the tub to relieve some soreness instead of a shower. "S'okay, about being spooked by drunks, you know. They scare me too."

"You didn't look scared."

"I was."

"I seem to recall you putting yourself between Kurt and me almost from the second he opened the door."

"Well," Adele admitted, "he was obviously smitten the moment he laid eyes on you. As far as drunks go, he really wasn't very freaky, which is why I left you alone for two minutes. I'm sorry about that, and I swear I wouldn't have if I believed you were in danger."

"You're not a bad actress." Natalie shook her head in disbelief. "For a minute I believed we were going to have to leave so you could find a restroom!"

Adele shrugged one shoulder. "I needed to get inside that house. But the whole evening still felt…it was odd." She shook her head. "It's been a while since I've questioned anyone, you know?"

Natalie nodded.

"Just talking to him, it made me excited, but uneasy too. I dunno. I suppose I'm rusty."

"You knew just what to ask, Ella. It's obvious to me that you're so very good at investigating, whether you're actually a detective or not. But maybe you're a little gun-shy?" Natalie laid her free hand on top of the one resting on her arm. "You'd have every right to be."

"Don't you mean knife-shy?" Adele joked weakly, regretting her words as they left her mouth.

Natalie didn't even crack a smile. "So why did you step between Kurt and me?"

Adele shifted uneasily and focused on their touching hands. "I didn't plan it. I just did it. Old habits, I guess." Her eyes flicked sideways. "Did it bother you?"

"The only thing that bothered me is that I didn't want *either* of us to get hurt."

Adele wrinkled her nose. "I might be rusty, but I'm not *that* rusty. But thanks for making me sound all chivalrous."

"I live to be the damsel in distress," Natalie deadpanned.

Adele laughed. "You were perfect. You distracted Kurt long enough for me to do what I needed to do even if the results were less than spectacular." She recalled how she'd told herself she couldn't think of Natalie as a real partner because she hadn't been trained as a cop. That, Adele realized, was all wrong. "Besides, we're a team in this…I gotta watch out for my partner, right?"

Natalie nodded enthusiastically. "So long as it's okay for me to do the same."

"Then that's how we roll…together. And by together, I mean that I hate searching for things on the Internet so tomorrow you can pick up my slack in that department."

Natalie laughed again. "Deal."

They both yawned, but neither wanted to be the one to officially put the long day to bed.

Natalie glanced down at Adele's extended leg and her cane, which was leaning against the sofa. Then she let her gaze trail up a slender leg encased in black yoga pants, not stopping until she reached her hip.

Adele felt Natalie's eyes on her as though they were fingers brushing her skin. Her pulse quickened.

"I hope this doesn't sound creepy, but if you'd like, I could massage your leg. My grandfather had terrible arthritis, especially in his shoulders, and my grandma showed me how to give a great backrub to help ease his pain. This wouldn't be too different."

It was a bold offer and Adele leapt at it. "Yes!" she said a little too loudly. "I mean, are you sure? Where…I…it might be awkward. You'd need to rub my thigh up high, near my hipbone." She forced herself to shut up so Natalie could absorb her words.

"I'm sure." Natalie smiled kindly and nibbled on her lower lip. "Do you have oil or lotion or—"

Adele nodded, her temperature rising so quickly she felt a little dizzy. "My God, the fire is too hot, right? I think it is. Yes. Hot." The words tumbled out in a rush leaving Natalie staring at her…dumbfounded. Adele stood and jammed the fireplace poker into the flames and separated a few small logs.

Dammit. That wasn't embarrassing at all. The temperature is the same as it was five minutes ago when we were both chilled! "Umm…I'll put on some loose shorts and get the massage oil." She hoped the oil didn't have an expiration date because she had no idea how old the bottle was. Okay, that was a lie. She knew exactly how old it was. The massage therapist from her physical therapy program, a tiny woman who was part healing fairy and part Nazi torture queen, had given it to her the day before she'd quit in a fit of anger, and fear, and self-pity. And she hadn't used it since.

With the tips of her ears still burning bright red, Adele quickly excused herself, but stopped only a few feet later. "Are you sure you—?"

Natalie blew out a frustrated breath. "Go!" She made a shooing motion with her hands, but it was also obvious she was holding in a smile. "Get the oil. Neither one of us is getting any younger, and yes, I'm sure."

Adele nearly tripped on her own feet as she made her way into her bedroom. After standing in the middle of the dark room for a full minute, not knowing what to do, she unzipped her gray hoodie and tossed it on the bed, leaving herself in a pale green tank top.

She brought the back of her hand to her forehead and felt the heat. She was already sweating, but at least in less clothing she'd reduce the chance of spontaneous combustion. Adele wiggled quickly into a different pair of underwear, and slid on a pair of loose, navy blue jersey shorts that were perfect to sleep in or for times when she needed to feel ultra cozy. Her clothes from Amelia's were undeniably beautiful, but not the best for lounging around the house.

Adele ran a hand over her thigh. Thank God she'd shaved her legs that morning.

Grabbing an old towel and blanket from the closet and the bottle of massage oil from the very back of her nightstand drawer, she padded softly back into the living room, shoulders straight, chin high. Not meeting Natalie's curious gaze, she spread out the soft blanket, then the towel on the floor between the sofa and the fireplace. "It, um, it will probably help if I'm stretched out when you do this." She finally dared to turn around, knowing her cheeks were as red as the embers in the fireplace. "Is the floor okay?"

"Of course," Natalie said distractedly, taking the oil with a hand that Adele was sure held a tiny tremor. Natalie knelt on the blanket and sat back on her heels as she patiently waited.

Adele situated herself on her back on the floor, positioning her bad leg on the towel and doing her best to relax. She stared at the ceiling, closing her eyes as she heard the lotion bottle top pop open and the sound of the liquid squirting. She expected to feel it hit her thigh in a cold rush, and when it didn't, she opened her eyes in time to see Natalie warming the oil on her hands, a thoughtful look on her face.

"Ready?" Natalie said, obviously doing her best to hold in a smile at Adele's nervousness.

"Sure," Adele said nonchalantly, forcing her fists to unclench. What was making her ready to jump out of her own skin wasn't the fact that she had a crush on Natalie. She was honest enough with herself to admit that was true, and handle it, even if it did make her act like a gangly teenager all over again. It was the mere idea of Natalie's hands on her after feeling so alone for so long. The very thought made even a simple massage seem so intensely personal. And, okay, it was the crush too.

Not reacting to Adele's little jump when she first touched her, Natalie drew her glistening palms up Adele's calf just past her knee, and midway up her thigh, applying steady, light pressure in order to spread the oil.

Adele's eyes fluttered closed at the tender touch. "Jesus Christ."

Natalie froze. "Everything okay?"

"Y-y—" Adele cleared her throat. "Yes. Fine."

"Okay." Applying more oil Natalie circled the sensitive skin on the back of Adele's knee and gently worked her hands up Adele's thigh, using her thumbs to press deeply along the muscle in slow, even strokes.

After a few minutes Adele began to relax. "This feels," her voice had dropped an octave without her permission, "*really* good, Natalie." She laughed at the hitch in her voice. "Like scary good."

"I've seen how you're hurting, and I've been itching to do something about it for days." Natalie ducked her head, her hands never stopping their soothing rhythm. "But I've held back. I…well, after I told you about my former girlfriend, I didn't want you to be uncomfortable or worry that I was hitting on you."

Disappointment. That's what she felt. Adele found herself actually disappointed that Natalie wasn't hitting on her. It was too bad too, because if Natalie were hitting on her, this would be a spectacular way to do it.

She craned her neck up to look Natalie in the eyes. "I don't think that. And you don't make me uncomfortable." And that was true except when Natalie smiled at her just so, making her heart squeeze tight in her chest. "You don't have to worry."

The strange look on Natalie's face was indecipherable, and Adele let her head fall back to the blanket, confused. Had she said something wrong?

Natalie frowned at the tightness in Adele's leg and added a bit more pressure. "Can I ask you something?"

"Of course."

"What exactly happened? I-I know you were stabbed. But what's wrong with your leg?"

Adele sighed. She was hoping Natalie wouldn't ask her anything to make her embarrass herself again more than she already had, but it appeared that tonight she was having no such luck.

"The blade was really long and went in near my hipbone. The crazy woman actually twisted it and tried to do as much damage as possible. It sliced through my ligaments and nerves and my iliac artery. I'd lost about forty percent of the blood in my body before I made it to the emergency room."

Natalie's strong hands stopped, but after a deep, shaky breath, the massage continued again, her thumbs edging slightly higher.

"I spent about three weeks in the hospital. The plastic surgeon did his best on the scar on my face the morning after I hit the ER. But within a couple of days, I got a wicked infection from the stabbing. Turns out the knife was not only a little rusty, but it had been recently used to cut raw meat."

Adele decided not to mention that the infection had gotten so bad that her father, the only practicing Catholic in the family, actually had a priest brought in for last rites. "Once I was well enough, I had reparative surgery on my leg. The muscles and ligaments have healed properly, or so the doctors think. But the scar tissue ended up being much worse than they expected. It puts pressure on the nerves and causes a lot of pain."

"The pain and your difficulty walking…" Natalie paused and spoke even more quietly. "It's permanent then?" She applied more oil to her hands and studiously avoided Adele's eyes. Adele knew it was to give her what little privacy Natalie could so she could speak freely.

Natalie's fingers dug into Adele's tense muscle and the heady combination of intense pleasure and a hint of pain caused her to gasp. "It's…complicated."

"What does that mean? Complicated?" Natalie leaned forward on her knees, expertly applying her body's weight to the task.

Adele tensed, feeling the familiar urge to flee and avoid the issue. But it took less internal convincing than she thought it would to be able to answer. "It means that I could have had another surgery to try to repair things further, and I could have continued with physical therapy and rehabilitation, but I didn't. I chose to move on with my life instead." She knew she was being vague and incomplete, but she hoped it would be enough.

Natalie frowned at Adele's words as she carefully rolled up the leg of Adele's shorts all the way to the hipbone, exposing the slender black string of a thong and a jagged scar that was at least three inches long.

Adele knew it was significantly worse than the scar on her face, and that was bad enough.

Natalie's voice was barely a whisper. "Oh, Ella."

"Pretty ugly, right?"

"No, it's just…" Natalie pressed warm hands, slick with oil, over the scar, letting her body heat soak into Adele. "That must have hurt so badly. I'm so sorry that happened to you."

The sweet words caused a rush of hot tears to fill Adele's eyes and her throat to close. "It…yeah," was all she could manage.

Natalie nodded to herself and began to run her hands along the pink scar and into the flesh around it. Her touch was gentle but strong. She glanced at Adele's face, watching for any reaction that meant pain. "Then let's try to make it feel better."

As Natalie worked, Adele waited for the inevitable questions about why she hadn't had the surgery and why she'd quit rehab. But they never came. Just when she was about to bonelessly dissolve into a puddle under Natalie's relentless, heavenly ministrations, Natalie spoke again.

"Can I ask you one more personal question?"

Adele was so deeply lost in a haze of pleasure that she didn't think twice about her answer. In this moment, she found herself willing to give

Natalie absolutely anything she wanted. Anything to make her happy. "Same answer as before, Natalie. Of course."

"Have you dated anyone since your divorce?"

Adele's heart thumped unevenly at the unexpected change in subjects.

When she didn't reply for nearly a minute, Natalie looked embarrassed and said, "I'm sorry if I poked my nose where it doesn't belong again. I know it's none of my business. But—"

"No," Adele assured her quickly. "It's okay. I was just surprised, is all. The answer is no. I haven't dated since my divorce."

Unmistakably bewildered, Natalie looked up from Adele's leg. "But why? It's been a couple of years and, I mean, you're gorgeous. You must get asked out all the time. Every day."

"I—" Adele stopped to smile at the use of the word gorgeous. "'Every day' is a big exaggeration." She was battered and scarred and limped. Nobody was signing her up to be a fashion model. But Adele wasn't stupid. She realized that despite those things, she still got her fair share of attention. Though that really wasn't the issue.

"I don't know," Adele finally replied. Then she hesitated and bit down on the inside of her cheek, debating. *Honesty.* "No, I do know. For a long time I was too much of a train wreck to even consider it. When Landry left…things had already been bad between us for months. But I would have never given up, you know?"

Natalie nodded, her expression boiling with anger that Adele understood was directed solely at her ex.

"I would have kept trying for as long as it took to make things right. I felt even more betrayed by him than I did by the NOPD. And *that* was like having my guts ripped out.

"Afterward, I could hardly force myself to venture outside the house," Adele admitted to the ceiling. "When I wasn't furious with the entire world, I was so despondent that it was only the fact that Logan needed me that kept me from crawling into bed and never getting back out. I certainly wasn't looking for a romantic partner. I had enough sense left to know that I couldn't subject someone else to my crap or ruin any more lives."

Natalie scowled. "Ella."

"It's true. Or at least I believed it was true at the time. When I finally started to feel better about myself, there wasn't anyone who captured my interest. When someone would ask me out, it was easy to tell him no. So I did. I guess I was waiting for someone to make me feel like I had to say yes."

Natalie carefully slid her fingers beneath the string of Adele's panties and dug deeply into the muscle surrounding the scar.

Heat flooded Adele's lower belly, and guilt at enjoying this a little too much piled on top of pleasure. Too soon, though, those magic hands ran down her thigh and began to work on her calf muscle.

Adele hadn't been touched by someone who wanted nothing more than to make her feel good in ages. Natalie's touch didn't just ease her aches. It connected her to another human being, something she hadn't even known she'd missed. It was as though all the tiny cracks that still caused her pain were being filled in with the warm oil and the sure hands that dug into her flesh and trailed over her skin leaving sparks in their wake. Adele's eyes slid closed and, unthinkingly, she arched her back and released a languid moan.

Natalie's mouth went slack. Then she licked her lips, her eyes glued to Adele's face. "Is it hard to capture your interest?"

"Not for the right person."

Natalie finally let go of Adele's leg and wiped her hands on the towel. Adele opened her eyes and squinted at the invasion of the firelight. She rose to her elbows in time to see Natalie making fists with both hands. A sliver of guilt pierced her. She'd allowed herself to get lost in the moment. In *many* moments. Natalie's hands were probably about ready to fall off because of it.

"I should have stopped you sooner, but I was too stoned from your magic hands to think straight."

Clearly pleased, Natalie dipped her head at the praise.

"Natalie, thank you. Nothing and nobody has made me feel that good in a very long time." Adele grinned and lifted her leg and gave it a little shake to prove her point.

Natalie beamed, white teeth gleaming in the flickering firelight. "You're welcome. Why don't we make a deal?"

A little hesitant, Adele lowered her leg. "Okay."

"When I want to remember Josh, I'll talk to you about him."

"Yes." Adele nodded immediately. She didn't need to hear the rest. She wanted to do that for Natalie, and she didn't need nor want anything in exchange.

"And you ask me to massage your leg whenever it hurts."

"But it hurts every day."

Natalie smiled softly. "Then I'll expect you to ask again soon."

Adele relaxed under Natalie's tender gaze. "You don't drive a very hard bargain. Don't you think I'm getting the better end of that deal?"

Natalie lifted a sassy eyebrow. "I beg to differ. And besides, I know what I want out of a bargain, Adele Lejeune."

"Then it's a done deal."

Natalie glanced at the antique grandfather clock that stood proudly along the wall. It was past midnight, but she didn't remember hearing a single chime. *Magic hands.* "I'd better get to bed."

Adele nodded. "Me too."

But neither of them moved.

"Ready?" Adele asked knowingly. It was nice to spend time with someone. Especially someone kind, and funny, and smart. She still didn't want it to end.

"No. You?"

"Nope."

They shared a conspiratorial smile, and finally, it was Natalie who relented. She stood and offered a hand, palm up, to help Adele to her feet. But her skin was slippery from the residual oil so when Adele took it and began to pull herself up, she only got about halfway before she started to slide out of Natalie's grasp.

"Whoa!" Natalie tightened her grip and reached out with her other hand...but it proved equally useless.

Arms flailing, Adele fell back onto the blanket and flat onto her back with a giant thud. "Uff!" The air was forced out of her lungs in a great rush.

"Oh my God." Natalie straddled Adele and dropped to her knees, hovering lightly above the bare skin of her stomach where her tank top had ridden up. "The oil! I tried...are you hurt?" Natalie ran her hands lightly down Adele's arms and worriedly searched her face. "You need to breathe, Ella. *Breathe!*"

Red-faced from a lack of oxygen, Adele finally sucked in a deep breath, then let out a choked laugh. "Ow. My...everything."

"It's not funny!" Natalie gave her a light swat on the shoulder, relief making her hands shake. "You scared me."

That only made Adele laugh harder, though it was still a little difficult to pull in a full breath. Warm brown eyes twinkled. "It's sort of funny."

Natalie shook her head indulgently. Then her face grew serious and her gaze blistering.

Adele's brows knit at the sudden shift in demeanor. "What?"

"Remember when I told you that since coming to New Orleans I was doing what I wanted and not what I should?"

"Yeah?"

Without further discussion, Natalie slid her hand under the nape of Adele's neck and gently lifted as she ducked down and pulled Adele into a bruising, open-mouthed kiss.

Arousal swept through Adele like an unexpected storm front as their mouths met in an explosion of sensation, a tangle of teeth and tongues. She drew her fingers up Natalie's neck and threaded them into silky hair, locking Natalie firmly in place. The resulting moan against her lips caused her stomach to flutter excitedly and suffused her with want.

"Is this—" Natalie muttered hotly into Adele's mouth after a sizzling minute. "Is this okay?"

Adele wrenched her mouth a few millimeters away from Natalie's to desperately suck in oxygen and whisper a quick, "God, yes," before smashing their lips back together. She was on fire.

For another long, blissful moment, nothing in the world mattered but their hammering hearts, their breathy sighs and their glorious kiss.

Finally, Natalie pulled away, her eyes dark with desire. Still breathing heavily from their ardent exchange, she ghosted her lips over Adele's one last time, as though she couldn't bear to leave them without a final, sweet visit. "You taste so good," she whispered, the very tip of her tongue darting out for a tiny, provocative sampling.

"You too." Spontaneous combustion was definitely back on the table.

Still straddling Adele, Natalie sat back and rested most of her weight on Adele's middle. Stunned by what had just happened, Natalie raised her fingertips to her own parted lips as if to confirm it had been real. She ignored Adele's groan of protest as she gently untangled Adele's hands from her hair. Affectionately, Natalie folded one of Adele's hands tightly between her own.

Concern was etched across Natalie's every feature. "Is it really okay? I mean that I'm a woman and—"

"Yes." Adele stared back at her from behind heavily lidded eyes. "It's more than okay. It's awesome. I promise. You aren't the first woman who's kissed me and who I've kissed back."

Natalie's eye-crinkling smile lit up the entire room, and Adele couldn't help but answer it with one of her own, her dimples popping out in spectacular fashion. In an uncharacteristic move, Natalie pumped her fist in victory. "Yes!"

Laughing, Adele's heart soared. "Nat?"

"Hmm?" Natalie threaded the fingers of one of her hands with Adele's and pulled their joined hands closer to her chest, as though the link between them was something precious and worthy of safekeeping.

"You've gone way, *way* past piquing my interest."

"I have?" Natalie responded hopefully, gently pushing some pale hair off Adele's forehead.

Adele could only earnestly nod. "Oh, yeah. So," she cleared her throat. "Will you go shopping with me tomorrow and have dinner with me afterward? After we do some computer searching, that is?"

With her index finger, Natalie traced their joined fingers, a small grin playing at her lips. "Are you asking me on a date?"

She thought that was obvious. A flash of uncertainty made Adele's stomach flip. Sure, Natalie had kissed her, and Holy Mary, mother of God could she kiss, but what if that's all she wanted? "Yes."

Natalie shrugged happily. "I'd love to go out with you…" She winked. "And not for the purpose of burglarizing someone's house."

Adele felt giddy.

"And, Ella, if you hadn't asked me, I was going to ask you. I couldn't wait any longer."

Adele couldn't keep herself from squirming with delight. "Good, because there is something very special that I need to buy. And I think you're the perfect person to help me."

CHAPTER TWELVE

The next day dawned sunny and temperate with a promise of hitting sixty-six degrees by midafternoon. That was the good news. The bad news was that finding Billy Hobson had taken longer than either woman expected. Google, at least in this instance, wasn't the messiah that Adele had proclaimed.

It was nearly lunchtime when Natalie found a cousin of Billy's who lived in Metairie, a suburb of New Orleans.

Adele made a quick phone call and provided the white lie—she was a dear friend of Billy's from the NOPD who was trying to reach him—and the cousin turned over all of Billy's address information without asking a single question. As it turned out, Billy now lived in Shreveport, which was nearly a five-hour drive.

Adele powered down her laptop and unplugged it from the outlet near the kitchen stovetop. She set it on the countertop. "I forgot how much I hate doing computer work. That was *horrible*!"

Natalie crossed her arms over her chest and glared disbelievingly. "I searched all morning. You helped for the last ten minutes."

Adele's voice was unnaturally cheerful. "But I picked out the new fixtures for the bathrooms and made sandwiches!" She passed a plate holding a sandwich and a handful of potato chips to Natalie, who rolled her eyes then stood with a groan, stretching shoulders that had been hunched over for too long.

Georgia stormed into the room looking murderous. "That incompetent, stupid, *stupid* man!" She threw a notepad and pen down onto the kitchen island.

"Landry's here?" Adele looked behind Georgia as though she expected him to enter the room any second.

"No. Ross."

Adele made a face and sliced her sandwich in half. "What about him? If he tried to pinch your butt again, you have no one to blame but yourself."

Looking anxious, Georgia said, "There's a problem with the paint on the back of the house."

Adele shrugged. "Ask him to correct it. He's had workmen crawling everywhere all day so it shouldn't take long. You're the one who wanted to use him because he's cheap." She waggled half a sandwich at Georgia, and a piece of lettuce fell out, causing the older woman to narrow her eyes at the messy gesture. "You get what you pay for," Adele continued, "and we are paying for a decrepit old pervert and his merry men."

Georgia leaned against the kitchen island and crossed her thin legs at the ankles. Today she was wearing the exact same dress as before, in yet another color. Gold.

This one was Natalie's favorite, by far, because it contrasted so wonderfully with Georgia's dark skin and made the older woman look exotic.

"Ella, that man only goes to his favorite store to buy paint."

"So?" Adele muttered as she popped a chip into her mouth. She held the open bag out invitingly to Georgia, who shook her head.

"That store doesn't carry the brand of paint we selected," Georgia continued, picking at her fingernails.

Adele took a bite of sandwich. "So he went to another store, right?"

"No. Ross decided to go with another brand of paint and another color." Georgia said the words so quickly they were barely decipherable. She winced. "Bright purple."

Adele began choking on her bite of turkey sandwich. Then she accidentally knocked her plate onto the floor, sending her sandwich flopping onto the cool tile. Natalie quickly moved to her side and began slapping her on the back. "Wh-wh-what!" Adele spluttered.

"Ross says that the color is authentic to the period and—"

Adele coughed a few times and waved Natalie away with a grateful look. "Grape Ape purple isn't authentic to this era house! Creole houses are usually earth tones. Today *that man* is wearing plaid brown pants and a striped black shirt. I think he's completely blind!"

Natalie sat back down and took another bite of her own sandwich. Her attention swung from Adele to Georgia, as though she was attending a tennis match.

Tsking, Georgia picked up the plate and sandwich from the floor and set them on the countertop. She spoke pointedly at Adele. "Save that bread for the birds and the meat for the dog next door. And just so you know, Ross is waitin' in his truck out front. I'm going with him to buy new paint and make sure there are no more surprises."

Placated, Adele nodded.

"But…well," Georgia looked upset, "I know you wanted Butterscotch Cream as the exterior color. But now it will take two or three coats of primer to cover up the purple." Her expression suddenly cleared. "But it will take only one coat if we decide to go with the Rust Red. Ross confirmed this. Then we could still use the Butterscotch Cream for the trim and most importantly stay on schedule."

Georgia held her breath, and Natalie watched in amused silence. Georgia was good. Really good. And Natalie would know. She'd been raised by Rose, the Queen of Manipulation. Natalie wondered idly when Adele would figure it out.

Adele puffed out a grumpy breath. "Fine, fine. Get Rust Red. And please make some calls to get an estimate on soundproofing my room today. I know we talked about doing it next weekend, but it's going to be a mess, so I want to start as soon as possible."

Clearly pleased with herself, Georgia nodded. "I know just whom to call. I'll get bids and have someone workin' in your room by tomorrow." Her voice held all the confidence in the world.

"Not Ross."

"Certainly not!" Georgia look mortally offended. "I would never let him in your room. I have a couple of other contractors I'll try right away."

"That'll be perfect, Georgia. Thanks." Adele smiled and gestured toward the loaf of bread. "Lunch?"

"Not today. Ross is so upset by his little mistake that I'm going to buy him lunch. You girls enjoy your lunch and shopping." Georgia waved over her shoulder as she strode out of the room.

Natalie snickered.

"That woman is the shepherd of the devil." Adele released a long-suffering sigh. "Somehow I knew this place would end up Georgia's preferred Rust Red come hell or high water. I guess I should be glad she didn't resort to something more drastic."

Natalie passed Adele half her sandwich so she wouldn't have to make another. "You knew?"

"Of course." Adele chuckled good-naturedly. "She used to do the same thing when she worked for my mother. She's like genius smart and was Mama's personal assistant for more than thirty-five years before she came to work for me. She never messes with anything important, but if it's something small, and she believes she's right, which she usually is, she has no mercy.

"When I was sixteen, and despised the truly hideous prom dress my mother sweetly but misguidedly purchased for me, it was Georgia who rode her bicycle to my high school and showed up just before prom with a different dress. The one I really wanted.

"She'd bought it for me with her own money, including matching shoes. I changed in the school bathroom, and my mother was none the wiser." Adele's expression was a mixture of genuine affection and wistfulness. "I guess it's only fair that Georgia turn her powers against me now." She winked at Natalie. "I probably even deserve it."

Natalie rested her chin on her upturned hand and soaked in Adele's every word. She was having a hard time not kissing her this very second. But here in the light of day, Natalie found herself more bashful and cautious than she'd been the night before. Though her lips still tingled at the memory.

Adele was the kind of woman Natalie could fall in love with, if she let herself. And she didn't want to mess things up by moving too quickly. For now, at least, she resolved to put out of her mind any of the numerous roadblocks that lay ahead of them, but most especially the fact that they lived in different cities. "You're sweet to let her have her way."

Appearing a little embarrassed for looking like a tenderhearted pushover, Adele shrugged and wiped the crumbs from her mouth with a napkin. "I don't always give in. But after what she's put up with these last couple of years, she's earned a lot more than her choice of paint colors. Just don't tell her I said so."

"It'll be our secret." Natalie finished her sandwich and rose to put her plate into the dishwasher. "Are we going to Shreveport to question Billy Hobson now?" she asked, trying to keep disappointment from coloring her words. The trip now meant no date tonight.

Adele's face fell. "We absolutely could." She nibbled her top lip. "On the other hand, Hobson's cousin said he wasn't due back home from a hunting trip until tomorrow night sometime. I thought maybe we could leave first thing in the morning. That way we could still go out tonight and be at Hobson's well before tomorrow night. It sucks, but bedtime or early mornings are the best time to catch someone at home." Adele shoved her hands into the pockets of her jeans and focused on her shoes. "But if you'd rather—"

"No!" Natalie said a little too quickly. She was sure she should feel guilty for not searching for Josh's killer with every second of her time in New Orleans. But she still had her own life to lead. She was grateful to have a chance at all the things that Josh would miss, and was determined not to waste it by ending up hopelessly trapped in the past. "I don't want to do anything other than go out with you tonight."

Natalie had never seen Adele so happy. The look on Adele's face brought to mind the impressive, enthusiastic woman she'd met more than five years earlier.

Adele's smile was blinding. "Really?"

Helplessly, Natalie nodded. "Really." She admired the way the sunlight streamed in through the window and brought out the dozen or so shades of light brown and blond in Adele's hair. "Just don't let it go to your head."

Adele stepped over to Natalie and looked her square in the eyes. "Then I'd better make sure our date is a good one."

Natalie's eyes zeroed in on Adele's lips.

"But, now we shop!"

Natalie jumped, a little startled. "We pretty much cleaned out Amelia's earlier this week. But I'm always game if there's something else you need."

Adele looked at Natalie as if she'd grown a second head. "Not for clothes, silly. This is way more important than that. C'mon, Amelia's going to meet us there. You can borrow a pair of my boots."

Scowling, Natalie allowed herself to be dragged out of the room by her wrist. She had several pairs of winter boots back home, and if she never wore them again, it would be too soon. "What do you mean boots?"

"You'll see."

Natalie suddenly remembered something. "Hey, since we're going shopping anyway, can we stop by a Best Buy or something? I need to get a phone charging cable."

"You can borrow mine. I saw that we're both Droid girls."

Natalie felt a tickle of dread deep in her belly. Until just that moment, she hadn't thought of Josh's phone since she grabbed it, and she hadn't told Adele about it. She licked her lips nervously. "It's not for my phone. It's for Josh's."

Adele stopped dead in her tracks. "Wh-what?"

"I found it in Misty's bedroom and I…well, I just took it. It was the last thing I ever gave Josh, and he loved it." Natalie shrugged. "I didn't want it ending up in the dump or auctioned off for nothing. But I can't power it up. It's an iPhone and my charger won't work with it."

A crease appeared between Adele's eyes. "And you didn't trust me enough to tell me right away?"

Natalie felt a sliver of pain in her chest. For Adele it always came down to trust. "No, no, no, Ella, it wasn't like that at all. Trust had nothing to do with it. I was going to mention it, and then I just didn't think of it again. That's the only reason. I promise."

Adele nodded slowly and Natalie allowed herself to breathe again. "Do you think it could be important?" Natalie asked.

"I doubt it. But there's only one way to find out." With a slightly impatient sigh, Adele glanced at her watch. "We need to head out now if we're going to make it on time. Georgia has an iPhone. We'll grab her charger tonight and see."

"Okay." Natalie could have kicked herself for bringing down Adele's playful mood. "I really am sorry."

Adele smiled a little. "You don't have to be sorry. Just start thinking a little more like Nancy Drew. Now, about those boots…"

* * *

"I can't believe we're doing this in this weather. This just seems wrong somehow. Like maybe even morally wrong." It turned out Natalie hadn't, thank God, needed boots. The ground was firm and dry. "No. Not morally wrong. Abnormal."

"What are you talking about?" Adele asked absently as she craned her neck in search of Amelia. "This is perfectly normal."

"It's more than sixty degrees outside and we're going to cut down a Christmas tree! I'm wearing a sleeveless sweater and you have on a short-sleeved blouse. We're supposed to do this in long underwear and knee-deep snow." Natalie pointed at a fat, white-bearded man. "And that Santa has on a Hawaiian print shirt, jeans and a giant alligator belt. At least he got the Santa hat right."

"That's not Santa. That's Gus. He owns the tree farm."

"It's called Santa's Village! He's passing out mini candy canes and an elf is standing next to him!"

"I'm telling you, that's Gus." Adele tilted her head toward the man in question. "I've been coming here my entire life, and I think I'd know if he was Santa. In fact, I have proof he's not. I remember when his beard was partly black." Adele's gaze dropped significantly lower. "That's Gus's big brother, Rob. I think Rob prefers the term little person over elf."

Natalie looked askance at Adele, sure that she was teasing. Almost.

"Amelia!" Adele spotted her sister, who was carrying a large canvas sack with her, and motioned her over to them. Three little blond girls, who looked to range in age from around six to ten, skipped along in tow.

"Aunt Ella!" the girls shouted, all vying for a spot in their aunt's arms. Adele bent down and set her cane on the ground before giving each child an enthusiastic bear hug and sloppy kiss on the cheek.

"We didn't think you were ever coming again, Aunt Ella," the tallest girl said. She glanced around. "Where is Lo—?"

"Ahem," Amelia interrupted, looking a little concerned. She gave the girl a tiny poke. "Remember our talk?"

But Adele met the words with a lopsided grin. "It's okay." She ruffled the now red-faced girl's hair. "Logan is with his dad, but will be home on Christmas Day. I decided that I missed our tradition so badly that I couldn't stay away." Her voice went a little serious. "I'm sorry that I was gone for so long. But I'm back and I'm not going anywhere again."

The news was greeted with loud cheers and three little bodies jumping up and down as though they'd never heard anything better in their lives. Amelia's and Adele's eyes met and instantly filled with tears. At the sight, Natalie's own vision began to blur.

Adele saved the adults from getting too maudlin by making introductions.

Natalie shook each girl's hand politely, then promptly confused their names. They looked so similarly adorable: all with brown eyes a bit darker than Adele's and varying shades of straight blond hair.

The oldest and the tallest of the girls was Amelia's. The other two belonged to Jackson, Adele and Amelia's younger brother. Jackson was a single father. Amelia's husband, Tony, had decided to take the day off from work, and send only the women to the tree farm this year for the Great Christmas Tree Challenge.

While Adele was busy catching up to the kids, Natalie moved over to Amelia, who was watching Adele with misty eyes.

"She looks happy, don't you think?" Amelia asked softly, voice thick with emotion. "She's crazy about her nieces. I think it hurt Adele even more than the kids when they stopped seeing each other regularly."

Natalie nodded, her heart melting a little at the sight of three little girls hanging on Adele's every animated word. "She looks great."

Natalie dropped the volume of her voice to barely audible and, as expected, Amelia took a step closer. "I was hoping you could help me with something. I mean, you've already done so much, I know. The items in your shop are so beautiful. I'll pay full price, of course. It's the only place that I know to shop at the moment, though I'm sure there is a department store somewhere in New Orleans."

Amelia's eyebrows rose as Natalie continued to struggle to express herself.

"I need to hurry, and I can walk to your shop from the inn." Then Natalie simply stopped speaking, and stared at Amelia expectantly.

Amelia waited a long beat before saying, "If there was a question in there, I'm sorry, but I missed it."

Natalie groaned at herself and did her best to push aside her nervousness about the night to come. "I need a dress." She *really* liked Adele and wanted to make the best possible impression. That meant showing a little leg and an effort.

Amelia cracked a knowing smile. "A dress?"

"For tonight," Natalie clarified. "Yes."

Amelia shifted her focus to Adele and the girls, her eyes suddenly dancing with what looked a lot like mischief. "Oh, well, you could always just borrow one of Ella's. I'm sure she wouldn't mind sharing."

Natalie frowned and selected her words with extreme care. She didn't know how Amelia would react to Adele going on a date with a woman, and she didn't want to find out this way. Natalie'd sooner gnaw off her own hand than be the cause of any family strife just when Adele was trying to find her place in the world again.

Only last night, she had awoken to Adele's soul-shattering screams for the second time. Adele had dreamt someone was after Logan, and she was unable to get to him before he was taken from her for good. While Adele projected sure and steady in her waking hours, she was simply terrified in her sleep.

The poor woman had been so drenched in cold sweat that she'd had to get up and take a shower in the middle of the night. Even so, this bout of bad dreams had been slightly better than the time before. Adele had recognized Natalie immediately and the gun never made an appearance.

If the entire experience had been exhausting for her, Natalie could only imagine how Adele felt.

"Borrowing something is a good idea, Amelia. Thanks. But I'd rather get a new dress."

"What's the occasion, and where are you going?" Amelia turned her hands palm up. "You know, so I'll know what type of dress we're talking about."

Natalie felt herself start to panic. She could hardly say she didn't know where she was going, but she still wanted to look devastatingly sexy.

"I-I-I'm going out to dinner and the clothes I've purchased already are…well, they're gorgeous." She looked down at the black, sleeveless cashmere sweater she was wearing and even while anxious, nearly swooned. "But I didn't pick any dresses. I was wondering if your shop was open today? With you here, I wasn't sure." That didn't come close to answering Amelia's question and she knew it.

Amelia pursed her lips. "I see. And you want to look pretty?"

No, I want to look hideous. "Umm…I want to look like I'm in a dress."

Amelia's face was unreadable. "So Ella asked you out on a date? Or was it you that got up the nerve first?"

Natalie went stock-still and her belly spasmed. "I-I'm going to dinner," she repeated, knowing she sounded like a dullard, but determined not to divulge more. She licked her lips nervously, and felt a little light-headed. *Abort!* her mind screamed. "Now that I think about it, I can just wear what I have on." She smiled an overly bright smile. "Never mind." Before she could rejoin Adele, Amelia's hand darted out and gently, but firmly, circled her wrist.

"Stop, Natalie. Please." Amelia chuckled. She kept her voice low. "I'm sorry. I was just teasing. You haven't done anything wrong, so there's no need for you to look like you're going to be sick all over your shoes. Ella told me that she liked both men and women when we were teenagers. I'm *not* shocked, and it's not a secret. In fact, I'm thrilled that…you asked her?" she guessed.

Natalie closed her eyes and willed her wildly thumping heart to slow. She was torn between being touched that Amelia felt comfortable enough to include her in what seemed very much like familial teasing, and being angry enough to punch Amelia in the nose for worrying her. But Amelia's apologetic grin seemed genuine, so she unclenched her fists. "Ella was the one who asked me." Natalie's expression went a little dreamy as she thought about it. "But I couldn't have held out much longer."

"Wow." Amelia hummed a little to herself, clearly impressed. "Go, Ella." She gave Natalie a conspiratorial grin and began to gush. "You'll look fabulous! I know just the dress to make her drool. I know what she likes. In fact, I can still picture that slutty, blue-eyed cheerleader that first turned her head when we were in high school."

Natalie blinked slowly.

At the look on Natalie's face, Amelia's own words seemed to register. She clamped her hand over her mouth. "Oh, Christ," she mumbled through her fingers, laughing a little. "Don't tell Ella I said that. And no offense. I'm sure you're not slutty. Well, I'm not *sure*, but I don't have a real reason to suspect otherwise."

"Gee thanks," Natalie said dryly, the only hint of the amusement she was feeling shining in her eyes.

"I'm sure you don't have blue—" Amelia glanced at Natalie's face. "Whoops. Never mind." She waved a hand at the trees around them, her cheeks pink with embarrassment. "Back to the tree hunt. I'll bring the dress by the inn tonight and make sure Ella doesn't see a thing. When she sees you in it, she'll swoon."

"Thanks, Amelia." Natalie's tone was filled with genuine warmth and a hint of envy. It must be nice to have a sister.

"The dress will only be the icing on the cake."

Natalie glowed at the compliment.

"You should know, Natalie, that if you're even a small part of what's putting the smile on Ella's face today, and I suspect you are, then that's worth a hundred dresses to me. I think I'm the one who should be thanking you."

Natalie had no idea what to say to that, but luckily, Amelia didn't seem to expect a response.

Amelia inclined her head to the side as if something suddenly occurred to her. Her expression shifted from thoughtful to wicked. "If Ella wants to sleep with you, and for some reason you're not into it, I'm willing to bribe you," she whispered happily. "Seriously, whatever it takes."

"Amelia!" Natalie burst out laughing.

Adele glanced up at Natalie and Amelia's laughter, but Natalie just shook her head. There was absolutely nothing about her current conversation that she needed to share.

Adele nodded in acknowledgment and refocused on her nieces, their chatter never slowing. "Ha!" Adele said to the littlest girl. "It's too bad your daddy isn't here for me to beat the pants off again this year. You make sure and tell him that he can sit home and drink all the beer he wants with Uncle Tony, knowing that I am the champion, okay?"

The girl nodded dutifully.

"Hey!" Indignant, Amelia protested. "You're not the supreme champion yet."

"It's only a matter of time. One hour, to be exact."

The sisters glared at each other, then burst into raucous giggles as they traded comments about tree hunts long since past.

Natalie blinked a few times, astonished, but entranced. Adele wasn't frugal with her laughter, but this time she actually *giggled*. This impish, open side of Adele wasn't just new and lovely; it called to Natalie on an almost primal level.

"Have you explained the rules to Natalie?" Amelia finally asked, adjusting the sack she was carrying, and pulling out a second tiny sack from her pocket. She handed the smaller of the sacks to the middle-sized child.

"Not yet." Adele turned and wound her arm around Natalie's the way an especially dear friend might. Partway through the move, she caught herself and glanced shyly at Natalie for permission.

Natalie hummed contentedly. Permission granted. She thrilled at the contact but tried not to show it. From the corner of her eye, Natalie noticed Amelia indulgently watching them.

"The rules are simple. We have one hour to select the most magnificent tree on the planet. The children will be impartial judges, no matter who might have bought them ice cream on the way to the tree farm as a bribe."

Amelia's gaze innocently tilted skyward.

"And they will judge the winner. She, I mean, *I*, will be crowned best Christmas Tree Picker in the Universe. The loser, I mean, *Amelia…*" Amelia's eyes turned to slits and the children giggled uncontrollably at Ella's bravado, especially Amelia's own daughter, who suddenly seemed thrilled by the prospect of her mother's demise, "…will host the entire family for dinner on New Year's Day," Adele continued, eyes wide at the thought of what Natalie could only assume would be a daunting experience.

Adele began ticking items off on her fingers. "That includes all the shopping, cleaning and cooking. And just so you know, I want pecan pies, not apple," she reminded Amelia tartly.

"Boo," the girls hissed. Apparently nuts were unwelcome guests.

"And, Amelia, no using a cleaning service to do the work for you. That was cheating!"

"That was years ago, and I was nine months pregnant!" Amelia protested indignantly, pointing at her daughter as though Adele somehow needed proof of the pregnancy.

"Excuses," Adele scoffed, allowing her sister no quarter.

Natalie clamped her hand over her mouth to keep from laughing.

"Please note, Ella, that I've won nearly every year since then."

Adele sneered. "All good things must come to an end. And since Natalie is a guest I assume it's acceptable that she gets the choice of weapons?"

Natalie's mouth dropped open. *Weapons?*

The girls conferred with each other in a hushed circle. Finally, the youngest poked her head up and proclaimed, "Acceptable."

Adele leaned close to Natalie's ear and whispered, "Reach into the bag and pick out a saw."

Natalie recoiled. "You want me to stick my hand inside a dark sack for a *saw*, not knowing exactly where the blade is?"

"Those are the *rules*," Adele hissed from the side of her mouth.

Natalie rolled her eyes. "Fine, but if I end up in the emergency room, I'm blaming you." Carefully, and so slowly that Amelia snorted, Natalie pulled out a decent-sized saw. Unsure what to do next, she held it up for all to see.

Adele nodded, apparently extremely satisfied. "Excellent choice."

Natalie examined the saw with a critical eye while Amelia extricated hers from the sack. "Is ours better?"

"No, they're exactly the same."

"What the—?" Natalie stared at Adele again.

"Now comes the tree choice," Adele proclaimed as though she was announcing the arrival of royalty at a formal ball. She took the smaller bag from her niece and held it for Natalie. "Go on. Reach inside."

"Um...what's in there?" Natalie inquired warily, keeping her hand as far from the bag as possible.

"Just colored beads. You know, from Mardi Gras." Adele gave the bag a little shake. "Pull out one and it will tell us what type of tree we have to chop."

"Fine, fine," Natalie murmured. Trying not to look like the wimp she was, she reached and prayed Adele had been telling the truth. Feeling around, she let out a relieved breath and pulled out a bead.

Five sets of eyes regarded her anxiously.

"A green one," Natalie announced, confused.

The girls sucked in a breath in unison.

"Yes!" Adele practically danced a jig. "Green! Suck on that, Amelia!"

Amelia groaned and hung her head low.

The judges glanced at Amelia with pity in their eyes.

"I take it that's the color you wanted?" Natalie asked hesitantly. *They are all crazy. Wonderful, but crazy.*

"Green stands for Leyland Cypress," Adele said as though that explained everything. She danced around with the middle-sized child, her cane only minimally slowing her down.

Natalie hadn't even heard of that kind of tree. "And that's good?"

Adele froze. "You're kidding, right?"

"Yes, I'm totally kidding."

Adele nodded approvingly. "Good one."

Next, Amelia dug into the small bag and when she looked at her bead, a slow cocky smile spread across her face, transforming it into a Cheshire cat's. The bead was blue. "Carolina Sapphire."

The girls tittered and released a series of "oooh's" and "ahhh's."

Adele gasped.

"What does that mean?" Natalie whispered in Adele's ear, acknowledging that sapphires were, at least, blue. "Is that even a tree?"

"Of course it is. But for some reason, no one ever picks it. It's a wild card. Who knows how the judges will react?"

"On your marks. Get set. Go!" Amelia cried then disappeared into a row of trees with the girls trailing behind her.

When her sister was out of sight, Adele gestured to their right. "C'mon, our trees are this way."

With arms linked, Natalie and Adele strolled at a leisurely pace. Apparently an hour was plenty of time, because Adele didn't seem to be in any particular hurry.

Natalie sucked in a breath of sweet, fresh air. The tree farm was about forty miles outside of New Orleans, but felt a world away from the languid, but still spirited city. With the sun shining brightly, the day seemed filled with possibilities.

"So, Ella, you've really been coming here and picking trees your entire life?" Her family didn't have any longstanding traditions that seemed so…joyful. It was nice, and Natalie vowed that if she ever had a family of her own, things would be different.

"Oh, yeah. My aunts and uncles and parents competed when I was little and me, Amelia, Jackson, and our cousins were their judges. Now it's my generation's turn to entertain the kids. They love it. Logan especially likes…" Adele paused, then seemed to let the thought skitter away without voicing it. She guided Natalie through the changing varieties and shades of green of the trees. "Here we go. These are the ones."

The trees didn't quite look like the pines or even blue spruce so common in Wisconsin, but they were beautiful all the same. One would undoubtedly look glorious all decked out at the Touro Street Inn. "Nice."

"If you see a tree you like, let me know, okay? I'm counting on your homespun Wisconsin background for a competitive edge."

"You do know that I'm from a city of almost 250,000 and not a farm, right?"

"A thousand people plus 249,000 mosquitoes?" Adele teased gently as she squeezed their linked arms. She glanced around, then apparently satisfied they were alone, snuck a quick kiss to Natalie's cheek.

Natalie's heart pounded quicker at the feeling of soft lips and warm breath against her skin.

"Let's find this tree, and get out of here so we can go on our date."

Without looking, Natalie walked up to the very next tree in the row. "This one looks perfect."

Adele's hungry eyes roamed over Natalie instead of the tall tree next to her. She shrugged lightly. "I agree."

CHAPTER THIRTEEN

Natalie, hair in a loose, low bun, with a few stylish tendrils flowing free, met Adele in the kitchen for their date wearing a lace jacquard pencil dress. It was black, short, but not scandalously so, and exquisitely fitted to every one of Natalie's curves, of which there were many.

Adele's mouth opened and closed a few times, helplessly, with no sound coming out, when she saw Natalie. Her gaze darkened a shade at the sight before her, and when she was finally able, Adele reverently whispered, "Wow. Just…wow. Amazing." She fanned herself.

Natalie basked in the thrilled look on Adele's face. "Thanks, Ella." *Worth. Every. Penny.*

With a thousand-watt smile, Natalie allowed her eyes to rake up and down Adele. Slowly. "You look beautiful." Her smile eased into a playful frown. "So beautiful, in fact, I'm not sure I'm in the mood to beat off the men and women who will be drooling over you. Maybe we should order pizza and stay in instead." She was only half kidding. The thought of spending the evening alone with Adele on the sofa made her heart race every bit as much as going out.

Adele's outfit wasn't quite as dressy as Natalie's, but she still looked stunning in snug, black leather pants, a red satin, cowl-neck blouse and a short black jacket. She normally favored light, barely-there makeup that complemented her naturally youthful look. But tonight she'd gone for something smokier with bold mascara and eyeliner that gave her a sexy air and caused her whiskey-brown eyes to stand out in a way that threatened to melt Natalie's knees.

Adele laughed. "Thanks, but I don't think so. You, in that dress, are too gorgeous to waste on a night at home. And unlike you, I have absolutely no problem beating off the competition."

Obviously noticing a change in their normal positioning, Adele looked down at her feet. "No heels for me, I'm afraid." Her hand clenched on the handle of her cane.

"Good." Natalie remained resolutely cheerful. "Then for once I'll be taller." Usually, Adele was an inch or so taller, but in three-and-a-half-inch heels Natalie had new perspective. Since Adele was showing a tantalizing bit of cleavage, it was one Natalie immediately enjoyed.

Adele grinned. "Don't get used to it. Are you ready to go?"

For years… "Ready."

The evening was still surprisingly temperate and Natalie opted to leave her coat at home. Slowly, and with heads leaned close together as they talked, they strolled up the block to a busier street and caught a cab. Within five minutes they were at Stella! and waiting to be seated.

When the hostess disappeared with Adele's jacket, Natalie finally peeled her eyes away from Adele long enough to make conversation. "The restaurant is lovely." *Romantic.*

An enormous vase of fresh, brightly colored flowers sat near the center of the room. The tables were covered in crisp white linens, and the heavy chairs were tufted and upholstered with cream-colored, buttery leather. Candlelight and two large, golden chandeliers delicately lit the space. The exposed, dark wood beams that crisscrossed the ceiling matched the plush brown and gold carpet.

Adele murmured her agreement. "We had Creole food at Galatoire's, so I thought American would be good for tonight."

Adele's hand found the small of Natalie's back as she gently guided her behind the hostess who seated them. The fingertips felt like they were searing Natalie's flesh and she bit back a delighted moan at the sensation.

Happily, they were seated close enough to the enormous vase that the aroma of fresh flowers hung lightly in the air. It was almost enough for Natalie to forget that it was the middle of winter.

After ordering and each receiving a cocktail, they settled in to talk and get to know one another better.

"So," Adele began, swirling her drink in her glass, the chunks of ice knocking together lightly, "I have to warn you that I'm a bit out of practice. I haven't been on a date with someone who wasn't Landry since

I was in my early twenties. Oh, shoot!" She looked ready to slap herself in the forehead. "I wasn't supposed to mention him."

Natalie paused with her glass midway to her lips. "You weren't?"

"Well, I mean, nobody wants to hear about someone's ex on a first date." Adele wrinkled her nose. "At least that's what Amelia told me."

Natalie laughed. "Well, normally, I'd agree with your sister. But you were married to him for a long time and he's always going to be a part of your life because of Logan. There's no reason talking about him should be off limits, unless it makes you unhappy, that is."

"You're perfect," Adele said dreamily, her eyes glazed over. Her eyes popped open wide when she realized she'd actually said the words out loud. "Oh, my God. I'm so sorry." She tilted her head back and found something very interesting about the ceiling. "What is wrong with me?"

"You mean I'm *not* perfect?" Natalie asked coyly. Even Adele's edginess was adorable. It meant that the evening was important to them both.

Adele's gaze snapped down. "You are. I just…" She grimaced. "It wasn't supposed to come out like that."

"How about this?" Natalie set her glass on the table. "How about we stop worrying about this being an official date, and just be ourselves?"

Adele let out a shuddering breath. "Yeah. Okay. That would be…just right. But I mean, it's still a date. It still counts, right?"

"Absolutely. And Ella?"

"Yes?"

"I'm nervous too."

Natalie could see Adele calm even further at her words, and it went a long way to calming the nervous fluttering in her own belly.

They each selected a seven-course tasting menu, one traditional and one vegetarian and accepted the waiter's recommendation of the accompanying wine pairings. By midway through the evening Natalie was feeling a pleasant, light buzz and one look at Adele's slightly glassy eyes told her she was in the same state.

They happily shared bites from each other's plates and the savory food and fine wine were nothing short of delectable. But it was the company Natalie reveled in.

It wasn't like any first date she'd ever experienced. True, there was a hint of awkwardness and the thrill of new discovery because there was still so much to explore about one another. But at the same time, so much was already familiar and comfortable. There was an energy between them, pulsing and alive, an invisible rope that tethered them together and drew them back to each other again and again. Maybe it had always been there, lurking in the background, biding its time until it was safe and appropriate to rise to the surface.

And that time was now.

Natalie tossed her napkin onto the table. "This is ridiculous! Your photo actually looks good. How is that even possible? Nobody's looks good. No way do you get to see mine."

Adele was immediately indignant. "That's not fair! What do you mean, no way? I showed you mine. Now you have to show me yours."

Their eyes met and they both burst into laughter. "Okay, okay, you win," Natalie murmured good-naturedly. Fair was fair. She handed Adele back the Louisiana driver's license and began rooting in her purse for hers.

Their waiter interrupted *again* to bring their fifth course: a tiny smoked lamb chop for Natalie and Parmesan gnocchi for Adele. Hot on his heels was a second waiter with two glasses of Merlot.

Adele scowled a little as she watched the waiters go. "If I'd known we'd have a waiter at our table every five minutes all night long, I wouldn't have suggested the tasting menu. Sorry about that."

"Don't be. You're great company, and I'm having a wonderful time. Even though I feel a little like we should offer our waiter a seat at our table just so he can rest."

Adele chuckled silently. "I know, right?"

"Now don't laugh." Natalie reluctantly handed over her driver's license. "The picture is a little…rough."

Adele glanced down, back at Natalie, then back at the license, her eyes a narrow slit. Then she repeated the sequence. "Rough?" Adele did her best to hold in her laughter, which turned out to be a less than valiant attempt. "Were you hung-over or still drunk when this was taken?"

"Neither!" Natalie sniffed haughtily. "My hair was merely windblown and tousled."

"And your makeup?"

"A bit smudged."

Adele lifted a single fair eyebrow.

"Fine." Natalie lightheartedly threw her hands into the air. "That was taken the day after that year's big departmental gala at the university, which also happened to be the night I finally broke things off with my ex for good. I spent half the evening having a good time and indulging in some surprisingly decent wine. That is, until I caught my ex in the ladies' room going at it with the skinny skank who teaches East Asian History."

Adele winced. "No!"

"Oh, yes. And now you've gone and made me talk about *my* ex. Amelia wouldn't approve," Natalie said drolly. She took a sip of wine before continuing, enjoying the way it warmed the pit of her stomach. "So I spent the other half of the night ending a relationship that was dead in the water anyway. My license was set to expire the next day and I couldn't drive with an expired license, so even looking like this," she pointed to the offending license, "I hauled myself to the DMV to immortalize my humiliation via photograph."

"Wow." Adele gazed at the horrid photo with open affection. "If more citizens were as law-abiding as you, I would have been bored as a detective."

Natalie noticed that this time Adele didn't seem so bitter when she said the word detective. Progress. "Luckily for you there seemed to be no shortage of horrible, horrible people. And hopefully now there will be no shortage of tourists who will flock to the newly renovated, historic, and *not* purple, Touro Street Inn."

"I'll drink to that!"

The women clinked their glasses together, and Adele handed back Natalie's license. "So did your ex make a scene in front of your coworkers at the departmental party? Or did you?"

Natalie's vision went a little hazy as she remembered. It was honestly something that hadn't crossed her mind in ages. "Neither. I just wanted to go home that night. Luckily, Hannah would never do anything intentionally to outright embarrass herself in front of her peers or underlings."

"Underlings?"

Natalie shifted a little uncomfortably in her seat. "She was, and is, my department chair."

Adele's mouth dropped open. "Your ex-girlfriend is your current boss?"

"You could say that." Natalie rolled her eyes at herself. "But I wish you wouldn't."

Adele made a face. "Eww."

"Hey, don't judge!"

"Okay, I—" Adele paused. "No, sorry. Still eww."

Their quiet laughter wove together and created a sound all its own that filled Natalie's heart as much as her ears. "Okay," she allowed grudgingly. "It was a stupid error in judgment that won't ever be repeated."

"Is she old? The title department chair makes me think of someone pruny and ancient." Adele clearly was warming to her hypothesis, her eyes taking on a lively glint as she teased. "She probably doesn't have to memorize dates from World War I and the Great Depression and stuff. She remembers them personally."

Confused and slightly distressed that Adele would assume she was that desperate, Natalie tilted her head to the side. "Why would I date someone ancient?"

"How should I know?" Adele's face beamed with an inner glow that Natalie had come to learn meant she was happy and having fun. "Everyone has quirks. Some people just hide them better than others. For example, maybe right around the time you figured out that you liked women, you developed a thing for your eighth-grade history teacher, who I'm sure was very nice looking for someone all shriveled up and old—"

"I'll bet there's not as much of an age difference between Hannah and me as there is between you and Landry. She's seven years older than I am."

"I knew you were competitive." Adele pouted. "Touché." But she brightened quickly. "You and I are only a couple of months apart in age. I've never been on a date with someone younger before."

Natalie smiled wickedly. "Then I take it back. You were right."

"About what?"

"Maybe I *do* have a thing for older, dried up—"

Adele narrowed her eyes in mock anger. "Ha, ha. Funny."

A few bites more, and they both decided they were too full to finish this course, and they abandoned the food.

Adele asked their waiter to box up the desserts. "Was your breakup bad?" Her words were spoken casually, but it was clear she was still keenly interested in the topic. She reached for the water at the table that had, up until now, been ignored in favor of the wine.

"Not really. Things the night of the party were a bit dramatic because of the alcohol and the skank. But Hannah certainly wasn't the love of my life and I wasn't hers. We'd been on-again, off-again for a while." She shrugged one shoulder. "Within a day or two after the breakup everyone was fine. And, happily, we never talked about it again." She shivered at the mere thought.

"A day or two?" Visibly stunned, Adele looked away. "I—I took longer than that to get over running over a squirrel last winter."

"Did the squirrel bang an East Asian History professor while you were getting its wrap from the car?"

"Umm…no."

"Well then."

The conversation shifted to lighter topics that included more tidbits about their jobs and favorite things, and lots of laughter. Some loud enough to turn heads. Of course, Natalie admitted privately with a combination of pride and jealousy, the rubbernecking could have just as easily been the product of Adele getting up to use the bathroom and walking away in those goddamn tight leather pants.

Not long after, the mood subtly changed again and Natalie could see that something was playing on Adele's mind. She rewound the evening in her head, and landed on one particular spot. Hannah. She wasn't sure if her comments about her breakup had made her seem callous or whether they simply highlighted Adele's more pain-filled break from Landry. Either way, she hoped to erase the pensive look on her friend's face and any misconceptions she might have caused.

She laid a hand on Adele's forearm and gently stroked satin-covered skin with the ridge of her thumb, feeling Adele's warmth seep through the thin material. "Ella," her voice was as gentle as she could make it. "What I had with Hannah wasn't even close to a marriage. If I'm honest, it wasn't *anything* like what I think you and Landry had together. If it had been, I wouldn't have been okay the day after losing it. Or for lots and lots of days after that."

Adele blinked a few times, and her eyes began to glisten in the candlelight. Her voice took on a vulnerable quality that had Natalie at the edge of her seat. "Can I tell you something that might sound a little weird?"

Natalie nodded then glanced over Adele's shoulder and surreptitiously waved away the waiter who'd arrived with their boxes. Now was not the time.

"I've never told anyone this, not even Amelia because it makes me feel sort of guilty. But I got over losing Landry the husband a lot faster than I got over losing him as a friend." Adele's brows furrowed with concern. "Does that seem strange?"

Natalie thought about her answer for a moment, giving the serious question the consideration it deserved. It was an interesting admission. Adele had loved Landry. There was no question about that. But people often had many friends but, presumably, only one husband. It would be logical to miss most that which is scarcest. Then again, love and logic were, oftentimes, complete strangers.

Natalie recalled the times she'd seen Adele and Landry together, how they'd interacted, and what was clearly most important to Adele. "He was your best friend first? Before you were even married?"

Adele nodded slowly, her eyes never leaving Natalie's. "For a long time, actually."

"Then I don't think it's strange at all." Natalie continued to stroke the soft satin, her mind easily replacing the material with Adele's warm lightly tanned skin. "You're so strong, and you're independent. Maybe when it comes right down to it, even though I'm sure there are things about it that you miss very much, and even though that might not be your preference, maybe you discovered that you're able to live without a spouse."

Even more slowly than before, Adele nodded again, not really confirming or denying what Natalie said, but silently urging her on.

Encouraged, Natalie continued. "But, Ella, maybe what you can't live without is at least one friend who is a true equal. Maybe you need someone that you can trust all the way and with everything. A best friend whose loyalty and steadfastness you never have reason to question, and who you're willing to let see every single part of you without shame or censor. And maybe giving up that, losing that, is what hurt most of all."

Adele somehow managed to look astonished, a little melancholy, and grateful all at once. "Yes. That's exactly…How—?" She swallowed thickly.

Natalie moistened her lips and wrapped her fingers around the forearm she'd been stroking. She gave it an affectionate squeeze and willed all the confidence she felt to show in her voice. "You don't know this yet. And maybe you're not ready to know this. I get that. But you can trust me. Really trust me." *All the way.* "When it matters most, I won't let you down. I promise."

Adele's smile was electric. So much so, that Natalie was convinced if she reached out and touched the air between them, she'd feel the crackling current. Adele's next words seemed to contradict her beaming grin.

"You're wrong, Natalie."

Instantly, Natalie's face fell. *But…* "I-I'm sorry. I—"

"I do know it, and I do trust you. I can't seem to help myself. Even though it scares me. I don't want to stop."

Before she could say anything else, Adele boldly leaned forward and pressed her lips into Natalie's smile.

* * *

Adele and Natalie exited a taxicab outside the inn. Their evening was set to continue at Snug Harbor, a jazz club just a few minutes' walk away on Frenchman Street. But they'd decided to stop by the inn first to drop off their boxed desserts from Stella!

Natalie shivered as she rubbed her hands over the goose-bumped flesh on her arm. The temperature had dropped during dinner and she was feeling a definite chill.

The move didn't go unnoticed by Adele. "Cold?" Adele wiggled her eyebrows, her nervousness from earlier in the evening, nowhere in sight. "We could skip the club and I could warm you up?"

"Nuh-uh. You've been talking about the music at this place all evening. I want to go." She smiled invitingly. "Besides, you can keep me warm when we come home."

"Make no mistake about it, I'm planning on it," Adele drawled sexily.

Natalie pressed her thighs together to relieve a delicious ache that had been slowly building, and had just spiked.

Patience. Tucking her small clutch under her arm, Natalie reached for the boxes Adele was balancing with one hand. "Give me those. I'll put them in the kitchen and then grab a coat and meet you back outside in a few minutes, okay?"

Wordlessly, Adele took them to the side gate that led directly into the inn's courtyard. She pressed the house keys into Natalie's hand and drew in a deep breath of cool night air as she tilted her head back to gaze up at the stars, her eyes glittering black in the moonlight. "It feels nice out here. I was getting too warm at Stella!" Adele's eyes slanted sideways. "Or maybe it was just the company that had me hot and bothered."

"Or maybe it was all that wine we polished off?"

Clearly relaxed, Adele's arms swung freely as they strolled through the courtyard. "No, it's the company."

"We can take a cab to the club if it would be quicker and easier on your leg. It's nice out, but I certainly don't mind."

"Nah." Adele smiled and spiritedly bumped hips with Natalie as they moved. "It's close, and my leg's feeling really good tonight. Let's walk."

Natalie stopped Adele's progress with a gentle hand and moved directly in front of her. "You're gorgeous when you smile." Without warning, she surged forward and brushed her lips against the dimple that had been driving her to distraction for days. "And walking sounds great."

Adele gave Natalie a look that said she was reconsidering whether they should leave the inn at all. She firmly pulled Natalie's body flush against her, their breath mingling. They fit together like two pieces of a complex puzzle. Flawlessly.

"If we must go, Nat, you should at least be comfortable. Although you look positively mouthwatering in that dress, how about you slip into some jeans and comfortable shoes while you're inside?" Her gaze moved to Natalie's lips and, convulsively, she swallowed. "It's a short walk, but I bet it would be a torture hotter than hell in high-heeled shoes."

Natalie ran her fingertips along Adele's jaw, willingly drowning in the heady sexual tension that filled the night air. Natalie toyed with the idea of changing her mind and asking Adele to forget the jazz club and take her to bed, but quickly decided against it. *Slowly*, she reminded herself. *She's worth the wait.* "Good idea. Jeans and comfortable shoes it is."

Their lips met again in what was meant as just the whisper of a departing kiss, but Adele was having none of that. The kiss deepened naturally to just below scorching, sorely testing Natalie's resolve.

When they separated a second time, they were both panting. "I'll only be a few minutes," Natalie rasped, knowing that if she didn't go inside this very instant, she wouldn't have the willpower to stop herself a third time.

"Let me see you in."

Natalie smiled at her friend. The back door was only a few paces away. Like a good racehorse, it appeared that some things had simply been bred into Adele and went bone deep. Good manners were one of them. "Sit and rest your leg."

With one hand, Natalie grasped Adele's shoulder and gently pushed her into a wrought-iron patio chair. "I'll be right back." But she couldn't leave without dropping a final kiss atop Adele's head. She nuzzled her nose into the silky-soft locks and greedily inhaled, enjoying the light clean scent of shampoo and Adele herself.

In a move that Natalie had come to expect, Adele kicked her feet straight out in front of her, stretching, and set her cane on the ground beside her.

"If you never leave," Adele said through her smile, her eyes fluttering closed at the sensation of Natalie nuzzling her head, "we can never go. And that means we can't come back and, um, warm each other up."

"I'm already gone."

Natalie entered the dark house quickly, humming a happy tune. There was no need to turn on the lights as she dropped the boxes off in the kitchen and then headed to her room. She wondered what she should wear to Snug Harbor, thankful Adele had suggested different shoes. She usually wore slacks or skirts to work and appropriate shoes, but her feet were not used to cigarette heels.

Tomorrow's blisters would be payment for tonight's folly.

When she flicked on the light to her room, her mouth dropped open in disbelief. "Oh, my God!" It had been ransacked. She stepped deeper inside, her eyes flitting from surface to surface. Every drawer had been opened and its contents dumped. The bedding had been torn from the bed and lay in a haphazard pile on the floor, and Natalie's clothes were strewn everywhere.

Natalie froze when she heard the bedroom door close quietly behind her and the heavy deadbolt lock click smoothly into place.

The voice was deep, male, and deadly serious. "Where is it?"

* * *

A bloodcurdling scream from inside the house caused Adele to start. *Natalie?*

Adele scooped up her cane and took off in a dead run, or as much of a dead run as her leg would allow. Her heart leapt into her throat, and the searing pain in her leg didn't even register as she tore across the courtyard and flung open the back door. It wasn't a police detective who responded to the terrifying sounds coming from inside the inn, it was Natalie's date. For a second she panicked, thinking that Logan might be inside and in trouble too. But she quickly remembered her son was with his father.

The screams continued and once inside she could hear the harsh sound of smashing glass. "Natalie!" Adele sped through the dark house, knowing every turn by heart.

"H-help!" Natalie screeched, but this time her voice was garbled. "St…st-stop it. Stop!"

Adele skidded to a halt outside Natalie's room, the last room at the end of the hallway, and furiously tried to open the door. It was locked. Frantic, she pounded on it with a closed fist.

Instinctively, she reached for the gun on her side…that wasn't there. She could run to her room to retrieve it, but she knew she couldn't shoot through the door, not when she wasn't sure where Natalie was on the other side. "Shit!"

"Natalie! Open the fucking door! Open it!" But she could hear fighting on the other side of the door, high-pitched gasps and Natalie's cries, bodies crashing against the walls and furniture and the sound of wood and glass breaking. Someone was in there with her. "Natalie!"

Adele's adrenaline levels spiked so quickly that she began to tremble and see stars. She realized in that split second that she didn't have the keys to the dead bolts on her and wasn't even sure where they were. With all the construction going on, she'd lost track.

She lifted her good leg and kicked the door with all her might. But she was off balance when she did it and it had little impact. Two kicks. Three kicks. Four kicks, and she finally heard the doorframe begin to crack. The inn's doors were over a hundred years old and made of solid wood, not the foam core pieces of crap people had today. A single kick would have splintered one of those.

"Ella!" Natalie cried out in clear pain. A red veil of fury draped over Adele's vision.

"Motherfucker!" Adele raged, her voice going high and desperate at the end. "Whoever you are, when I get inside, I'm going to blow your head off!" It was a lie. Though she was most certainly going to kill whoever it was. Just with her bare hands.

"No! Stop!"

Trying to kick the door in was taking too long, and she wasn't convinced she could even manage it. Her bad leg was giving way.

Backing up halfway down the hallway, Adele ran at full tilt and flung her entire body against the door, her shoulder and good hip taking most of the impact. Violently, she bounced off it and ended up flat on her back on the cool wood floor.

Again, she saw stars and felt warm blood begin to trickle down the back of her neck from where her head had impacted the floor. But quickly, if wobbly, Adele stood and threw herself at the door again and again, cursing the entire time and calling out Natalie's name.

Eventually, the doorframe cracked again.

At the exact same moment, the fighting stopped, and the room went eerily quiet. Adele's hands flew to her ears when an explosion of glass shattered the silence. *The side window.* Whoever was in that room was making his escape.

Out of breath, Adele lost track of how many attempts she made at the door, but finally, thankfully, the doorframe came apart completely. "Natalie!" With wild arms, she knocked away the splintered wood and pushed the door aside to slide in between it and what was left of the frame. A shard of wood sliced into the skin a couple of inches above her wrist like a scalpel.

She hissed in a breath.

The room had been destroyed. The desk chair was in pieces. Broken glass, from the window and several pictures that had been knocked from the walls, was scattered all over the room and shimmered like tiny diamonds against the bed's dark duvet. On the rug next to the bed lay Natalie, quiet and as still as a corpse. Her face was partly covered with matted, bloody hair. The cord from the lamp was wound tightly around her neck, her tongue protruding, her eyes partially open and fixed.

All the air rushed from Adele's lungs, as though she'd been punched in the chest. "Oh, God." She flew across the room and fell to her knees at Natalie's side, glass crunching beneath and cutting through her leather pants. "No, no, no!"

For a second, time stood still. Adele's hands hovered above Natalie, not touching, her eyes not believing what was before her. *Too late. Too late*, her mind chanted cruelly. *She's dead*. But a heartbeat later and time not only resumed, it propelled her forward into frenzied motion.

With shaking, but lightning-fast hands, Adele unwrapped the cord from Natalie's neck, not missing the bright red ligature marks and a large open-fingered handprint that had already started to bruise. "Breathe! Breathe!" Natalie's body was limp as a wet noodle and unmoving. Adele bent down and placed her cheek to Natalie's mouth, her fingers moving to her neck. *No breath sounds. No pulse. Dammit!*

Her chest hitched with a loud sob. She sealed her lips around Natalie's and gave her several large breaths. *This can't be happening. It can't!* Then she scrambled to the phone that was tucked behind an overturned nightstand and the wall. Following the cord back to the base, she punched in 911, misdialing once before the call went through.

She barked out her address and the nature of the emergency, then simply dropped the phone and went back to give Natalie several more breaths and begin chest compressions, muttering words of encouragement the entire time. "Don't die. Don't die. Don't die. Breathe again. You can do it, dammit! Breathe!"

It seemed as though she'd been doing CPR for a million years when paramedics finally arrived on the scene. But instead of bursting into the room, they entered cautiously, and far too slowly for her tastes.

"Dammit, move it! The scene is clear!" She paused to blow into Natalie's mouth twice more, dizziness almost overtaking her. The wound near her wrist had been bleeding steadily the entire time she'd been giving CPR, and she hadn't had a chance to bind it. "The intruder is gone. Attempted strangulation." *Attempted? No. Actually strangled.* Her stomach clenched painfully.

Adele cursed. Talking to the paramedics had caused her to lose count of the chest compressions. "Blunt force trauma to the head. Most of the blood on her is mine."

"Police?" The paramedic looked around as he crouched down at Natalie's head.

"NOPD will be behind you." *If they ever show up*, she thought bitterly.

An Ambu bag quickly took over for Adele's mouth while the second paramedic pressed a stethoscope to Natalie's still chest.

"How long?" The man at Natalie's head squeezed the Ambu bag in a steady rhythm.

Gasping for breath and sweating from exertion, Adele moved aside so the men had room to work. She stared at Natalie's pale, bloody face in shock.

"Ma'am, how long?"

"No pulse." The second paramedic was already reaching for the defibrillator.

Adele's head snapped up sideways and she shook the sweat out of her eyes. "She was only down for one or two minutes before I called it in and started CPR." She glanced at her watch. To her astonishment, it hadn't taken the paramedics a million years to arrive, only ten minutes or so. A remarkably good response time. But she was well aware that in situations like this every second mattered.

"Ma'am? Your wrist? It's bleeding bad—"

"It's fine." Adele clutched it against her stomach, feeling the blood pulse sluggishly between her fingers. "Just take care of her."

"But—"

"Just do it!"

Scissors cut through the top of Natalie's dress and bra like butter and paddles were pressed against her chest. "Clear!"

Tears spilled down Adele's cheeks. She squeezed her eyes shut tightly and began a series of prayers she hadn't said since childhood as hundreds of volts of electricity sought to do what she could not—bring Natalie back.

CHAPTER FOURTEEN

"Detective?" A salt-and-pepper-haired nurse with a sharp chin and penetrating black eyes spoke softly. "We need to get that stitched up and find you a new shirt. You're scaring the other people in the waiting room."

Adele shifted in the hard plastic chair in the emergency waiting room of Tulane University Hospital. Crushed by the weight of the day, she looked down at her blood-soaked shirt and found it impossible to care.

What she did care about were the people. Even though it was well past midnight, the waiting room was packed with visitors and a few non-serious patients in various stages of waiting, anxiety and grief. It was noisy and smelled of cloying sweat and harsh cleaning supplies. A nearby toddler, whose sleep schedule had undoubtedly been thrown off by some family tragedy, hadn't stopped wailing for the past twenty minutes.

Everyone and everything was too close and she felt nauseous.

"It's Adele, and I appreciate your offer. *Again*. But I'm not the scariest looking person in this waiting room tonight. You can try to bully me all you want, but I'm not leaving this spot until I get an update on Natalie."

The paramedics had been able to restart Natalie's heart on the floor of the inn at about the same time police had poured into the room, whispering about Hurricane Lejeune who did more damage to the NOPD than Katrina. Then everything was chaos.

After refusing to take no for an answer, and a big dose of pleading, the paramedics allowed Adele in the back of the ambulance for the longest ride of her life. Natalie had coded while en route, and there was nothing more Adele could do than sit back and watch in horror as it took three attempts with the defibrillator to shock Natalie's heart back to life.

The police, thankfully two young officers she'd never met, had already come and gone from the hospital. Their questioning had been exceptionally quick and easy. Adele hadn't seen or heard anything at the inn other than Natalie's heartbreaking screams, so she had almost nothing to say. She'd provided a list of valuables, and directed the cops to Georgia for more detailed information. For now, it appeared the NOPD was treating this as a routine break-in that had been interrupted and turned violent.

That was nearly an hour ago. Despite repeated requests, Adele hadn't heard a single word on Natalie's condition. It was taking too long. Dread brewed hot and thick in her belly, and when her mind's eye flashed to a scene of Natalie on the floor with the lamp cord wrapped around her neck, Adele stood on unsteady legs and lurched to the nearest trash can where she heaved up her stomach contents. Sour wine and her dinner burned her throat and sinuses and splashed against the bottom of the metal can.

The nurse glowered at Adele, who was so wrapped up in her own misery that she'd forgotten the older woman was even there. She limped back to her seat and wiped her mouth with the back of her hand. "The ER doctor will find you to give an update on your friend while we attend to your wrist. You won't miss anything."

"My *cousin*, not friend," Adele insisted for the umpteenth time. She didn't want to be kept away because she wasn't family. She would have said sister, but after years of hospital visits while working for the NOPD, she knew she was recognized by too many of the hospital staff to pull it off.

"And my cut isn't that bad." In truth, Adele was feeling woozy from blood loss and anxiety. It was only mind-numbing terror for Natalie and a healthy dose of stubbornness that kept her upright at the moment.

"Then why are you bleeding all over my floor?"

Adele glanced down to the small puddle at the base of her chair and the sluggish dripping that was making it grow a tiny bit larger with each passing minute. "Oh."

An enormous male nurse with a Fu Manchu mustache appeared at her side with a wheelchair. "Best get in before the mess gets any bigger or you pass out."

"Hmm…" the female nurse looked Adele over with a critical eye. "She's a little shocky."

"I can hear you talking about me," Adele groused, but decided that she couldn't sit out here with all these people for another second anyway.

With a sigh and slightly trembling hands, she tried to push herself to her feet, and then promptly keeled over.

The next time Adele opened her eyes she was lying on an examination table and felt the sharp prick of a needle at the damaged skin near her wrist. Momentarily disoriented, the entire evening rushed back to her in an avalanche of emotion.

"Natalie!" She tried to sit up, but Nurse Fu Manchu held her down with enormous, but gentle hands. With the second prick of the needle an IV was inserted into her free hand. "Hey!"

"Relax, sister, you fainted into my arms," he said calmly, sufficiently distracting Adele long enough for the young doctor by her bedside to pick up a pair of tweezers from his instrument tray and remove a surprisingly large sliver of wood from the flesh near the base of her thumb. Nurse Fu Manchu winked. "I felt a little bit like Prince Charming."

Adele gave him a small smile, profoundly grateful for his reassuring grin when she felt on the verge of falling apart.

The doctor, a resident most likely, who looked like he hadn't slept or shaved in an entire month, began examining her wrist. "No tendon or nerve damage," he murmured, then began stitching. "For a cut this deep, you were extremely lucky."

Adele didn't feel lucky. She felt alone. Desperately alone. What if Natalie felt the same all while she was sitting here doing nothing? "What's taking so long? Why won't anyone tell me anything?"

The doctor looked more than a little insulted. "I want the stitches to be small to reduce scarring. That takes time. But I'd be happy to explain your wound aftercare."

Was he kidding? She wanted to burst into tears, but instead she bit her tongue and tried to imagine that every passing second didn't feel like eons.

"Okay. All finished with the stitches." The doctor secured the gauze bandage firmly in place. Then his meticulous gaze found the bloodstains on the collar of her blouse. "Now let's look at the back of your head and you can tell me about anyplace else you were injured."

Finally, when he was finished, he snapped off his gloves and tossed them into a nearby trash can. "Do you need something for pain?"

Adele's shoulder and hip had grown impossibly stiff and were throbbing in time with her heartbeat. She'd pushed her bad leg beyond all endurance, and even with her cane, she doubted she'd be able to stand in the morning. "No. Can you check on Natalie Abbott, please? We came in at the same time."

"I'll see what I can find out."

Sixteen stitches near her wrist and three in the back of her head, one diagnosis of a mild concussion, and an IV bag full of replacement fluids later, and her doctor and Nurse Fu Manchu left the room, only to be replaced by a second doctor.

This older man wore dorky glasses and had a grim countenance. He was otherwise so nondescript looking, that Adele found herself forgetting his face while she was still looking at it.

"Ms. Lejeune…" He glanced down at the chart in his hands, and then regarded Adele over the thick black frames of his Buddy Holly glasses. "Ms. Abbott's family?"

Adele's heart nearly stopped. "Y—yes."

"I'm Doctor Garner. I apologize for taking so long with an update. We've been very busy."

Adele pushed her next words through a throat that was closing fast. "How—how is she?" *Say anything but dead. Anything…*

"She's stable."

Adele blew out a loud shaky breath and roughly scrubbed her face with one hand, silently thanking gods from religions that hadn't even been invented yet.

"Ms. Lejeune, you look extremely pale." The doctor frowned. "I'd like to check your blood pressure. And—"

"Where's Natalie right now? She was attacked tonight and can't be left alone." Adele began to panic and started to unhook her IV, but the doctor stopped her by covering her hand with his own.

"Whoa! Hang on."

"You don't understand!" she growled and wrenched his hand away. "It's not safe for her to be alone. I—"

"We're moving her to the Intensive Care Unit in just a few minutes. Trust me, she's not alone." He took out a penlight from his breast pocket and shined it into Adele's eyes.

Annoyed, she jerked her head away.

He sighed. "Our ICU ward is secure. Only family members and medical staff are allowed inside. Visitors have to be cleared and then buzzed in."

Feeling only slightly better, Adele nodded quickly. She should have remembered that from the last time she was here. Then again, her time in the ICU as a patient was nothing but a jumbled blur.

The doctor pushed his glasses farther up the bridge of his nose. "I understand that Ms. Abbott was the victim of an assault tonight. She presents just about every textbook sign of strangulation. This isn't my first rodeo, Ms. Lejeune. Her clothing has been bagged for the police and we've collected as much physical evidence as is possible at this time. Her chart has been tagged to notify."

He didn't bother explaining further, but Adele knew that meant the police would be contacted when Natalie's doctors believed she was even remotely fit enough to talk to them.

"I don't know what exactly happened tonight other than Ms. Abbott was strangled and badly beaten." He paused and the skin around his eyes briefly tightened. "But we haven't done a rape kit yet."

Adele blinked slowly, the words not quite registering.

"We need consent for that."

"Rape kit?" The earth tilted on its side. "I d-don't. But-but she hasn't…wasn't…" Hot tears leapt into Adele's eyes so quickly she couldn't blink them back. She understood with revolting clarity that while Natalie wasn't in the room long with her attacker, it only took a few seconds to be violated. *Jesus.*

"Ms. Lejeune?"

"*Shit!*" Adele hissed, her blood turning to ice. "I never even con-considered…" Rage flared inside her once more, its embers being stoked to life by images of what might have happened behind that heavy door that made Adele ill.

Fire and ice.

"We don't have to do it now," Dr. Garner said kindly. "And maybe not at all, depending on what she says. So long as the evidence is preserved, when she wakes—"

"She's *still* unconscious?"

"She was awake earlier, but was so agitated we couldn't adequately test her neurological function. We had to restrain her."

Adele's eyes flashed dangerously. She opened her mouth to speak, but the doctor beat her to the punch.

"It's only temporary, I assure you. I've given her some nonnarcotic medication to help calm her down and for the pain. When I left her she had just fallen asleep."

He quickly referred to the chart in his hand again, flipping through the pages too quickly to really be reading. "The good news is she doesn't have any rib fractures or breaks. Those commonly occur during CPR. There also doesn't appear to be any lasting damage to her esophagus or jaw. We'll know more about the larynx when she wakes. She was negative for facial fractures. She's badly bruised and swollen, has sustained numerous lacerations to her face, arms and hands, but none of them so severe as to require stitches."

As the tears pooled in Adele's eyes, he softened his voice. "Those things will all heal." He smiled sadly. "She put up a hell of a fight."

"And the bad news? You said good news, that means there's bad."

The creases in his forehead deepened and he drew in a deep breath.

Adele's vision swam.

"Ms. Abbott has a grade three concussion and a skull fracture of the parietal bone. The bones are just barely displaced, which normally means they'd heal without surgical intervention. Despite that, her intracranial pressure is a bit higher than normal, and holding steady. If it doesn't drop on its own by morning, we'll likely put her into a medically induced coma. That will help with sensitivity to swelling and pressure. If that doesn't work, we'll be forced to operate."

Her brain. Fuck. "And in the meantime?"

"We monitor her closely and watch for complications." Asking for consent by his ultra-slow movements, he laid a comforting hand on Adele's shoulder.

She bit back a painful groan. Her shoulder was on fire.

"Her body needs to heal, and if we can get the intracranial pressure down, chances are she'll be just fine."

If? Chances are? Adele couldn't stand even the thought that there was anything less than a one hundred percent chance that Natalie would be fine. She still had trouble believing this was happening at all. Adele gulped back the acrid bile that had risen in her throat. "Can I see her? *Please.*"

The doctor seemed to consider the situation for a moment, then nodded. "ICU will need a few minutes to get her settled. In the meantime, I'll check with your doctor, and then I'll have a nurse take you up." He looked over Adele carefully and added, "In a wheelchair."

Adele merely nodded, unwilling to do a single thing that might hurt her chances of getting into Natalie's room. As the doctor excused himself, her head spun with thoughts of everything she needed to do. Most of all, she needed to plant herself at Natalie's bedside, and grasp her soft hand and pepper it with kisses. Adele needed to see for herself that Natalie was alive and fighting to get better. And if for some reason she couldn't fight for herself, then Adele would find a way to fight for her.

Tiredly, Adele closed her eyes, and her face went hard. And, oh yeah, she really needed her gun.

* * *

One of the ICU nurses stole quietly into Natalie's darkened room. There was the constant flow of nurses and the humming and beeping of machines, but the ICU felt controlled and peaceful, the opposite of the emergency room.

Adele, who had pulled her chair as close to Natalie's bed as possible, immediately lifted her head from the mattress to watch the nurse as she worked. She refused to let go of Natalie's hand.

It was still a few hours to sunrise, but it felt like the night would never end.

The young nurse spoke without looking up from her task. "Your sister just arrived. She's waiting for you outside ICU."

Upper lip between her teeth, Adele glanced between Natalie, who was calmly sleeping, and the door.

"Go," the nurse urged kindly, her voice barely above a whisper. "I need to change her IV fluids, record her stats, and wake her for her next neuro check. This would be a good time for you to go talk to your sister and maybe get a cup of coffee, if you're not going to try to sleep."

Adele smiled politely and allowed the nurse to try to convince her, but knew she wouldn't leave the area.

"You could even get cleaned up a bit. We'll be drawing more blood soon and then taking Natalie down for another CT scan. We'll buzz both you and your sister back in when you're ready."

Still uncertain, Adele nodded. She knew Amelia would be frantic to see her and she was desperate for her own phone. "You'll come get me if anything—"

"Of course."

Adele liked this nurse. She was professional, concise and took extra care to speak to Natalie as she worked.

Adele rose with a moan she couldn't have held in if she'd tried, and dropped a tender, ghost of a kiss on Natalie's swollen cheek. She tried not to let her gaze linger on her friend's spectacular black eye. The longer she sat in Natalie's room, the more guilt crept in. If she'd only…

"Your sister?" the nurse reminded her as she wrote down Natalie's vitals.

Adele nodded and squinted at the harsh fluorescent light as she exited Natalie's room and entered the ICU ward at a snail's pace to meet a very worried-looking Amelia in the deserted hallway.

"Oh, my God!" Amelia's eyes widened as Adele limped closer. "Jesus, you're covered in blood! You didn't say you were hurt!" Panicky, she dropped the duffel bag she'd brought that had Adele's cane sticking out the top, and ran her hands lightly down her sister's arms, assessing her more intently than even her doctor had.

"I'm just bruised, and I cut myself breaking in the stupid door," Adele muttered unhappily. "It looks worse than it is. Natalie's the one…" Her words trailed off to nothing.

Amelia studied Adele with a critical eye and lowered her voice even though they were alone. She cupped Adele's cheek. "How is she?"

Adele spoke past the lump in her throat. "The same." Then her eyes brightened a fraction. "But…we spoke when the nurse woke her up for her last neurological exam. She knew me, but was hazy-sounding. But she aced the neuro check anyway. She knew the day of the week, the month, and the name of the vice president."

"That's way more than most people in New Orleans know."

Adele laughed. "I—I—know." Then she burst into uncontrollable sobs, bending at the waist and wrapping her arms around herself in mute comfort.

"Oh, Ella." Amelia moved to hug her, but acting on pure instinct, Adele stumbled backward and out of reach. "No." Amelia's voice was as hard as Adele had ever heard it, pure granite. "I'm not letting you do that ever again. You aren't alone. Stop running."

Her sister was right. She wanted to bolt. The urge rose up inside her like a tidal wave, seductive and strong, an addiction to be obeyed. But despite that, her feet were cast in cement. The words she'd avoided so many times since her world crashed down around her ears finally cut through the clutter in her mind. And sunk in. And stayed.

Amelia's breathing hitched as Adele gave her a tearful nod and allowed herself to be pulled into her waiting arms.

Adele felt cool lips press firmly against the fine hairs at her temple again and again as she came apart at the seams.

Amelia murmured into Adele's hair, "Let it out. It's going to be okay, sweetie."

Desperately, Adele wound herself around her big sister, and buried her face into Amelia's neck and let everything go. "Bu—bu—but what if it izzzzn—n—nt? The doctor…he s—s—said rape and I t—tried, but I couldn't get in—inside for too lo—ong!" She hiccupped a few times in quick succession. "And there are n—n—no co—coincidences. I—I—I couldn't help her. Some—s—s-someone *strangled* her, Am—Amelia. *Strangled* her in my—my house!"

Amelia tightened her grip, a few of her own tears leaking out. "You didn't do anything wrong. You tried your best."

Adele's entire body shook as she cried. "She al-almost di-di-died!"

"But she didn't."

"But—"

"The police were still at the inn when I got there, Ella. They told me that you saved Natalie."

"No, I—"

"Yes!" Amelia corrected fervently. "Nothing is perfect, but it was enough, and that's all that matters."

Adele continued to weep for several long minutes and her sister didn't interrupt. She needed this more than oxygen at the moment. Her body and head hurt, everything felt fuzzy around the edges and far more daunting than usual.

Finally, Adele shook her head fiercely, her words barely intelligible. "I-I don't think I-I can do this."

Amelia's brows drew together. "Do what?"

"Ca-care about her. Be…maybe be fa-falling in lo-love with her."

"You're afraid that you'll let her down." It was more statement than question.

A jerky nod was Adele's answer.

"Or that she'll do the same and break your heart."

This time the nod was accompanied by a broken whimper that spilled out without Adele's permission.

Amelia sighed softly and tightened her hold. "You're braver than you think, Ella."

Adele wanted to believe the words. But she'd put everything on the line and failed before, and so it was easier to just believe it would happen again. Something in Amelia's voice, however, was impossible to ignore.

"And I don't think you have a choice when it comes to falling in love. It just sort of happens whether you like it or not. I've seen you two together. She's good for you and a good person herself. Do you really want to stop it?"

"I—I…" Adele's sobs began to wind down. She took several slow breaths and started to sound more like herself. "No," she admitted to herself and Amelia. She sniffed loudly. "I don't want to stop it."

"That's what I thought." Amelia pulled away long enough to examine her sister's tearstained face and wipe futilely at her drenched cheeks. "Are you done for now?"

Amelia's expression made it clear that it would be okay if Adele hadn't finished crying. That she had all night. And somehow that made all the difference. Adele nodded.

"Then, c'mon. You're a hot mess." With one arm around Adele's shoulders Amelia guided them both into a ladies' room that was only steps away, grabbing the bag she'd brought as they went.

Once inside, and with head down and eyes shut tight, Adele braced herself over the sink and took a few more deep breaths while Amelia disappeared into one of the stalls. She collected her scattered emotions long enough to be embarrassed that she'd just dissolved like a sandcastle in the surf. Adele couldn't remember the last time she'd cried like that. If ever. She felt…more in control. Better. "I'm sorry for doing that, Amelia."

"What? Are you kidding? Considering what happened tonight, that was totally normal." Amelia emerged from the stall with a giant wad of toilet tissue in her hand. "It's the scary, withdrawing-from-the-world crap that's not okay, all right?"

A firm nod. "Okay. No more of that." It was a promise not just to her sister, but also to herself. Natalie needed her and even more than that, Adele desperately needed to come through for Natalie.

Adele lifted her head and opened her eyes to look in the mirror. "Fuck me sideways." She barely recognized the woman looking back at her.

Amelia chuckled weakly. "I know. Your mascara was undoubtedly waterproof, but, apparently, nothing is typhoon proof."

Adele rolled her eyes at her sister's quip, even though it was clearly true. Her face was tearstained and bloodstained from touching herself with bloody hands all night. Her bawling had caused the dried blood on her face to rehydrate and smear, and her mascara had dripped all the way down her cheeks to her chin in crooked charcoal streaks.

Adele looked like the most pathetic accident victim-slash-hooker-slash-sad clown ever.

With Amelia's help, and after enduring several of her sister's gasps at the bruises covering half her body, Adele dressed in fresh clothes. She trashed everything she'd been wearing, brushed her teeth and cleaned up her face. Feeling horrible, but like a horrible *new* woman, Adele rummaged through the rest of the duffel until she found her phone.

"Did you find Natalie's too?" Adele took a few twenties from the billfold in her purse and shoved them into her jeans pocket.

Amelia shook her head. "Her purse wasn't anywhere to be found. The police think the burglar took it with him."

Adele grunted unhappily. "And my gun?"

"Even if it was still there, I couldn't get to it. The intruder trashed all the guest rooms and your entire apartment, Ella. The police were being dicks and I wasn't allowed to remove anything. Not even your toothbrush. The only reason I was able to get your purse was because you'd left it outside in the courtyard. I plain old stole the cane while no one was looking."

They shared conspiratorial grins.

Amelia dug into her own purse. "I brought you my gun from the shop." She pulled out a nickel-plated .357.

"Goddamn, Amelia!" Adele exclaimed, eyes wide. That particular model gun was a beast and about as scary looking as they came. "Where did you get that? I thought you believed in gun control."

Amelia smirked. "I do, for everyone else." Her gaze strayed to the door as though they somehow might be overheard. "Just don't tell Tony. You know how squeamish he is."

Adele smiled softly, and for the first time all night, it reached her eyes. "I *really* love you." She took the heavy weapon and made sure the safety was on before she stuffed it into the duffel bag.

"I know. Oh, and here." Amelia pulled a small box of bullets from her handbag and passed them over. At Adele's raised eyebrows, she said, "What? Just in case."

"Thanks for all this, sis." Adele gestured to the bag that contained a new full set of toiletries, an iPad still in the box—apparently Apple products could be had at any time day or night in the City of New Orleans—another change of clothes and a windbreaker.

Adele's mind drifted back into the ICU. Her heart had never left. For a second, a look of fear overtook her.

Amelia rubbed Adele's back with one hand. "She's going to be okay, you know."

She has to be. "Let's go make sure for ourselves."

When they entered Natalie's room, her doctor was there and Adele's stomach dropped. "What's wrong?" She moved quickly around the bed to be close to Natalie.

Seemingly distracted with one of the machines hooked to Natalie, the doctor motioned for the nurse to be the one to tell Adele.

Even Amelia's face paled.

Unexpectedly, the nurse smiled brightly. "The pressure in her head has gone down significantly since our last check. It's almost back to normal."

Adele finally exhaled, a little surprised that she was still upright.

Amelia mumbled, "Thank heavens," and found a place to stand out of the way against the far wall.

The doctor finally joined the conversation. "Ms. Abbott is doing very well. I've reduced her medication and she should be much more alert soon. At this rate, it's likely her intracranial pressure will be normal by morning. I'll be back after her CT scan to check on her again."

Light-headed with relief, Adele gently squeezed Natalie's hand. "Good job, Nat."

The doctor leaned closer to Adele. "Ms. Lejeune, if you remember our conversation from earlier? I can do it, of course. Or if you'd prefer to ask…?"

The smile dropped from Adele's face. "As soon as I'm able, I'll find out."

With a short, but sympathetic nod, he left the room.

Natalie began to stir.

"Natalie?" the nurse called softly, leaning down so she could look directly into Natalie's eyes. "I need you to wake up and talk to me." She turned to Adele. "I went to get the doctor before, so I'm just now getting to her neuro check, though the doctor did a preliminary check when he arrived."

Natalie grumbled in protest, but her eyes dutifully fluttered open. She looked dazed and doped up, but managed to automatically mumble, "It's still the same date and the vice president is still the same. And if something has changed, I don't really care."

The nurse chuckled, and Adele's smile could have lit up the city. This was the most lucid Natalie'd been all night.

After a few routine questions that Natalie successfully answered, the nurse left and Amelia went with her in search of coffee and to track down a phone number for Natalie's parents.

For the first time that night, Natalie's eyes didn't immediately close when the nurse finished her evaluation. The capillaries in one of Natalie's eyes had ruptured and it was splotched with red, heavy-lidded and half-mast.

Adele's heart clenched. She threaded their fingers together and brushed her lips against Natalie's clammy forehead. "How ya feeling?"

"Honestly?" Natalie's voice was raw and raspy. "Not great, but not too bad." She tried to narrow her eyes, but it was a sad attempt that ended up somewhere between an awkward wink and squint. "I think I'm high."

Adele chuckled silently.

"I think my head hurts."

"You think?"

"It does." Natalie's voice went a little dreamy. "I just don't care."

This time Adele laughed softly.

Natalie glanced down at Adele's bandaged wrist and slowly let go of their joined fingers so she could gently graze it. Her eyebrows knotted. "You're hurt. What happened to you?"

"Shouldn't that be my line?" Adele asked affectionately.

Natalie just waited.

"I scraped it on the door. It's nothing."

"Not nothing." Natalie sighed. "You're important."

Adele nearly came undone.

Natalie slowly licked dry lips, and her eyes began to drift closed. "That bastard…we fought…but the cord. I knew you'd get in. I could hear the door breaking. He was afraid of you. I could tell. You were awesome… like a girl Incredible Hulk."

Adele wasn't sure whether to laugh or cry. "I wasn't." She rested her forehead against the mattress and slammed her eyes shut tight, feeling like a fraud. How could Natalie think that? "I'm so sorry."

"Why?" Natalie whispered, dragging her fingers softly through Adele's short blond hair that had somehow gone a little messy again.

"Because I didn't get in sooner."

A faint smile curled sleepy lips. "Didja blow his head off?"

Adele snorted as she remembered her frantic threat. She sat up. "No. I didn't have my gun with me. He'd gone out the window by the time I got into the room."

"Bummer." Natalie brought her hand back near the bandage on Adele's wrist.

No wonder Amelia liked Natalie. They were both sweet on the outside, but sweet *and* mercenary on the inside. "I agree."

Adele couldn't meet Natalie's eyes. "I need to ask you something, Nat." She wrung her hands together and her heart started to slam against her ribs. "I'm sorry, sugar, but the doctor needs to know."

The endearment slipped out and she tried not to think about it as she swallowed hard and glanced up at the ceiling before forcing herself forward, dreading the answer. "Do—do they need to run a rape kit on you?"

The words made Natalie's eyes pop open wide very briefly, but she relaxed again almost immediately. "No. No, he didn't want *that*."

Adele didn't know when it had happened, but tears were sliding down her face again. She swiped at her cheeks, wholly without words to describe how grateful she was. So she didn't even try.

"Aww...don't look so sad." Natalie pouted. "I'm sorry about our date too."

"I don't care about our date," Adele said hoarsely. She couldn't help but kiss Natalie's protruding lower lip. "We'll go on another one. An even better one."

Natalie smiled wistfully. "With even more kissing?"

Adele's body jerked with a laugh. "Yeah. With nonstop kissing."

Natalie's sloppy smile was big enough to show teeth. "Good."

"You kept saying *he* before. Who was the *he* that did this to you?"

Natalie shook her head a tiny bit and grimaced at the movement that was obviously painful. Her eyes slid all the way closed again. "I dunno." Her voice began to slur from fatigue. "He had...err...a mask 'n' gloves."

Adele bit back a curse. "What did he want?"

Natalie's face went slack.

"Natalie?" Adele prompted gingerly. She felt guilty for pressing her, but her mind was already whirring with ideas and suspects. The burglary and assault *had* to be connected to Misty and Josh. First on her list of suspects was Kurt Mosley, though she didn't know how he would have tracked Natalie to the inn and what motive he might have. "What did the man that hurt you want?"

"Mmm?"

"Natalie. Focus, hon."

"Phone."

"But...why would someone want your phone?"

"Nuh-uh...Josh's." Then Natalie's hand fell away from Adele's wrist and she began to lightly snore.

CHAPTER FIFTEEN

Twenty-four hours later…

It was the middle of the night again and a single light above the bed was enough to see by, but still dim enough to be soothing. Adele changed positions in the chair next to Natalie's bedside for the hundredth time. There was no point, really, as true comfort lay beyond her reach. And that's all she was hoping for at this point, just being able to rest and relax, but not necessarily sleep. Adele was exhausted, but she needed to keep watch, not to mention the fact that the looming specter of her own dreams frightened her more than she cared to admit.

Adele stood, and her eyes immediately slammed shut from the pain. After a few deep breaths to gather herself, she moved to the head of Natalie's bed and ever so gently traced Natalie's face with her fingertip, admiring well-shaped, full lips and the dark brows that were relaxed in sleep. She carefully drew a stray strand of hair from Natalie's face, frowning at the random speckles of dried blood that were still caked along the scalp line and disappeared into thick hair.

Just as the doctor had predicted, Natalie's intracranial pressure had stabilized to well within the normal range just a few hours after it began its decline. She'd been monitored closely for the rest of the day, but, thankfully, every test had come back with good results and she'd been moved into a private room where she could rest and continue to heal.

Confused and wounded, Adele found herself wanting to touch Natalie constantly, but at the same time, draw away. She didn't understand how Josh's phone played into the break-in at the inn.

Georgia had given Natalie her charger after they'd returned from the Christmas tree lot. But Natalie never mentioned the phone again. Surely if Natalie had found something on it that would help their investigation she would have come to Adele with the information. Or would Natalie "forget" to mention that the same way she had the phone in the first place?

Adele had so many questions, but they all needed to wait. Patience had never been her best virtue.

Stretching, she bent and kissed Natalie tenderly on the lips and smiled when her friend released a gentle, contented sigh. Adele's heart clenched. She needed Natalie safe, but she was fighting an unknown foe and so knowledge was power. They had almost nothing to go on, but Adele was determined to leverage what little they did know. That also meant achingly hard choices, but ones that Adele was prepared to make.

Quietly, she retrieved her phone and stepped out of the room. Taking a few steps away, she ducked into an empty room that still allowed for a view of Natalie's doorway. Adele leaned heavily against the wall and dialed Al's home phone number, her stomach tight with tension.

The phone rang seven times before a sleepy-sounding woman answered the phone. "Latisha?" Adele said, pleased that Al's wife had answered the phone. "I know it's late. I'm so sorry." A pause. "No, you're the one I need to speak with."

* * *

Thirty-six hours later…

Natalie shifted in the bed of the nicest hospital room she'd ever seen and wondered whether Adele's and Amelia's repeated, emphatic phone calls to persons unknown had anything to do with it. She supposed she'd worry about what her health insurance would actually cover later.

She was in significantly less pain than the day before. Once her doctor was sure there was no additional danger from her head injury, he'd switched her to a mild narcotic painkiller that she'd have to give up all too soon.

Natalie lifted her fork to her mouth and scrunched up her face. The green beans were slimy and the chicken thigh, while drenched in shockingly yellow gravy, still managed to be dry. As she chewed and took a painful swallow, she only half-listened as Adele and her doctor discussed her pending discharge.

If the doctor said she could leave in the next five minutes, it wouldn't be soon enough for Natalie's tastes. She needed to leave, if not for herself, then for Adele, who had refused to leave her bedside and stood guard like the most dedicated of sentries, but looked utterly spent. Adele had also grown increasingly…distant wasn't quite the right word. Guarded. That was better. And it was starting to frighten her.

Natalie was the tiniest bit groggy. It was the sluggish sensation one's mind had when you first woke up, only she wasn't able to shake it off fully. Not yet. She was also beyond drained herself, although she wasn't sure what was the bigger contributing factor, her injuries, or the recent, highly stressful phone conversation with her mother.

Rose had been understandably worried, but she also hadn't missed the opportunity to harshly scold her daughter for not disclosing that she'd gone to New Orleans in the first place, and then for foolishly remaining in a city "where everyone gets murdered." Natalie had listened patiently to her mother's rant, then Rose's apology for her rant, then a *new* rant, before hanging up with a promise to call later. By later she meant as long as she could possibly put it off.

Natalie pushed her plate and rollaway cart away with a little grunt and sat up a little straighter as her doctor finished his conversation with Adele and exited the room. Adele did not look happy.

Adele took her usual position in the chair beside Natalie's bed and picked up her iPad. "They're discharging you tomorrow after breakfast."

Thank you. "Isn't that a good thing?" Natalie rasped, her throat still raw, but much better than the day before when she sounded like a cross between a drag queen and a phone sex operator.

"You *just* got hurt!"

Irritated they were having this discussion again, Natalie smoothed the edge of her blanket. "I can't believe you talked them into keeping me until then. There's no way my insurance will allow me to be here ten seconds longer than…" Natalie's eyes turned to slits when a guilty look flashed across Adele's face. "You offered to pay to keep me here, didn't you!"

"You almost died!"

"I'm only lying here, Ella. My doctor wouldn't let me leave if it would endanger my health. There's no reason I can't recuperate at home."

Adele swallowed hard and trained her eyes on the far wall. "You can't fly for a week to ten days. I asked. Something about absorbing gas and the pressure in your head."

"I didn't mean home to Wisconsin."

Adele began to smile at the implication, but her face quickly went flat.

Natalie could sense the progress they'd made together on a deeper relationship begin to slip through her fingers. This was the Adele she'd first encountered when she came back to New Orleans this most recent time, not the mostly open, bright woman she'd come to care so much about. "I'm not giving up on finding out what happened to Josh either. This slowed us down, but it doesn't have to stop us."

She saw Adele's jaw work, and when there was no reply, Natalie hesitantly added, "I don't have to go back to the inn. I know this has been awful and that you're probably tired of…all of this. But I've got almost a month before I have to be back at work. I know my week's prepay at the inn is basically over."

"Christ," Adele mumbled. "Do you really think I want your money? And neither one of us are going back to the inn. Not until I figure out what happened."

The lack of the word "we" in Adele's last sentence didn't go unnoticed. "What's wrong, Ella?" She grasped Adele's arm and while Adele didn't shrug her hand away, she felt the muscles beneath her fingers turn to iron. "I'm tired of waiting for you to be ready to tell me, so I'm asking."

"You mean besides the fact that a man broke into my inn and then tried to murder you?" Adele fired back, swiping her finger over her iPad screen with more force than was necessary.

Her feelings are hurt. Natalie could see the shuttered pain and frustration lurking behind Adele's eyes. She just had no clue why. "Yes," she challenged just as strongly. "Besides that."

Adele's knuckles turned white as she gripped the iPad. "Why are you so calm?"

"Because you aren't, and one of us should be."

Adele's mouth snapped shut.

Natalie wanted to keep picking and picking until she discovered exactly what was bothering Adele, but she schooled herself in patience. Besides, everything had grown so complicated—like a giant spiderweb where every fact, emotion and multiple crimes were somehow tied together with translucent wire, its pattern still a mystery—that she assumed whatever was haunting Adele was part of the same, enormous mess.

"Ella, are we ever going to talk about what happened at the inn?"

Adele ran her hands through her hair. She had dark circles under her eyes and her cheeks were sunken, and Natalie thought it was a little unfair that the other woman was still undeniably beautiful.

Adele sighed long and loud. "The doctor said…I mean, I don't want to upset you. You're supposed to be resting and getting better without stress. Not worrying about any of this."

Natalie gave her a wan smile. "So you're doing all the worrying for both of us?"

"I'm not the one who's hurt."

"You can barely walk, and you haven't slept more than a couple of hours at a time in almost three days!"

"That's hardly the same."

Natalie bit back an exasperated grumble. "I can see the wheels in your head turning. I thought we were a team, remember? Talk to me."

"Fine!" Adele's face turned red with what at first appeared to be anger, but then dissolved into something more complex. "Why didn't you tell me something was on Josh's phone?"

"What are you talking about?" Natalie was reminded that the day before Adele had specifically asked her *not* to mention Josh's phone to the police, then refused to discuss it further.

"You know, the phone that was somehow worth almost getting killed over? Why didn't you tell me what was on it? When I said you needed to think more like Nancy Drew that didn't mean for you to try to solve this on your own!"

Natalie drew her head back. She had no idea what Adele was talking about. "I'm not."

"I can't believe you would have forgotten to tell me. Again. You're not *that* stupid."

Natalie's blood began to boil. "When you get hurt or angry you lash out, Ella. And that's not okay."

"I know that! But—"

"I have no idea what's on Josh's phone."

Adele leaned forward, eyes intense and vulnerable, as though she desperately wanted to believe Natalie but didn't know how. "I saw Georgia give you her charger before she went home for the day."

"She did, and I tried to use it. But her charger is for the new iPhone. Josh's is more than five years old. The chargers must be different because hers didn't fit. When it didn't work, I put the phone back in my purse so I could take it to the store with me to find the correct charger."

Adele could only stare, dumbstruck.

"And I know what you're going to say next. I wasn't keeping this information from you." She gave Adele a stern look. "But somehow discussing my dead brother's cell phone in the middle of our first date didn't seem like a good choice." Natalie grimaced in pain and lowered her voice. "I'm sorry if that isn't enough like Nancy *goddamned* Drew for you."

"Natalie." Pale-faced, Adele dropped her face into her hands. "I'm… I'm…shit! I'm so sorry that I used the word stupid. I'm sorry I said all that. I'm…I don't even know what I'm doing. I'm so angry and worried! And I feel sick and stupid that I didn't go charge the phone the second you told me about it. If I had, maybe, somehow you wouldn't have gotten hurt. Christ, sometimes I'm just an asshole."

Natalie pursed her lips. "You're not an asshole. But, Ella, you claim to be concerned about my trust in you, when really it's you who's afraid. Not the other way around."

Eyes glistening, Adele looked up directly into Natalie's gaze. "I am trying."

Natalie did her best to reassure with a smile. It was easy to forgive Adele when she knew her worry and anxiety was on her behalf. "I know."

"But…there's still something I don't get. If you didn't think there was something important on the phone, why didn't you just turn it over to the intruder in your room when he asked for it?"

"You think I *didn't?*" Natalie said, suddenly angry again because maybe Adele really did think she was an idiot. "I gave it to him instantly, and offered him my wallet, and anything else he wanted. I also started screaming my head off!"

Natalie's heart began to pound as she remembered the terror that felt like an icy-hot shock wave. "He stuffed Josh's phone in his pocket and turned to leave, but you were already outside the door, banging on it. That's when he froze, like he wasn't sure what to do next. Then he spun around and…just came at me."

Adele's jaw dropped, her eyes widened. A look of pure horror settled over her. "Oh, my God. He attacked you because I was blocking his way out?"

"No!" When Adele looked away Natalie cupped her jaw firmly and turned her head back so they were facing each other again. "Listen to me as I say this. There is no way to know this asshole's reasoning. He's a criminal and all you did was save my life."

"I—"

"Don't you dare make this about you and your irrational need to feel guilty for anything that happens within a twenty-mile radius of me!"

That shut Adele up instantly. She floundered for a second and Natalie let her. Adele needed to understand for herself that she wasn't responsible for other adults. "I-I…I didn't know I was doing that and I'll try not to do that again," Adele whispered finally, looking a little like a deer in the headlights.

"Good. Because I won't let you."

Natalie's voice filled with tears when her mind settled on a particularly difficult moment, but she refused to cry. "We fought." The statement seemed so inadequate when what she had done was punch, kick, block, claw, flail, anything to try to stay alive.

"He pinned me on my back with his knees on my chest and wrapped his hands around my throat. When he leaned forward and squeezed everything started to go fuzzy. Even then, I could hear the violent banging as you threw yourself against the door, and the sound of wood cracking."

Adele closed her eyes, visibly disturbed by the vivid picture Natalie was painting.

"It must have been taking too long to choke me, because he grabbed the lamp from the nightstand and hit me with it." She shivered. "Everything went black, and the next thing I remember is waking up in the hospital." There. It was over.

Adele perched on the very edge of the bed next to Natalie and moved her IV tubing out of the way before she wrapped her in a gentle hug. "It's okay now." Adele stroked up and down Natalie's back with one hand, her body vibrating with an intense, dark energy that Natalie could literally feel through her thin hospital gown. "I'm going to make sure he can't hurt you again. One way or another."

Natalie pulled away so she could see Adele's face. "Wha-what do you mean hurt me again? Why would he do that? He has what he wanted."

"Maybe he thinks you saw something on the phone that's incriminating. Or maybe the fact that you know it exists is the problem. It could be a lot of things. But there is one constant: you are someone very bad's loose end."

* * *

After a long nap, Natalie awoke feeling surprisingly alert. Adele was lightly dozing, the blonde's body horribly contorted in the small hospital chair. Natalie hated to wake her, knowing that Adele's body must have simply given in to its demands for rest. She also knew how much pain Adele was already suffering through. And this would only make it worse.

"Ella?" she whispered. "Wake up. Ella?"

Adele bolted upright, then sprang to her feet. "What?" She limped around in a circle, looking for the danger and reaching for her phantom gun. Seeing none, she grasped the bed railing for support, her head hanging down between her arms as she steadied herself before her legs could give way. "Dammit."

"I'm sorry. I know you're hurting and worn out." She gave Adele a sympathetic look. "I didn't want to wake you, but I was afraid you were going to end up as a lifetime chiropractic patient if I didn't."

"I'm okay," Adele murmured, looking anything but okay. She twisted her neck and winced.

Natalie scooted over and patted the bed next to her. "Come up here with me. It's not the greatest mattress in the world, but it has to be better than that horrible chair."

"No. I'll hurt you. You—"

"Then go to a hotel."

"What? I'm not going to a hotel! You know I'm not going to do that. You're stuck with me."

"You're stuck with me too, and that means sometimes I actually get my way, Ella. Get up here before I have to drag you up." Natalie suddenly had an idea. She was going to kill two birds with one stone. "And bring your iPad."

Reluctantly, Adele kicked off her shoes and shocked Natalie by actually climbing under the covers with her. "You said you wanted me in here," Adele reminded her teasingly.

Ecstatic, Natalie said, "I did indeed. And if I'd known I'd get you under the covers, I would have asked a long time ago." She glanced down at Adele's mouth, but before she could decide whether she should kiss her, cool lips whispered adoringly over hers.

Natalie couldn't stifle her soft moan at the sensation that both excited and calmed her. Her lips had never been treated with such reverence.

After a moment, Adele backed off a little sheepishly. "I'm sorry. I couldn't resist."

The grin that stretched Natalie's cheeks felt wonderful. "I think it's safe to say that's nothing you ever have to resist." She gestured to the iPad. "Now show me what you've been poring over while you think I'm asleep. If it's pornography, I'm a little insulted that you're hoarding it." Natalie was hoping to earn at least a small smile, but was met with a serious look instead.

"We don't have to—"

"I'm well enough for you to read to me, Ella."

"Okay," Adele agreed uneasily, and she opened up her notes.

Natalie was shocked to see pages of what looked like theories, timelines, lists of names and other scraps of information.

Adele scrolled a few pages, then stopped. "This is the one I need your help with. It's a list of everyone who knew you were in New Orleans. The motive for your attack, at least in part, was to get Josh's phone. We know that, though that doesn't really help us. We know the means for the crime. Now, we need to know who had the knowledge and opportunity."

The "we" was back in Adele's sentences and Natalie was thrilled. She was tempted to comment, but Adele was still so easily spooked when it came to risking her heart that she didn't dare. There would, she promised herself, be time to be effusive in the future and really let Adele see all that she felt.

Her eyes never leaving the screen, Adele lifted one of Natalie's hands and pressed her lips against the slender bones. The move was done so matter-of-factly, so absently, that Natalie was sure Adele didn't even realize she was doing it. Adele kept hold of her hand, placing them both in her lap, her thumb tracing a soothing pattern on the back of Natalie's hand.

"Oh, wait," Adele said, sounding a little excited and letting go of Natalie's hand.

Natalie felt the loss immediately.

Adele bent down, retrieved her duffel bag, and plucked out a simple pair of brown-framed reading glasses. "I asked Amelia to pick these up for you at the gift shop yesterday."

Natalie knew Adele was leaving off the words "because I wouldn't leave you."

"They won't be as good as your own, of course, but until we can retrieve them, I figured these would be better than nothing."

Natalie's chest constricted with a feeling so overwhelming it made her gasp. "Ella…"

"Hang on…yeah…just turn your head…let me help put them on." Adele carefully slid them onto Natalie's face, taking great care to make sure they didn't upset the bandage coiled around her head. "There." She gave Natalie a delighted, slightly dopey grin and kissed the tip of her nose. "You look beautiful."

It was a small gesture, almost insignificant in comparison to others Adele had readily made on her behalf, which somehow managed to bowl Natalie over completely. And in that moment she knew. She could feel it from the top of her head to the tips of her toes. It was so simple and beautiful it made her want to cry. They *fit*. Natalie would travel a million miles for this woman, all of them baby steps, if that was what it took.

"Hey, are you okay?" Adele asked softly, concerned. "You look weird all of a sudden."

Natalie laughed. The fact that she was hurt and lying in a hospital bed was all but forgotten in the wake of the heady moment. "I'm wonderful. I promise."

With a sigh, Natalie refocused on the iPad screen. The tiny letters now appeared blessedly bigger. As she scanned the names, she blinked stupidly. "I-I don't know what to say. Amelia? Georgia? You can't think they'd hurt me."

"It's just a list. Sometimes it's not the name on the list that's important, but who they might tell, accidentally or otherwise." They were touching from shoulder to foot, but Adele somehow found a way to scoot a little closer.

"But, no," Adele shook her head resolutely. "Of course I don't think they had anything to do with it. Besides, they're off the list because they're female. I know what you told the police, but you're sure your attacker was male?"

"Very. He had a man's voice, and he was way too strong to be a woman."

Adele hummed to herself. "Kurt Mosley is an obvious suspect. As Misty's boyfriend, he might have known about the phone all along."

Natalie shook her head. "I don't think he could have held me down. I think I would have noticed if the man who attacked me was rail-thin."

Adele nodded. "Plus how would Kurt have found you at the inn? You didn't tell him where you were staying, right?"

"I...oh, no." Natalie's hands shaped fists. "Oh, my gosh. He could have found me through you. I told him your name." She felt like a fool. "While you were inside looking around Misty's house, he asked, and I panicked. I didn't think it mattered, or that I, or we, were hiding."

"It's okay. We weren't hiding. But let's leave him on the list for now. Wiry men can still be deceptively strong. And when you're scared, whatever is scaring you can seem bigger than it really is."

Natalie was doubtful, but it was Adele's list. "Okay."

The next name made Natalie laugh out loud. "Ross? The contractor at the inn? He's ancient. There is no way he could have fought like that."

"Okay," Natalie allowed grudgingly. She pressed a couple keys and lined through his name. "But what about one of his men? He had a crew of at least three strong, young guys at the house all this week."

Natalie nodded unhappily. "I never spoke to any of them. But, fine. They stay."

"Next are the officers who responded to the call to Misty's house."

They discussed the two men for a moment, keeping one name, but eliminating one due to size. Natalie's attacker was bigger and taller than she was, but not by a hundred pounds and eight inches.

"Why would the police be involved in this at all?" Natalie asked, fighting off a shiver not only from thoughts of the attack, but also from her hospital room that was perpetually kept as cool as a meat locker. And Adele's warm body felt so good that Natalie wanted to burrow underneath her friend's skin and take up residence there.

"I dunno, but I don't think we can exclude them just because they're cops."

Now that Natalie thought of it, she wondered whether them being cops, considering the corruption in the NOPD that seemed so endemic, made them prime candidates on the list. But as angry as Adele was at her former colleagues, Natalie knew in Adele's heart she didn't want to believe the worst.

The next name was another Natalie hadn't expected. Sgt. Jay Morrell. The rat who was first on the scene to Josh's murder and who had beaten Crisco within an inch of his life and set off the firestorm that ended Adele's career. If Natalie could run him down with her car and not go to prison for it, she wasn't sure he'd see another day. "What connects him to Misty now? Misty said she left the Dixie Brewery right after Josh's… right after it happened. I don't think she saw Morrell, and if he'd seen her, surely she would have been arrested."

"I don't know the connection. As much as I'd like to pin Josh's murder on him, Morrell didn't do it. I was able to confirm that he and his dumbass rookie partner, Billy Hobson, were still across town at the time of Josh's death. Apparently, they stopped for gas on the way to the diner where they were headed when they got dispatched to the brewery. During the PIB investigations, Morrell was able to produce a receipt proving where he was and when."

"Wow. The police actually shared this information with you?"

Adele snorted and turned just enough to rub her nose against Natalie's cool cheek. Even with the grim subject matter, Adele seemed to be relaxing a tiny bit more with each passing minute, which had been one of the reasons Natalie had coaxed her into bed in the first place. "Hardly. Al dug it up for me. I've been thinking of Morrell ever since I realized Misty's house was in his stomping ground…the Tremé."

A kiss was added to the mix and caused Natalie's lips to curl.

"Because Morrell works the Tremé, he could have easily spotted you when you were at the station giving your statement about Misty. Or he could have spoken to the cops from the crime scene. Word travels like wildfire within the PD. If Morrell found out about you, and he's still in touch with Hobson, he could have told him, too."

Natalie rubbed at the creases her scowl was making in her forehead. Their net was cast too wide to be useful. "Using that logic, every male police officer in the NOPD who isn't a giant or a midget is a suspect."

Dejectedly, Adele clicked off her iPad. "I know."

There was one name that Natalie hadn't seen on the list, and it made her uneasy to bring him up, but… "If we're including everyone, why isn't Al's name on the list?" She kept her voice more curious than accusing. "He saw me at the inn my first day back in town."

"He didn't do it," Adele said dully, glancing at the dark iPad screen.

"Okay. I trust you, and if you trust him, I do too."

"I don't trust anybody," Adele growled suddenly. "Not when it comes to your safety. I didn't put him on the list because I ruled him out before I even made the list. I had a feeling…my gut told me your attack wasn't random. The night after your attack, I called Al's house."

"But if he was involved, you couldn't think he would just confess because you called him."

"I didn't call *him*. I called his home phone and his wife, Latisha, picked up. She's who I was after. We spoke for a minute or two, and she confirmed that Al had been home that entire evening. Then she figured out there couldn't really be a positive reason that I was trying to pin down Al's whereabouts, all without talking to him, and she hung up on me." Adele's exhausted frown made her look years older. "Not that I blame her."

"Oh, Ella." Natalie tried to wrap her head around what that single call had likely cost Adele. It was enough to make her queasy. How many more relationships would Adele have to lose? Natalie vowed to reach out to Al on her own. Maybe she could smooth things over. "I'm sorry." Her already hoarse voice broke.

"Hey, remember what you told me?" Warm brown eyes were suddenly fierce and protective. "Don't make this about you when it isn't. I decided how to handle it, and I'm not sorry. I didn't set out to burn that bridge, but I had to be sure. And now I am."

Just then, a nurse walked into the room. She stared at Adele and Natalie, who were sitting side by side in bed, but she managed not to comment. "I'm here to check your IV, Ms. Abbott. I hear you're going to be discharged in the morning."

With a groan from the movement, Adele flung off the covers and moved off the bed to pick up her phone. "We'll be ready."

CHAPTER SIXTEEN

Adele slowly pushed Natalie's wheelchair toward the elevator, using it to steady herself as they made their way out of the hospital ward. She backed them into the elevator with great care, but instead of pushing the button for the ground floor, where patients normally stopped to leave the hospital, Adele selected the lower level that held the hospital's kitchens, laundry, storage facilities, laboratories and pharmacy.

Wearing a comfortable pair of full-length yoga pants and a thin velvety-soft sweater, courtesy of Amelia, Natalie clutched Adele's duffel bag to her belly. She tried to look over her shoulder at the former detective. "I already have my prescriptions. I thought we were leav—"

Two men entered the elevator at the ground floor and began the ride with them to the lower level.

"Shh…" Adele breathed discreetly. "We are."

Adele assessed the men carefully, more confident due to the weapon she had tucked into the back of her pants and hidden beneath her windbreaker. The gun was too large to carry comfortably this way for long, but it was all Adele had for now. She leaned close to Natalie's ear and whispered. "You'll see."

They exited the elevator as a small group.

The men walked ahead of them until they reached the pharmacy where they stepped inside and went about their business. Adele and

Natalie continued past them and down a long corridor that began to slope uphill. Body on high alert, Adele ducked them into a deep doorway and waited, hand on gun, in case the men were intentionally following them.

They weren't.

As the women moved farther down the corridor the number of nonhospital staff dwindled to nothing. They were stopped several times by nurses asking if they needed help finding the pharmacy, but Adele assured the helpful strangers that she was merely stretching her legs. After all, the area wasn't technically restricted to staff.

Finally, Adele wheeled Natalie into a bustling kitchen where a middle-aged man with a severely receding hairline and a beer belly that made him appear pregnant intercepted them almost immediately. "You're later than I expected," he said casually as he motioned for Adele to follow him.

Adele maneuvered Natalie around an enormous vat of what smelled like applesauce. "You know how it is with bullshit hospital paperwork."

The man grunted his agreement.

Natalie listened to the bewildering conversation with wide eyes.

He led them through the kitchens and out to an open delivery bay where a white bakery truck was already backed into the dock. "Leave the wheelchair here and I'll take it back upstairs after you're gone." He disappeared back inside.

The sun seemed overly bright after several days inside and Adele and Natalie both squinted. "Okay," Adele said, glancing around. "This is where we leave."

Puzzled, Natalie looked for a car.

"No, this is our ride." Adele gestured toward the truck. "And we should get inside quickly."

She helped Natalie to her feet, noting enviously that even after everything that had happened, Natalie actually had better mobility than she did. Insecurity nagged at the back of Adele's mind. How long would Natalie want to be limited by what Adele could or couldn't do? Maybe once all of this was over, she'd visit the rehab center again or talk to her doctor about possible surgeries. It couldn't hurt to consider it, even though it probably wouldn't help, right?

A trim man somewhere in his early thirties with a thick shock of straw-colored hair and wearing worn jeans, a black faded T-shirt, work boots and a New Orleans Saints baseball hat, climbed out of the truck. "Do you ladies need any help getting in?"

Adele breezed by him without a second glance. "We're good." She helped Natalie into the truck through the rear bay doors. "Careful." The cargo area was empty, except for a few wooden crates that had been covered with heavy wool blankets and would serve as their seats.

The man shut the doors behind them, then climbed into the driver's side door and made his way between the front seats and into the cargo area, wearing a big smile. He stopped in front of Adele and lifted an eyebrow. "Well?"

"It'll do," Adele said in an unimpressed voice, then grinned broadly and allowed herself to be hoisted into a full body bear hug that lifted her off her feet and felt almost as good as it did bad. "Uff! Careful. I'm still sore!" Adele's smile belied her words and she was lowered carefully until her feet touched the ground. "This is perfect. And you look just right. Though I'm not sure I recognize you without the Armani suit you were born in."

Natalie narrowed her eyes at their embrace.

"Natalie," Adele laughed a little as the man finally released her, but slung an arm over her shoulder. She hadn't missed Natalie's sudden pique. "This is my brother Jackson."

Natalie's face immediately brightened. "Oh, my gosh. It's great to meet you." She self-consciously smoothed her hair, clearly a little embarrassed by her appearance.

Jackson gently shook her hand. "It's a pleasure to meet you. Amelia and my girls have told me all about you. All great things, I might add, including that you helped Ella try to find a winning Christmas tree this year. I love it when anyone at least tries to beat Amelia at anything." He winked good-naturedly. "Too bad it's so rarely successful."

"Your daughters are darling and so smart. They helped make the day even more fun."

Jackson flashed Natalie a brilliant smile, then he turned and guided Adele a few steps away, their backs to Natalie. He lowered his voice to a whisper, but it still came out as an angry growl. "You're going to get the animal, son-of-a-bitch who did that to her, right?"

Adele's gaze drifted back to Natalie and she did her best not to frown. They'd been together constantly, and she'd almost forgotten how bad Natalie would look to someone with fresh eyes. Adele was so grateful that Natalie was still among the living that everything else, while important, was secondary.

Natalie still had visible ligature marks around her neck, along with a lurid bruise in the shape of a hand. One of her eyes was pink. The tiny cuts that marred her normally smooth skin had scabbed over and her black eye had gone from deep red to a spectacular purple-yellow mix. All of these things, as bad as they were, were substantially better than a few days ago.

Adele's eyes glinted terrifyingly. "Oh, I'm going to find him, Jackson. Don't you doubt that."

Brother and sister shared a nod of understanding. While it was true that Adele had always been closer to Amelia than Jackson, that didn't mean they didn't have each other's backs. Family was family.

"I have another bag of goodies in the back to supplement what Amelia gave you," Jackson said. "Keys to your new place are in the side pocket. But I still don't know why you can't stay at my house."

"With your girls there, Jackson? C'mon." Adele patted his chest. "This is safest for us all."

Reluctantly conceding Adele's point, he moved back to the driver's seat and started the truck. "We'd better get going."

Adele sat down next to Natalie, who was unusually quiet. "Are you okay, Nancy goddamned Drew?"

Natalie laughed silently. "Just tired. I know I shouldn't be, but I am. And my head hurts."

Adele opened her mouth to speak, but Natalie pressed her fingertips against Adele's lips. "It's just a headache. Nothing more."

Adele reluctantly nodded. "If you're sure."

"Are you finally going to tell me what's going on?"

The truck began to move.

"Yes, and I'm sorry about the cloak-and-dagger stuff. I don't want us to go back to the inn. Whoever hurt you could come back, or track us and try again later. The inn is too big for two people and there are multiple entrances and first-floor windows. There's no good way for us to keep it secure if someone really wants inside. We're going to a safe house that Georgia and Amelia arranged and rented under a fake name."

"And you didn't tell me we were going to escape from the hospital like Bonnie and Clyde because…?"

"Loose lips sink ships?"

Natalie pinched her. Hard.

"Ouch. Shit. Okay, okay." She chuckled and swatted away the still-attacking hand. "We just finalized this all this morning while you were getting your endless aftercare medical instructions. And I figured the less you knew, the less you'd have to worry about."

"Don't make a habit of that, okay?" Natalie received an immediate, sheepish nod in reply. "How did you do all this?" She gestured to the empty vehicle. "The truck, the man in the kitchen, a safe house? All in a few days?"

"Georgia is a master planner. If she were on the president's cabinet… well, actually, Georgia should just be president. When Amelia talks, people listen." Adele broke into a lazy, crooked grin. "Plus, she bribes the hell out of them."

Less than ten minutes later, the truck pulled behind a smallish—for the neighborhood—but gorgeous, white Greek Revival-style home in the Garden District and stopped in front of its carriage house. Jackson helped Natalie and Adele out onto the stone driveway. He leaned close to Adele. "You'll call if you need anything, and be careful?" He glared pointedly at the thick bandage near her wrist.

She nodded and leaned onto tiptoes to kiss his cheek, using one hand on his shoulder for balance. "Smooch my gorgeous nieces for me and remind them which aunt is the best?"

"Duh."

"Then, yes."

Jackson left the women staring at the carriage house. Its upstairs had been converted into a large apartment. Adele examined their surroundings closely, impressed. The yard was fenced, and there was enough shrubbery for privacy but not so much that someone could be lurking in every shadow.

"Does it meet your requirements, Your Highness?" Natalie sassed, taking one of the bags from Adele and ignoring her protests. "Before you say anything, our temporary hideout looks better than my actual townhouse."

"Well, let's see. The owners of the main house are gone to Hawaii for the winter, so that's privacy." She made a check mark in the air. "Second floor, quiet street, one point of entry only." Three more checks. "There was only one more thing on my list, and we won't know if we got that until we get inside. Now we just have to brave those stairs." The last few days were catching up to Adele quickly, and the thought of hiking up the stairs made her whimper out loud.

"Wait," Natalie reached out and tugged on Adele's jacket. "Who is already here? Amelia or Georgia?" A new white Ford Fiesta sat in the driveway.

"Nah. That's ours. I'm amazed Amelia stuck to the plan and got something inconspicuous. I had to talk her out of both a Hummer and a Land Rover. Now, c'mon. You go ahead of me. I'm seriously ready to drop, and I don't want to take you with me if I do."

The inside of the carriage house was simple but lovely. It was an open floor plan, and despite the historical building, there was nary an antique in sight. The appliances were gleaming stainless steel, and the furniture was modern, immaculate, and done in tranquil shades of blue and cream. The scent of fresh flowers filled the room from the several overflowing vases that dotted the space.

"Well?" Adele inclined her head toward Natalie. She wanted her to be happy even in their temporary digs.

"Anyone would be comfortable here. It's lovely, Ella."

Adele considered retrieving her cane from the duffel bag, but gritted her teeth and decided she could last just a few more minutes. She opened what she assumed to be the bathroom door and wasn't disappointed.

The shower was large with multiple heads and a teak bench. It was already stocked with spa-quality toiletries, and encased in opaque glass. Across from it and the toilet, sat a deep Jacuzzi tub that was big enough for two with room to spare. Fluffy white towels filled a rack near the sink. Adele smiled broadly, her heart racing at even the possibility of eventually sharing it with Natalie. Amelia and Georgia had found a way to find every single thing on her list. They rocked.

Natalie moved alongside Adele and stared at the tub with open lust. "I would kill for a bath." She groaned and wrinkled her nose. "I feel disgusting. My hair is filthy and I'm pretty sure I stink."

"Well, I *know* I stink." Adele shook her head woefully. "And my muscles are in knots. God, I'm going to owe Amelia forever for this." Georgia, she could pay. Amelia would demand something, well…more demanding.

Natalie wiped at the drool that had pooled at the corner of her mouth with the back of her hand as she continue to ogle the tub. "I'm willing to have her baby."

Adele burst out laughing. "Gross! Don't let Amelia hear you say that. You don't know my sister. She was a whiny pregnant woman and might take you up on that offer."

Natalie set her bag on a side table. "Tub first or sleep?" As they pondered which pleasure was more compelling, they continued deeper into the apartment. Several large Chinese screens separated this area from the rest of the apartment. In the corner was a tall, king-sized bed that looked decadent enough for an actual king.

Adele rolled her eyes. "One bed?" *Amelia, you goddamned meddler.* "I take back what I said about my sister," she groused, but was too tired to feel embarrassed or anxious at the idea of sharing a bed. "Would you like me to take the sofa?" Her bloodshot eyes pleaded with Natalie not to take her up on her offer.

Natalie drew her hand across a plush comforter, a slight frown pulling at her lips from Adele's words. "Don't be silly. If anyone has to end up on the sofa it should be me. It'll be nice not to be pestered throughout the night by nurses."

Adele snorted. "Like I'd have you sleep on the couch."

"This bed is huge. My head hurts, and I can tell by the way you're walking that you're sore all over. We both need a good night's sleep. I'm okay with sharing, if you are." Natalie grinned tiredly. "I'll even keep my hands to myself."

Adele wasn't sure whether that was really a selling point, but it didn't matter. Without further discussion, Natalie gingerly climbed onto the bed. Taking the hint, Adele followed.

They lay down on top of the covers with twin sighs.

"I'm just trying it out," Natalie mumbled, her eyes already closing. She moaned in pleasure and shifted to her side. Her voice went faint. "Just for a minute…"

"Yeah," Adele agreed, sinking into the luxurious comforter and snuggling so close to Natalie's side that they shared the same large down-filled pillow. She exhaled deeply, her breath ruffling Natalie's hair. Adele's aching body finally began to relax. Warm. Safe. Together. She gently placed an arm around Natalie's waist and pulled their bodies flush. "We'll get cleaned up eventually…"

But Natalie was already fast asleep.

* * *

A gentle shake. "Ella?"

"Nooo…" Adele muttered. "Go 'way. Sleepin'."

This time her shake was firmer. "Wake up, sweetie. Your phone is ringing." Natalie thrust the cell phone at her. "You're going to want to take this call. It's Logan."

Blearily, Adele pressed the phone to her ear. Her confused gaze traveled to the darkened windows and then to the clock. She'd slept for ten hours without moving an inch.

"Hey, Lo-Logan!" She cleared the sleep from her voice and smiled a gorgeous smile that transformed her face and made Natalie's knees buckle. "I've missed you, buddy. Are you having fun with your dad?" She sat up a little in bed and gave Natalie a grateful look. "Are you excited about Santa's visit soon? Only another week."

Natalie moved into the kitchen to give Adele a little privacy and hopefully to find something she could put together for a light meal. They'd slept through lunch and dinner and she was starving.

She'd been awake for the past hour and when she couldn't comfortably lie in bed any longer, she'd padded to the nearest window and cracked it open for a bit of fresh air. She stood there, star gazing, and feeling more at peace than she had in a very long time.

It was far quieter in this area of town than at the Touro Street Inn. She couldn't hear the sounds of tourists laughing or passing cars. Just the wind in the trees—she laughed quietly as she remembered—and Adele's light snoring.

Amelia, or perhaps it was Georgia, didn't disappoint. The kitchen cabinets and refrigerator were packed with fresh groceries and on the countertop sat a half-dozen bottles of good wine and an opener. Natalie debated between a California zinfandel and a Chianti. And for a second, she longed equally for both options. Deciding this wasn't really *Sophie's Choice*, she eventually selected the zin. She took a healthy sip and, murmuring her approval, gave herself permission to fully live in the moment.

A beautiful woman who Natalie wanted to get to know much, much better, was in her bed. The wine was delicious. And right now, they were safe. She sighed in pleasure.

Deciding on some pasta and a green salad, Natalie pulled out a large can of crushed tomatoes from the cupboard, along with some dried herbs and spices and a box of spaghetti noodles. After about ten minutes of work the salad was ready, and she poured the tomatoes and spices into a sizzling pan of sautéing onions and shredded carrots. Oregano and basil scented steam rose up and tickled her nose.

Satisfied, she turned the stovetop burner to low. Natalie's second glass of wine was nearly to her lips when Adele limped slowly into the kitchen with a raised eyebrow.

"Don't give me that look," Natalie warned. "I'm not being bad. I took my last prescription pain tablet this morning. As of now, I'm on ibuprofen and can safely drink in moderation." She said her last words in a surprisingly good imitation of her doctor's slightly southern, but mostly condescending tone.

Adele neatly plucked the glass from Natalie's hand and took a dainty swallow of wine, claiming the glass for herself. "What a coincidence. So can I."

"Hey!"

"Mmm." Adele smacked her lips a little and chuckled as Natalie playfully scowled in her direction and retrieved a second glass from the cabinet. "This is one of Georgia's favorites. Oooh…whatcha makin'? It smells fantastic." Adele stuck her nose into the pot of sauce and inhaled deeply, her eyes rolling back in pleasure.

"Just some spaghetti. I hope that's okay." At Adele's nod, Natalie poured herself a fresh glass, and added pasta to the boiling water. "You're walking so much better tonight." She'd noticed that Adele's forehead wasn't pinched in pain, as it often was when her leg was hurting.

"That's because I'm feeling so much better. Sleep does wonders. Though if I'm being honest, I could go back to bed in an hour or two and probably still sleep through the entire night."

Natalie felt the same way. "Then that's what we'll do." She added black pepper to the sauce. "How's Logan?"

Adele leaned against the cabinet, her voice a tiny bit more subdued than before. "Excited for Christmas. Happy. Enjoying his time with his dad. Missing me."

Concerned, Natalie glanced sideways. "You miss him too."

Adele shrugged one shoulder, and swirled the wine a little in the glass before bringing it to her mouth. "Pretty much all the time."

Natalie thought of the beautiful Christmas tree sitting undecorated and alone at the inn. "What are you going to do about Christmas with him?"

Adele let out a resigned breath. "He'll have to stay with Landry until this is over."

"What does that mean?" Natalie was suddenly a little panicky. She didn't feel any closer to finding Josh's killer than the day she'd arrived back in New Orleans. Even though her attacker clearly felt differently. "We might never find out who killed Josh."

Adele's brow puckered. "We won't give up."

"No. No. Jesus…" Natalie ran a frustrated hand through her hair, wincing when she encountered a few stitches that were now sans bandage. "I'm not that selfish…I mean, I guess I must be to have done this to you so far. But I shouldn't be. I'm dangerous to be around at the moment. But Logan's so excited about the holiday, and you miss him terribly. I'll leave town before you and Logan miss Christmas together. And—"

"Natalie, stop rambling." Adele's voice was full of warmth. "I don't want you to go." At Natalie's wide eyes, she added, with a little less confidence, "At least not yet, okay? We still have time." Adele drew a finger down the stem of her wineglass. "You haven't *done* anything to me. I'm doing this for myself too. Not just you."

"But now you're in danger."

"The second I said yes to investigating Josh's murder that happened. I was a cop for almost my entire adult life. A little danger isn't going to make me melt. Besides, I'm not sure you leaving town would put an end to things. If someone tried to kill you over something on Josh's phone, why wouldn't he come after me, too?"

Natalie's stomach dropped through the floor.

"The phone was in my house, after all. And we were clearly investigating this together. Anything you could or would know, I could know." Adele's gaze darkened. "I can't risk Logan. But I have to see this through, with or without you."

"Bu-but…" Natalie's mind whirred. It seemed unlikely someone would go after Adele, and yet, everything that had happened so far seemed that way. "Shit!"

Adele looked skyward, as though she was asking for some sort of heavenly intervention. "Or maybe we'll get lucky, and *my* Christmas wish will come true, and we'll figure out all of this before Christmas Day."

Suddenly tears swam in Natalie's eyes. "I'm sorry. I never meant to take time away from you and Logan."

"Hey." Adele moved to stand next to Natalie and gave her a gentle peck on the cheek, artfully avoiding a small scab that sat atop her cheekbone. "That hasn't even happened yet. Even if it does, none of this is your fault.

I'm glad you're working with me. I was tired of being alone, Nat. And I don't feel like I am when we're together."

Natalie couldn't help a tremulous smile at the heartfelt admission.

"The only thing I'm unhappy about is that you're hurt. Let's not worry about Christmas yet, and focus on one thing at a time."

Natalie turned her back to Adele and tested the spaghetti. She tried to keep the worry out of her voice as she thought of the coming days. "So, we're going to talk to Billy Hobson tomorrow?" Natalie knew she should be more enthusiastic about the prospect, especially now that she was officially the Grinch but she still felt weaker than normal and mentally frayed around the edges. It seemed a stretch that the rookie officer who responded to the crime scene *after* Josh's murder would know anything that could help them.

"If I can go alone, then yes, absolutely."

"Alone?" God, this woman could be infuriating! Natalie suddenly wanted to shake Adele until her teeth rattled. "No, absolutely!"

"Natalie—"

"No."

Adele gave her a challenging look. "Fine. If you're going to be anywhere near me when I catch up with Billy, you need to be able to run if something unexpected happens." She lifted her eyebrows in question. "Can you run?"

Natalie blanched. The thought of running and the pounding it would cause her head made her stomach roil. "Yes."

The challenging look turned into a disbelieving glare.

Natalie wanted to stamp her feet when she realized that Adele could already tell when she was lying. "I said yes."

Adele continued to stare.

"Oh, my God, fine! If I only have to go six steps and then it's okay for me to stop and puke, then, yes, I can run."

"Stopping to vomit won't slow your escape down at all."

Natalie bared her teeth at the sarcasm.

"And before you ask, I know I can't run either. But I'm willing to use my gun, if necessary."

Natalie winced at the word gun. They made her impossibly uneasy. Even though Natalie's parents had gone as far as purchasing her one, insisting that a single woman living alone needed protection, she'd refused it.

"I hate to put off going to Shreveport as much as you do, more maybe, but we don't need any more disadvantages when we confront Billy. And let's be honest. He's a sheep compared to Morrell. How about we reevaluate how we're feeling in the morning and take things from there?"

Natalie already felt like the weak link on this team. Now she felt even worse. "You mean how I feel."

"Trust me, I don't. But you could always carry a weapon when we meet Billy, just to help even the odds?"

Natalie knew the way she felt was showing on her face by Adele's I-thought-so expression. "Does this really need to be a confrontation?" Natalie asked. "Can't it be like what we did with Kurt Mosley? A conversation?"

"That will depend on Billy. But I really think a different tactic will work best with him. This guy is still in his midtwenties. He's not too many years older than your students. When was the last time one of them didn't announce their every move on Twitter or Tumblr or whatever?"

"Never."

"Exactly. The fact that it took us so long to find him online, and that he's completely absent from social media, tells me he doesn't want to be found. That makes him dangerous. Plus, he was a police officer, even if he wasn't a very good one. Chances are he's got a weapon somewhere."

Natalie acknowledged Adele's words with a sigh and a change of subject. "Dinner's ready."

The meal was slow and easy and filled with much lighter conversation. Instead of sitting across from each other, they sat side by side, heads unconsciously tilted toward each other, drawn together like magnets. Afterward, Natalie half-filled each of their glasses then threw away the empty wine bottle.

Looking supremely relaxed, Adele wiped the corners of her mouth and set her napkin on the table. "That was awesome, and I ate way too much."

Natalie felt a tickle of pleasure at the compliment. She liked to cook, but cooking for one seemed so pointless. "No big deal. It was easy."

"I'm not a good cook, as Logan and Landry will be the first ones to tell you. And I can't remember the last time someone cooked for me. So it was a big deal. I—" She stopped and broke into a yawn so big her jaw cracked.

Natalie's expression filled with sympathy. While she'd been in the hospital bed, it was easy to forget that Adele had literally beaten herself black-and-blue getting through the door of her room at the inn and had her own concussion, albeit a mild one. Add to that several nights without sleep, and it was going to take more time for her to recover, too.

"Ella, how about a bath and then bed?"

"God, yes."

* * *

Adele and Natalie stood in front of the large tub, not quite knowing what to do. Adele had filled it with hot water and had even added a bit of bubble bath that her nosy but well-intentioned sister had thoughtfully provided. She knew exactly what she wanted out of this bath, but she was far less sure of what Natalie was thinking.

Natalie drew in a deep breath and looked for a place to set their wineglasses as Adele lit several candles and turned off the lights. The room glowed with the perfect mix of relaxation and sensuality. Unnoticed on their earlier tour, a skylight above the tub allowed moonlight to drape over them and provided a lovely view of the stars.

Natalie licked her lips and looked longingly at the steaming water. "I-um…you can go first. Do you want some privacy?"

Face hot, Adele swallowed back her nerves. "I don't need privacy." She turned to face Natalie. "It's okay if you do though."

Natalie shook her head slowly. "I don't."

Natalie's smoky voice seemed to drop an octave and Adele felt it twist its way through her like a hot blowing wind. "I—I, I mean, I know you don't technically need it or anything, but, if you want, I could help you wash your hair."

"I'd like that. And, Ella?"

"Yeah?"

"It's just a bath. You don't need to be so nervous." Natalie set both glasses on the tiled floor alongside the tub.

Adele chuckled uneasily and glanced at Natalie from behind thick lashes. "It's that obvious?"

Natalie's grin was warm and inviting as she stepped into Adele's personal space, not stopping until their faces were only a few inches apart. Her pale eyes looked almost colorless in the combination of candle and moonlight. "A little. But that's okay. We can be nervous together."

Natalie reached up and traced Adele's cheek with the soft pads of her fingers.

The tender touch caused Adele's eyes to close halfway and her nostrils to flare. The bathroom was hot and steamy, and Natalie's unnerving fingertips gently drew along the fine, damp hair at Adele's temple and over her scar, treating it to an even gentler touch.

Adele settled her hands on Natalie's hips and lightly squeezed.

"You're so beautiful," Natalie muttered, enthralled, her hand never stopping. Her fingers trailed down Adele's throat. She turned her hand so that the backs of her fingers trailed lightly over delicate collarbones. She gave Adele's shirt a tiny tug. "Can I see more? Please?" Natalie whispered, brushing her lips over the tip of Adele's nose.

Adele's heart thudded in her chest and her knees felt weak. Her tongue seemed to be frozen in her mouth so she just nodded and allowed

Natalie to slowly strip off her shirt, fingers trailing from her shoulder and down her arms, leaving a trail of goose bumps in their wake. Adele's shirt puddled on the floor.

Natalie lifted Adele's wrist and gently brought it to her mouth where she lovingly kissed the bandaged flesh. "We need to keep this dry."

"Okay," Adele answered, her voice soft and breathy.

Warm hands trailed down Adele's slender middle and around to the front of her belly, and sure fingers dipped beneath the waist of her jeans and stopped. Adele sucked in a breath.

"Can I?" Natalie asked, watching Adele's face closely, her lips curled in a small smile.

Adele nodded and heard the dull pop of a button on her jeans and her zipper being lowered, inch by inch. She held in a moan. Natalie dropped slowly to her knees in front of her and looked up. *Holy shit.* Her nipples hardened at the sight.

Natalie grasped Adele's hands and laid them on her own shoulders for balance. "Step, please."

Dutifully, Adele stepped out of her jeans and Natalie whisked them away.

Moist lips dropped tiny kisses all around Adele's belly button, causing her to shiver in anticipation and a flood of warmth to pool between her legs. Okay, maybe it was time to rethink what she wanted out of this bath.

"You taste good."

The words tickled her skin, and Adele felt her chest flush hotly.

Unexpectedly, Natalie dipped her tongue inside Adele's navel.

Unable to stop herself, Adele shrieked and squirmed away laughing.

Natalie joined in, clearly delighted, her eyes dark with arousal. "I found a ticklish spot."

Adele felt a large portion of her nervousness fade. She reached down and pulled Natalie to her feet. "Isn't that everyone's ticklish spot?"

Natalie grinned coyly. "Wouldn't you like to know?"

"Yes," Adele whispered, "I actually really would." Standing in front of Natalie in only a white bra and mismatched red panties, she wrapped an arm around the other woman and pulled her close.

Natalie gave her a saucy wink. "Well—" Her gaze dropped to a massive bruise that started at Adele's shoulder and went all the way down to the middle of her thigh. "Oh, my God, Ella!" She moved to touch the injured flesh but clearly unsure of what was safe to touch, she hovered in place.

Adele captured Natalie's hands. "I'm okay. And the water is getting cold." That was a lie. The tub had a heater. But that wasn't the point. She was drifting in a lovely, erotic haze, and didn't want it spoiled by focusing on the grim reality of what had happened.

Natalie looked like she wanted to protest, but Adele squeezed her hands to signal that she really was okay. Adele threaded one of her own hands into soft hair, feeling the silky strands move between her fingers, and kissed Natalie firmly, but resisted the urge to rush things and deepen it. Natalie clearly got the message because Adele felt warm hands drop to her waist and linger there for a moment before moving to her panties.

And that's where Adele stopped Natalie's progress.

"Nuh-uh." Adele shook her head and smiled. "Now it's your turn."

Without a trace of hesitation, Natalie took a step back and stripped out of her sweater and yoga pants, leaving Adele to watch, mouth parted, breath coming in fast bursts. Chin held high, she stood before Adele in a royal blue bra and panties, her pulse visibly pounding in her neck.

Adele's hungry perusal started at hot pink polished toenails and worked its way up pale, toned legs, across womanly hips, and stopping briefly at a firm belly that had, to her surprise and delight, a very unprofessorly belly ring. Adele's money was on a spring break in the late nineties being the culprit. She would be asking about that later.

Perfect breasts, encased in dark silk and lace, captured Adele's attention for even longer before her eyes bid them a farewell, for now, and continued their journey upward. High on Natalie's chest were a smattering of tiny freckles in a pattern that Adele suddenly wanted to map with her tongue.

Natalie's chest rose and fell quicker under the weight of Adele's unabashed and appreciative scrutiny.

Adele snapped out of her trance when she realized that she'd been quiet for so long that Natalie was beginning to shift awkwardly. She wiped her mouth with the back of her hand, hoping she wasn't actually drooling. "Holy Christ, Nat," she breathed reverently. "You're perfect."

Natalie finally exhaled. "I'm not," she said, moving close to Adele again. When their bra-covered breasts and naked bellies pressed together, they both groaned. "But I'm glad you think so. And that thought goes doubly for me."

With a parting kiss, Adele reached around herself and unhooked her bra, allowing it to fall to the floor. She wondered how long it would take Natalie's gaze to drift downward. *Huh. Five seconds.* She was impressed, knowing that was about four seconds longer than she could have managed. Then she stripped off her panties and stepped into the steaming water, moaning the second it hit her skin.

The delicate scent of jasmine rose up from the tub and swirled around them.

Natalie looked a little stunned as Adele settled in with a sensual groan, leaving the arm with the bandage out of the water and casually resting on the side of the tub. She tilted her head and regarded Natalie's slightly open mouth with affection. "You can come in wearing what you have on, if you like." Though there was no denying she hoped Natalie wouldn't.

Natalie's gaze finally jumped up to meet Adele's eyes. "I…um…" She licked her lips. "What?"

Adele laughed, flattered. "Are you coming in?" Her eyes were heavily lidded. "The water feels awesome."

"Oh, right." Still preoccupied by Adele's naked body that was only *just* covered by the bubbles, Natalie unhooked her bra and let it fall carelessly to the ground. Next came her panties.

The light worshiped Natalie's skin as she climbed in behind Adele and it was all that Adele could do not to reach around and pull Natalie into her lap. *Too soon*, her mind scolded. She bit her lower lip.

The water rose with both women in the tub and twin, satisfied sighs filled the room.

"I need one of these tubs at home," Natalie said softly as she rolled her shoulder. "Do you think my neighbors will mind if I tear down their kitchen to make room?"

Adele frowned at the thought of Natalie leaving New Orleans. What did Wisconsin have over New Orleans? Well, except the job Natalie worked so hard for, and her parents, and her friends, and no reminders of where her brother was murdered, and her townhouse…but other than *that*. Adele rolled her eyes at herself.

Adele stretched out her legs and enjoyed the way the hot water instantly began to relax stiff muscles. Desire battled with fatigue and her continued craving to have her hands pretty much anywhere on Natalie's body. "Nat, can I still wash your hair?"

"I'd love that."

"But how are we going to do it without getting your stitches wet?" she wondered out loud. "Maybe we can put some tape or…" The water in the tub shifted dramatically and Adele turned around to see Natalie dunk herself fully underwater. A few seconds later, Natalie came back up sputtering and slicking her long hair back with one hand.

"Oh, God, this feels good." Natalie wiped some bubbles from her lips. "Were you saying something?"

Adele shook her head at her friend's blatant disregard for doctor's orders. She'd have to keep a close eye on her. "Nope." She made a spinning motion with her index finger and was promptly presented with Natalie's back. It looked strong, utterly feminine, and the bare, glistening skin called out for Adele's touch, as though it had a voice of its own.

Natalie's dripping arm snaked out of the tub as she reached down and picked up her wineglass. Taking a deep swallow, she wordlessly offered it over her shoulder to Adele, who polished it off, enjoying the warming sensation as the liquid slid down her throat and into her belly. She set the empty glass aside.

Natalie squared her shoulders. "Ready."

Adele squirted a healthy dollop of shampoo in one hand and very gently began massaging it into Natalie's hair, taking care to stay away from the neat row of stitches.

Natalie groaned out her approval, and asked in a quiet voice, "How bad is it? The spot they shaved, I mean."

Adele scooted closer, the water next to Natalie's body somehow seeming even warmer. She pressed her lips to Natalie's shoulder and tasted her skin, her hands stilling. "Not bad at all. Your hair completely covers it. They only shaved a small spot." She felt Natalie release a long breath and wondered if that had been bothering her for a while and whether she should have reassured Natalie earlier. Adele reminded herself to be more thoughtful. Natalie wasn't some gruff guy. She deserved more tender treatment.

It took a while, but with the help of a sprayer, they finished each other's hair. Adele felt herself growing sleepy. The heavy sexual tension that had permeated the room even more completely than the steam had melted into something softer and more soothing, and Adele's eyelids began to droop.

"Now you turn around," Natalie commanded softly, her smile audible in her voice.

Adele obeyed without thought, and Natalie scooted in close behind her and wrapped her legs around Adele's. She wound an arm around Adele's belly and gently pulled their bodies flush, resting her chin on Adele's unbruised shoulder, keeping her arm and hands just below full breasts.

Adele leaned back and her eyes closed at the sensation of soft mounds pressing into her back, lean legs encircling her, and warm breath caressing her neck and ear. "I can't believe you're so soft," Adele murmured.

"You're soft too."

"Your arms are so light around me," Adele said almost absently. She traced Natalie's forearm with a fingertip, sending bubbles sliding from heated skin.

"I guess you're used to someone so much bigger. Landry is not a small guy."

Adele grunted her agreement. There were many times she enjoyed the physical contrasts between her and Landry. But being with Natalie like this was different in an altogether delicious way. It was new and exciting, and familiar and comfortable all at once.

"What have your other girlfriends been like?" There was a long pause before Natalie added, "Amelia told me that you came out to your family as bisexual when you were a teenager. I hope that was okay."

Adele's expression turned thoughtful. "I don't care who knows." She felt Natalie's relieved exhale. "Does it bother you that I don't identify as lesbian? I've never heard you mention anything other than a former girlfriend, so I'm assuming there are no ex-husbands in your past."

Natalie's arms tightened around her and let go. Her words sounded strained. "No ex-husbands or boyfriends. The only thing that would bother me is if you wanted to date men...or actually *anyone* else at the same time that we see each other."

"Speaking of that...there's something I should probably tell you." This confession would probably be a little embarrassing, but Adele knew this was the right time to bring it up.

Natalie's whimper was barely audible.

Adele's forehead crumpled, and she wished she could see Natalie's face as she spoke but Natalie held her firmly in place. "Hey, what's the matter?"

"It's not that I'm not willing to compete for your attention," Natalie growled, her voice taking on a slightly possessive tone Adele hadn't heard before. "I *am*. And I know it's too soon to be talking about being exclusive, but I just don't think I can handle the thought of you and someone else together. The thought of you kissing..." The words trailed away softly, and Natalie shivered.

Adele pried Natalie's arms away and spun around, a little shocked to see stormy eyes peering back at her. "What on earth are you talking about? I'm not trying to tell you I want to date anyone but you. I want to see where things can go for us. Just us. Okay?"

Natalie exhaled noisily but still seemed a little wary. "You're sure? Because I've been there before, Ella, and I didn't like it."

Adele's nostrils flared. "The thought of you with someone other than me makes me want to lose my mind. We're on the same page. Trust me."

Natalie didn't bother to hide her relief.

"But," Adele paused to draw in a deep breath. "I should tell you that I haven't been romantically involved with a woman since I was in high school. I guess technically it was a girl. Or girls. There were two of them."

Natalie's eyebrows lifted.

"I mean, we were all girls, not women. So it was okay. And the two girls weren't at the same time. And even though we kissed and stuff...we never..." Adele's cheeks heated. "We never, you know."

Natalie's brows drew together. "You mean...?" She gave Adele a significant look.

Adele shook her head. "Nope."

"Never?"

"I'm pretty sure I would remember. But there was lots of kissing," Adele said hopefully, as though that might somehow change Natalie's perception.

Natalie still looked a little stunned. "Nothing past that?" She leaned forward and bypassed Adele's lips in favor of a kiss to her jaw and then lower.

Adele shrugged, enjoying the tongue that began to lave the sensitive place where her neck met her shoulder. She laid her hands on Natalie's thighs. "I always assumed there would be more women in my future, which is why I told my family about my orientation at all. I've always appreciated women, and some men."

"So you prefer women, but are attracted to both sexes?"

"In theory, if I only had to limit myself to one gender to find arousing, then yes, it would be women. So I guess you could call that a preference. But men have never been off the table for me, sexually or emotionally. Just by happenstance I dated a few guys before Landry while I was in college. It could have just as easily been a woman."

Adele stroked the soft skin beneath her hands, relishing the closeness. "And Landry…it's sometimes hard for me to remember this now, considering how things ended for us, but he really did sweep me off my feet. He's older and was so respected on the force. He has a really strong, charismatic personality that drew me in. Maybe more important than anything was that he taught me more about being a detective than anyone else."

Natalie huffed. "Plus, he's gorgeous."

Adele sniggered and supposed she owed the devil his due. "There is that."

"So you were hot for teacher?"

Adele hadn't thought of it that way, but it did sum it up nicely. And here she was, hot for teacher again. Apparently she had a type. "I guess so."

"Did you regret it? Not having any deeper relationships with women before settling down?"

Adele moaned a little when teeth grazed her skin again. "Not while I was married, no. I was happy. But now…now, I'm a little embarrassed that my experience with women consists only of what you can do under the bleachers during halftime at a football game."

Natalie chuckled throatily. "I've been on the receiving end of your kisses, Ella. You have nothing to be embarrassed about. I only wish I had gone to your high school."

Adele nibbled on Natalie's earlobe, feeling a little smug and relieved, but also exhausted. She shifted and pressed her cheek to Natalie's and they both slouched a little deeper in the hot water, any remaining tension drifting away.

This was as far as Adele was ready to go tonight. If there was ever a time to back away before she got in over her head, this was it. But

Natalie's arms were wrapped loosely around her and when they started to move to draw her closer, Adele knew deep in her soul that she didn't have the willpower to deny herself something she wanted so badly.

"So you've never been with a woman, and yet you're in this tub with me now, naked as the day you were born, kissing and nibbling and generally driving me mad, and you're as cool as a cucumber?" The words were said sleepily. "I'm clearly not as brave as you."

Adele almost burst out laughing. Natalie thought she was being cool about this?

Natalie captured Adele's lips in an almost chaste kiss. "Let's go to bed."

Adele's mouth went dry.

"But just to sleep, okay?" Natalie added softly, sounding a little apologetic and self-conscious. "It's not that I don't want to do more. God, how I want to do more. But the water has me so relaxed, and my ibuprofen has started to wear off. I don't want to mess this up by going too quickly. And—"

"Shh. That's more than okay." With a final very gentle nose-to-nose nuzzle, Adele pushed herself to her feet. Water cascaded down her in warm sheets and she extended her hand, palm up. She smiled broadly and let a little of her growing adoration show. "To sleep, together, sounds perfect."

CHAPTER SEVENTEEN

The next day…

"Are you sure you want to do this?" Adele gripped the steering wheel tighter and willed Natalie to change her mind.

Natalie clutched a plastic shopping bag from Home Depot against her chest. "I—I, yes."

"Then remember what I said, okay?" Adele pulled up in front of a ratty 1950s Shreveport roadside motel that had been converted into studio apartments. Most of the parking spaces were empty, but a couple of beater cars that were more rust than metal, and an ancient jalopy motorcycle that sat in pieces, dotted the parking spaces in front of the units.

Adele checked the GPS on her phone. She killed the headlights and eased the car deeper into the night's shadows before shutting off the engine. "This is it." She cringed and couldn't help but feel a tiny bit bad for Billy Hobson. Not only did he live in a shithole, he was about to have a *really* bad night.

"Oh, God, this is awful," Natalie murmured. Heavy clouds overhead blocked out the moonlight and stars, and there were no streetlights to speak of. But even without getting a good look, it was clear that this run-down old motel was scraping the bottom of the barrel when it came to lodging. "This makes the trailer park back home where Misty's mom lives look like Beverly Hills."

From inside the car Natalie and Adele could hear a couple in one of the units arguing and cursing, their bellows interspersed with a relentlessly barking dog. "Welcome to the deep South."

Natalie patted Adele's hand.

A long dormant sense of excitement began to pound through Adele's veins. "When we're both inside, I'm going to have to check on the car periodically. I'm afraid it we leave it empty too long, it won't be here when we're through."

"I don't think we could get a cab to come to this area."

Adele snorted. "You're right about that. It's apartment sixteen. Should be the one on the very end. It's even the most secluded, which is good."

Natalie craned her neck to see past Adele. The blinds were closed and no light shone from behind them. "It doesn't look like he's home."

"Good. Then we go with Plan A. Okay, I'm going to go inside to wait. You wait here and if anyone starts messing with you or the car, lay on the horn and I'll be out in a flash. But it looks quiet here tonight." She smiled reassuringly. "You'll be fine."

"I could always come inside with you now."

"No way. But soon." Adele took the sack from Natalie, grabbed her cane from the backseat, and handed over the car keys, wrapping them in Natalie's palm.

"Ella?"

Adele was halfway out of the car, but stopped at the soft pleading in Natalie's voice. "Yeah?"

Natalie's eyes shimmered with worry and the look made Adele's heart lurch. "Be careful."

* * *

Less than an hour later, an old pickup truck pulled in front of the last unit, backfiring a couple of times as it rolled to a stop. A man exited, taking care to lock the truck. With a paper grocery sack in his arms, he disappeared inside apartment 16.

Natalie felt lightheaded and forced herself to breathe so she didn't pass out, praying she wouldn't hear a gunshot. The minutes ticked by slowly and she found it almost impossible to sit still. What if Adele, who had been lying in wait inside Billy's apartment, needed her? What if at this very second Billy was hurting Adele? What if she was injured so badly that Adele couldn't flash the apartment lights to signal Natalie to come inside?

With every mile closer to Shreveport, Adele had grown more and more serious, quiet even. She'd said she was just getting her game face on, but it still made Natalie uneasy and anxious. *What if—?*

The lights in the apartment flashed. Natalie had to look hard to make sure she was seeing what was actually happening and not merely what she wanted. She opened the door with a trembling hand and locked the car, shoving the keys deep into her pocket. She didn't feel the biting wind against her skin or hear the vicious growl of the dog as she quickly walked by its apartment. Her mind was on one thing only: Adele.

When she reached the last apartment Natalie sucked in a shuddering breath and let herself inside.

She was promptly horrified by what she saw.

The apartment, which was unconscionably messy and furnished like a college crash pad, was lit by a single floor lamp in the corner. There had clearly been a struggle as the coffee table that was covered with sticky-looking bottle rings, now only had three legs and was tipped over on its side. Groceries were scattered across the floor and sofa. And the furnace had been turned on to full blast, and the room was somewhere between roast and broil.

Billy had a dingy green pillowcase over his head that was held in place by a thick coil of duct tape wound around his neck. A wet bloodstain, the size of a silver dollar, marred the cloth near his mouth. He was seated in a rickety-looking kitchen chair, his wrists bound behind him. His shins, chest and thighs were also secured to the chair by bands of tape. He wasn't going anywhere.

Adele was nursing a bloody nose that had dripped down her chin and onto her white button-down shirt, speckling it in red.

Appalled, Natalie sucked in a surprised breath. When Adele had insisted on subduing Billy before Natalie came inside, Natalie hadn't expected to walk into something that looked like a Middle Eastern hostage crisis.

"Looks like we've got company, Billy!" Adele announced loudly, mouthing an "I'm fine" to Natalie, who stopped in front of her to examine her nose.

"Who?" He craned his neck in all directions, panicked.

"None of your goddamned business!" Adele snarled from her place behind him.

"I'm sorry. I'm sorry!" Billy cried, his voice a little muffled by the cloth over his face as he struggled against his bindings. Sweat stains ringed the armpits of his T-shirt and had begun to form on his chest and stomach. "I won't come back to New Orleans again. I *swear* it. Please!"

Adele just shrugged, indicating she had no idea what he was ranting about or why he was this upset. She hit the back of Billy's chair with the metal ball end of her cane, startling him and causing him to jump.

The man was plainly terrified. Natalie wrinkled her nose at the pungent odor of perspiration as sweat poured off him in rivulets and mixed with the scent of dill and vinegar from a broken jar of pickles near the front door.

"I'm s-s-sorry," he carried on brokenly, his body quivering. "I haven't been back in all these years. A few days ago was-was the first time. I pr—promise. I won't do it again. Jesus, I can't believe he sent a woman after me."

Adele's eyes turned feral and her glare unconsciously drifted to Natalie's bruised throat, then back to Billy. She drew her gun from the waistband of her jeans. "What were you doing in New Orleans a few days ago, Billy?"

Adele's voice was deceptively calm, but Natalie swallowed hard at the sound, hearing the fury behind the words. If he admitted to being the one who broke into the inn and tried to strangle her, well, she wasn't completely sure what Adele would do.

"I-I—"

"Spit it out!" Adele growled, moving around to stand in front of Billy. She wiped the remainder of the blood from her nose on her shirtsleeve.

Natalie's heart rate tripled. Seeing someone with such a naturally gentle persona looking so fierce, had thrown her.

"I went to t-t-take care of her."

Adele's grip on the .357 turned white. "You son of a—"

Faster than she thought she could move, Natalie was back at Adele's side, calming her with a hand on the arm. "It's okay," she murmured, just loud enough for Adele to hear.

Their eyes met briefly, dueling, then Adele nodded and exhaled with exaggerated slowness, and visibly calmed herself. "Who were you coming to take care of in New Orleans? I want a name."

"Oh, Jesus! *Fuck.* I-I can't tell you."

Adele mouthed an "I'm sorry" to Natalie and then placed her gun right alongside Billy's ear so he couldn't mistake the sound of her cocking it.

His entire body jerked.

"That was the wrong answer." Adele's purr sounded deadly, and her face was so close to his her breath ruffled the pillowcase.

Holy shit. Natalie was about to wet her pants. She didn't know how Billy already hadn't.

His hands gripped the metal chair railings so hard the metal began to creak. "I can't tell you her name. But she doesn't know anything. Honest. My girlfriend. She's pregnant. She usually comes here bu-bu-but her car broke down. I'm sorry. I know I was supposed to dis-disappear, but I had to go back just this once."

Adele relaxed and straightened.

Natalie felt dizzy with relief.

"Billy," Adele began, scrubbing her face, which was slick with perspiration, "I don't give a crap about your girlfriend, or about you coming to New Orleans to help her. Do you understand?"

"Uh...no."

"Then let me explain it to you. I'm here to ask you some questions. You can make things easy on yourself by answering them. You're obviously in some deep shit. I might even be able to help you out of that shit. But you have to help me first."

"I...no one can help me."

"But I can try. Now, you said you couldn't believe he sent a woman after you. Who is he?"

Billy turned his head to follow Adele's voice as she paced in front of him. "You mean, you don't know?"

Adele and Natalie shared a worried look. Seconds ticked by and Natalie was sure Adele had no idea how to respond. Finally, Adele said, "Your old partner, Jay Morrell."

"I knew he sent you!" Billy began struggling wildly against his bonds.

"Whoa. Okay, you can relax now that we're getting somewhere. Just take a deep breath. I don't want to hurt you." Adele crooned, in a soothing tone, "One more breath now, so you don't hyperventilate and pass out."

He obeyed instantly.

Natalie wasn't sure whether to be impressed or freaked out by Adele's Jekyll & Hyde performance, and she had no idea how Adele had picked Morrell's name out of the hat. She blinked at the tender quality Adele's voice suddenly adopted.

"Jay Morrell didn't send us, Billy."

"What?" he said incredulously, his voice rising to a near yell. "Then who the fuck are you, you crazy bitch?"

Natalie wondered why Billy hadn't recognized Adele on sight. Then again, maybe she'd gotten the bag over his head before he got a good look or maybe she'd gotten to him before he'd turned on the light. Natalie was also astonished at how Billy had gone from sniveling captive to calling Adele a bitch, in a matter of seconds once he believed Morrell wasn't part of what was happening.

He'd just given Adele all the leverage she needed.

Adele tapped Billy's knee gently with her cane. "Do I need to remind you what I said would happen if you got too loud?"

Natalie actually heard Billy's teeth snap together as his mouth closed tight like a steel trap.

"Now, to answer your question, I'm the crazy bitch you're going to answer with the truth, the whole truth, and nothing but the truth, so help you God. Got it?"

Silence.

"You can speak, Billy."

"Wh-why should I-I answer your questions?"

Adele tucked her gun back into her jeans and gave Natalie a long-suffering look. "Considering your position, I would think it's obvious. But in case that's not incentive enough, if you don't answer me, I'm going to tell Morrell exactly where you are and that you've been coming back to New Orleans."

"You can't do that!" Billy insisted, utterly unnerved. "He'll *kill* me."

"Why?"

Billy's bony shoulders sagged. "How…if I tell you, how do I really know you can help me?"

"You don't have a choice." Adele let him stew over that for a full minute before asking, "Do you remember the night of the Joshua Phillips murder?"

Billy cocked his head like a curious puppy. "Yeah."

"Tell me what happened at the Dixie Brewery. And don't leave out a single detail."

He was quiet for several seconds. "Detective Le-Lejeune?" His voice was high and tight.

Maybe Billy wasn't as dense as he seemed.

"Tell me!" Adele demanded, ignoring his question. She didn't seem particularly bothered that he'd guessed who she was. Natalie was now certain that the pillowcase on Billy's head had been placed there for her benefit. "Tell me and I promise to help you."

Then the dam broke and the words rushed out of him in a tidal wave. "When we got to the brewery, the vic was already dead, just like we said! And Crisco was there passed out. I don't know *anything* about the actual killing."

"You didn't see anyone else there that night?"

"No. The place was deserted."

"What happened between Morrell and Crisco?"

"Morrell told me it was obvious that Crisco did it, so we needed him to confess. Then he woke Crisco up and started beating the shit out of him. Crisco tried to fight back, but it wasn't any use. The old drunk just started crying and repeating everything Morrell told him to say. I-I-I didn't know what to do. It had never been that bad before! Then you showed up."

Natalie smiled sadly, feeling a flash of guilt. Adele had been right all along and not a single person, herself included, had cared enough to stand by her.

"If you didn't have anything to do with it, why did you lie to the Public Integrity Board for Morrell? If you hadn't, you wouldn't have ended up in some dead-end job and living in this dung heap."

"You don't get it, do you?" Billy growled brokenly, his spittle bleeding through the pillowcase. "I was just trying to stay alive. I was right too. When Crisco crossed Morrell, he ended up facedown in a ditch."

Natalie sucked in a breath.

Adele's back stiffened. "Morrell murdered Crisco?"

"Maybe it wasn't him," Billy allowed with a shrug. "But if it wasn't, it still wasn't an accident. I wasn't taking any chances. Morrell made it clear what would happen to Crisco if he took back his bullshit confession. Crisco took it back and then ends up dead. What would you think?"

Adele dragged her fingers through her hair in rapid, frustrated movements, sending the short, slightly wavy locks into disarray. "How was Morrell dirty, besides what you've told me?"

Billy shook his head. "I…he hurt lots of people. Got off on roughing them up. Made him feel like a big man, I guess. Sometimes he'd run drugs or money. A couple of times he helped one of the gangs by letting them know just before a bust was about to go down."

"The drugs and money weren't for him?"

"Morrell liked to act the big shot, but he was just somebody else's bitch." That fact actually seemed to make Billy a little happier. "You think I'm worried about Morrell? He's petrified of his boss. And before you ask, I dunno who it is. Morrell never trusted me enough to tell me."

"So you helped Morrell with the drugs and gangs?"

Natalie watched in awe as Adele rattled off her questions so fast that Billy didn't have time to do anything but spit out the answer. There was no time to think of a lie.

"No! I mean…not like you think. I covered for him, yeah, if he smacked around some jerk or something. He was my partner. I couldn't help it if he actually enjoyed doing it."

Adele winced.

"I never worked the drug or gangs angle. Not that I would have anyway, but Morrell never asked me to. He said he couldn't trust me not to screw something up, and he wasn't going to get banged up because of me." Resentment invaded Billy's voice. "My only job was to shut up and follow his lead like a good *boy*. Racist, asshole."

"But you took a plea bargain and left the force…"

"That was bullshit! Morrell said I was a weak link. He wanted me gone. I'd already agreed to leave town, even though I'm born and raised in New Orleans and my girlfriend is there. But then the bastard went to the PIB anyway, and told them *I* was the one roughing up suspects. Got a couple of his confidential informants to back him up, and before you know it, I had to take a plea just to stay outta jail."

Adele groaned. She clearly wasn't getting everything she wanted. "Tell me again what happened that night at the brewery."

Billy repeated his story and it stayed the same, only he seemed to grow more upset during the second retelling.

Natalie felt a stirring of pity. Then she remembered what had happened to poor Crisco while Billy stood by and watched, and what had happened to Adele while he continued to lie, and her pity evaporated.

"I told you everything," Billy said urgently, his chest rising and falling unevenly. "Just like you asked. Now you promised to help me."

"But what you told me didn't help me. I already knew Morrell was an asshole and that Crisco's confession was crap." Adele sighed and gathered the bag she'd brought that had held the duct tape. "I think it's time for us to go now."

"Wha-what!" Billy looked around the room as though he just remembered a second person was with them. "You can't leave me like this?" He tried to stand, but the tape held firm.

"Sure I can. I'll just tape a sock in your mouth and then come back in a few days and see how your story has changed." The dog a few units down barked loudly again, and Adele listened at first with visible annoyance, then something else. "In fact, I think I'll go buy that noisy dog off your neighbors and then leave him in here with you. I wonder how long it will take him to get really hungry? Is he a Doberman or a pit bull? With a deep bark like that, I'm betting pit bull."

Natalie's jaw sagged. She knew Adele was lying and it was still hard not to believe her.

Billy whimpered loudly. "But I told you everything!"

"Tell me something I don't already know," Adele roared, slamming the end of her cane down on the floor near Billy's feet. "Start at the beginning."

"I already told you. Morrell got a call to come to the Dixie Brewery. We were going to dinner and—"

"Whoa. Whoa! Hold up." Adele leaned closer, her focus like a laser. "Morrell got the call? Personally? Or your car was dispatched to the scene?"

"I-I...we were in the Tremé when he got a call on his cell phone. He hung up and said we had to go to the brewery to deal with...he said it was a disturbance, I think. I figured that meant a drunken fight or somethin'."

Billy hesitated and Adele rumbled, "Keep going!"

"After l-l-like half an-an hour, the weather had the streets half flood-ed, and it took forever to get across town. We pulled into the brewery and then Morrell said he wanted to let the weather get better before we got out of the car. Maybe fifteen minutes later, the dispatch went out. We took it, the weather was still shit, and went in anyway."

The blood drained from Adele's face. She stepped away from Billy and whispered directly into Natalie's ear, "It was a cop."

CHAPTER EIGHTEEN

Adele glanced uncomfortably over at Natalie as she pulled their car up to the Hilton Shreveport Hotel. It was almost nine o'clock and too late to make the nearly five-hour drive back to New Orleans tonight.

Adele had interrogated Billy for longer than expected and ended with a series of questions about what happened to Natalie at the inn and Josh's cell phone. Reasonably certain Billy had nothing to do with any of that, she'd insisted that he text Morrell and demand a meeting in New Orleans in forty-eight hours' time. She needed that much time to prepare. Adele would be the one who showed up to that meeting, not Billy.

Satisfied with the text, and Morrell's profane, but surprising prompt answer, Adele had come to an agreement with Billy and a plan. She cut the tape from one of his wrists and then left him to deal with the rest as she and Natalie drove away.

Adele had been on the phone nonstop since, but all the arrangements had been made. Tomorrow, Billy's girlfriend would board a Greyhound bus to Shreveport. Billy and the pregnant woman would then take over the room she and Natalie would vacate in the morning. He would be safe, and out of the way, while Adele worked to bring down Morrell, along with whoever was pulling his strings.

Unbeknownst to Billy, a private detective would be watching him the entire time to make certain he didn't run. Adele didn't want to involve the DA just yet, but soon they would need Billy's official statement.

Natalie shot Adele an aggrieved look that Adele knew she sorely deserved. Adele had been in a rotten mood since driving away from Billy's hovel. Her mind raced with future scenarios and plans, and her stomach twisted with shame and disgust at the thought that a cop had killed Natalie's brother. She endured a lot at the hands of her brothers and sisters in blue, and even Landry. But this... For one of her own to have inflicted this boundless suffering on someone she...on Natalie. It was almost unthinkable.

"You don't have to keep looking at me like that, Natalie."

"Yes, I'm looking at you. But I don't know what looking at you 'like that' means, Ella."

Adele tossed the keys to the valet then impatiently waited for her valet ticket.

"Ma'am, are you okay?" The valet, who looked all of eighteen years old and had braces on his teeth, glued wide, frightened eyes on Adele's chest.

Adele lifted an eyebrow. "Eyes up, kid!"

"She's fine," Natalie interjected smoothly, exiting the car. "She gets nose bleeds from time to time. It's the dry weather." Her charming smile disarmed the young man immediately.

Natalie's confidence had improved with her appearance and nearly twenty-four hours of continuous rest. The bruises on her neck and around her eye were still there, but they had faded to the point where they could be covered with makeup. The valet didn't seem to notice that she'd slipped on a pair of sunglasses even though it was dark outside. "We'll take care of the bloody nose inside."

"Oh, okay, then," he said, suddenly unconcerned. "Enjoy your stay, ladies."

Adele rolled her eyes at the love-struck expression he directed at Natalie.

"The weather isn't dry. It's supposed to rain tonight," Adele said under her breath as she held open the hotel lobby door for Natalie. Her cane sounded unnaturally loud as it struck the marble floors with every step.

"Should I have said that you got all that blood on you when you were punched in the nose by our kidnap victim?" Natalie adjusted the strap of their bag on her shoulder as she walked.

"It might have made junior think twice about drooling all over you." Adele skipped the line at the front desk and headed straight for a kiosk in the lobby where she ran her credit card through the machine. She felt a hot flash of irritation. "It wasn't a punch. Just a lucky elbow."

After a few seconds of processing, a screen prompted her with the option to upgrade to a suite for thirty more dollars and a choice of two beds or one. Adele's finger hovered over the touch screen, unmoving, as her mind began replaying the night's events.

"Ella?"

Billy's words ran through her mind on a high-speed loop as she tried to work out the identity of Morrell's boss.

"Ella?" This time the word was laced with worry.

"Huh?" Adele's unseeing eyes never left the screen.

Natalie snaked a hand around Adele, selected a king-sized bed and declined the suite option with the touch of a couple of buttons. When a room key popped out of the dispenser at the bottom of the machine, Natalie grabbed it and looped her arm around Adele's. She guided them toward the elevators.

Adele's attention was suddenly drawn back to the present. "Hey! How did you know I didn't want a suite?" She looked over her shoulder at the kiosk with a frown.

"Because you didn't reserve one to begin with. I picked the king bed because I want to share a bed with you tonight." Natalie's eyes cut sideways. "Do you have a problem with that?" Her voice was stern, but Adele didn't miss its teasing undercurrent or the hint of concern in her blue eyes.

"No, Professor. No problems." Adele couldn't help the tiny grin that twitched at her lips. She appreciated that Natalie had given her some space and silence on the drive over so that she could brood, but her friend clearly wasn't going to let her dwell in dark places for too long. Adele also knew Natalie had questions about what Billy had said, and her pronouncement that they were looking for a cop. Natalie was patiently biding her time, and Adele felt a wave of affection nearly bowl her over. She was lucky to have Natalie in her life and she knew it.

They were barely through the door of their room when Adele kicked off her shoes and began to wriggle out of her jeans. "I feel gross." She made a face. "I had the heat in the apartment cranked to put the screws to Billy, but it wiped me out too. I'm going to take a shower."

Next Adele stripped off her socks, using the desk for balance. Then she remembered they hadn't eaten, and Natalie needed to keep up her strength. "Will you get us something to eat from room service for dinner? Just pick whatever. I like everything."

Natalie flopped back on the bed, letting her arms rest above her head. "Yes. And some ice for your nose. It could be broken, Ella. Maybe you should see a doctor."

"Nah." Adele left the bathroom door open as she spoke. She winced at her reflection in the mirror, and her eyes welled with tears. "Unfortunately, I've taken hits to the nose before. It's not broken, just a little tender." She stripped out of her bloody shirt and stuffed it into a garbage can too small to be useful.

Adele turned the shower to the hottest setting and let the water pressure and heat beat into the sore muscles in her shoulders and back. Her breath hitched into a sob. *Everything* was riding on her questioning of Morrell. Failure wasn't an option.

Anger, fear, resentment and worry all built up and simply overflowed. She had her proof that Crisco had been coerced, but with so much still hanging over them, the victory felt hollow. Adele let the tears come, her forehead pressed against the cool gray tile of the shower as she silently wept and her body released its pent-up stress and burned through any lingering adrenaline. By the time she was finished, she felt significantly better.

Forty-five minutes later the women sat cross-legged, in flannel pajamas, on their bed, both freshly showered and taking their last few bites of dinner. Natalie's stolen, concerned glances told Adele her tears hadn't gone unnoticed. But thankfully, neither seemed to be in the mood to dredge it up now that the storm had passed.

Natalie cleared their plates and wheeled the room service tray outside while Adele gathered the plastic bag full of ice and pressed it against her nose.

They both sat back down on the bed. "Lemme see it." Natalie scooted closer and examined the body part in question with a solemn expression. "The swelling is already almost completely down."

Adele smirked. "Will I live, Doctor?"

"Too bad for you, I'm not an MD and have no idea whether it's really broken, but I'm pretty sure you'll live. However, you have a cute nose, and my not-so-esteemed medical opinion is that you need to let me kiss it to make it all better. Stat."

Adele softly laughed, but apparently Natalie was serious because she framed Adele's face with warm palms, and dropped a feather-light kiss against the abused flesh. She hugged Adele tightly against her chest.

"Nat…" Adele's heart constricted. "I'm sorry about tonight. I know it was…scary. I—" She buried her nose in Natalie's neck. "I'm not like Morrell, I don't get off on making people suffer."

Natalie eased away with a gentle kiss on the cheek, her eyes brimming with equal parts adoration and understanding. "Of course you don't. You're the most caring person I've ever met, Ella. Yes, you frightened Billy, but you didn't hurt him, and you did what needed to be done. You don't have to apologize for that. Not to me. It's not like you didn't warn me about what you were going to do. I just…" She lifted one hand then let it helplessly drop to the bed.

"It's just different to see it with your own eyes?"

A sigh. "Something like that. C'mon. Let's get ready for bed. You look wrecked."

"Gee, thanks."

Natalie bumped hips with Adele as they walked to the bathroom. "Okay, a gorgeous wreck then."

Bedtime routines completed, Adele clicked off the light. The room was cool and she snuggled under soft, clean-smelling sheets and a comforter with a wiggle of pleasure.

Natalie settled down half on top of Adele, tucking her face into the side of Adele's neck. Soft hair tickled Adele's chin, and Natalie slung one leg over her in a slightly possessive pose that made Adele smile.

Adele wrapped a contented arm around Natalie.

"Why would a police officer have killed Josh? It just doesn't make sense."

Adele's eyes closed tight at the aching quality to Natalie's soft, raspy voice. "Sweetie, it sounds like he and Misty were just in the wrong place at the wrong time that night. They saw a drug deal or something equally shady go down. I think Josh caught his killer's attention, and then the killer eliminated him as a potential witness. But it's *never* going to make sense."

"But-but what kind of witness would he have even been? They were inside a dark warehouse, and Josh was stoned out of his mind."

"A terrible witness. Who knows what goes on in someone's demented brain before they do something so…so wasteful and horrible."

Adele rolled onto her side and took Natalie with her, spooning them snugly together. It was an act of giving comfort, but also of receiving and accepting it because the contact she craved with every fiber of her being was so lovingly offered in return. "You're the first person I've got to be the big spoon with."

"It feels good."

"To me too." Adele greedily absorbed Natalie's warmth, and sucked in a deep breath of soap-scented skin. She rubbed her cheek against the silky skin at the nape of Natalie's neck.

"Why are you sure the killer is a cop? Because Morrell is one?"

"Anyone could have called Morrell after the murder and told him to head to the Dixie Brewery to clean up his mess, but only a cop would have been able to make sure the dispatch didn't go out until Morrell and Hobson were already in place to take the call instead of a Mid-City police cruiser."

Natalie tugged up the sheet and tucked it beneath her chin. "Misty said she called the police from outside a strip club."

"The club she's talking about is called the Pink Pony, and it's about a five-minute walk from the brewery, less if you're hurrying. She said she told the police there was a fight of some kind so they'd come?"

"Right. A fight the police needed to break up."

"That call would have been dispatched right away," Adele said confidently. "Even though it sometimes takes officers a while to get to the scene, the dispatch goes out immediately."

Adele bitterly recalled when she'd needed backup the most, but the minutes had ticked away with no help. "According to Billy's timeline, the dispatch didn't happen until maybe forty or forty-five minutes after Morrell got called on his personal cell and was told to head to the brewery. That means, even allowing Misty five or ten minutes to make the nine-one-one call, there's thirty-plus missing minutes."

Natalie snuggled deeper into Adele's embrace. "But if this person had the power to have the dispatch delayed, why not just kill the call from the very start?"

"Misty's call created the perfect excuse for Morrell and Hobson to be at the scene, it just came too quickly. Even the storm helped." Adele vividly recalled the lashing rain, the explosive thunder, the flashes of brilliant white light that lit up the crime scene, and Josh's body in gruesome detail. "On nights like that the emergency calls flood in, and a supervisor triages them before dispatch. He or she would be the perfect filter."

"But…how did the killer know Misty would call?"

"He couldn't have known. My guess is that he was making sure that Morrell and Hobson didn't get dispatched to someplace back in the Tremé while on their way to the brewery, and then also made sure no other patrol units ended up at the brewery."

Natalie rolled over in Adele's arms, her mouth so close to Adele's they were sharing the same minty-flavored breath. "We're getting closer, aren't we?"

Adele felt a surge of short-lived excitement that came with the thrill of the chase. "So close."

Natalie drew her hands up between her and Adele and traced her collarbone with a light touch. "I don't want to talk or think about dirty cops or what happened to Josh any more tonight, okay?"

Adele shivered at the tender touch and dropped her voice to match Natalie's barely-there whisper. "Deal." She yawned, her body coming down hard from the roller coaster of emotions. "Aren't you sleepy?"

"I should be, I guess. But after getting so much sleep over the last couple of days, I'm really not. I slept all the way to Shreveport while you drove, remember?" Natalie's finger moved to Adele's lower lip where she continued her gentle stroking. "But you need rest. Relax. There's nothing more to do or think about tonight. Just let your mind float."

Natalie's voice was hypnotizing. "I…" Adele sighed and felt herself sink deeper into the mattress.

"Good ni—"

Adele silenced Natalie with a slow, lingering kiss, designed to show affection rather than entice.

Even so, Natalie moaned quietly.

Rather than escalate the contact, Adele drifted there for a moment with their lips pressed softly, warmly together. Then, ever so delicately, she sleepily nipped and sucked the delicious lips so tantalizingly close. "You know I'm crazy about you, right?"

"Likewise."

Adele could feel Natalie's smile against her lips.

"Only sweet dreams tonight," was the last thing Adele thought she heard before the sandman stealthily dragged her under.

* * *

The next day…

"You're not listening and you're not being reasonable!" Breathing hard, Natalie slammed the carriage house's refrigerator door closed, causing the few bottles that were in the door to careen across the shelf and crash together violently. She tried not to wince. She was furious, but she hadn't meant to do that.

They'd been arguing off and on ever since they'd gotten back to New Orleans and Adele had casually announced that she wouldn't be taking Natalie with her when she confronted Morrell the following afternoon. After politely disagreeing, but neither one yielding, things had finally come to a head. Both women had brick-red faces, and the volume of their voices had inched upward with each passing minute.

Adele's eyes narrowed to angry slits. "Pitching a fit like a three-year-old when you don't get your way doesn't look good on you, Natalie."

"And being a dictator doesn't look good on you, Ella." Natalie squared her shoulders and forced herself not to burst into tears. "You don't just get to say no and then expect that I'm going to obey without question, like I'm your pet. We need to talk about this!"

"We really don't."

Only a few feet separated them, but it felt like miles.

Natalie knew a confrontation with Morrell was inevitable; that had always been the plan. But it all seemed so much more terrifying now that she wouldn't be there to see it. Fear for what could happen was making her nauseous.

Both her and Adele's emotions were running high and close to the surface. It would have been the perfect time for each woman to back away and take a deep breath.

Neither one did.

Adele ran both hands through her hair. "Argh! You are the one who is being unreasonable, Natalie! As much as you want to be there while I question Morrell, I can't worry about your safety and my own. The thought of you being in danger paralyzes me!" The words were spat out harshly like a deep dark secret that was never meant to see the light of day.

Natalie felt a twinge of guilt for pushing but not enough to make her stop. "We both know that's not true, Ella. When I was in danger at the inn you were far from paralyzed."

"But I didn't make it to you in time. Don't you see? You were dead! If the paramedics hadn't shocked your heart you would have stayed dead." Adele looked suddenly bereft.

Natalie tried to calm her voice and queasy stomach. "I won't do or say anything while you question Morrell. I could stay hidden or even at a distance. Morrell never has to know I'm there. If I'm not personally close enough to help you if something goes wrong, at least I could call for help."

"Anywhere near me talking to Morrell is unsafe. I'm sorry, it just is."

"I thought we were doing this together."

"We are. But Kurt Mosley and Billy Hobson are *nothing* compared to Morrell. You need to understand that they're pussycats to Morrell's wolf. A dumb, mangy wolf, but one with sharp teeth and claws. I've known him for years. When he feels threatened, and he will, he won't hesitate to bite. He's not smart enough to be predictable."

"Ella…" Natalie sighed and looked skyward, eyes welling. "What you're asking isn't fair. We're supposed to be a team. You would never stay back if it was me going to meet Morrell."

The look on Adele's face was guilty but defiant. "You need to trust me." The challenging look fell away and was replaced by genuine fear. "Please."

At that, Natalie's angry insistence began to crumble without her permission.

"I'm going to be fine with Morrell, Nat, I'm not doing this alone."

They'd been trying to reach Al all day but either he wouldn't or couldn't answer his cell. Adele had explained he was a Vice detective and sometimes they went undercover for days or even weeks at a time and were unreachable. The worry that he was unforgivably angry with her was written all over Adele's face as clearly as if it had been etched there in black ink.

They'd even tried using the disposable phone Natalie had purchased for herself until they could retrieve her personal phone, in case he'd blocked Adele's number. But as before, there was no answer. Natalie couldn't really blame him for being upset. It wasn't every day a dear old friend wanted to make sure you hadn't broken into her home and strangled someone.

Across the room, Adele's phone began to ring. She shifted back and forth on her feet, clearly wanting to answer it, but also not about to abandon their argument.

"Go," Natalie said quietly. "It might be Al." She hated the idea that she wouldn't be with Adele and Morrell, but at least if she couldn't be with her, it would be someone Adele trusted.

With a grateful nod, Adele retrieved her phone. She stared at it for a long beat, lower lip caught between her teeth, before she closed her eyes and answered, "Hey, Landry."

Natalie's eyebrows rose in surprise.

"Yeah, everything is okay. I know I missed my call with Logan last night. I…I got tied up. " Adele licked her lips and shot Natalie an apologetic look. "I need your help with something tomorrow. It's important, Landry."

Natalie's mouth sagged.

Adele's gaze skittered away from Natalie.

Him? Natalie was dumbstruck. *After everything?* Adele didn't believe he was dirty like Morrell, but how could she be certain? Why take the risk? At the very least Landry had already shown himself incapable of standing by Adele when she needed him. And yet he was who Adele chose to have by her side?

Anger tinged with jealousy burned hot and sick in Natalie's belly.

"Logan can stay with Amelia." Adele nodded at something Landry said, looking relieved. "Me too. Okay, here's what's up and what we're going to need."

Seething, Natalie grabbed a sweatshirt and headed for the door.

* * *

The sun had set and storms were moving into New Orleans once again. Adele had only turned on a single light since Natalie'd been gone, too engrossed in her thoughts to notice the growing darkness. She'd been waiting by the open window the entire time, although it only allowed a view of tree branches and a tiny sliver of sidewalk along the driveway.

The breeze carried with it the fresh scent of bruised grass, charcoal from someone's winter BBQ and ozone. Adele tapped her foot and peered at her watch for the twentieth time. Natalie had been gone for more than two hours and she cursed herself for not going after her immediately. She wasn't raised under a rock and actually had been to the movies. She knew what she should have done. *You* always *go after the girl.*

Please be okay.

Adele knew she could have handled their argument better, tried to be more flexible or at least have explained that if Landry hadn't called her, she was going to call him, regardless of whether Al was available. But she hadn't gotten that far, and eventually she'd reasoned that she'd rather have Natalie angry but safe.

She firmly believed that Morrell had already had his filthy hands around Natalie's throat once and she wouldn't allow that to happen ever again. Still, their terse words and Natalie's obvious hurt and worry left Adele feeling truly awful.

Adele acknowledged with a deep sigh that Natalie had been especially right about one thing. Were the shoe on the other foot, there was no way in hell she would allow herself to be sidelined, no matter the risk. "So I was a jerk and a hypocrite," she mumbled to herself, rolling her eyes. "Great."

The door to the carriage house opened just as the first raindrops began to spatter against the windowpane. Adele held in a growl as she slowly walked past Natalie. She locked the door, woozy with relief. *Thank God.*

Neither woman made eye contact and Natalie was uncharacteristically quiet.

"Where were you?" Adele burred, her voice low and angry. Her back to Natalie, she gripped the doorknob tightly with one hand and the deadbolt with the other.

With cheeks pink from the cool wind and tousled hair, Natalie headed to the back of the apartment and behind the Chinese screens. "There's a tire swing in the backyard," she said softly. Her words lacked the heat and sting they'd carried earlier.

Adele perched on the sofa arm and watched Natalie move behind the screens. She wasn't sure whether she was resentful that Natalie had stormed out and left her to stew, or simply grateful that she was back safe and sound. She settled on both. "You left like that before. You just marched out and never came back."

Natalie stripped out of her sweatshirt, then folded it and put it into one of the dresser drawers. When she was finished, she tilted her head, her hair falling softly over one shoulder. "What are you talking about? Since the hospital—"

"You went back to Wisconsin. I tried to do the right thing and you— you left."

Natalie turned and faced the screen, arms hanging loose at her side, and for a moment Adele wished she could see her face to know what she was thinking. "That was years ago."

The lamp next to the bed, on its lowest setting, cast the area of the room behind the tall screen in a golden glow. All that was visible of Natalie was her dark, but well-defined outline behind the delicate paper. As she moved, Natalie's outline grew larger or smaller, and when she bent, as she did to remove her shoes, her silhouette on the angled side panels became slightly distorted.

Fascinated by not being able to really see anything, but also the illusion of seeing everything, Adele's mind was split between the provocative feast for her eyes and their conversation. "I thought maybe you'd done the same thing tonight. Run away."

Finger-combing her long tresses, Natalie gathered her hair as though she intended to put it into a ponytail. Instead, she twisted it into a low, haphazard knot. Wisps of hair immediately escaped to frame her face.

Why did Natalie seem to be moving in slow motion? Adele's nostrils flared.

"Ella, yes, I'm angry," she sighed as she admitted, "and even a little bit jealous of Landry. But I wouldn't do that to you."

"You don't need to be jealous."

"I believe you. I was just having a moment."

Adele lifted an eyebrow, the tension in her belly growing at the sight of Natalie gently tugging her shirt from a pair of snug jeans, then slowly releasing each blouse button from the bottom up. *So goddamned sexy.* Hating herself a little for her body's undeniable reaction while she was still irritated, she swallowed, her mouth suddenly dry. She looked away. "A moment? You let me worry about you for hours."

A pause. "I needed to cool off before I said something I would regret." Natalie squared her shoulders and let her shirt slide down her back and into a puddle on the floor behind her, revealing the outline of her tantalizing curves and dips in far greater detail.

Crossing her legs and relentlessly bouncing her top foot, Adele covered her mouth, nose and chin with both hands. She drew them slowly down her face as she muttered a quiet, "Christ."

"Did you say something?" Natalie began peeling out of her Levi's.

Completely distracted, Adele fought to remember what they were talking about. "I-I needed to know that you were okay." She bit back a groan as one long naked leg revealed itself, and then another.

Natalie lifted her hands high over her head and arched her back in a languid stretch. She put her hands on her hips in a pose that signaled frustration. "I was only in the backyard. I—"

"It's called a safe house for a reason." Adele's voice cracked on the last word and she prayed for strength at the same time she prayed for more clothes to be shed. "To be safe, you're supposed to stay inside it. You could have at least called or texted me." *Had it always been so hot in the apartment?*

Natalie reached behind her and unhooked her bra. As she shrugged out of it, Adele could picture it in her mind as though it danced before her very eyes, a scarlet red lacy number that her sister had declared a masterpiece of function and art. Goddamn Amelia was always right.

When Natalie twisted to the side to toss the bra onto the bed the outline of full, perfect breasts came to life on the screen and Adele felt a corresponding rush of warm wetness between her legs. What had begun as a gentle ache at her core had escalated into a deep throbbing sensation that was low, hot and impossibly heavy.

"Ella, you could have called or texted me, too."

Adele couldn't think of a comeback to that. Of course she'd considered calling Natalie. She'd been irrationally afraid that she'd catch her at the airport in the midst of leaving town. But it was okay that she didn't have a good reply, she wasn't sure she could speak anyway.

Natalie turned and bent deeply at the waist to pick up the jeans and blouse, and Adele had to close her eyes and grab the arm of the sofa to keep from sliding to the floor.

Adele's skin suddenly felt too tight for her body. Somewhere in the far reaches of her mind she wondered whether Natalie knew she was providing the sexiest-ever-peep-show-for-one. Maybe. She was certain Natalie was just that wicked.

"I was fine in the backyard." Natalie disappeared for a few seconds and Adele could hear her dump her clothes into the hamper. When she came back into view, Adele's heart did a double thump at the sight. Natalie was completely nude, and her hair had completely escaped its loose knot.

Adele felt her toes curl.

Toned arms gestured as Natalie spoke, her breasts slightly bouncing with each emphasized word. "You need to stop worrying about me like I'm going to break."

Quicker than she thought she could move, Adele strode across the room, barely feeling the twinge in her leg. She moved around the screen in a blur of motion and gathered Natalie in her arms. In a surprise move that left both breathless, she yanked Natalie as close as humanly possible. "I couldn't agree more," Adele said in a hushed, reverent voice, relishing skin so smooth it put the finest silk to shame.

A tiny smirk played at the corners of Natalie's lips and her eyes danced. "Took you long enough to get back here. I was beginning to think I would have to go out in search of a pole."

Adele lowered her arms and reached down to grab two full hands of Natalie's remarkable ass. Hands gripping tightly into firm flesh, she ground their centers together. Adele shivered at the sensation, but managed to choke out a laugh. The want she felt for Natalie eclipsed anything she'd ever known. "I knew it! You tease."

Natalie's face softened into something a lot like tender adoration. "Ella, I-I—"

Adele held her breath. *Tell me you love me...*

Instead of finishing her sentence, Natalie wrapped a hand around Adele's slender neck and roughly pulled her into a scorching kiss that temporarily caused Adele's mind to go utterly blank and threatened to send her legs wobbling out from underneath her like a newborn foal's.

After a few insanely hot minutes, Natalie pulled away gasping. She placed a gentle peck to the corner of Adele's smiling mouth. Natalie's face and chest were flushed with arousal and Adele could feel the heat in her own cheeks. "I'm sorry for our argument," Natalie began earnestly.

Adele's body buzzed with so much raw energy it felt as though she'd grabbed hold of a live wire, and it took a few seconds for Natalie's words to penetrate the sensual haze that clouded her thinking.

"You need to be safe when you meet with Morrell. You need to do it the right way. I trust you. I was just afraid for you...terrified, actually. I-I still am. And I'm not at all happy about it. But I do understand."

Adele melted. "Natalie—"

Two cool fingertips pressed against Adele's lips to stop her from speaking. "I'm not finished yet."

Adele nodded and felt Natalie's body somehow inch even closer. She could feel every breath, every twitching muscle, and the quick, strong beating of Natalie's heart.

Pale eyes gleamed with unshed tears and Natalie removed her fingers from their position against Adele's mouth and drew them down Adele's chin and throat, stopping at the base of her neck to dip them in the notch between collarbones. "I won't run out on you. *Ever*. But that doesn't mean that sometimes I won't need some space so I don't let my mouth get away from me, okay?"

Adele nodded slowly.

"I'll always come back."

"You'd better," Adele said fiercely.

Natalie slid her hand back to tickle the fine hairs at the back of Adele's neck. "I need you to really believe me."

The clear sincerity in Natalie's words penetrated deep into Adele's chest and settled there, working to soothe away lingering doubts and frustration. It would take time to believe without fear, but she would get there. "I'm sorry too. I do want to talk about Landry and everything that's going to happen."

Adele dragged her fingers from Natalie's ass to her waist and released a tiny growl of pure lust. "Just not right now." Not when they were so close it was hard to tell where one ended and the other began. She ground their hips together once again to make her point.

Natalie nodded and released a shaky breath. "Not right now."

"By the way," Natalie paused and gave Adele a gentle poke in the ribs, "one of us is way overdressed, and it's not me." She began to nibble at Adele's lips, each separately, then together as she whispered against them. "I know you've never been with a woman before and—"

Adele propelled them forward onto the bed where they landed with a soft thud on the mattress. She latched her mouth onto the skin below Natalie's ear and sucked. "I'm sure I'll figure it out as I go."

Adele reached up to fondle one of Natalie's breasts, and elicited a throaty moan. "So soft," she whispered reverently. In that instant she made it one of her life's missions to hear that exact moan again. As often as possible. But then a wave of panic hit her. Natalie wouldn't have mentioned it if... "I *will* figure it out, right?"

Natalie burst into happy laughter, her eyes crinkling with joy. "Yes." She let her gaze drift down their bodies and a lifted eyebrow told Adele she was doing just fine so far. "I'm confident that you will."

"Whew." Adele nodded, a full, dimple-inducing grin stretching her cheeks as wide as they could possibly go as she chuckled. They tried to kiss again while still laughing, and their teeth collided lightly. Their kissing was sloppy and urgent but impossibly sweet, hot tongues swirling against each other, tasting, exploring as though they could discover each other's innermost secrets through touch alone.

Natalie slipped her fingers just beneath the hem Adele's T-shirt and tugged upward. "Off. I want to feel you too."

Adele pushed herself up from the bed and stripped off her shirt, taking only a second to make sure she didn't tear off the bandage covering the laceration near her wrist, and her pants in record time.

Propped up on elbows, Natalie watched delightedly, her lower lip between her teeth, a low purr of approval vibrating through her like an inordinately pleased jungle cat.

Adele stopped moving altogether when she got a good look at Natalie's body in all its glory. Natalie's nipples seemed to harden further under her laser-like gaze.

In the bath there had been bubbles to slightly obscure her view. Though they'd dressed and undressed in the same room several times, they'd turned their backs, affording each other a modicum of privacy. But this unabashed, unobstructed view…Adele's heart threatened to pound out of her chest. Natalie was brazenly on full display, and it took her breath away.

"You're…" Adele had to swallow around a lump in her throat. "Nat, you're so gorgeous, I think…It hurts to look at you," she whispered not bothering to hide the fact that she was simply in awe of the goddess before her.

Natalie sat up on her knees, her eyes brimming with raw emotion as she reached for Adele's hand. Her wish was granted immediately. "Ella," she murmured softly, bringing the hand to her lips, then tugging gently so that Adele ended up in her waiting arms. "C'mere." They fell back on the bed, together.

Their next kiss was wild and incendiary, the flames threatening to reduce Adele to a pile of smoking ash. Adele had no idea how long they kissed, but it was finally Natalie who moved things forward by tracing Adele's bra. The bolt of heat it caused between her legs jerked Adele from her hedonistic haze.

Lower lip between her teeth, Natalie glanced at Adele in question and received a smile and a nod in return. It took Natalie three tries, but she finally unhooked Adele's bra and slid it down her arms, their madly roaming hands never stopping. Adele shivered at the sparks cast from Natalie's fingertips.

Adele tightly wound her hands in soft brown hair and gently pulled Natalie's head back long enough to issue a quiet command. "Turn over onto your belly."

Natalie mewed at the loss of Adele's lips and looked confused. "Wh-what?" Her hands had been spread wide and possessively around Adele's waist and were purposefully inching toward generous, bare breasts.

"There's something I want to do." Adele leaned forward and brushed her tongue along Natalie's jugular, being supremely gentle in deference to her bruises and feeling the rush of hot blood beneath it. She needed to replace every mark made in anger with one given in adoration. "Please."

Natalie complied and lay on her stomach, groaning as Adele straddled her bare bottom, painting it with searing wetness.

Adele swept Natalie's hair to the side and gently nuzzled her nose into the chestnut mane. She inhaled deeply before placing hot, open-mouth kisses down Natalie's spine. "You smell so damn good…all the time." She ran her tongue over her spine, kissing each valley and ridge, murmuring her exaltation as she went.

Natalie writhed beneath her.

Nothing is as good as this. Adele allowed her bare breasts to slide down Natalie's back, two hard tips trailing smoothly over lightly perspiring skin.

Both women groaned at the sensation.

"God, Ella," Natalie whimpered when Adele's lips and tongue hit the base of her spine and she licked one of her vertebra, then sucked on it hard enough to leave a tiny welt.

Adele lifted her leg and scooted over to straddle one of Natalie's thighs. It took every ounce of her considerable willpower not to grind down on it.

Natalie showed no such restraint, and with a drawn out moan, pressed her hips into the mattress, seeking relief any way she could get it and spreading her legs in invitation.

Adele hummed at the taste of salty skin, and drew just the very tips of her fingers through Natalie's slick heat. Her stomach knotted pleasantly. "Jesus."

Natalie convulsed, and a gravelly moan exploded from her chest as she tried to open her legs even wider to coax Adele along. "Puh-please, Ella."

"You're soaked."

Adele ran her fingers through Natalie's wetness once more, her own center twitching in empathy when Natalie cried out. Adele's body was ready to combust. Dear God, she was going to come, and so damn hard, just from touching Natalie. She would have been embarrassed if she weren't too blissed-out to care.

"El...Ella." Natalie grabbed two fistfuls of sheet. "Ple—" A third, excruciatingly slow pass of Adele's fingers robbed Natalie of speech completely.

In a burst of movement, Natalie thrust her buttocks off the bed, and Adele with her. Panting, she managed to flip onto her back beneath Adele.

Adele opened her mouth to protest, but then felt sure hands palm her breasts. She let out a ragged breath that turned into a hiss when Natalie squeezed both her nipples in tandem. She fought not to come undone in that instant, her entire body quaking, her chest flushing red and perspiration gathering at her hairline and trailing down the nape of her neck.

Natalie's eyes were black with desire, and her voice was honey and gravel. "Ella, sweetheart, I promise that I am going to have my mouth on, in, and around every inch of your body," she rasped, her chest rising and falling fast. "All. Night. Long."

Adele moaned loudly, suddenly dizzy.

Natalie cupped Adele's saturated panties with one hand and pushed forward, grinding the heel of her hand where Adele was most sensitive. With her other hand, she twisted Adele's nipple gently, but firmly.

Adele cried out, her hips thrusting forward of their own accord.

"But if you don't fuck me right now, I'm going to die."

Her own center bursting with need, Adele lunged forward and drove two fingers into Natalie's dripping core, burying them to the hilt. Feeling their sweat-slicked bodies pressed together as Natalie's head thrashed from side to side, sent Adele careening to the razor's edge where she hung on for all she was worth. *How is she doing this to me?*

Adele slid her hand under one of Natalie's trembling thighs and gave a tiny tug upward. She shook a drop of perspiration from her brow and it splashed onto Natalie's nipple, causing Natalie to jerk and hiss at the sensation. "Nat, is this—?"

Natalie arched her back, pushing their bodies closer. "Yes." Her raspy voice was a cross between a command and outright begging. "Yes to *everything*."

The words landed directly between Adele's legs, flooding her with arousal, and filling every crack and crevice inside her with molten desire. With a growl, she lifted one of Natalie's thighs over her shoulder, opening Natalie further to the steady thrusting motion of her hand. Adele placed a hot kiss on the tender skin behind Natalie's knee and then dragged her teeth along her pale inner thigh. She was so close to coming herself that when Natalie reached between them and lightly touched Adele just where she needed her most, Adele released a strangled shout.

"Nat, if you...Jesus! I won't be able...I-I'm gonna come..." It was hard to speak with her teeth gritted together and while fire consumed her.

"Good."

Adele threw her head back when the maddening touch returned, but then quickly retreated. "Oh, my God!" She was on the verge of plunging headlong into insanity.

"You are exquisite." Natalie's voice overflowed with lust and reverence. She lightly ran her index and middle fingers on either side of Adele's clit once again and ever so gently squeezed.

This time she couldn't stop herself. Adele came. *Hard.* Head thrown back in pleasure, mouth opened in a silent scream, she was blasted in a volcano of pleasure. Her body shook from a gratification so intense that she, and the world around her, were enveloped in a euphoric white light. For several long seconds, the only thing holding her upright was Natalie's thigh as she leaned against it, floating at a rarified height she'd never experienced and that had to be heaven. The hot rush of release and relief that pushed outward from her center, and extended to her fingertips and toes, was so profound she couldn't quite wrap her mind around it. So instead, she opened her arms to it and was willingly engulfed.

Eventually, Natalie swam into view.

Beaming, Natalie leaned up and ran her fingers through Adele's hair, tucking a strand of the sexily mussed locks behind Adele's ear. She gently held Adele's face between two warm palms. "I adore you," she whispered breathily, unbidden tears shimmering in her eyes.

When Adele finally came back to her senses, she grinned a little sheepishly and wiped at a few tears that had escaped with her thumb. A lump in her throat kept her from speaking, so she expressed herself in another way. She curled the fingers that were still buried deep inside Natalie.

Natalie gasped, and her eyes widened as she was wonderfully reminded where Adele had left off.

Outside the rain began to pour in earnest, beating loudly against the roof.

The devouring kiss that Adele delivered next unraveled them both. Their lips clung hotly together.

It didn't take Adele long to reestablish a rhythm that had them both panting, her own desire rising again like the tide. Then there was a look on Natalie's face. *Jesus. Her face. I've never...* It was wide open. Sharing her pleasure. Holding nothing back as she moaned, and whimpered, and sighed. Adele's heart clenched with joy that bordered on pain it was so intensely beautiful.

Hips helping her hand thrust forward, Adele increased the speed of her plunging fingers, and she added her thumb to gently caress Natalie's slick clit with each stroke. The result was immediate. Adele's eyes found Natalie's, untamed but trusting, and she was sure she'd never seen anything more stunning.

Natalie bowed her back even more, the flush on her chest darkening. "Yes, yes, yes," she chanted brokenly. "So...fuck!"

Adele felt the smooth walls around her fingers contract hard, as Natalie's eyes slammed shut and she let out a loud staccato moan. Her body trembled violently, then stiffened as she came apart at the seams. She collapsed in a winded, helpless heap.

Carefully, and with as much tenderness as she possessed, Adele lowered Natalie's leg and snuggled up alongside her. She inhaled deeply, reveling in the light scent that was uniquely Natalie.

Noticing she still had her own panties on, Adele pushed them off and flung them somewhere over her shoulder. She trailed her finger down Natalie's face and whispered soft words of devotion to the recovering woman as she tenderly kissed each eyelid, then each cheek, her chin, and finally deliciously pliant, soft lips.

Natalie released a contented hum, and with what appeared to be an inordinate amount of effort, wrapped a limp arm around Adele's ribs and squeezed. Tendrils of sweat-dampened, matted hair were stuck to Natalie's face and neck, her eyes were heavily hooded, and her cheeks glowed.

Gorgeous. Adele felt her rising desire shift from a simmer to something infinitely hotter, and deeper. "Hi there," she crooned quietly, willing herself the patience required to keep from diving in and devouring Natalie whole. She sat up on one elbow and smiled down at Natalie with a mischievous, faintly smug smirk.

"Hi," Natalie whispered back, playfully rolling her eyes when she caught sight of that cocky grin.

Adele rolled atop Natalie and laughed, her movement shaking them both. She dropped a tender kiss to Natalie's glistening breastbone, unable to stop her tongue from darting out to taste the damp skin. "What?"

"Happy with yourself?"

"Yes."

Natalie chuckled and aimlessly waved a limp hand. "You earned it."

Adele kissed the very end of Natalie's nose, then her smile. This kiss was achingly soft and sweet, and neither woman made a move to deepen it.

A surge of affection rose up in Adele and then spilled over. The urge to drop to her knees and confess to Natalie that she loved her was nearly overwhelming. It was there on the tip of her tongue, itching so fiercely to be said that Adele had to take several calming breaths to keep from simply blurting it out into the scorching air between them. But she didn't want to leave any room for doubt. Didn't want the first time she said it to be in some post-coital, clichéd moment of hormonal ecstasy. That's what she was feeling—a high so sumptuous it couldn't be legal. Though she knew it was far more than a rush of hormones. *Tomorrow*, she promised herself. Tomorrow would be soon enough.

Adele lifted her head and her eyes met Natalie's. The air around them, once again, became electric and heat blossomed low in Adele's belly.

With a beaming smile, Natalie sank her hands into Adele's hair and pulled her into a bruising kiss. Tongues dueled, savored, and conquered. They kissed long and hot enough for Adele to forget her own name and for her blood to reignite as though she hadn't already been reduced to a nearly boneless pile of quivering flesh only moments before.

"Flat on your back," Natalie finally instructed, her voice smoky. She sank down on top of Adele when she complied. Both women sighed loudly as bare skin met from head to toe. They melted together, losing themselves in each other.

"I haven't…" Natalie's hot breath danced over Adele's skin, causing a riot of sensation. "God, I never want to stop kissing you." Natalie worked her plundering kisses down Adele's throat and sharply nipped the skin where Adele's neck and shoulder came together. "I love...the way you taste." Her voice quivered with want.

"Oh, sweet baby Jesus…" Adele's guttural groan was one of pure pleasure and a rush of wetness slicked her thighs. "You're a b-biter?"

Natalie laughed quietly. "Problem with that?" She punctuated her question with another sharp nip to Adele's collarbone. At Adele's gasp, she laved the red mark she'd made with a wet, soothing tongue.

Adele almost came out of her skin. "Yes!"

"Yes?" Natalie stilled, lips hovering just over Adele's chest, hot puffs of moist air causing goose bumps to erupt on the skin below and Adele's nipples to tighten to an almost painful degree.

Adele was certain her brain was about to short-circuit. "I mean n-no! Don't stop!"

"Never," Natalie swore, smiling. She tightened her hold on Adele and marked her territory with abandon. She drew her cheek along the top of one of Adele's breasts, her long tresses tickling Adele's shoulders, then chest. Adele dug her fingernails into Natalie's back and caused her to stutter. "Mmm. I can't…I can't get enough of you."

Happiness bubbled up inside Adele and infused her every syllable. "Good thing I'm here all night." She glanced down and found a pair of sexy, mischievous blue eyes looking back up at her through dark lashes. The women shared a smoldering look that made Adele idly wonder whether the entire world was ablaze.

"Remember you said that." Natalie's voice dripped with seduction and was as sultry and hot as the steamiest New Orleans night. "Now hold onto something, love."

Adele immediately fisted the fitted sheet with both hands and planted the soles of her feet firmly on the bed. Her body felt like it was spinning out of control as Natalie moved lower and lower and dragged her tongue over her scar and along the sensitive crease of her inner thigh. Adele didn't recognize the primal groan that burst from deep in her chest and throat, and she wondered for a quick second whether she'd live long enough to see the sunrise. The sound of the blood rushing in her ears was starting to drown out everything else.

Natalie chuckled wickedly. "I've got a promise to keep." She moved her mouth a few inches and a low keening sound was torn from the pit of Adele's stomach.

Adele's heart slammed against her ribcage as she held on to the sheet for dear life, her body and mind thrust helplessly into free fall. Head spinning, she felt more than heard Natalie's deep, erotic hum of pleasure and the flutter of her voice.

"Mmm…Ella, you're delicious."

Lightning flashed and thunder boomed, and the only thing they knew was each other.

CHAPTER NINETEEN

The next day…

Adele unlocked the gate to Lafayette Cemetery No. 1 and left it open. The old cemetery was founded in 1833 and located right in the heart of the Garden District. It was filled with the wall vaults and above-ground tombs that New Orleans was so famous for.

Adele found it both peaceful and haunting in its beauty. The wind whistled through the grounds in gusts and fits, and bordered on cold. The sky was heavy with dark clouds, making it seem closer to twilight than it actually was, but so far it wasn't raining. Adele made her way to a specific bench near the rear of the cemetery and set her cane down near her feet.

The cemetery had officially closed to the public almost ninety minutes ago, in the middle of the afternoon, but Adele's mother and sister were former presidents and existing board members of New Orleans's Save Our Cemeteries Organization, so getting a key to the gates for this private meeting hadn't been a problem. Once Sgt. Jay Morrell entered the cemetery, the gates would be locked behind him, securing them both inside and guaranteeing they wouldn't be disturbed.

Adele's phone vibrated in her jacket pocket and she reviewed the text with a nod. She sent a one-letter reply before sticking the phone back in her pocket.

He was here.

Morrell's shaved head came into view. He'd gained weight since she'd last seen him, had gotten soft with his new supervisory role. His neck was as thick as his head, giving him a fire hydrant-like appearance. She wrinkled her nose and wondered if he could even button the top of his shirt. She was relatively confident that he couldn't run from her if he tried. Disgust slithered through her veins at the very sight of him.

She would be a totally new experience for Morrell. He'd never needed to be fast or quick because he didn't fight fair and spent his time preying on those who were weaker. Things would be different today.

"What the hell?" Morrell spluttered when he saw Adele, and not Billy Hobson, on the bench waiting for him. He stopped dead in his tracks, his dark, narrowed eyes flitting from tomb to tomb, as though he half-expected someone to jump out and grab him.

The cemetery was completely quiet except for the sound of the wind. Morrell tried to cover his surprise with a smug look, but he hadn't been quick enough. She'd caught a glimpse of his confusion and worry, and knew his feeble mind was racing as he wondered why and how she was here instead of Hobson.

"Hello, Morrell." Adele didn't stand and didn't address him by his rank. He was a disgrace to cops everywhere. She just waited, staring at a crepe myrtle tree that was particularly old and beautiful.

"Well, well, if it isn't Hurricane Lejeune," Morrell sneered at her, his thin lips twisting. "Aren't you a dark horse? Popping back up when I least expect you."

Adele felt a burning sensation in the pit of her stomach but refused to take the bait. "Have a seat."

"Gimpy bitch, I don't—"

"Sit!" She enunciated the word preciously, harshly, thoughts of this man in her own home, lying in wait for Natalie, and then making her scream, caused her blood to boil and her pulse to pound. Adele's palms began to sweat.

Her gun was tucked into the back of her pants, but she kept her hands folded casually in front of her, right where he could see them. Adele wasn't going to persuade this pig of a man to give her what she wanted by brute physical force. She needed to appear less threatening than she was, not more. *God*, how she wanted to simply shove her weapon as far down his mouth as it would go and demand answers.

"Morrell, we have something to talk about."

His eyes scanned the space around them again. Worried. Nervous. But curious, too. "What could you have to say that I want to hear?" Reluctantly he sat down, his gut coming to rest over his belt, his weapon visible beneath his ill-fitting navy blue suit coat. "I take it you found that sniveling shit Hobson."

She nodded, unwilling to disagree with his assessment of the man. "You know what I hate more than a dirty cop?" she asked conversationally.

"Dick? I hear you're batting for the other team now."

Adele couldn't help it, she laughed. "Nope. Well, maybe *your* dick, yeah. But other than that, I can't really think of a single thing I hate more than a dirty cop. They're like cancer, and need to be cut out with a sharp knife." Adele sat up a little straighter. Today, she was that knife. "How did you know I had a friend staying with me?"

He snorted derisively, watching her closely, wariness seeping from every breath. "Every cop in town knows your place got robbed. And how you went crazy over your 'friend' when the ambulance arrived." Morrell faux pouted. "Paramedics gossip worse than cops. Anyway, I was so sorry to hear about her unfortunate accident."

Adele felt the growl rise up inside her like a rocket, only barely able to hold it in at the last second. "I'll bet you were. But somehow I think you're going to be more sorry about the talk I had with Hobson." Adele's grin was genuine. "He rolled over on you."

"Bullshit."

"Oh, yes, he really did." She reached into her inside jacket pocket and Morrell jerked away, his own hand coming down to rest on his gun.

She stopped moving. "Relax. I have something for you." Slowly, she began to pull out an envelope. "See? Nothing dangerous."

"For me?" Morrell looked skeptical.

She nodded, and passed it over, refusing to let it go for a second until he looked her in the eye. "You really deserve this."

"Is it from Hobson? I don't—" He opened the envelope and pulled out a thick stack of twenty-dollar bills bound together with a rubber band.

"It's not from Billy. It's from me. It's an offer in case you want to do things the easy way. I was wondering if now I could have you on my payroll the way your boss on the NOPD has you on his?"

"Go to hell," Morrell snarled and threw the envelope back against Adele's chest, the stack of bills bouncing off her and landing on her lap.

She ignored it.

Morrell's eyes flashed. "If Hobson said anything worthwhile, not that there is anything to say, mind you," he clarified in a sarcastic voice, "I'd be in custody right now and not wasting my time jerking off to your moving lips in some graveyard. Fuck you. I'm outta here."

He moved to stand, but Adele grabbed his sleeve. "You were right about him. About Billy. He told me you always said he was the weakest link."

Slowly, Morrell relaxed back to the bench.

Adele released his sleeve and scooted a bit farther down the bench, far enough that he would have to lean to reach her. She had his undivided attention.

"He really was the weakest link," she went on conversationally. "And that weak link is currently in Baton Rouge. He decided to take a little drive there yesterday seeing as how I have a friend on the force in Baton Rouge who was willing to help by taking his statement. I understand Hobson has been very, very talkative. Not that it matters. I already had a long talk with him myself where he explained how you tried to pin Joshua Phillips's murder on poor Crisco."

"Not that shit again." Morrell rolled his eyes. "You just can't leave it alone, can you?" He shook his head mockingly. "Didn't you see what happened last time you fucked with things you shouldn't have?"

"I guess I didn't learn my lesson," Adele admitted with blunt honesty. "I can be stubborn that way."

"Crisco is dead and buried in some potter's field. The word of a disgraced cop against mine won't mean shit, especially coming from you." Morrell snorted. "If this is why you called me out here, you wasted both our time."

"Trust me, it gets better. Even though he was wetting his pants while he was doing it, Billy then explained how you got a private call on your cell instructing you to go to the Dixie Brewery that night."

The blood began to drain from Morrell's face.

Bingo. "And how you sat there, someplace you should have never been to begin with, and waited at the brewery until you could pick up the dispatch. And that gave me an idea!" Adele tapped her temple lightly. "I thought, 'wouldn't it be interesting if I found out who had been the dispatch supervisor that night?'"

Despite the cold breeze, sweat formed on Morrell's heavy brow. "You're not on the force anymore, those records can't—"

"I couldn't get them. But a cop from another town can make a simple phone call to check on it...for a case. As a courtesy, NOPD supplies it in an instant. It was easy. Don't you remember when the Police Union insisted all schedule records be retained to ensure cops didn't get screwed out of overtime? Everything is on computer. It took like five minutes. The dispatch supervisor is being picked up for questioning tonight."

Morrell looked like he might barf.

Excitement sang through Adele as she continued to speak. "And then I had *another* idea! I thought, that dispatch supervisor did someone a *really* big solid that night, holding that dispatch call until you and Hobson were on the scene, I wonder if she got paid a little bonus for her efforts?

I wonder whether her bank account will show a bump in the next day or so? And—"

"Bitch!" Morrell seethed. He made a move that was perilously close to his gun.

"Freeze!" she shouted, eyes wide.

His smile was arctic as he looked down at her empty hands. "Why should I?"

"Because you'll be dead before it's out of the holster. Look at your chest, nice and slowly."

He frowned, but did as she asked. And in the center of his chest was a glowing red dot. He glanced around wildly but couldn't see anyone.

"That's courtesy of my ex-husband Landry. You remember him, right? The homicide detective who was also Marine Recon with sniper qualifications?"

"Fuck me."

"No, thanks. We've already established I find even the thought of your dick repulsive."

She slowly pulled her phone out and pressed a few buttons. "Now, I just told Landry that you're being very threatening. If you try to get up or go anywhere near your weapon, he will shoot you." That wasn't what she'd texted, but Morrell would find that out soon enough. "In fact, you know what, hands in the air."

Adele moved around behind him so that she was never in Landry's line of fire and removed Morrell's gun before taking her seat back at the other end of the bench.

Morrell crossed his arms over his chest. "You don't know the shit you're playing in."

"Oh, yes, I do. Did you ever make those domino chains when you were a kid?"

"Who the fuck cares?"

"You know, where you line up the dominoes and then push one and they all start tumbling down in a big line? That's what's already happened. Hobson was the first domino. The dispatch supervisor was next. They're all falling down, and they're all leading to you. And best of all, you can't stop it."

The fear showed plainly in his eyes now. "You don't understand!"

"I understand that you are filthy, fucking dirty and on the take!"

She pointed an accusing finger in his face. "I understand that you ran drugs and money for your boss and got off on roughing up suspects. I understand that your boss killed Joshua Phillips and then called you to come cover it up by blaming Crisco. I understand that your boss had the dispatch held until you could guarantee you'd be the first and only cops on the scene. I understand that I walked in and saw you in the middle of convincing Crisco that he'd better go along with your plan."

Defiant, Morrell sat there, his face hard as stone. Only his eyes were savage, like a beast desperately seeking a way to break free from his cage.

"I understand that you tanked Hobson's career and scared him into leaving town and staying away. I understand that when Crisco recanted his confession and was released from jail, you killed him."

"I didn't!" Morrell denied hotly, and for a second, Adele was surprised to find herself wondering whether he might actually be telling the truth. It was the first thing in her laundry list of his misdeeds that he'd even bothered to deny.

Adele shrugged carelessly. "I don't believe you."

"I'm not going down for murder…" he mumbled to himself repeatedly, looking shaken this was really happening.

"Then we come to poor Misty. She had Joshua's phone and your boss wanted that phone."

He made a face. "I hate those nasty junkies, but it wasn't me that killed her."

A slight narrowing of her eyes was Adele's only outer reaction. He'd just confirmed another homicide. She still didn't know what was on the phone that was so important, but that didn't change the chain of events. "Then you broke into *my* inn and you…" She had to stop to swallow thickly. "And you strangled Natalie."

"Dammit! I didn't do that either!"

Adele's hands shaped into fists and she leaned close to his face, too close, well within his meaty reach, unable to contain her fury. Her voice was low, and deadly, and sounded foreign to her own ears. "I'm going to make sure you get the needle. I'm going to be there when they stab it into your arm and push in the poison, you son of a bitch. I'm going to watch and smile while you twitch, and gasp, and writhe as you try to draw in a deep breath but your body won't listen to your feeble, mushy brain anymore."

Sweating freely, Morrell glanced down at his chest again. That red dot was still there, mocking him, never moving.

Adele could feel that he wanted to rip her throat out, feel the hatred rolling off him. She smiled. "You want to come at me, right? Shut me up. It must hurt that a woman is doing this to you, right? Bringing everything down. Embarrassing you. Making you feel small and shriveled," Adele taunted mercilessly.

His chest started to heave.

"I was better than you at the academy, and as a cop, and I'm better now. Go ahead! Do it!" she shouted and spread her arms open as far as they would go. "Save the state the trouble of killing you later!"

He looked at her with his mouth hanging slightly open, panting, as though he was seeing her for the first time.

Adele caught a glimpse of a distorted version of herself reflected back in his livid gaze…and she applied the brakes…and slid a little farther down the bench. *Jesus.* Her heart was jackhammering and she felt a little ill that she really *did* want Morrell to make a move so Landry would shoot him. *Too close.*

Her phone buzzed and she ignored it.

"But, Morrell," she paused to lick her lips, her mouth dry, "there's a way you could avoid the needle, you know. Just give me a name. I'll help you get a deal."

He shook his head, resolutely. "No."

"Surely your boss isn't worth dying for?"

"Giving you a name makes me as good as dead anyway. I'll take my chances with a New Orleans jury."

Adele sighed. "I thought you would say that." She pulled out her phone and looked at the screen, grinning broadly. "By the way, I made a new friend this morning. He's well and truly awful."

"Are you a psych case or somethin'?" Morrell wondered aloud, drawing his head back.

"Do you read the *Times-Picayune*? Though I really doubt you're smart enough to understand more than the comics."

His face turned an interesting shade of purple. She'd struck a nerve. "I read! I mean, I read the paper in the shitter every day!"

She raised both eyebrows doubtfully. "Sure you do. Then you'll know all about my new friend Winston Benoit."

Morrell's eyes bugged out. "The fucking prick reporter who hates cops?"

Adele shivered. "I know." Benoit had crucified the NOPD in his articles after Hurricane Katrina. He might be the only person in town less popular with the police than she was. "Benoit is almost as vile as you. Anyway, he's superexcited about these."

She slid her phone down the white stone bench. It didn't quite make it all the way to Morrell and he began to reach for it, but stopped, his hand frozen in midair. The red dot had followed his every move.

"It's okay," she assured him softly. "You can take it."

Morrell picked up the phone and his jaw sagged as he looked at the crystal clear photograph of him taking an envelope from Adele.

"Be sure to scroll. There are several. My favorite is the last one. It got my dimples."

With a dry swallow, Morrell swiped his meaty finger across the screen. The next photo was of him opening the envelope with Adele's gaze turned sideways as if she was worried they were being watched. The last photo was of him taking out a big wad of cash with Adele looking on and beaming like a fool.

Morrell closed his eyes.

"Can't you see tomorrow's headline? It will for sure include the words 'Dirty Cop' and 'Rat' and 'Cover-up.' You know, shit like that. I'm going to make sure that everyone in New Orleans knows you've been throwing me tidbits of info about your crooked boss as I investigate what really happened at the Dixie Brewery, and that because of you, I'm almost onto him."

Flabbergasted, Morrell sputtered, "You can't do that!"

"Of course, I can. I'm not an officer of the court nowadays. I can lie and cheat. I don't wear a white hat anymore thanks to you. My hat's more gray, and it lets me do horrible shit like this."

"Bu-but-but—"

"Here's what's going to happen: Landry can take you into the protective custody of the Baton Rouge Police Department where no terrible 'accident' will befall you and where you can make a dirtball deal with the DA. Or…"

"Or what? I can't do that! I can't."

Adele felt a twinge of satisfaction. Hobson had been right. Morrell was gnawing on his lower lip so hard she wasn't sure there was going to be much left by the time he was through. He was terrified of whoever was pulling his strings.

"Or, Landry is going to take you into custody, but he's going to hand you right over to the NOPD. He's going to give them the details of Hobson's confession. He happens to have a written copy with him. It's more than enough to hold you. Unlike me, Landry managed to leave with at least a few friends on the force.

"He's going to make sure they all know that I want revenge for my career going down the tubes, and that you've been stringing me along with details about someone corrupt and high up in the force, but you haven't spilled all the beans quite yet. You'll spend half your night in an interrogation room where so many people know who you are that your dirty boss won't be able to save you, and the other half of the night in a quiet cell away from the general jail population, where your boss or one of his minions can easily get to you."

She let that soak in for a few seconds and nodded to herself when she saw the horror dawn on Morrell's stupid face. "Remember what I said about those dominoes? Landry's friends are going to 'confidentially' tell their friends, and their friends will tell their friends. Soon everyone is going to know that you have a big secret that is just bursting to be set free so you can make a deal with the DA."

"No one will believe you," he cried desperately, though Morrell didn't look as though he could even convince himself. "I'm no narc!"

Natalie inclined her head in disbelief. "Seriously?"

Still rebellious, he nodded.

"You're a greedy dumb bastard. Your boss paid you to do disgusting things, and you did other grotesque things just *because you liked it.* Do you really think your boss is going to believe you wouldn't sell him out to me on moral grounds? Besides, how is he going to doubt that I've been buying information from you when it's there in living color in the newspaper?" She let out a low whistle. "It's going to crank the heat so high…"

"He has people at the jail!" Morrell blurted frantically.

Yes! She pumped a mental fist.

"I-I-I won't last the night!"

Adele shrugged one shoulder, looking utterly unconcerned even though her stomach was rolling over on itself. "Probably not. But that's your problem, not mine. Now decide what you're doing. I don't have all day."

She texted Landry—who was comfortably perched on the second-floor balcony of a home across the street, his rifle trained at Morrell's chest—that it was time to come in. Adele had picked his location very carefully. This was her childhood neighborhood, and she knew people in most of the houses up and down the street lining the cemetery. She'd had her first kiss on the very balcony where Landry was packing up shop and was well aware of its view into the cemetery.

"What?" Morrell screeched, voice uncharacteristically high. "I can't decide right this second. I need to think." He began gesturing wildly. "I need—"

Adele pulled her gun from the back of her pants and trained it on Morrell. "Hands on your head!" she barked, rising to her feet. "I need a name."

Morrell was torn. She could see that. Confusion emanated from his every sweaty pore, but he obeyed immediately and clasped his hands on his head. "But—"

"No buts!" This was the time to press. He was starting to crumble. He'd believed everything she'd said even though much of it was a pack of lies.

Adele had never contacted Winston Benoit. Landry had taken the photos of her and Morrell with a high-powered camera and sent them to her burner cell from his. The phones and the camera's memory card would disappear after this conversation so Morrell wouldn't have proof for a claim of coercion.

Adele hadn't even tried to find the dispatch supervisor from the night of Josh's murder yet. She didn't want to tip anyone off that she was looking.

Billy Hobson was still tucked safely away in the Shreveport Hilton, most likely tearing through the minibar, and certainly not talking to any Baton Rouge cops.

But, the offer for Landry to take Morrell into custody in Baton Rouge was true. Well, it was more than an offer. Landry was going to pop Morrell and haul him back to Baton Rouge one way or another tonight. Morrell just didn't know it yet.

"Tell me your decision, Morrell, or deal with the NOPD and a boss who has no problem committing murder." She gave him a look of revulsion. "I'm done with you. Your boss is going down one way or another, and so are you. Do you really want to wonder for the rest of your short life how he's going to finish you off?"

"I…" It began to rain and Morrell looked up at the sky and let the drops hit his face. His big body was trembling. "Shit. Shit! Fine!"

Adele's heart stopped. "Who?"

"Swear it! Protective custody. No way he can touch me."

"I swear."

His face turned bright red as though his mouth and brain couldn't agree on whatever he was about to do next. "Argh!"

"Your lieutenant? Luna?" she prodded gently. Who better to protect Morrell from himself long enough to make him useful? Who else would ignore his incompetence and cruelty and allow him to rise to a sergeant? Why else would his lieutenant have outright refused her request for an investigation into Crisco's beating?

Morrell glared up at her and, unaccountably, his mouth distorted into an awful smile. "You're not as smart as you think you are."

Adele lifted an eyebrow, her gun never wavering as she waited, the cold rain plastering her hair to her face.

"It was never my boss. It was yours."

She could only stare. The respected leader who'd run the Juvenile Division for almost twenty years? The boss who took her under his wing and gave her her first break as a detective? The beaming man who'd showed up at the hospital when Logan was born with Godiva chocolates for her, Jack Daniel's for Landry, and a teddy bear as big as a real bear cub for her son?

Adele's mind ruthlessly rewound the clock and replayed other events too. He'd also completely shut down her claims of Morrell's violence. He'd callously egged on Landry's worry about the damage her claims could do to their lives and careers. God only knew what he'd told

Lieutenant Luna behind the scenes. Maybe that's why no one, including the PIB, had listened to her.

She'd always thought her boss wanted to sweep police brutality under the rug in an effort to save the NOPD's badly damaged image. She'd thought he played by old-school rules and valued the thin blue line above everything else.

In reality, he was covering for murder.

"Lieutenant Peter Xavier?" she whispered, believing it the second his name passed her lips.

Morrell nodded, his sinister-looking grin still frozen in place.

Landry strode up behind her and roughly pushed Morrell down on the wet bench headfirst. Morrell's belly made a loud squelching sound when it hit the wet stone. "Hands out above your head, ass hat!" When he didn't see Morrell's gun, he wordlessly reached out and Adele passed it to him.

Landry continued to pat him down and removed a baby Glock from Morrell's ankle holster. "Who?" he grunted, knowing by the look on Adele's face that Morrell had told her.

"Xavier."

"Shit." Landry sighed. He cuffed Morrell then jerked him upright to a sitting position, as though the large man weighed no more than a child.

Adele texted Natalie: *It's done and he talked. I'm okay. Details soon.*

She was rewarded with an instant reply. *Thank God! Come home. We both need a hug. And wine.* ☺

Adele smiled affectionately, running her finger over the text.

Morrell suddenly released a surprise cackle. "Hey, Lejeune, don't you want to know the rest of the story?"

She and Landry exchanged worried glances. Morrell looked way too happy. Something was very wrong. His paralyzing fear had shifted into something that dripped with gleeful hatred.

Landry gave Morrell a rough shake. "What else? Spit it out," he said in an eerily calm voice. "I'm not as nice as my wife. I'll beat your fat ass from here to Texas."

Morrell cocked his head to the side. "Don't you mean *ex*-wife?"

Landry lifted his fist but Adele intercepted him by grabbing his bicep. "What else Morrell?" She stuffed her weapon into her jacket pocket and wiped her sodden hair back off her forehead. She collected Landry's cell phone from his pocket and lifted the large camera off from around his neck, ejecting the memory card.

They worked and moved easily together. Time, it seemed, had erased most of the awkwardness since their split. "Morrell, if you have something to say, it's now or never."

"I told you that I didn't hurt your girlfriend or kill Crisco."

Landry's head snapped sideways at the word girlfriend. He looked at Adele in question, and she mouthed "later."

"So what?" she said out loud to Morrell. "You're a dirty liar."

"Yeah, I guess," Morrell allowed easily. "But I was never the muscle for Xavier. I just ran small jobs." He squared his shoulders proudly. "But I did it well. Xavier has a gorilla for the truly nasty stuff."

"Enough of this," Landry groaned, frowning at the darkening sky. "Save it for the judge and your prison résumé."

Adele collected the envelope with the money and stuffed it next to her gun.

Landry jerked Morrell to his feet and started walking. Morrell craned his head backward, obviously desperate to get in the last word. "The henchman for Xavier is your good buddy. The newly minted Vice detective. Alonzo Rice."

Adele held up a hand and Landry stopped. "Wh-what did you say?"

"Don't listen to him, Ella," Landry said, smacking Morrell hard on the back of the head and beginning to walk again. "He's just trying to get to you."

"It's the truth!" Morrell protested shrilly, digging in his heels and sending tiny bits of white rock from the gravel path everywhere. "I'm not lying."

"Landry, stop. I want to hear this." Adele removed her gun and pointed it right at Morrell's head. She strode forward, not stopping until the barrel was pressed tightly against the space between his eyes. "Now, what did you say?"

"Ella…" Landry's voice rumbled deep in his chest. An urgent warning.

"I-I…" Morrell began to trip over his words, his eyes crossing as he stared at the barrel of the gun. "Uh, I didn't mean to…"

"What. Did. You. Say?" Eyes blazing, Adele spat out the words.

"It's the truth." Morrell began to struggle wildly. "Rice is the muscle when Xavier needs someone to disappear. Not me. You promised me protective custody! You promised!"

"Shut up and quit spazzing out when there is a gun to your head," Landry barked, wrestling Morrell back into control with hands made slippery by the rain. They were all soaked. "Or protective custody for you is going to be the morgue."

Adele searched Morrell's eyes for the lie, but all she saw was malice and terror that she'd renege on her part of the deal. Her mind raced, and suddenly it lit on an omission that she hadn't thought important until now. She'd thought it was trivial. When she'd questioned Billy about the night at the Dixie Brewery she made him recount the evening in detail, over and over. While she'd never asked him about it specifically, he'd never mentioned…

"The night you were headed to the Dixie Brewery, tell me what happened after you got the call. Everything." Adele tasted bile.

"Ella—"

"Quiet, Landry!" she nearly shouted, her glare drilling into Morrell. Her phone buzzed again but she left it in her pocket.

Morrell yelped as Landry pushed his cuffed hands farther up his back when he didn't respond quickly enough. "You already know." He recounted the events exactly as Hobson had.

Adele grew more agitated.

Obviously trying to hit whatever it was she was searching for, Morrell added, "We were never gonna eat at Betsy's Hole-in-the-Wall diner. Her chili makes me shit fire for days. I just said that as an excuse for why I was in Mid-City."

Adele squeezed her eyes shut. *No. No. No!* "There has to be more."

"Huh?"

"Tell me that you stopped for gas on the way to the brewery."

Morrell and Landry both looked truly bewildered. "But, we didn't."

"Tell me you stopped for gas! Tell me you kept the receipt and showed it to PIB during the investigations."

"The fuck? I don't know what you're even talking about. We had to haul it to make it to the brewery during that storm! You think I stopped for a Big Gulp along the way? Xavier would have put a bullet in my head himself."

Tears leapt into her eyes but were quickly washed away by the rain. Al had told her about the gas stop to shut her up. To keep her from looking deeper into Morrell. He'd known she couldn't prove or disapprove his story. And it had worked.

"Ella?" Landry looked between his ex-wife and Morrell. "What does that mean?"

"He's telling the truth," she said brokenly, bending at the waist and turning her back to the men. *Oh, God.* She was going to barf on some poor Confederate soldier's grave. "Al…"

"Shit!" Landry's eyes welled as fast as Adele's. "I'm sorry, Ella. I am." He shook his head roughly as if to order his thoughts. "Okay, you don't do anything about this. We'll get him. Al doesn't know we're on to him, and we'll get him just like that SOB Xavier. Just don't do anything yet. We don't want to tip either one of them off."

Adele didn't respond. She couldn't.

"This has to go down at the exact same time." Landry ran a hand over his short dark hair, scattering more water droplets. "Just like we talked about for whomever Morrell's crooked boss turned out to be, we'll bring in the Baton Rouge PD for the bust. But first I have to take this piece of shit back home, and you have to pick up Logan at Amelia's."

Stunned, Adele let his words roll over her. *Not Al. Please no. This has to be a mistake.* She loved him like family. He *was* family.

"Too bad—" Whatever Morrell was going to say next was cut off by Landry's hard smack to the face.

"Ella?" Landry questioned worriedly. "Did you hear me? You cannot go near Al."

"No…I mean, yes." She was going numb on the inside as though someone had injected her veins with novocaine. She'd helped Al since he was a boy. Like Al said, they were *tight*. After everything, he was the only one who had had her back. And somehow it was all a lie. How was that even possible?

"I-I won't go after him," she said, her voice feathery light. *I don't think I can even look at him.* "You're right. We can't risk Xavier finding out or vice versa." Her jaw worked. "They go down tomorrow, together."

Landry reached out and laid a comforting hand on her soaked forearm. "I'm sorry."

Tears burned her eyes and carved a path down her cheeks. "Me too." She sat back down on the bench. "Go." She made a shooing motion. "I'll go get Logan right from here. I'll see you tomorrow."

Landry nodded but didn't move. "I'll leave the keys in the gate. Are you—?"

"I'm not fine. But I will be." Adele closed her eyes and heard them walk away. She knew that Landry had borrowed a black-and-white cruiser so he could secure Morrell for the trip to Baton Rouge. And she imagined that she heard the cemetery gate open and close and the cruiser pull away.

For a few minutes she sat there, cane in hand, letting the rain pound down on her, her arms wrapped around herself in misery, when her phone buzzed again. "Goddammit, Landry! What now?" But it wasn't a missed call. It was a text from Natalie that had been sent moments earlier.

Al called my phone back. Wants to meet w/me. Cabbing to his house now. Be back soon. XOXO

Adele's blood turned to ice. "Christ!" She phoned Natalie back, her entire body in motion as she frantically willed her to pick up. But there was no answer. In a panic, she texted several messages, but didn't get a reply.

She sprinted for the gate, quite sure neither her feet nor her cane ever hit the ground.

CHAPTER TWENTY

Detective Rice lived in a small area of the Algiers neighborhood called Algiers Point. It was located across the Mississippi River from the rest of New Orleans and accessible only by ferry or bridge. Adele had her foot flat on the accelerator of her hopelessly gutless Ford Fiesta the entire way across the bridge, using every swear word she knew and twisting them into increasingly vile combinations.

During the drive, the pain from Al's bone-deep betrayal had evolved into a raw fury that was barely containable. She gripped the steering wheel so tight her fingers ached. How dare he try to kill someone she loved!

And if he'd harmed Natalie again…what? The new threat died as quickly as it was born. She could haul him to jail to face the music for his crimes, yes. Without question. But hurt Al? It would be like hurting Logan or Amelia or even Natalie. Inconceivable.

She'd texted Natalie a half-dozen more times and called nearly that many. Nat's phone had to be off because the messages were now going directly to voice mail.

Adele pulled onto Oliver Street and slowed down, finally yielding to the pouring rain. Her windshield wipers were on full speed, and they still weren't doing enough. The last thing she wanted was to crash the damn car.

It was fully dark when Adele came to a stop behind a new, tricked-out, black Escalade she didn't recognize, and in front of a cheerful pale blue Queen Anne-style home with several palm trees dotting the small front yard. Al's wife's minivan was nowhere to be seen. The porch light was off, but lights inside the house were on, and an enormous Christmas wreath decorated the front door.

Adele drew her gun and turned off her own phone, stuffing it into the back pocket of her jeans as she moved up the front walk and stood next to the porch swing, and a coffee can full of sand that served as an ashtray. For a moment, she wasn't sure how to proceed. Things could be calm inside and Al could be simply chatting with Natalie, or it could be a nightmare. Unwilling to take any chances with Natalie's safety, she kept her gun out and assumed the worst.

She mentally reviewed the layout of the house and had almost decided to head around to the back when she heard the sound of children in the front room. Her heart clenched so hard that it threatened to send her to her knees. She gasped.

Her mind flashed to a ramshackle house almost three years ago, and darkness began to invade the edges of her eyesight. Images and sensations from the past merged with the here and now and yanked her back through time: a cloudy night sky, children's voices, the weight of her weapon clenched tightly in her hand, stinging sweat in her eyes, the feeling of her feet sinking into mud, the scent of damp wood and cigarettes. Suddenly she was back inside *that* house, only Natalie was there too, and they were separated. How?

Adele swallowed hard and drew in several shaky breaths. *Calm down. Calm the fuck down.* Abruptly overheated, she rested her forehead against the cool wooden front door as her vision swam. She was melting down, and she hadn't even made it inside yet. *Don't get her killed. Don't!*

Her eyes slammed closed of their own accord. *This house is different. This is now. This is different. This is now. This is Al's house.* It took an embarrassingly long time, but she repeated her mantra again and again until she could look around and see and smell and feel only what was happening today. Although she had regained some semblance of clarity, she didn't feel much better.

Three years ago she'd been dealing with strangers. This was infinitely more horrible. These were people she loved.

A few seconds more, and Adele's heartbeat slowed to something close enough to normal that she was certain she wouldn't pass out. *Think.* Al had three kids. The littlest was still in diapers and the oldest was the same age as Logan. There was a boy in the middle. It had been so long since she'd seen them, she was sure they wouldn't recognize her, but she had to get them out of the house. Despite her overwhelming need to find Natalie, Adele needed to do that first.

Thankfully, the front door was unlocked, and she silently slipped inside, putting her gun away and dripping heavily on the dark hardwood floors. Adele crept into a small room off the main entry and Al's oldest child, a pretty girl named Monique, glanced up from a Lego tower she was making with her little brother, Damien. Oddly, both children were wearing coats.

"Hi, Monique," Adele said quietly, bending down so she was on the same level as the child.

Monique's eyes widened and she looked like she might scream for help until her brother intervened.

"The lady from the picture!" he said excitedly. He grabbed Adele's hand and pulled her over to a side table to see a photo of Al in cap and gown at his high school graduation, his muscular arm wound around Adele's shoulders as they smiled happily for the camera. Adele had the photo's twin in her living room.

"That's me," Adele said in a cheerful but quiet voice. "I'm your daddy's friend, Ella." When she'd detached herself from just about everything good in her life, she'd stopped visiting with Al's family too. She hadn't seen his kids in more than a year, and now she was a stranger. "We've met before, but you were too little to remember."

Monique instantly relaxed. "You're Logan's mama. His picture is on our refrigerator. Are you a police detective like Daddy?"

"I-I catch bad guys sometimes." Though she knew she was going to lie like a rug to get the children out of the house, for some reason she found herself unable to lie about that. "Where is your mama and baby Michael?"

"Gone Christmas shoppin'!" Damien answered excitedly. He looked up at Adele with his father's pretty eyes, and she wanted to burst into tears. "Daddy's mad cuz Mama's not answering her phone again."

Adele looked over her shoulder nervously. "I need you kids to come with me."

"We can't," Monique informed Adele seriously. "Daddy says we're going on a car trip and to wait here and not move an inch until he's finished talking to the pretty lady. She's coming on our trip too. He already put our suitcases in the car."

Adele licked her lips and nodded. "We're all going on the trip together. That's why I have my coat on too. Your daddy sent me to get you."

"You're all wet," Damien said, wrinkling his nose.

"It's raining, but we'll run fast so we won't get too wet. Let's go."

Monique hesitated, and Adele quickly pulled out her phone. "You can play with this in the car while I get your daddy. It's brand new and it has a game on it." Temptingly, she held it out and smiled.

Monique looked skeptical and unimpressed, and Adele felt a tiny rush of pride at the girl's intelligence.

Damien elbowed his sister. "Say yes, Mo! I wanna play. Puh-leeze!"

"It's Angry Birds," Adele enticed, smiling so wide anyone but a child would have known it was unnatural. "You can try to beat your daddy's score. If you're good enough, that is."

Monique's dark eyes narrowed. She hadn't missed the challenge in Adele's voice. "Okay," she finally agreed, taking the phone in one hand and Damien's hand in her other.

When the children were tucked safely in the car, Adele wiped the rain from her eyes and ducked her head inside. "Now stay here and wait for us."

"In the dark?" Damien asked, clearly realizing this might not be so fun.

"When you're playing with the phone it will light up the car. See?" She quickly turned on the game. "You need to stay right here, or your daddy is going to be super mad." She pinned each child with a serious glare. "Got it?"

Two sets of wide eyes gazed back at her, and the children nodded simultaneously.

Unable to stop herself, Adele pressed a kiss to each head. Eventually those trusting eyes would be filled with nothing but hatred for her. She would be the woman who destroyed their family.

"Have fun and be good." She locked the car doors, knowing that Monique could probably open them without any trouble, but praying that she wouldn't.

For a moment she thought about calling the NOPD, but she didn't know whom she could trust. She should have called Landry and had him come back right away, but she hadn't and now it would take him too long to get here for her to wait.

Alone and with a sickening sense of déjà vu, she hurriedly slipped back inside the house, gun at the ready.

* * *

Al ushered Natalie into his house with a blindingly white smile that instantly put her at ease. He looked more casual than she'd ever seen him, in a pair of dark jeans, a black cashmere sweater, and designer shoes so shiny she was sure she could see her reflection in the Italian leather.

The house was immaculate and more impressive on the inside than it was on the outside. Maybe he got that from Adele.

"C'mon in." He clasped her shoulder like an old friend and gave it a tiny shake.

She laughed. "I'm glad you invited me, Al. I was hoping we'd get a chance to talk." Natalie breathed an inward sigh of relief. She was worried he'd be angry about Adele's late night phone call to his wife, but if his bright smile was any indication, he wasn't holding a grudge.

Al took a moment to introduce his kids, and then he whispered something in Monique's ear before she nodded and headed back to her brother and their Lego tower.

"C'mon, Natalie, let's get comfortable. Oh, and would you mind turning off your cell phone? Mine's been going off all day and if I hear another ring I'm going to strangle someone." He flashed her a boyish grin. "I don't want us to be disturbed. I've been waiting forever to have an ally that I could talk to about Ella."

Natalie nodded politely. She had to remind her students to turn their phones off every single day, and understood how annoying the constant interruptions could be. She punched the power button and tucked the phone back into the purse Amelia had loaned her. Al hadn't offered to take her jacket, so she unzipped it in deference to the cozy warmth of the house.

They passed by a living room with two overstuffed leather sofas and Natalie's brows drew together.

Al motioned for her to walk in front of him. "Like I said on the phone, I was hoping to talk to you without Ella so we could discuss her injury. Did she tell you about how she up and quit rehab and never had the last surgery her doctor recommended? Her asshole ex never even encouraged her to go back. Said it was her decision and to leave her be." Al extended his arm and pointed. "Turn here. We're headed upstairs."

Natalie felt a prickle of unease. Al's kids were busy playing and Ella wasn't with her, so why the need for more privacy? Then again, she knew these old homes had lots of interesting nooks and crannies. Perhaps there was a den that Al especially loved upstairs. "She's mentioned rehab, but not in detail."

"Ahh…if she didn't tell you about it, then she doesn't trust you."

"Excuse me?" His blunt words dragged her from her thoughts. She stopped at the top of the stairs and gave him a strange look.

"You can't think you can just breeze back into town every few years and expect to be top dog. You gotta earn that. And that takes more than a drive-by. Looks like she doesn't trust either of us."

Natalie frowned. His voice was calm and pleasant, even though what he was saying wasn't. He didn't seem angry at all. He seemed jealous. "I don't think anything like that. I know Adele feels horrible about calling your wife and asking about you. She was just worried for me."

He shrugged a massive shoulder. "She wasn't always like that, you know. Distrustful. Things were different before."

"Her injury must have been very hard on her."

"I'm not talking about her getting hurt. Yeah, that was a bitch. I mean before she married Landry." He said Landry's name as though it was a curse.

"Their divorce—"

"No!"

Eyes round, she automatically backed up a step.

"Landry's been trying to control her since before they even got married. It got worse after they did, and then worse again when Logan was born."

Something dark invaded Al's expression and a chill raced down Natalie's spine. "What does that have to do with her injury, Al? I'm not here to talk about her marriage. That's not my business. Or yours."

He gave her a curious look. "I assumed you two were close. She's helping you. She's risking her life for you."

"We are close. But…I don't understand."

Al smiled sadly. "That's too bad. That you're close, I mean. I hate that she's going to hurt even more. Though it does work out well for me today. Here we are." Al reached around Natalie and pushed open a door with an arm so thick with muscle that it reminded Natalie of a large boa constrictor.

The shift of his muscle struck a familiar chord in her and suddenly she didn't feel well.

"Natalie?"

Natalie didn't move. She glanced past Al and back down the stairs, but he was blocking her path. She was more than uneasy now. Something was very wrong. "I-I think we should go back downstairs."

Without answering, Al roughly grabbed her by the elbow and shoved Natalie into the room in front of him.

"Hey!" she shouted and lurched forward a few steps, only barely able to keep from falling flat on her face.

Al snatched her upright by the lapels and snarled so close to her mouth that she could feel the heat of his breath against her lips and smell the stale odor of coffee. "Be quiet and don't move." He yanked her purse from her shoulder, snapping the leather strap like a rubber band. Carelessly, he chucked it behind her.

Shocked and confused, Natalie glanced around the large room that was obviously the master bedroom.

Keeping one eye on her, Al pulled a pair of matching duffel bags from the closet and began stuffing clothes into one of them. "Tell me what Morrell told Ella." The look on his face was warning enough for Natalie to know that she should obey him without question. His eyes had gone from welcoming to dead.

"I have no idea."

He rooted around in his sock drawer, distracted, and unable to find whatever it was he wanted. "Where is it?" Al wondered aloud.

The tiny hairs on Natalie's body stood on end and a primal fear so ferocious it was nearly debilitating ripped through her veins like a speeding bullet. Those exact words and the feeling of his powerful hands brought back the night of her attack in stunning detail.

A hot rush of adrenaline made her tremble. "Oh, my God. Y-you?"

Out of the top drawer of his dresser, Al pulled a pistol with a long cylinder attached to the end. Natalie had seen something like it before in movies and assumed it was a silencer.

"Yeah. I'm sorry 'bout that. It wasn't personal. If you hadn't fought like a fuckin' wild hellcat, I could have just broken your neck and it would have been a lot less painful for you in the end." He actually seemed a little impressed by her, or maybe just amused.

Natalie bolted for the door. Just as she was about to reach for the knob, a hand flew out of nowhere and exploded against her face, knocking her clean off her feet and onto her back, stealing the air from her lungs.

When her head hit the wood floor it felt like the business end of a sledgehammer.

"I told you not to move."

Everything was fuzzy: her sight, how things sounded, even how she felt lying on the floor when she tried to lift her hand. Like she was trying to push her way through a thick sea of molasses. Was Al speaking? It was hard to understand his angry rasp over the sound of her phone ringing and ringing and ringing. It took her a full minute to realize the sound was coming from inside her head.

"Don't get too comfortable down there. We're not staying."

His grip was cool and painful on her wrists as he hoisted her up by her hands and her ponytail and unceremoniously dumped her on the bed. She let out a painful squawk. It hurt like hell, but it did make the world come into slightly sharper focus. Natalie couldn't tell whether she'd lost consciousness or not. She assumed because she wasn't sure, that she had.

It seemed like no time had passed, but Al had already finished packing one of the bags and was now quickly working on the second. A picture from the wall behind him was on the floor, and when he dug into the wall safe, his hand emerged with several thick stacks of cash and papers.

She swallowed and gagged on the bitter taste of blood. Her tongue tentatively swept over her badly cut bottom lip. It would need stitches. Awkwardly, she pushed herself into a seated position, dizzy.

"Jesus, don't bleed on Latisha's bedspread!" He tossed Natalie a clean white T-shirt to wipe her mouth. "She will kill me."

Natalie clumsily caught the shirt and blinked a few times. The room was draped in fog again. Al was only a couple of inches taller than she was, but he was made of solid muscle. The thought that he was afraid of his wife made her want to giggle. An inward voice that sounded very far away informed her that wasn't quite the appropriate response to her situation, but for the life of her she couldn't figure out why.

"Al, you have Josh's phone…you have wh-what you wanted. Why am I here?"

Al pulled Josh's phone out of the safe and dropped it into one of the bags. "This baby is leverage. You never did hear what was on it, did you? I nearly shit my pants when I took it from you and then found out it wasn't even working. I thought we'd busted it wrestling around your room. Luckily, it just needed a charge."

His full lips turned down in a sympathetic frown. "Somehow that skinny bitch Misty accidentally recorded audio from the night your brother was killed. The storm drowns out a lot of it, but you can still hear all the voices. Did you know computers can identify voices the same way they can fingerprints? It's all *CSI* and shit. Trust me, since it's your brother, you don't want to listen."

Blood dripped down her chin and Natalie wiped it with the T-shirt. "Your voice is on there?"

"I didn't kill your brother."

Natalie tried her best to remember, but she couldn't recall Misty saying anything about Josh's phone. "How-how did you even know Misty had it?"

"Ha! She called into the Tremé Police Station and asked to make an appointment to talk to whoever was in charge because she had some sort of evidence of a big crime. Bad luck for her, she ended up talking to Morrell. Afterward that fat moron said I was supposed to grab *her* phone…once I took care of her."

Natalie shivered at the casual tone of his voice.

"So I took Misty's phone, and it turned out to be the wrong one. Morrell said *her* phone, not *Joshua Phillips's* phone. The dumbass! I went back for it, but it was gone. I knew you'd taken it."

Natalie spit into the T-shirt, blasting it with red spray. She angrily tossed it aside, trying not to throw up, darkness edging the corners of her vision. "But you have what you want! Why do you still need me?"

"I'd like to know the same thing."

Natalie's head jerked sideways at the sound of Adele's drawl. She'd never been so glad or horrified to see anyone in her entire life. It was too dangerous to be here.

Adele walked slowly into the room, limping, gun gripped expertly in two hands and pointed straight at Al.

Not thinking, Natalie stood and took a quick unsteady step, putting herself directly between Adele and Al.

"No!" Adele shouted, but it was too late.

In a flash, Al grabbed Natalie and yanked her against him by the hair, his own gun pointed at Natalie's temple.

"My kids?" he growled to Adele, his breath tickling the side of Natalie's head and cheek.

Adele looked insulted. "Safe in my car."

Al breathed a shuddering sigh of relief. "For now only. They're coming with me tonight."

"What the hell are you doing, Al?" Adele asked softly, sadly. "Why have you done any of this? How could you have put your hands on her?"

"Fuck, Ella, you really got Morrell to tell you everything, didn't you?"

She nodded slowly.

"You always were the best."

Natalie could have sworn she heard a smile in his words. "Al?" she spoke up, surprising both him and Adele by speaking at all. "Your wife said you were home the night I was attacked. I don't…I'm confused. How could you have been b-both places at the same time?"

"Damn, bitch, you think my girl doesn't know when to lie to the police when she's asked about where I've been? Adele Lejeune may not be wearing a badge anymore, but she will always and forever be a cop."

"Don't you call her a bitch!" Adele snapped furiously, her lips pulled into a snarl.

"I apologize," Al said, immediately contrite, like he'd just been caught with his hand in the cookie jar instead of kidnapping and attempted murder.

Natalie felt like she was in the *Twilight Zone*.

Adele tried to move closer, but Al warned her away by pressing the gun harder into Natalie's head.

Natalie yelped loudly.

"Nat, sweetheart, are you okay? You don't look so hot." Adele's keen eyes surveyed every inch of Natalie, her lips compressed in a tight line.

When Adele focused on her split lip, Natalie could see the unadulterated rage in her eyes, ready to erupt into something deadly. "I'm…my head is…" Natalie's head throbbed as though her ear was pressed against a rock concert stereo speaker on full blast. "I don't feel very well."

Adele tightened the grip on her gun. "Let her go, Al. She's obviously hurt, and you must have somehow lost your mind to do this. *Twice*. It's all over now. Let me help you."

"Help me?" He snorted. "I don't think so. Your friend is my insurance policy to get my ass out of town. I knew you'd figure things out, but shit,

I thought I'd at least be outta New Orleans first. Drop your gun. Let me go and I'll leave her by the side of the road when I'm outta the city. You'll never see me or mine again, Ella. I promise."

Adele's eyes swam with tears, then overflowed and streamed down her cheeks. Her weapon stayed as steady as a rock. "Why?"

The word was pure pain and betrayal, and Natalie felt the stabbing sensation in her own chest.

Adele looked utterly lost. "I don't get any of this. It can't just be the money, Al." Her voice shook. "You only ever needed to ask and anything I have would be yours. How did Xavier get his meathooks into you?"

"Do you really care?" Al suddenly sounded much younger than his years, a wounded child, bitter.

Adele flinched and her shining eyes softened. "Alonzo, I care so much it's killing me."

Al sucked in a quick breath and then hesitated. Natalie caught a whiff of his pungent sweat and her stomach roiled. She felt his body tense as he spoke. "I'd only been with the NOPD a few months when he came to me and told me that he'd do me a favor, if I did one for him. And that was the start."

"A favor?" Adele swiped at her eyes with the back of her hand and flung the tears onto the floor. "What favor could possibly—?"

"He knew who killed my mother."

Adele's mouth sagged.

"He'd known for years! But who cares about a dead New Orleans hooker, right? So he just sat on the information, waiting. He does that all the time, you know." Agitated, Al tightened his grip around Natalie's chest until it felt like a steel band, forcing her to work to drag in every single breath. "He keeps things quiet and then uses information like a razor blade."

"Al, honey, your mom—"

"Was a *whore*, but she was still my mother!" he thundered, peppering Natalie's cheek with warm spittle. The barrel of the gun slid from her temple to her jaw. "My *mother*, Ella! He knew who killed her, and he told me. And it turned out it was one of my stupid punk friends who was just a few years older than me. He wasn't even sixteen and he was one of her regulars!"

"Christ," Adele hissed under her breath.

"So right after he tells me, Xavier drives me to this nasty shack in the Ninth Ward and says the guy is inside all alone and getting ready for bed after a long day of doing jack shit and running dime bags for a livin'."

"He just *gave* him to you?" Adele was obviously appalled. "Like a present?"

"In a pretty pink bow," Al agreed hoarsely. "Then Xavier asked what I wanted to do. I told him I wanted to kill the prick. He said, 'Okay. Do it.' And he pulled a gun from his glove box and said to use it instead of my police issue." Natalie could feel Al's heartbeat now, pounding against her back, strong and fast like a steam engine gathering momentum. "And so I-I did. I wasn't thinking right, and I gave Xavier the gun back when I was finished. He never mentioned it again, but I know he kept it, and he knew that I knew." Al snorted a little. "I've been his ever since."

Adele's eyes fluttered closed for just a half second in misery and she rasped, "Fuck, Al. Why didn't you come to me? I could have—"

"Arrested me?"

"I-I…" Adele's mouth worked helplessly, but it was clear she couldn't deny it.

"Xavier has wanted you for years, you know. So bad I think he tasted it. But I told him you'd never go for it and made sure he left you alone. I could at least do that much for you."

Adele could only stare, her pain palpable.

In that moment, Natalie realized that she'd never understood someone less than she understood Detective Alonzo Rice. Were it not for his arm holding her firmly in place, she was sure the look on Adele's face alone would be enough to send her crashing to her knees. How could he stand it, knowing he was the cause of that look? Knowing that he'd wrecked her?

Al took a handful of heartbeats to collect himself. He lifted his chin. "You've been a cop long enough to know that everyone has a shitty story, Ella. So what?"

"You could take me with you instead. One hostage is as good as the next."

Natalie's skin turned clammy and panic seeped into her bones. "No."

Al openly scoffed. "You're kidding me, right, Little Mama? You'd be more trouble than this one, and that's saying somethin'."

"Al, for God's sake let me help you now! Please. *Please*," Adele begged without hesitation. "There's got to be some deal to be had. I'll tell the DA you helped me bring down Xavier. I'll tell him we've been working together to take him down because you want to make amends. You can give up whoever the other stooges are under Xavier's thumb. The DA will need that and will be willing to work something out."

"I'm not spending the rest of my life in jail." Al's voice made it clear that he thought Adele had lost her mind. "I'm going to fuckin' Florida! Put down the gun. You *know* I'll shoot her if you don't."

Natalie whimpered, too stunned to even cry. Adele wasn't going to talk him out of his gun. He really was going to kill her and all she could think about was that she couldn't die now. Everything in her life was still unfinished. She'd only just started with Adele. It couldn't be over before it had really begun. Yet Al was tearing out the remaining pages of their story faster than they could write them.

"Al, sweetie, we both know you won't leave her on the side of the road," Adele admitted quietly. "She'll end up facedown in some swamp with a bullet in the back of her head if you walk out of this house with her tonight. That can't happen. I won't let it."

Suddenly, Al removed the gun from Natalie's head and pointed it straight at Adele.

Natalie began to struggle but his grip was like iron. "No!" The room began to spin. "Don't shoot her!"

"Don't make me shoot you, Ella!" Al sounded as desperate as Natalie felt. "Don't make me!"

"Let her go. I love you, and I will always help you." Adele's words were astoundingly gentle in contrast to Al's coarse bellow. They were a mother's comforting hug, a sister's warm kiss on the cheek, the extended hand of a true friend. "Even now it's not too late. You just have to let her go."

Al sniffed and Natalie wondered if he was actually crying. "You know I can't. I passed 'too late' years ago. Put down your weapon." There was something in his tone that hadn't been there before. Finality. They were done talking.

Tears streamed down Adele's cheeks and when her glistening eyes found Natalie's they looked right into the bottom of her soul. An icy fist closed around Natalie's heart.

"I love you, Natalie, and I'm sorry."

And then she understood.

No! "Don't! Don't put the gun down! He'll shoot you!" Natalie began to thrash wildly against Al's grip with renewed strength. She opened her mouth but before she could utter a word, a gunshot detonated like a bomb between her ears and the floor flew up to meet her.

Natalie's ears rang with a continuous buzzing sound. For a terrifying second, she thought the wall behind her had collapsed. Then she realized that it was Al lying on top of her, his body pushing hers into the floor. Unable to breathe, and rattled beyond all reason, she panicked. "El—la. S-s-say something!" Natalie lifted her face off the floor and could tell that it was painted with hot blood.

It took another few seconds to fully understand that most of it wasn't hers. "Ella?"

Wriggling madly, Natalie shoved Al's heavy, limp body away and pushed herself to her knees.

Across the room, Adele was lying flat on her back. A bright red blood spray pattern marred the wall behind her and a bullet hole was visible in the plaster.

Jesus. Jesus. Jesus. Natalie's head spun. She tried to push all the way to her feet, but quickly ended up back on the ground. She braced her arms against Al's bed to keep from toppling over.

One gunshot, but they were both down? How?

Natalie heard pounding footsteps downstairs and then Adele's voice, gravelly and urgent. "Shut the d-d-door."

Snapping out of her haze, Natalie scrambled over to Adele on her hands and knees, eyes like saucers. "You're alive! But, oh God, you're bleeding, Ella. A lot."

Footsteps were on the stairs now.

"The door!" Adele screeched an octave higher than normal. "Monique and Damien. They can't...they can't see this!"

She's alive. She's alive. Natalie staggered to her feet, but before she could make it to the door, Landry burst into the room, his gun leading the way. He grasped Natalie by the forearms and held her firm so she wouldn't fall. "Ms. Abbott?" His tone of voice made it clear she was the last person he expected to see at Al's house.

Adele awkwardly sat up, using only one hand for leverage, and slipped a little in her own blood. Her face contorted in pain. When she was steady, she wrapped her hand tightly around her bicep. Blood poured between her fingers, and her face wrinkled in confusion. "Landry?" she croaked. "Wh-what are you doing here?"

Landry let go of Natalie, moving her a little behind him as he continued to scan the scene for danger.

Nonsensically, Natalie's mind stalled on a tiny detail. Landry's sideburns and the edges of his temples had turned silver since the last time she'd seen him.

Landry shut the bedroom door behind him and ran a hand over his bristly chin. "Jesus Christ." With a disbelieving expression, he surveyed the room again. "I called Amelia to make sure you went straight over to pick up Logan, and when she said you hadn't been by yet, I turned right back around. When you didn't pick up your phone, I knew in my gut where you'd gone."

He looked furious with Adele until he took a step around a chair that was blocking his full view of her. "Are you—? Shit, Ella, I can't believe... Al shot you? Should I—"

Adele waved him off.

"Let me—"

Adele just glared.

For a second Landry looked like he would argue, but he bit his lip instead. "Keep your hand on it then." His outraged gaze swung over to Al and to the gun on the floor next to him. "A silencer? Damn."

Still wobbly on her feet, Natalie rushed back to Adele's side and dropped to her knees. Hands quaking, she ran them down Adele's body, her groggy mind finally able to start to make sense of things. She'd only heard one gunshot because of the silencer. Adele had been shot in the arm, not the body or head. She wouldn't die unless she bled to death. But there was so much blood. *I can't lose her now.*

Natalie pressed her hand over Adele's, directly on top of the wound. She interlaced their fingers, the cloying scent of gunpowder mixed with blood making her gag.

"Nat? Your face?" Adele glanced up and instantly went frantic. "Did I—?"

"Shh…no." Natalie realized how she must look and with her other hand sluggishly lifted the hem of her shirt to wipe her cheek and hair. "I'm okay. Most of this is Al's blood. You didn't shoot me." At Adele's uncertain look she said, "I promise."

For a split second Adele's entire body relaxed, then contracted in obvious pain. "Landry, the kids in my car?" She hissed as she scooted back to lean against the wall, taking Natalie and their joined hands right along with her. "Shit! This hurts."

"Safe and sound with an old neighbor who was coming home just as I pulled in." Landry pulled out his phone. "That prick Morrell's still locked in the squad car."

"Watch out for Al's wife." Adele grimaced and the cloudy, faraway look on her face told Natalie that Ella was thinking of another crime scene. "If she finds us like this, there will be trouble."

"Ella?" Natalie watched her closely. Adele's breathing was growing faster and faster and her eyes had the same glazed look they held when she was fresh from a nightmare and still half dreaming. "Stay right here. Right here, Ella! With Landry and me. Today."

Adele's eyes darted to Natalie at the sound of her voice. "Yeah," she said quickly, licking her lips. "Okay. Today. Right."

Landry nodded at Natalie and locked the bedroom door so there wouldn't be any surprises. "What happened here?"

It was Natalie who answered, though her thoughts and words were slower than normal. "Al…he asked me over. He didn't want…he tried to kidnap me to keep Ella from coming after him. Which is so stupid. That would only make her c-come faster. He-he was going to shoot her. Or me. Or both of us." She shook her head, willing away the muddled feeling. "There was no choice. I mean, Ella had no choice."

Landry sucked in a breath between clenched teeth.

Adele scrunched her eyes tightly closed, devastation marring her beautiful face. "*Damn-Dammit!*"

The broken roar caused Natalie to jump and her guts to boil with an awful sensation—hatred. She despised Al for hurting Adele so profoundly that it was sickening to watch. She felt a beast inside her chest clawing to be free and howling with rage. Irrationally, she wanted to bring Al back to life so she could kill him herself.

"Gimme your belt," Natalie instructed Landry, her voice a low growl as she extended an impatient hand.

Adele shifted in a futile attempt to get more comfortable. Landry's eyes found the startlingly large pool of blood that had formed next her and partially soaked her jeans. He instantly abandoned his phone and unclipped his weapon, holster and gold shield from his belt and tossed them on the bed. He yanked off his leather belt so quickly it cracked like a whip.

He passed it to Natalie, who dragged a pillow from the bed and stripped off the pillowcase. She inadvertently decorated it with bloody red handprints, and it looked like a messy child's macabre art project.

"Move your hand, Ella." She began to pry Adele's fingers from the wound, swallowing hard at the sight of the torn flesh. "I need to put this on so we can stop the bleeding."

Without warning, Adele bent at the waist and groaned, her face tinged green.

Natalie knew what that look meant, and there was nothing to do but scramble out of the way.

"I'm gonna…" Adele turned her head and vomited violently on the floor.

"I know. It's okay," Natalie murmured, doing her best to hold the pillowcase tight against the wound with one hand, while rubbing small circles against Adele's back with the other. The damp jacket hydrated the blood on Natalie's hand and made an even bigger mess.

"So-so-sorry about that," Adele said roughly when she was finished, obviously embarrassed as she wiped her chin against her shoulder.

Natalie affectionately ran her fingertips down Adele's cheek. "Honey, I don't care about that." With quick but clumsy hands, she continued to bind the bullet wound.

Landry dialed 911. "This is Detective Landry Odette, Baton Rouge PD, at two-oh-four Oliver Street. I need a bus." He moved back toward Al and continued to speak in hushed tones.

"How is Al?" The wistful hope in Adele's voice was nearly more than Natalie could bear. She knew Adele knew the truth, but had to ask anyway.

Unable to stop herself, Natalie glanced over her shoulder at Al. She was blocking most of Adele's view of his body. The bullet had hit him just above the eye and blown a small fist-sized hole out of the back of his head. The wall behind him was covered in gore and gray matter, and still the anger she felt toward him didn't lessen. If anything, it grew and expanded like she'd swallowed hot coals that were scorching her throat and belly, their heat spreading wider and wider. Of all of the possible outcomes tonight, this would hurt Adele the most.

Natalie exchanged worried glances with Landry as Adele tried to peer over her shoulder. Natalie repositioned herself even more fully in front of Adele and rose off her haunches so her lover couldn't see behind her no matter how she shifted. "No, Ella. Look at me. At me."

Adele's eyes were glassy. "But, I need—"

"No, you don't. You need to look at me instead," Natalie commanded as she adjusted the belt around Adele's arm. The wound was still bleeding, though not as badly as a moment ago.

The coppery scent of the hot blood...Adele's blood...rushed up into her nostrils and Natalie fought hard not to add to the vomit pool. *Keep it together,* she told herself. Her mouth filled with saliva, a precursor to throwing up, but she gulped it back, pushed through the nausea and tied off the belt as best she could.

Hands finally free, Natalie cupped Adele's cheeks and, ignoring her split lip, pressed a firm kiss to Adele's temple, leaving behind a bloody pink imprint. The much-needed contact grounded her, but Adele seemed to soften under her touch. "Al is dead, honey."

Tears spilled over pale cheeks. "Maybe..."

Lower lip trembling, Natalie shook her head resolutely. She pushed Adele's rain-matted hair from her brow and placed a lingering kiss there, then a third kiss on the cheek, letting her lips graze Adele's skin as she spoke. "*No.* He's dead. I'm so sorry he made you do that. I'm so sorry that I came here tonight and that you had to follow."

Guilt nearly swallowed Natalie whole.

"You couldn't have known," Adele whispered, visibly starting to unravel.

Adele's chest lurched with a sob and Natalie pulled her into a crushing hug and held her tight, pressing their cheeks together. "He's dead, and this is all over. And...and...and this is a horrible time to tell you," Natalie whispered brokenly, burying her nose in Adele's hair and sucking in a greedy lungful of air that smelled faintly like sweat and rain and Adele. Heaven. "I love you, too. So very much."

They sat that way for a long moment, with Adele silently weeping and Natalie simply holding her close, feeling helpless and wishing somehow she could turn back the clock.

Landry awkwardly wandered over and squatted down next to Adele, rubbing the back of his neck with a large hand. "How are you, darlin'?"

Natalie reluctantly eased away from Adele and sat back on her heels, but not before wiping away Adele's tears with shaky fingers.

Adele smiled gratefully, and turned her attention to Landry. "I sh-shot…I…" Her words seemed to trail away without her permission. With a grimace, she redirected the conversation and glanced down at her own arm. "Through and through. Burns like there's a hot poker in there, but the bleeding has slowed. And thank Christ, because you know how much I like the sight of my own blood. I'm sure I'll be upchucking again soon."

They shared a watery private smile.

Adele patted his shoulder weakly. "You need to go, Landry. Go get him now so we don't lose him."

Their eyes dueled fiercely before he nodded and rose to his feet. He retrieved his gun, holster and badge from the bed.

"What do you mean go?" Natalie leveled a blistering glare at Landry. "What about all the cops that are going to show up here any minute? They hate her!" She couldn't believe he would even consider leaving when Adele was hurt and before the ambulance arrived. "What if the police arrest Adele instead of taking her to the hospital? They're going to see a dead police detective and she won't be safe!"

Landry slid his badge in his front pocket, and removing the gun from its holster, tucked it in the waist of his pants. "I didn't tell them about Al. I said Ella was bleeding from an injury to her arm, and then my phone went dead. That pesky cell phone reception," he deadpanned. "You'll want to tell the ambulance crew what happened, and the police will come, but hopefully you'll be on the way to the hospital by then."

"Landry," Adele scolded, but looked pleased. "You're going to get into deep trouble for that."

He lifted a challenging eyebrow. "We need every minute."

Adele took Natalie's hand and started to stand.

Landry steadied both women as they rose.

Adele straightened with a broken groan. "Natalie, we're going to go downstairs and wait for the ambulance. I can't be in here with Al for another minute and not go crazy, okay?" Her face was tense with physical and emotional pain.

"Anything you need." Natalie would have promised to rob a bank to make Adele feel better.

"We're both going to wait for an ambulance. You probably have another concussion. We gotta take care of that beautiful brain of yours."

Adele's tender concern made Natalie want to cry.

"Am I going to have to buy you a helmet?"

Natalie sighed. Another concussion. Of course. No wonder she felt so awful. They started slowly walking toward the door. "Only if I get to buy you a suit of armor. They're going to run out of thread stitching you up tonight. Your other cut, which hasn't even had time to completely heal, is soaking wet and looks like crap." The bandage near Adele's wrist hung from her in a bloody wet pile.

"Deal. But now Landry has to go arrest my old lieutenant before word gets out about what happened here."

"Take Al's bags," Natalie told him. "Josh's phone is in there with a voice recording you'll want, and a bunch of papers Al took out of his safe, and more cash than anyone would normally keep at home."

Adele pinned Landry with a severe look as he darted across the room to collect the bags. "You can't take on Xavier alone."

"I won't. It's good not to be the only cop in my family. I'll call my brother and cousins." His green eyes flashed with determination and poorly veiled rage. "My lieutenant, and anyone else who he decided to bring with him from Baton Rouge, are already on their way, too. We're going to get Xavier, Ella, and he's going to pay for what he's done to us all."

And then Landry was gone.

Natalie wanted to unzip Adele's skin and climb inside. She couldn't get close enough, but she settled for gently wrapping an arm around her waist.

Adele glanced back in the direction of Al's body, but not directly at it. She had to clear her throat a few times before she could speak. "There is no payment big enough for what he's done."

CHAPTER TWENTY-ONE

Three days later…

Adele and Natalie waved goodbye to Adele's lawyer, one of the best criminal defense attorneys in the state of Louisiana, courtesy of Adele's parents, as they exited the police station. They climbed into the backseat of Amelia's car so they could sit together.

"Bastards," Amelia seethed, sending a death glare to the building and its occupants, as she slammed down on her accelerator and pulled away from the curb.

Natalie couldn't agree more. The moment Adele had been discharged from the hospital she was taken into police custody for questioning. Eighteen grueling hours later, she was released without being charged for Al's death.

Amelia asked whether they wanted to be taken to Ella's inn or the rental carriage house. Exhausted and ambivalent, Natalie just shrugged, but Adele immediately selected the carriage house.

Amelia made a U-turn, and Natalie laid a hand on Adele's knee and began to trace a lazy pattern with the tip of her finger. She snuggled deeper into the buttery leather seats, and began to replay the last three days in her mind.

The first forty-eight hours after the shootings were a blur of doctors, nurses and police interviews, with plenty of breaks in between for each woman to sit in her own hospital room on separate floors, miss the other, and watch the local news in awe. Lieutenant Peter Xavier had been arrested the same night as Al's death, and the press gobbled up the story.

The next morning, Xavier was found hanging dead in his holding cell from a state-issued blanket. So far the police were calling it a probable suicide. And just like that, everything changed again, and the twisted trail of corruption that had only just begun to come to light, was plunged back into darkness.

All hell broke loose at the NOPD, and Natalie couldn't even find it in herself to be surprised or care. So long as Adele was alive and free, none of the rest really mattered. They needed time to heal and figure out what would happen next. Now it finally appeared that they would have it.

Natalie's lower lip was treated with a butterfly bandage rather than the stitches she'd predicted, but she did have a concussion. It was diagnosed as mild to moderately severe, and because it was Natalie's second head injury recently, her doctors were extremely concerned.

After two-and-half days of close monitoring, good test results, and nearly having to tie her to the bed to keep her from sneaking out to visit Adele, Natalie was released from the Tulane University hospital. She was now free to take the elevator two floors down and openly spend her time in Adele's hospital room.

Adele had surgery to repair the bullet wound and its damage. The round had struck her basilic vein, but missed her humerus and the most critical nerves. Still, she faced at least eight weeks with her arm in a sling and physical therapy to deal with the muscle damage. Even worse, this was the arm she needed to use her cane.

It was going to be a long, hard winter, and while Adele was grateful to be alive, to Natalie's eyes, she was struggling. She'd overheard one of Adele's nurses asking if Adele had ever talked to someone about PTSD. Adele's negative response had been blunt and definitive. And Natalie knew that, for a while at least, she might need to have enough faith in Adele and her recovery for the both of them.

Then there was the sensation of dread that had been brewing in Natalie since the first morning she woke up in her hospital room all alone. It left her slightly ill and hollow. The solitude of the empty room was quiet agony. It reminded her of the way she awoke every day back home. How had she learned to crave something so different in such a short amount of time? This new sense of belonging and connection seemed so critical to her very survival that she didn't know how she was going to get along without it.

As the car smoothly navigated the streets of the Garden District, Adele gently nudged Natalie with her shoulder. Her voice was low, the words for Natalie's ears only. "What are you thinking about? You look so serious."

"I'm thinking that if I never see the inside of a police station or hospital again, it will be too soon. I'm thinking about…everything." Natalie rubbed her temples with her fingertips, the dull headache she'd had for the past three days only just starting to fade. "I still can't believe what happened."

Adele stared out the car window, her smile strained. "You and me both."

Natalie saw the start of tears in Adele's eyes and was certain it would be her undoing. Adele both warmed her heart and broke her heart at the same time. She took Adele's hand and brought it to her mouth, kissing the palm and resting it against her cheek. "I know you're a little lost right now, but please let me help you find your way back."

Adele's watery gaze looked skyward, then back at Natalie. "I'd really like that."

"You solved Josh's murder and got justice for Crisco and Misty, too. I'm so, *so* proud of you. Anyone at the NOPD who doubted you is going to know just how wrong he or she was. They lost the best when they lost you, and they all know it. Take your moment, Ella. It's well deserved."

Adele actually looked a little embarrassed. "You might be a little biased."

"You saved my life and you're pretty much my own personal hero. I'm a lot biased. But that doesn't mean I'm not right."

"I just wish I could have managed to do it without getting myself shot." Lovingly, she traced Natalie's bottom lip with the pad of her thumb taking extra care around a cut that was already nearly healed. "And without you getting hurt." She frowned. "Plus you were up all night at the police station waiting for me when you should have been in bed. You need to rest."

"I wouldn't have slept while you were at the station anyway. Besides, starting right now the both of us are going to rest and heal. It's just going to take a while. Maybe we can all finally stop looking backward and just move forward?"

An unexpected, eager look dropped years away from Adele's face and put a twinkle in her eyes that Natalie hadn't seen for too long. "Forward sounds really good."

The corner of Natalie's mouth quirked as she nodded. "To me, too."

"Besides, we make a great team."

A team. Natalie's stomach sank like a stone. A team whose members had put down roots in cities a thousand miles apart. Like it or not, she did have a life back home and Adele's was here and included a business and a child. She needed this to work. She needed them to work. But how?

Adele shifted in obvious discomfort and adjusted her sling.

Natalie checked the clock on her cell phone, torn between willing time to stand still and wanting to push it forward for Adele's sake. Today was Adele's first day off prescription pain meds, and the transition to simple ibuprofen obviously hurt. "You can have a tablet in just a half an hour more."

Adele nodded, her mouth set in a grim but determined line.

Amelia, who had been uncharacteristically silent during the drive, slowly eased down the white stone driveway of the rented carriage house and stopped as close to the stairs leading up to the apartment as she dared. "Okay," she announced, shifting the car into park. "Here we are. Mama figured you'd want to spend at least one more day here until Logan comes home tomorrow, so she put on fresh sheets and brought by some milk and food this morning."

Natalie unbuckled her seat belt then reached over and helped Adele by unbuckling hers. "But how did she—?"

"She knows everything," Adele told Natalie seriously, shivering as though someone just walked across her grave. "Just leave it at that, or you'll drive yourself mad wondering."

Amelia nodded furiously. "Our witchy motherly powers aren't nearly as advanced yet."

Natalie chuckled, thinking that she'd like to witness this nascent witchy power in Adele herself.

Adele leaned forward to grasp Amelia's shoulder. "Thanks for the ride, sis. See you soon?"

Amelia reached over her shoulder and patted Adele's hand. "Landry mentioned he was bringing Logan back late morning tomorrow. I was thinking of bringing your nieces by tomorrow in the late afternoon or early evening. That will give you time to open Christmas gifts with Logan and still let the kids play together before it gets too late. What do you think?"

Adele nibbled the corner of her mouth and turned to Natalie. "Natalie, what do you think?"

Natalie blinked a few times. "About what?"

Adele's smile was gentle. "About what Amelia suggested. It would mean having three little girls plus Logan all hyped up on Christmas candy running through the inn tomorrow afternoon and evening."

Suddenly this felt like a test. And Natalie had no idea what the right answer was. She wrung her hands together. Adele needed to rest. On the other hand, time with people who unconditionally loved her was probably better than medicine. "I-I…it's up to you."

"I know it is," Adele said patiently. "But I'm asking your opinion. It might get kind of loud and with your head and all…"

"I'll be fine." Any chance for Adele to continue to reconnect with her family, Natalie decided, was too good to pass up. She was grateful, but felt a twinge of nervousness that Adele had cracked the door open for her to play a tiny role in anything that had to do with Logan. "Let the kids come. After picking out the Christmas trees, it's obvious they're dying to spend more time with you. Besides, the inn is plenty big and I can make myself scarce, if necessary."

The skin around Adele's eyes tightened and her voice dropped to a deeper register. "I don't want you to be scarce."

The intensity of Adele's expression caused Natalie to sit up a little straighter. "Then I won't. Logan would like to play with the girls, right?"

Adele nodded.

"Then the answer is easy. Christmas should be spent with family."

Adele frowned a little at that, but said, "Okay."

Amelia finally exhaled, looking supremely satisfied. "Good. I'll see you both then." She patted Adele's hand once more. "Now get inside and into bed."

Adele rolled her eyes. "Seriously, Amelia? It's the middle of the day. I think I can decide when I'm sleepy and when I'm not."

Natalie had no idea why Adele was stubbornly protesting. She'd been up all night being questioned by the police, and then spent the morning repeatedly yawning. She was clearly dead on her feet.

"You're all banged up, and you look wretched." Amelia scowled at her sister. "Well, *you* look wretched. Natalie just looks adorably worn out. So no shaggin' each other's brains out until you're at least semi-recuperated. I am not spending another night in the hospital waiting room because of your lack of self-control, Ella."

"Amelia!" Adele groaned, covering her eyes with one hand.

Natalie felt her face grow hot.

"What?" Amelia waved off her sister's concern. "Just continue with the eye-sex that you two have apparently perfected. That's nice and safe."

Natalie burst out laughing.

"O-kay," Adele pushed open the door, "time to go inside. I apologize for my family, Nat. They're barbarians." She stood with a soft moan.

"They're wonderful," Natalie countered a little wistfully as she exited the car. She already adored Amelia. And while in the hospital she'd spent a little more time with Adele's reserved but sweet younger brother Jackson. She'd met Adele's parents yesterday. They were levelheaded and a bit more serious than both Amelia and Adele, but also involved, openly supportive, and so warm that just talking with them felt like being wrapped in a loving hug. In short, they were the type of parents she had absolutely no experience with. That reminded her, she needed to call her mother. "You don't know how blessed you are."

"Yeah, Adele," Amelia piped up from her open car window, grinning like mad. "You're blessed. And don't be such a prude. There's nothing wrong with a little good old-fashioned eye-fu—"

"I know how lucky I am," Adele broke in. Her eyes met Amelia's and they traded knowing grins.

With a wave, Amelia drove away.

Natalie fell into stride alongside Adele for the few paces to the stairs, then wrapped an arm around Adele's slender waist to help her walk. She carried a small bag of things they'd accumulated while in the hospital and that Georgia had supplied. Natalie opened the door and peered inside… and gaped. "Holy…"

"Christmas." Adele let go of a contented sigh as she took in the room. "Holy Christmas."

The fresh scent of pine rolled out of the apartment like a tidal wave as they entered. In the very center of the room was a tall, completely decorated Christmas tree, colored lights gently twinkling. Beneath it on a deep red Christmas tree skirt were several wrapped packages and two Christmas stockings. Adele's name was sewn on one that looked well used, and Natalie's name was written on a Christmas card and pinned to the fabric of a new one. The stockings were full.

Natalie's throat closed. They'd stopped putting out Christmas stockings at her house when she wasn't much older than Logan. She never knew why and had never asked. Even as a child, she sensed it was something best left alone. One year the stockings simply weren't there. Now, as an adult, she suspected that the holiday had arrived during one of their leaner times, and there was nothing to fill them. After that first disappearance, despite their financial situation going from bleak to simply poor, they were never used again.

It was the same with the Christmas tree, though her mother always made sure she had a gift of some kind, and a special holiday dinner, no matter what the circumstances. "Is that for me?" Natalie felt a tingle of excitement for the holiday that she hadn't experienced since she was a child.

"You're the only Natalie I know. C'mon." Adele reached for her hand and dragged Natalie away from the tree and to the sofa, where they both kicked off their shoes and dropped down with heavy sighs.

Natalie tucked their bag alongside the sofa, noticing that her belongings had been retrieved from the inn and neatly piled on the kitchen table. "I can't believe your parents did this," she whispered, a little overcome. Adele's family was thoughtful and kind and seemed to accept her without question, simply because Adele did. After a lifetime of doing her best, and going far, but somehow always managing to disappoint, she wasn't quite sure how to process something as simple and profound as acceptance.

"Don't be silly. It's just a tree and a few gifts," Adele chided, but her voice was gentle and full of understanding. "They love the holidays, and they really liked you. Trust me, they were happy to do it. Tomorrow is Christmas, after all. And I hope you can enjoy being here." Adele's brow creased. "Unless you're going home tonight and just hadn't gotten a chance to mention it?"

Natalie shook her head. She'd thought about it, but couldn't bring herself to do it. She wanted more time together. She gestured to the tree and gifts. "You knew about this?"

"Someone had to give them the keys." Adele nervously fiddled with her sling and her gaze slid away. "Besides, I, um, I thought if it was nice enough, you might not want to leave just yet. I know you said that Christmas should be spent with family, but I'd love it if you'd spend it with Logan and me. I will understand if you'd rather go home. I'll hate it, but I'll understand."

"I-I didn't book a flight. It's so close to the holiday and—"

"I can get you on a red-eye flight tonight. Coach is sold out, but there's one seat left in first class. It would be my Christmas gift to you. You'd have to stop in Chicago first, but you could be home by morning." Adele audibly swallowed and couldn't quite stop the wishful note in her voice. "Or you could stay?"

"What do you want me to do?"

"Nat," Adele paused and thoughtfully cocked her head to the side, "how can you not know? I want you to stay. I never really believed in that bullshit 'if you love something set it free' expression. I want to chain you to the sofa. Seriously, I'm only barely holding myself back. If I still had my handcuffs you'd be in deep trouble."

Natalie's deep peal of laughter felt good, and Adele's hopeful, teasing expression made her want to kiss her. So she did. "I would love to spend Christmas with you," she murmured against now-smiling lips, the surge of happiness singing all the way down to her toes.

"It's sort of romantic, don't you think?"

"What? The tree? Or your threats to handcuff me?"

"No." Adele bumped her shoulder against Natalie's. "You and me. Here. Or, really, wherever we are so long as we're together."

The sudden ache under Natalie's breastbone was unbearable and she let out a half laugh, half sob. "Are you trying to make me kiss you again?"

Adele chuckled softly and batted her eyes. "You should pretty much assume that's the case going forward."

With a satisfied murmur, Natalie pressed her lips against Adele's. She couldn't help but deepen the kiss, feeling the familiar, heady rush of heat and longing as their tongues danced together. If she hadn't already been sitting, she wasn't entirely sure her legs would have held her. The kiss tapered off slowly, and it took a few seconds for Natalie to gather her wits and remember that they'd been talking about...something. Kissing Adele was enough to make her forget...everything.

Natalie fanned herself with one hand. "Are-are you ready for Logan tomorrow?"

Adele accepted the end of the kiss graciously but not without a slightly smug pout. "Oh, yeah. He's getting a bicycle, complete with training wheels, and a super cool helmet. It's in the garage all ready to go for tomorrow. Santa will come to Baton Rouge tomorrow morning while he's with Landry. And my house next year when Logan will be with me. So the bike is from me."

Natalie snuggled close to Adele's side, their thighs pressed tightly together as she glanced up at the pretty lights. "I remember my first bike. My mom bought it from a neighbor's yard sale. It was really old and had a banana seat and yellow flag on the back. I loved it. I was maybe six or seven years old."

"Sounds nice." Adele brushed her lips to Natalie's head, warm breath tickling her scalp.

"It was. Sadly, I forgot to lock it up one night that following summer and it was stolen."

Adele gasped. "There are actual thieves in Madison?"

Natalie delivered a devastating poke to Adele's thigh causing her to yelp, then laugh. "Madison is not Mayberry!"

"All right! Ouch. Ouch!" Adele swatted Natalie's hand away. She grimaced in pain when she moved her arm the wrong way.

Natalie's brows drew together with worry and she gave Adele's good arm a sympathetic squeeze and didn't let go. The contact felt good and she didn't have the heart to deny herself or Adele. "Almost time for a pain reliever. What are you going to tell Logan about your arm?" Natalie found herself nervous about meeting him again and hoped against hope that they would share even a sliver of the connection she felt with his mother.

The body next to hers went very still before Adele exhaled noisily and unhappily. "I'm going to lie and say that I fell."

"He's really little, Ella. I don't think you have a choice."

"I know. But I still hate to lie."

"How are you going to explain me being at your house?"

Adele turned sideways so they were fully facing each other. "I'm going to tell him the truth."

Natalie's pulse began to race. "Which is?"

Suddenly Adele's unease was so strong that Natalie felt its presence like a third person in the room. "We should talk about that."

Natalie's palms grew damp and she let go of Adele's hand to rub them on her jeans. "Okay." She was amazed the word came out without cracking. She drew her legs up underneath her.

Adele took a few seconds to compose herself before speaking in a penetrating voice that captured Natalie's attention completely. "These past few days in the hospital, I had a lot of time to think about things. The first thing that was on my mind, always, was you. I missed you." She looked a little bewildered with herself. "I mean, we saw each other at some point every single day, but I still *really* missed you."

Natalie melted a little. "I missed you too."

"And I-I thought a lot about the things that I want…that I *need* to be happy. I'm not an innkeeper."

Curious, Natalie could only nod. The statement was undeniably true. Running an inn was a fine profession, and if Adele were merely trying to make a living, it would be a good one. But it would never touch the core of who Adele was, or capture her drive and hunger to be there for someone who needed her. "No, honey. You're not."

"I can never be a cop again either, even if I have the surgery on my leg and get back into physical therapy. There's a good chance I would be able to use my cane less and a small chance that I will be able to ditch it altogether, if I work hard enough and get lucky. But my doctors were clear; I'll never be able to pass a police physical."

Natalie's stomach clenched with worry. "Will you do those things anyway? The operation, the rehabilitation, even if it's not to be a cop?"

"I'm not ready."

Natalie's heart sank, and she opened her mouth to protest, but Adele stopped her with a look.

"Not until my arm gets back into shape, that is. Before, well, I didn't think I had any reason to make myself get better. I was an idiot. Being with you has made me see that I do have a reason. As much as I care about you, and *God* how I do, the reason needs to be that I have to do it for myself. And I will." She nodded as if confirming it to herself. "I will." There it was. Definite. Absolute.

Natalie closed her eyes in profound relief and felt the sting of impending tears. Adele's word was as good as gold. It would happen. "Thank goodness." She wiped at her eyes. "I thought I was going to have to drug you and kidnap you to get you back into rehab."

Adele narrowed her eyes. "You would have teamed up with Amelia and Georgia, wouldn't you?" She sounded shocked, but also impressed.

"It might have been discussed." Natalie grinned sheepishly, a little giddy from the sudden release of anxiety. "Once…or a few times."

Adele snorted softly. "Underestimating you would be a mistake, Natalie. One I won't make." She drew in a deep, but still shaky, breath.

"Okay, so I'm going to get my act together and get as well as I can physically, and then I think I want to use my social work degree. I can still help kids and use my investigatory skills, just in a different way. Those jobs pay nothing, are high stress, and I will spend my days fighting the system and trying to make lost causes a little less lost. Most of the time I will lose."

Natalie's chest filled with pride and fondness. "You'll be the best." Her smile turned wry. "Within a year you will have six adopted children and twelve foster kids of your own. You'll need to keep the inn just to have enough bedrooms."

Adele chuckled guiltily. "I'm not good at saying no when I want something." She threaded the fingers of one hand into Natalie's hair and looked her square in the eyes. "I'm going to need a little help with that. I'm going to need…I do need and desperately want you. Us. And I want you to desperately want and need me too."

"I-I do," Natalie breathed solemnly. "But how?" She didn't trust her voice to say more. She wanted Adele so much she could hardly think straight. But it felt wrong to even consider turning her back on everything she'd worked so hard to achieve. Tenure, especially in her specialty, was nearly impossible to get nowadays, and walking away from it was tantamount to career insanity. It meant giving up the stability she'd worked so hard to gain. Yet, wasn't that exactly what she'd been considering even before coming to New Orleans this last time?

"Listen to me, okay?" Adele's powerful gaze burrowed into Natalie, wrapped around her heart, and squeezed. "I don't want to let you go. I know the circumstances that brought us together have been so far from perfect that it's not even funny."

Wordlessly, Natalie nodded, hanging on her lover's every word.

"I get that in an ideal world we would have more time together before we needed to figure things out and make big decisions. We would have had lots of dates full of stolen kisses and heavy-lidded glances, and so much less worry and pain. There would have been heartfelt discussions about practical things like PTSD, what it's like to have a child in your life, and long-distance relationships. We can still have those discussions. And should."

Natalie couldn't bring herself to do more than nod, her eyes riveted on Adele.

"But I don't need an ideal world, or a situation that's perfect or easy. I just need you."

Adele's words were so passionate, so earnest, that Natalie thought she might pass out.

"It's happening all out of order, but you said it earlier, we need to move forward. I'm asking you to stay here. Give us a chance. You're smart and talented. Find a job here. This apartment is paid up for the next six months because that was the shortest rental term Amelia could get. It was what we needed, and it's all yours. Or you could stay with me while you figure out what you want or longer than that, and I would cherish every single second of it."

Adele took Natalie's breath away. For a moment, she didn't know how to process what Adele was saying and the cascade of feelings that were bubbling up inside her.

"I want a real relationship with you and that means us together. In the same place. In the same bed as often as humanly possible. Doing all the mundane, domestic, wonderful things that couples do. I want to take care of you when you're sick. I want to grocery shop with you, and have picnics in the backyard."

"Sleep late together on Sunday mornings and argue over whose turn it is to make breakfast?" Natalie's voice was soft and filled with so much longing she barely recognized it as she made her own contribution.

"Yes." Adele nodded fervently, and a bolt of sudden optimism splashed across her face. "Yes. All that and more. I'm asking you to try to make things work here in New Orleans because I can't move out of state without getting a modification in my custody agreement with Landry." She cupped Natalie's cheek with a warm, smooth palm. "It would be nearly impossible to do, but-but I would try."

For once in her life Natalie wanted to be just that selfish. But…God. "Ella…"

"I know. I know," Adele interrupted. She glanced away. "But I want…" She seemed suddenly frustrated. "I would move heaven and earth for you, if I could. If you'd let me." She stroked Natalie's cheek with her thumb.

Like a moth to a flame, Natalie leaned into the irresistible touch, and her eyes fluttered closed. Love. Fear. Tenderness. Hope. They all collided inside her. She wanted to break into joyous laughter and sob at the same time.

"Give us a chance. Take the leap. I swear to God I'll catch you."

Natalie's tongue was frozen and her mind reeled. Never in her life had someone so plainly and vehemently laid out her feelings before her like an offering. It was in that very second that she realized they both wanted two very different things.

Adele wanted back the life she had in a city she loved before violence cast its shadow over her. New Orleans was ingrained in her, just like her family. Just like Al. The last thing Natalie wanted was to be the reason that Adele gave away another piece of herself. She had lost too much already.

Natalie had gotten nearly everything she wanted, career-wise, only to find out there was still something missing. Something she hadn't realized she didn't want to live without. What she needed was something fresh and new, something she'd only had the barest taste of but was somehow already addicted to. She opened her eyes to see Adele's heart showing plainly on her face. It was right there for the taking, if Natalie was only brave enough to reach out and grab it.

"So what do you say, Nat?" Adele's eyes blazed. Adoration and attraction arcing between them. Crackling. Alive. Magnetic. "It's your move."

Natalie's natural inclination was to be ruthlessly pragmatic and continue single-mindedly down the path she'd already started. It was how she'd always lived. It was how she'd built her life. She never quit. She endured. Natalie had never put all her hope and trust and faith in another person. She'd never thrown herself willingly into that abyss. But this time her heart was demanding something different, and it wanted a path for two.

All she could think of was Adele's kindness. The dedication and loyalty that was woven through her every fiber. Her soft throaty laugh, gentle nature, and a fierce protective streak. Those damn dimples she wanted to kiss every minute. And that *voice*.

The smile reached all the way to Natalie's eyes and beyond. A sense of peace enveloped her as realization hit home and sank all the way into her bones. To stay. There was so much more to talk about. More to work out. Details to organize. Priorities to address. But there was really only one answer when logic rightly, and *finally*, yielded to love. "I'm all in."

EPILOGUE

Four months later…

Adele's mind drifted peacefully and then parked itself on her two favorite subjects, snippets of time playing one by one behind her eyelids like a flickering movie on a screen.

Natalie wrapping up her research project early one afternoon so she can help Logan learn how to tell time on a clock with hands.

Logan and Natalie snuggled up on the sofa watching The Lion King *and Natalie crying harder than Logan when Mufasa dies.*

Logan coloring Easter eggs at the kitchen table and then not believing Natalie when she tells him that chocolate eggs do not come from chocolate chickens.

Natalie finally agreeing to move in with them the same day the Touro Street Inn officially becomes Georgia's.

She and Natalie in bed. Natalie's lips and teeth making a slow trail up her leg. Each sensual kiss flooding her with desire. Every love bite burning with pleasure and stinging with just a hint of pain. A kiss. A bite. A kiss. A bite. A harder bite. Ow. Another bite where there is only pain. Ouch! Her leg!

Adele's eyes fluttered open, and for a moment, she was confused. The room was still mostly dark, and Natalie was sitting in a chair next to the bed reading, not on the bed tangled up with her. They weren't naked. And the room had a faintly medicinal smell…

"Well, hello." Natalie beamed a smile down at Adele that dissolved her into a puddle. She loved it when Natalie wore her reading glasses. "Welcome back."

"Hey." Adele licked dry lips and immediately felt a plastic straw pressed to her mouth. She drew in a sip of cool water with pleasure and reached over to pick up the hospital bed controls so she could sit up a little. She let out a hiss when she stretched too far.

"Let me." Natalie reached for the control box. She pressed the button and the head of the bed lifted. "How are you feeling?"

Adele grimaced and mentally focused on the area just below her hip. It felt hot and throbbed in time with her heartbeat. "It hurts, but I'll live." She glanced at a large clock on the wall, giving her eyes a few seconds to adjust. It was almost eleven p.m. "It's late, and you're still here."

Natalie's eyebrows rose and she pushed a shock of hair off Adele's forehead as she deposited a kiss to the newly exposed skin. "Where else would I be?"

"At home. In bed. Asleep."

Natalie carefully took Adele's hand in hers and traced the ridges of her fingers. "Don't be silly, I'm not going anywhere."

Adele's face showed her intense adulation, and she knew it, but couldn't help it. Natalie's presence always seemed to make everything better.

The surgery on Adele's leg was the last scheduled operation of the day. It had taken longer than expected and hadn't wrapped up until after eight p.m. After an hour in the recovery room, she was wheeled to the private room where she lay now. She couldn't recall a second of the trip, but she vaguely remembered talking with her family, and then Natalie, before she slipped back into oblivion. "I fell asleep in the middle of talking to everyone, didn't I?"

Natalie smiled indulgently. "Don't worry about that. You lasted for a good fifteen minutes before you conked out again."

"Tell me I didn't say anything stupid." Drugs did terrible, humiliating things to her. Even though she knew they were holding the worst of the pain at bay, she hated the groggy state she was in now.

"You didn't say anything stupid."

Adele was pleasantly surprised. "I didn't embarrass myself? Really?"

Natalie chewed her lip. "I didn't say that. I mean, what you said wasn't stupid, but had you not been under the influence, I don't think—"

"Just tell me."

"Ella…"

Adele steeled herself. "Tell me."

"You sang me a love song, then proposed to me, all while trying to pull me in bed with you."

Adele's face went scarlet.

"In front of your family."

Like a car hitting a brick wall at sixty miles per hour, everything came to a screeching halt. "Wh-What?"

"You asked me to marry you and—"

"Oh, my God." Adele was horrified. "That's what I thought you said!"

Natalie burst out laughing.

Adele moaned. "You're really serious, aren't you?"

A nod.

Adele closed her eyes. Well, she did love Natalie. And it's not like she hadn't dreamt of putting a ring on her finger someday. Just not now. And certainly not in this train wreck scenario. Why didn't someone smother her with her pillow to stop her? "I'm so sorry."

Natalie was clearly trying not to laugh again. "Honey, why are you sorry? It was really sweet. Honestly."

"What song did I sing?"

Natalie's lips turned down. "I don't think—"

"What song?"

"'My Heart Will Go On.'"

"But-but, I hate Celine Dion music!" Maybe this wasn't really happening and she was still dreaming. But one look at Natalie's grin, and she wondered if things could possibly get worse. "I don't even know all the words to that horrible song."

"I know." Natalie gave her a sympathetic look. "You made up a lot of the lyrics as you went along."

The tips of Adele's ears burned as red as her cheeks. "I suppose this was all recorded on Amelia's cell phone?"

"Well, hers…" Natalie began counting off names on her fingers. "Jackson's, one of the nurses', and your mom's. Your dad tried too, but he couldn't figure out how to do it, and somehow he ended up accidentally turning on his phone's camera flash and taking picture after picture instead. But it did give the room a strobe-lighting nightclub feel while you sang your heart out."

"Christ," Adele wheezed, choking a little on her own tongue. Natalie was probably sweet enough to ignore that this ever happened. Maybe. But her family would never let her live it down. Thank goodness at least *one* person hadn't stooped so low as to record her humiliation. She couldn't count Logan because he didn't have his own phone yet. "At least Georgia didn't—"

"Oh, yeah. Her too."

Adele closed her eyes. "Fuck."

"You swore a lot in your song, too, Ella." Natalie smirked and smoothed Adele's blanket across her chest. "For some reason, the drugs really give you a potty mouth." She winced. "Your, um, mom is going to talk to you about that later. She wasn't happy about the curse words, and I think you're in trouble."

Adele rolled her eyes.

"If it helps, I made them all promise not to put it on YouTube."

"Uh-huh. And how many hits does it already have?"

Natalie sighed. "Four hundred and seventy-eight."

"In only a couple of hours?" Adele gaped. Maybe she wasn't still dreaming. Maybe she'd died during surgery and this was Hell. "How is that possible?"

"Well, one of your nieces posted it and—"

"No." Adele held up a hand. "Don't tell me. I don't want to know." Adele threw her arm over her eyes. She couldn't think about what she'd done for another second and not die. "I hate hospitals. And I hate my doctor."

"Ella," Natalie scolded quietly, accepting the change of subjects gracefully. "The man is allowed to have a life. He did a great job on your bicep last winter, didn't he?"

Adele reluctantly nodded. Her arm had healed completely and with no lingering effects except for the scar.

"Everyone needs a little time off now and then."

Adele moped. "He made me miss it."

"You didn't miss anything. I recorded it for you and Landry." Natalie couldn't suppress her smitten smile. "Logan was wonderful and to-die-for cute. Seriously. He was disgustingly adorable."

"Tell me."

And so she did. Logan's first-grade class put on an end-of-the-year school play, and he had the part of a growly lion, complete with a fake fur mane, felt claws and a long fuzzy tail. Adele hadn't wanted to miss it, but it was either schedule her operation for today or wait six weeks until her doctor returned from a world cruise.

Like a trusty second in a duel, Natalie had agreed to go to Logan's play in her stead. She'd gone early enough to get a seat in the front row and cheer on Logan then hustled him and Amelia back to the hospital for a quick visit. He was spending the night with his aunt.

Adele licked her lips again. Why were they so dry? "How did he do with his line?"

Natalie clamped a hand over her own mouth to cover a short laugh.

"Uh-oh." Adele shook her head, doing her best to smile and forcing herself to ignore the throbbing sensation in her leg that was growing with every minute. "Don't tell me he forgot it. You've been practicing with him all week. It was only ten words. It's burned into my brain, so I know he knows it!"

"Ella, you should have seen him." Natalie was practically vibrating with pleasure. "He remembered the first few words perfectly, then walked to the front of the stage, put his hands on his hips, exactly the way you do when you want something, and called out to me in the audience to remind him of the rest. Amelia laughed so hard I think she wet her pants a little."

Adele laughed softly, but felt a pang of guilt and sadness that she'd missed it. "Was Logan upset?"

"Nope." Natalie chuckled. "When the audience laughed, he did too. After that, the show went on for an hour more. An *hour* more, but Logan was great."

Every night last week Logan had said good night to his mother, but then mysteriously asked that Natalie be the one to tuck him in bed. Adele had assumed Natalie was reading to him, something they both loved and that had become routine. One evening, when Natalie was especially engrossed in her sabbatical research project, Adele had offered to tuck Logan in bed instead. Logan had steadfastly refused, and so Natalie put her project aside and met him in his room. That's when curiosity had gotten the best of Adele, and she'd wandered to Logan's bedroom and stood outside his partially open door to listen and peek inside.

He and Natalie had talked about his day, the chicken nuggets at school and how they were somehow better than the ones at home, and why stars were only visible at night. And every few minutes during their chat, Natalie had unexpectedly given Logan his cue and he would roar ferociously and blurt out his line with the enthusiasm that only a six-year-old could manage. In response, Natalie would *baaa* like the frightened sheep and cower in terror under his blankets, causing him to laugh hysterically and beg her to do it again.

Adele's first reaction had been such an overwhelming burst of love for them both that it left her speechless. To her surprise, the rush of affection was immediately followed by a hot spike of jealousy. She wasn't used to sharing her son with anyone other than Landry, and she wasn't used to sharing Natalie with anyone at all. It took a gentle reminder to herself that this was a good thing. She wasn't giving up anything special with either one of them, and there would always be more than enough love to go around.

"I can't wait to see the recording, Nat. Thanks." Adele's body jerked a little as she felt a sudden stab of pain. "Ow."

Natalie ran her fingertips across Adele's forehead and down her cheeks in a soothing motion. "Try to relax and rest now. You'll feel better tomorrow."

Adele heard the beep of her self-controlled medication pump and knew that Natalie had pressed the button for her, administering a dose of narcotics. She wanted to scowl. Pain meds made her sleepy and dangerously goofy and she wasn't ready to be pulled back under yet. It wasn't long before a cool, dreamy sensation eased through her bloodstream, and the pain began to fade into the background, and all was forgiven. Her body grew impossibly heavy and she relaxed into the mattress, her eyes easing closed.

"That's it," Natalie murmured reassuringly. "The doctor said everything went really well with your surgery." She dropped her voice to a mesmerizing whisper. "I'll be here when you wake up."

"I…Nat?"

"Hmm?"

"I like really, really jusss…" Adele's voice began to slur. "I love…"

The last thing Adele remembered was a soft laugh, the feeling of warm lips at the corner of her mouth, and the words, "I love you, too. So, so much."

* * *

Two months later…

"Is this the last one?" Natalie asked, looking tired but satisfied. She put a large box on the floor and stepped away from it.

"Finally and yes!" Adele set a box down in the middle of their new living room. The walls were bare and beautiful, and it felt like a blank canvas for the rest of their lives. Sunlight streamed in from tall windows and bathed everything in a cheerful glow.

The owners of the main house that went along with their carriage house rental had decided the month previous that they liked Hawaii so much they were never coming back. Adele immediately made an offer on the main house and carriage house apartment, and today was moving day.

Adele had to jump out of the way as Logan zoomed by at a full run, chasing one of the neighbor boys he'd only just met. They made a loop around the room, then the neighbor disappeared out of the room and the front door slammed. "Bye, Brian!" Logan called out loudly.

Adele's eyes narrowed. "Logan!"

Natalie's arm snaked out and she pulled Logan to a stop. She wrapped her arm around him and pulled him tight against her to hold him still for a second so his mother could address him.

Adele pinned him with a serious look. "How many times have I told you not to run in the house? And yelling like that? Since when is that okay?"

"Sorry, Mama," he said solemnly, staring up at Adele with the same honey-brown eyes she saw in the mirror every day. Both women smiled.

Logan had the good graces to look ashamed, but it would only last a few seconds. He was full of his mother's twitchy energy, only in even greater measure, and that wasn't about to change anytime soon. Asking him to stop running was akin to asking the wind not to blow, though Adele felt obligated to at least try.

She sighed dramatically. "Go." Adele made a shooing motion. "Run as much as you want. In the backyard."

He smiled brightly, his eyes alive with renewed excitement. "Okay!"

Natalie ruffled his hair and released him, and like a shot, he was off again. "Careful on that tire swing this time," she called after him. He'd already bruised an elbow jumping off the swing, and they'd only been in the house a few hours. She turned to Natalie and gave her a resigned look. "You do know that he's going to jump off that swing again, and we're going to end up in the emergency room."

"Really?" Natalie's face was suddenly awash with dread. "Maybe you should make him wear a helmet."

"All the time? C'mon, Nat." Natalie was surprisingly protective of Logan, and Adele absently wondered how much of that had to do with Josh.

Natalie smiled fondly at the doorway through which Logan had disappeared, seeming to draw her calm acceptance of Logan's nature from Adele. "He can hardly contain himself. New house. New bedroom. New kids to play with."

Adele flopped down heavily on a sofa they'd moved over from her living room at the inn. It was one of the few pieces of furniture she'd brought with her. She wanted to start fresh with Natalie and to pick out things together. They just hadn't seemed to find the time yet. She had the sudden urge to go see her stained-glass windows, which she'd pulled out of storage to install in the kitchen, but it hurt to think of walking that far.

Her leg felt like it was on fire, and it was only the middle of the day. She'd been foolish to think she'd make it the entire day without her cane, having only recently retired a pair of hospital-issued crutches.

Her physical therapy sessions were grueling, and daily, and so far she wasn't much better than she'd been prior to the surgery. Still, her doctors were hopeful, and she was doing her level best to be patient through an arduous, and sometimes torturous, recovery process. But while she was excited by the prospect of improvement, she was also tired of the constant pain and work it took just to move around. It grated on her and wore her down. She knew it made her moody, though she tried to fight it.

As if reading her thoughts, Natalie dusted her hands off on the back of her cutoff denim shorts and sat down next to Adele. She nudged Adele with her shoulder. "You okay?"

Adele nodded, but could tell by Natalie's obvious concern that she wasn't very convincing.

"I wish you wouldn't strain your leg. You paid movers for a reason."

Natalie's concerned tone held just enough annoyance to fully capture Adele's attention.

"Ella, when you hurt, I feel awful. Please take it easy on yourself. For me?" Natalie pulled two over-the-counter pain tablets from her pocket and handed them over.

Adele knew she was being gently manipulated but was unable to stop the sharp pang in her chest at the thought of Natalie hurting for any reason. "I-I just feel stupid standing around while you're working." She took the pills, swallowing them without waiting for Natalie's certain offer to get up and bring her some water.

Natalie grimaced at the action. "You've hardly been standing around, Ella. You've been working all morning, but you shouldn't be walking at all without your cane yet. Remember what the doctor said? You're not healed enough."

While in the middle of her scolding, Adele was surprised to receive a firm kiss on the lips that went on long, and was passionate, enough to leave her breathless.

"Please?"

Adele found herself nodding without realizing it. Inwardly, she rolled her eyes at herself. She leaned back and wrapped an arm around Natalie's shoulders, her fingers running back and forth across the smooth skin of a bare shoulder. Summer was in full force, and today was a scorcher, but seeing Natalie slightly sweaty and lightly clad in a snug white tank top and shorts was easily worth the perspiration.

"I can't believe I'm going to be living here." Natalie glanced around the room looking half-pleased, half-terrified. "I've never lived anyplace even close to this nice."

"It's gonna be great." Adele was every bit as excited as Logan. She just wasn't able to run around like she was on fire to show it. Now their bed would really be *theirs*, and she intended to do everything she could to make her girlfriend so happy she'd never want to leave it. That reminded her, their new bed would be delivered later that afternoon and it would, hopefully, be the first of many new additions that would start to make this place seem like home.

Despite her aching leg, and the moodiness it caused her, Adele felt more content than she had in weeks. She drew in a deep breath of lemon wood polish-scented air and shifted so that her leg felt a bit better.

The house had three large bedrooms upstairs, a fourth smaller room downstairs that would make an excellent home office, high ceilings to help keep the place cool, and a double-tiered porch that both women adored. They'd had the upstairs painted a soothing, cream color. The rooms downstairs were each done in a different, deep, jewel-tone color with bright white trim. The yard was big enough for Logan to be in heaven, and they could rent out the carriage house for additional income or keep it for guests. It was perfect.

Adele frowned when, out of the corner of her eye, she caught sight of Natalie's unusually contemplative expression. "What's the matter?"

"Nothing's…wrong." Natalie paused and knotted her fingers together. "Well, that's not quite true. Something is bothering me."

A solitary vertical crease appeared in Adele's forehead when she tried to puzzle out what it was without being told. "If you're still mad because I—"

"I want to put more money toward the house."

Adele relaxed a little, even as her frown deepened. It was nearly impossible to outright win an argument with Natalie. In the face of defeat, Natalie would strategically retreat to live and fight again another day. "That's not necessary, and we've already fussed about this like three times, Nat," she whined.

"Yes, it is necessary," Natalie persisted, taking both of Adele's hands in hers. She squeezed hard and long enough for Adele to know that she was serious, and irritated, before letting go. Natalie stood and began pacing in front of the couch, her high ponytail swinging indignantly with each step. "Even though I didn't have as much equity in my townhouse as I'd hoped, the sale price was good. I can contribute more." She gestured with her hands as she moved. "Not a huge amount, but still more."

"Look, I know you're stressed about your sabbatical ending next week and quitting your teaching position without another full-time job already in the bag. But there's no hurry for you to jump back into a new job. I can support us in the meantime. Besides, we already agreed that once you're working again, you'd pay for groceries and utilities. And Logan and I eat…every single day."

Natalie stopped squarely in front of Adele, her hands on her hips. "I'm being serious."

"I know you are, but you don't have to be. This doesn't need to be a big deal."

"Then don't make it a big deal by being stubborn, Ella. You put my name on the title, and I've barely pitched in seven percent! It's obvious that you and your family aren't poor, but nobody can just drop that much money and not think twice. This house may not be as large as the neighbors', but it's really nice, and the neighborhood's gorgeous. Georgia also told me that she couldn't talk you out of giving her a fabulous deal on the inn."

Dismayed, Natalie looked truly upset. "I get that I can't really afford this place or come close to paying for half." She began pacing again. "But I should be contributing everything I can."

Adele could suddenly taste the beignets and coffee she'd had for breakfast all over again. Once Natalie had seen the prices for homes in the more desirable or historical neighborhoods, she'd insisted that they could simply buy a smaller place or even a townhouse or condo. But Adele had already seen how she'd reacted to this house. It wasn't lavish, but it was undeniably beautiful. It was what they both wanted, and that was all the reason Adele needed to make it happen. "Can't we just forget about the money thing for now?"

"No. We can't. We haven't had a chance to discuss it, and I was going to wait until I knew for sure before I mentioned it, but I've been putting out job feelers, and I got a call back from a former colleague who now works for MacDonald Education Press."

"That's who you were talking to for so long on the phone this morning?" Adele felt a sense of foreboding swell within her. There was no MacDonald Education Press in New Orleans. She was sure of it.

"They're publishers who specialize in college course books, and they're looking for an author for a series of books in my specialty area." Natalie's smile exploded into life. "I'm meeting with them next week to discuss writing them."

Adele's elation for Natalie was instantly tempered by anxiety. "But from here in New Orleans, right?"

Natalie gave her a funny look. "Buh…of course from here."

Adele began to breathe again.

Natalie's brow furrowed and her voice softened. "Hey."

"It's okay." Adele's smile was small, but genuine. Crisis averted. Things were going so well between her and Natalie that sometimes she forgot she didn't need to wait for the other shoe to drop. There was no other shoe. "Go on."

Natalie studied Adele for a moment, looking a little perplexed, before nodding. "One of the reasons I'm so interested is that I can work right from home. It's potentially years' worth of work and several of the focus areas are subjects that I've been dying to explore in more depth."

Adele gave Natalie a lovesick grin. "That's so awesome, Natalie. I know how you love doing research. The job sounds fabulous. You're so friggin' smart, and I'm proud of you whether you get the job or not."

Natalie's return smile was electric. "Thanks." She continued to gesture as she walked. "It's not a done deal yet, of course, but they're interested. If it goes through, I'll get an advance that I can put toward the house."

Adele reached out and wrapped her fingers around Natalie's slender wrist, pulling her to a stop. "Your pacing is making me dizzy. I can see you aren't going to let this go." She made a face and bit the bullet. "So let's really talk about money."

Looking worried, Natalie immediately dropped to the floor on her knees between Adele's legs and searched her face.

Adele's eyes grew round. "I'm not going to tell you that I rob liquor stores for extra cash, sweetheart."

With visible effort, Natalie let her arms hang loose at her sides. "Okay."

"C'mere." Adele scooted to the end of the sofa and patted a cushion at the opposite end. She felt a stab of guilt for making Natalie worry. When Natalie sat down she motioned for her to spin around so she could rub her feet. "It's nothing bad. So relax."

Adele began to massage a single socked foot as she spoke. "Both sides of my family have been in New Orleans a long time. Since the 1750s."

Natalie excitedly leaned forward at the mention of the time period that was her area of study. "Do you have family documents or records from back then?"

Adele grinned and only just held back from rolling her eyes at the immediate interruption. "We've got tons of old papers and stuff. Talk to my mom."

Natalie squirmed happily in her seat and made a motion that she was zipping her lips.

"My family has been everything from farm laborers to ferrymen to bootleggers to shopkeepers. It was my great-grandparents' generation on Mama's side that bought several shoe stores with their ill-gotten bootlegging gains as a way to go legit after Prohibition. Since then, the main family occupation has revolved around retail of some variety. When my sister, brother and I graduated from college, we were each given our own shop in the Quarter as part of the family business."

"'Amelia's'?"

"Yes. Though it's a lot fancier now than it was when Amelia took it over. 'Jackson's' started as a small fine jewelry store on Decatur Street. He now owns four jewelry stores around town."

Curiosity filled Natalie's eyes and Adele didn't have to try hard to guess what she was wondering.

"'Adele's' sells antiques on Chartres Street. But I never wanted to go into retail, and my parents have always known that. They offered it to me, mainly as a formality, because we instantly struck a deal where they kept 'Adele's' but invested in 'Amelia's,' and later 'Jackson's,' on my behalf instead. That investment let me pursue a career that made me happy. Today I own twenty-five percent of each of my siblings' stores. It's not like I'm super rich, and the money is wrapped up in the businesses, but I could probably live reasonably comfortably for the rest of my life from those investments, even if I didn't work at all. I could easily support you, too. I sold back some of my shares of 'Jackson's' to buy this place."

"But…wow." Natalie blinked a few times. "I didn't realize so much was yours personally. I thought maybe your parents…I mean, I've never even known someone who didn't have to work at all."

"Sure you have." Adele winked. "Biblically." Natalie flushed a lovely shade of pink, which Adele found delightfully endearing, especially considering that Natalie was the opposite of shy in the bedroom.

"Why didn't you tell me?"

"We would have talked about it eventually. I just…I was just happy to put it off. The guy I dated before Landry was a business major who was more interested in the family business than me. By the time I figured that out, I was deep enough into the relationship that it not only hurt, I was embarrassed. So I learned to keep my finances private. Money was a bone of contention in my marriage from the very start, and I didn't want that for us."

Natalie pulled the elastic band from her hair and shook her head. It was damp with perspiration at the temples from hefting boxes. "When you and Landry were together you had a nice house and nice things, but you weren't living like rap stars."

Adele snorted. "No matter what, I would never live like a rap star, darlin'. Anyway, when I was engaged to marry Landry I found out that he had a ton of credit card debt that he'd carelessly racked up while he was in his twenties. I made the mistake of casually mentioning to Georgia that I was going to pay it all off after we got married, and she went right to my folks with the information." Adele smiled wanly. "The downside to a close-knit family is the lack of privacy.

"My previous gold digger boyfriend had made my parents wary of my choices, but they quickly got over their worries about Landry when they saw that I was happy, and that he truly loved me. Landry, on the other hand, never completely forgave them for their initial concerns. He never wanted anything to do with my money. So except for me paying off his debt, which was necessary if we wanted to qualify for a mortgage, I really didn't touch most of my investments while I was married. Over the years my folks have given me some nice gifts." She gestured toward the watch on her wrist. "But that's about it. My salary added to Landry's was still a modest amount, but enough to live on, and real estate prices then weren't what they are today."

Adele lifted one shoulder. "In the end, Landry got his wish about the money, because we had a prenuptial agreement in place. I kept all my family business assets in the divorce."

Natalie wrinkled her nose. "Most guys would consider themselves lucky to have a wife who could pay them out of debt."

"He was proud, and I think it just made him feel small, knowing that I was bailing him out of his poor decisions." Adele gently set down Natalie's foot and picked up the other.

"But, Ella, none of this explains why I shouldn't contribute more to the house. I don't love you for your mon—" Natalie groaned when Adele hit a tender spot in the arch of her foot, "money. Ugh, God, that feels so good! Surely you know that."

"Duh."

Natalie's eyes twinkled. "But I can't lie. I do love you for your clothes and especially the purses you let me borrow."

Adele laughed. She pinched Natalie's big toe and earned a high-pitched yelp for her efforts. "If 'Amelia's' ever goes out of business, I'm in deep trouble."

Adele sobered. "You've already contributed financially what's reasonable based on what you can afford. That shows me you're serious about us and you're fair. I don't want a bunch of percentages between us. I don't want a roommate where I own everything and you live in my house. I want things to be equal between us regardless of who contributed what and when. In my mind, they already are." Adele thought about it for a second before adding, "I'd actually like to enjoy not having to live on a couple of cops' salaries for once. Can't we just consider the house ours and take things from here?"

Natalie mulled over what Adele said long enough that the blonde began to fidget. It was clear Natalie wanted to argue, but the words seemed to stall in her mouth. Instead, what eventually emerged was simple, but heartfelt, "I love you, and I accept."

Adele was too shocked to do more than blink stupidly for a few seconds. Then she pumped a fist in victory. "Yes!"

"But," Natalie held up her index finger, "only on one condition."

Adele's eyes narrowed in challenge. Her mind raced, but she was unable to think of a single thing she wouldn't do or give up to get what she wanted. "Anything."

"If we ever sell the house, and don't buy something else together, we each take out the percentage that we chipped in."

A rush of happiness chased its way down Adele's spine, making her shiver. She had no intention of letting this place or Natalie go. Ever. "Deal. I love you, too. Just so you know, I'm well aware that what you do contribute is something I can never buy. It's priceless. That's your fair share."

Natalie moved so quickly that Adele didn't know what hit her as her body, and Natalie's right along with it, flew deeper into the corner of the sofa with a loud *oomph*.

Adele's eyes rolled back when Natalie nudged her chin up with her head and attacked her throat with wet, sucking kisses, hard enough to leave faint marks. Warm hands flew beneath her shirt, and then her bra, and began massaging her breasts before she could register what was happening. "Wh-what...oh, God!" Adele arched her back, pushing harder against Natalie's insistent touch.

"I'd like to..." Natalie nuzzled closer, murmuring against tender skin, "continue my relationship contributions right now."

Suddenly feeling hot all over, Adele moaned. "Yes, yes, yes...g-g-good idea." A leg slid between hers and pressed upward. Adele gasped and her head swam.

Light footsteps banging on the wooden floors interrupted them.

Natalie quickly pulled her hands out from under Adele's shirt and moved to sit up, but Adele held her firmly in place and linked their hands together in plain sight. Natalie eased her leg from between Adele's.

With a steadying exhale, Adele smiled calmly at Natalie's slightly panicked expression. "It's okay for him to see us together."

Logan came to a stop in front of them, tears in his eyes, completely unfazed by their current intimate position. "I need Band-Aids." He winced and looked down at both skinned knees.

Adele cringed.

Natalie hissed in a breath between her teeth. "Ouch! You sure do. And more than one." She shifted. "Just let me move so your mom can—"

"You can do it, Nat," he said earnestly. "I like it when you blow on the scrapes. It feels really good. I'll go get the Godzilla Band-Aids!" Without waiting for confirmation of his request, he hobbled quickly in the direction of the bathroom.

Natalie looked worriedly at Adele and bit her bottom lip. This would be the first time, while they were both available, that Logan had asked for her comfort instead of his mother's.

Adele's face relaxed into a devastatingly wide smile. They were becoming a real family. "How about you patch up Logan, and then join me in the bathtub upstairs?" She watched, mesmerized, as the words registered and Natalie's eyes darkened and then smoldered.

Natalie licked her lips and her voice sank deeper. "We, um, don't have any towels unpacked yet. Or a bed."

Adele chuckled a little wickedly as Natalie rose to her feet, and then offered a hand up. "Hon," she drawled, "the only things that are not optional in this scenario...are me and you."

* * *

Six months later...

Natalie, Adele and Logan sat around a large firepit they'd recently added to the backyard, the women side by side on a wooden bench, and Logan in his own New Orleans Saints folding chair. The sky was crystal clear and blanketed with a million stars, and the night air was brisk and growing colder by the minute. Snug in jeans, warm sweaters, and with blankets slung over their laps for extra warmth, they peered into the dancing flames and spoke in low voices. Logan dug into the fire with a long stick, causing the wood to pop and snap and ashes to rise up in a plume before disappearing into the inky sky.

Adele's eyes turned to slits. How could this have happened again? "This is impossible! Impossible!"

Natalie and Logan laughed at how distraught Adele was over losing another Christmas tree hunt to her sister. Earlier in the day, Jackson had been even more vocal in his displeasure. The claim of fraud had caused an argument that Adele's parents finally had to break up.

Adele gritted her teeth. "Amelia must be bribing the kids. Or putting them under a spell or something."

"Aunt Amelia told me you'd say that. She doesn't bribe us, Mama!" the second-grader insisted. "Her tree was way taller."

"But my tree was perfect. Size isn't everything!"

Natalie failed to cover her snicker.

"But hers was wider too," Logan added, tossing his stick into the flames and watching intently as it caught fire.

Adele gave her son an incredulous look. "That's it? That's her secret? That's what you kids like? Just something huge?"

Logan yawned. "Well, yeah, I guess."

Adele crossed her arms over her chest with a playful grumpiness that left both her girlfriend and her son smiling at her.

With a soft giggle, Logan looked up at the stars. Seeing their twinkling lights reflected in his sleepy, soulful eyes seared itself into Adele's memory. He was happy. He loved their home. He loved Natalie. His relationship with both Landry and her was stronger than ever.

Life was verging on spectacular.

"Don't worry. There's always next year, Mama." Logan had recently lost his two middle front teeth and his words now held a slight lisp that continually made Natalie grin. Tonight was no exception.

Adele sighed, already wondering what it would cost to ship in the tallest tree ever from California or Montana or wherever it is they grew enormous trees. She would ask Natalie about Wisconsin later. "I know, buddy." She turned to Natalie with an arched eyebrow. "Was Amelia's tree really better than mine?"

"Impossible, sweetheart."

Adele laughed. Natalie always played along seamlessly. Adele rose and plucked the blanket from her son's lap. "Bedtime."

"But—" His protest was interrupted by another mammoth yawn.

"No buts." Adele nudged his chair with her foot. "It's already late. I'll walk you inside."

With a sigh, he jumped to his feet, his sneakers thudding lightly against the ground. He hugged his mother, while she pressed a kiss to the top of his head. Then he went to Natalie, who regarded him fondly and happily accepted her goodnight kiss on the cheek.

Natalie snuggled deeper into her blanket and swept her legs up underneath herself. "Night, Logan."

"Night, Nat."

"Be right back." Adele rested her hand on Natalie's shoulder and gave it a little squeeze before following her son inside.

Once inside, Logan turned around excitedly. "Are you ready?"

Adele nodded slowly.

"Nervous?"

"A little."

"Don't be nervous. She's gonna be happy."

"Fingers crossed. Don't forget to brush your teeth." Adele snorted to herself as Logan took the stairs two at a time and with boundless energy, despite the long day they'd all had. She paused before heading back outside, and with a deep breath, opened the back door. She could feel Natalie's eyes riveted on her as she moved. She naturally squared her shoulders a bit and lifted her chin under the frank perusal. The closer Adele got to Natalie, the more Natalie's smile grew and grew until it finally exploded and was blinding.

Adele's heart skipped a beat. *God, I can't believe that look is for me.* "What?"

Natalie sighed dreamily. "Your swagger is back."

"My what?" Adele's ears felt hot and her palms sweaty.

Natalie gave her a look. "Don't play dumb with me, Ms. Lejeune. You know you have a sexy strut and that I'm helpless against it. When I first met you, I thought you swung your arms out as you walked to keep them from hitting the gun on your belt." She pursed her lips. "Though that never explained the sexy sashay in your hips. But it wasn't the gun, or even the job. It was just you."

Adele knew exactly what Natalie was talking about, but it wouldn't do to admit that out loud. It was wonderful to once again enjoy the relaxed, confident feeling that went along with her normal gait.

Two months ago, Adele rounded a significant corner in her physical therapy. While running still brought out a slight limp, her walk was almost back to normal.

"I'm so proud of you, Ella. I know how hard you've worked for this."

Adele felt herself glow under the praise.

Natalie reached down and picked up Adele's cane, which was lying by her feet. Her eyes twinkled. "Are you ready?"

Adele nodded and took the cane. With a shuddering breath, she tossed it on the fire. She snuggled down next to Natalie beneath the blanket, and they watched in silence for a few moments as the cane caught fire, and the rubber tip smoked.

"Wow," Adele said thickly, a tornado of emotions suddenly grabbing hold and spinning her hopelessly in its grasp. She recalled the first months that had melted into years after her stabbing, and the numb, confused feeling of going through the motions of a life so foreign it was as though she was watching it from afar rather than actually living it. There was an ever-present sting, like walking around without any skin to protect her, constantly raw and hurting. Trust became something she no longer recognized, and was a commodity too scarce to trade. She thought of her failures and how she'd let self-pity bury her and damage the relationships she held dear. And, oh God, the precious time she'd squandered while she flailed and floundered.

Adele considered her physical therapy and how many instances in the past months she'd been reduced to tears of frustration when nothing seemed to be working, and the tears of pain because things were working, but it felt as though she had to be ripped apart before she could be rebuilt again. She remembered the nights when sleep wouldn't come because of the searing ache in her leg, her ego, and her spirit. The nights when sleep did come, she was often snared in a web of nightmares so sticky it was nearly impossible to tell what was real and what wasn't.

And then she watched all those things rise up in a plume of smoke and drift away into the night's sky and she realized she hadn't been rebuilt at all, but reborn.

"Are you okay?"

Adele just nodded, though in truth she was a little shaky. She felt a soft kiss pressed into her cheek, the lips warm and silky on her chilled skin. The gesture grounded her. She thought of Natalie's words on the night of Al's shooting, compelling her to stay in the here and now. Natalie grounded her.

"Now, Ella, are you going to tell me what you and Logan have been whispering about all evening?"

"You saw that, huh?" She nuzzled Natalie's neck and drew in a deep breath. Natalie's skin and hair smelled like flowers from her shampoo. Adele hummed her approval and couldn't help but place a kiss just below Natalie's ear, using her tongue to repeatedly tickle the tender skin.

"Ella..." Natalie wriggled and laughed under the sweet torture, but wouldn't be distracted. "Spill it."

Adele went serious. "The call came in this afternoon while you were talking with Amelia."

Natalie's eyes widened slightly and her body tensed in anticipation. She turned to face Adele. "They offered you the job?"

Adele couldn't hold in her grin in any longer. "They offered me the job."

Natalie let out a loud whoop and pulled Adele into a bone-crushing hug. "I knew it! I knew they would."

Adele laughed and allowed herself to be, quite literally, smothered in affection. "If I say yes, you'll be living with the head of Louisiana's new Missing and Exploited Children Task Force."

"So you'll be *Agent* Lejeune?"

Adele nodded.

"That's superhot."

Adele burst into laughter. "If you say so."

She had received a call from the New Orleans Chief of Police and the Louisiana Attorney General to discuss the position several weeks ago. Unlike the investigation she'd ignited years ago, the press and the NOPD leadership had uniformly supported her through the months of investigations revolving around Lt. Xavier and Sgt. Morrell and others. While there were those at the NOPD who believed she'd simply embarrassed them all over again, this time she'd emerged more hero than villain, and now the NOPD was desperately trying to save face.

That they would use this new offer, instead of any sort of real apology, to somehow smooth over years of pain and a ruined career infuriated her. On the other hand, the offer was solid, the task force was needed, and it would give her the opportunity to do more good than she ever could have as a police detective. And in the end, she decided, those things were more important than the NOPD, pride or politics.

The new job meant she would lead a three-person team that would liaise with multiple state agencies and police departments to work on clearing the backlog of cold cases, as well as current ones, involving crimes against minors, missing children, child trafficking, abuse and exploitation. She would carry a task force badge, have a special weapon's license, and because she wasn't technically a member of the NOPD, she was exempt from their physical exam requirements. Technically, she would only answer directly to the governor, though it had been made clear that one of the governor's lackeys would actually be her normal point of contact.

All that was left was for her to give her answer.

"What do you mean *if* you say yes?" Natalie cocked her head to the side. "Why wouldn't you? It's a fabulous opportunity."

Adele felt a gust of nervousness. They'd talked about what the job would mean for her personally and professionally, but never what it would mean for them as a couple…as a family. "Working on the task force means there will be times that I'll be away from home. Not just overnight, but maybe for several days at a time while I'm working on a case. I won't be able to control the hours. That part will be a lot like being a cop. I'll get calls on the weekends, holidays, during dinners, and in the middle of the night. And you need to know that I tend to get so focused on what I'm doing that sometimes I forget normal things, like that I was supposed to buy toilet paper and—"

Natalie held up a forestalling hand. "So you'll have periodic business travel, sometimes you'll have crappy hours, and you'll be as dedicated as you possibly can?"

That was one way of putting it, sure. "Yes."

"In that case, you should definitely decline."

"Really?"

Natalie rolled her eyes. "Of course not!" She pinched Adele in the side.

"Ouch! Christ, woman!"

"This is a once-in-a-lifetime opportunity. Take it! When you travel, I'll be home waiting for you when you come back. I'll make sure Logan gets dropped off at school on time, and for his weekends with Landry, and that you don't get rickets, or scurvy, or whatever it is a person gets from living on pizza and frozen dinners alone." Natalie gave Adele a reassuring smile that brimmed with love. "I'll always be here, Ella. And most importantly, I'll always have toilet paper."

Adele laughed as her heart sang. Though there was a tiny part of her that had to be sure. "I just, I just want to be sure that you're happy and okay with everything before I go disrupting it. Because I'm really…I just…" She threw her hands in the air, helpless. "I've never ever been happier, Natalie. I love you. I feel so wonderful that I want you to feel the same way."

Clearly smitten, Natalie rested a hand on Adele's chilled thigh and began to stroke the soft denim. Her eyes shimmered with happy tears that looked a heartbeat from falling. "I already do. So that means we don't have to worry about keeping things just the same to stay happy. We can do and want more and it will still be okay between us." The corner of Natalie's mouth quirked upward. "I'm afraid there's just no getting rid of me now."

Adele's expression softened and a sense of certainty settled deep and irrevocably into her bones. "Okay." She nodded to herself. "I'll accept the job. Just not tonight."

Natalie tugged the blanket up around her shoulders. "Mmm..." She yawned. "I guess it's a little late to call."

"That's not it. Tonight I want to focus on another once-in-a-lifetime opportunity."

"And what would that—?" Natalie froze when Adele, whose heart threatened to pound out of her chest, slid off the bench and onto one knee.

From her pocket Adele pulled out a platinum ring with a single sparkling clear stone in the center.

"Ella," Natalie gasped and their eyes met and held.

"I had a dream the other night that I was in a hospital bed, and the most beautiful woman I've ever seen was at my bedside, reading, and stroking my hair. I was so in love with her that I couldn't help myself, I wanted to spend my life with her, so I asked her to marry me. My entire family was there, but instead of answering out loud, and probably embarrassing me even further, she whispered something into my ear."

Natalie's eyes shimmered with bright tears, and Adele could see the flames of the fire reflected in their depths. It was achingly beautiful.

"Do-do you remember what she said?" Natalie said, her voice thick with emotion as she cupped Adele's jaw with a tender hand.

Adele smiled wistfully. "I didn't until the night of my dream, but I do now." Warmth crept up her cheeks as she remembered. "You said, 'Ask me again someday when you mean it, beautiful. My answer will always be yes.'" Adele reached out and tucked a strand of dark hair that was suddenly caught in the light breeze behind Natalie's ear. She took a deep breath. "Nat?"

"Yes, Ella?"

Adele's smile stretched muscles she didn't know existed. Or maybe she knew, once upon a time, and she'd just forgotten...until now. "I really mean it."

Bella Books, Inc.

Women. Books. Even Better Together.

P.O. Box 10543
Tallahassee, FL 32302

Phone: 800-729-4992
www.bellabooks.com